The Berlin Connection

A Novel

**by
Lily Scheel**

Copyright © 2009 by Lily Scheel
All Rights Reserved.

This is a work of fiction. All of the characters and events in this novel are either products of the author's imagination or are used fictitiously.

ISBN: 1-4392-4654-8
ISBN-13: 9781439246542

Visit www.booksurge.com to order additional copies.

To My Children

Acknowledgments

This book was fifteen years in the making. I couldn't have finished it without the help of many relatives and friends along the way who gave me encouragement and helpful suggestions, including but by no means limited to: Ruth Staab, Janet Wilkins, Tim Staab, Karen Huntington, Char Sanborn, Bernice Macchia, and the Lake Forest Park Third Place Books Writers Group under the direction of Frances Dayee, with special thanks to Steve Houchin, Janette Lemmé and Karen Brattesani, who had the authenticity expertise I needed and received at precisely the right time.

CHAPTER ONE

1969– In the spring of the fourth year of their marriage, Dee and her husband Dennis left their home in Seattle and went to Europe on vacation. They made love in every city they visited. In Rome, Italian mandolin music played everywhere; scented fresh, colorful flowers bloomed everywhere, and she was caught up in the romance of it all. Dee sensed destiny in the air like perfume. She knew it was the right time of the month to conceive, and although Dennis had said he wasn't sure he was ready for children yet, she dreamed of the day when she could tell this child who already existed in her heart that he or she had been conceived in Rome.

In Amsterdam, they visited the Anne Frank House, where Jewish families had hidden from the Nazis during World War II. This time she was caught up in the tragedy of Anne's shattered young life, of the hope Anne had expressed for the human race in spite of experiencing such atrocities and repression. Dee longed to reassure her own beloved future child that life was worth living.

Then on to Berlin, the city of her heritage. She had grown up hearing stories from her grandfather about family life in old Berlin, stories that had brought her forebears to life. When her mother had reminded her before their trip that these ancestors were buried in a cemetery now located behind the Wall in East Berlin, a surge of excitement rose in her.

"I want to go see their graves," she had said impulsively.

Dennis shot her a perplexed look.

"But you'd need papers," her mother told her.

As it turned out, it was relatively easy to get the papers before the trip. She told the authorities she was interested in researching family history, and she and Dennis were given a visa for a few hours. They also received strict written instructions on how to conduct themselves and what they might expect, such as confiscation of any western reading materials in their possession. Even so, Dee looked forward to the big adventure they faced.

But now, excitement turned to anxiety as they rode a noisy, rickety train from the bright, colorful districts of West Berlin into an area of gray desolation and rubble.

"The Reichstag." Dee pointed to the huge, damaged building they passed that she had seen in books. A vast, open area of weeds and dusty earth surrounded it.

Dennis craned his neck and peered through the dirty train window. They passed more city blocks of stark desolation, then everything went dark and the train came to a slow, rattling stop at Friedrichstrasse Station. They made their way among the crowd out onto a platform and down a set of stairs. Dee caught a brief glimpse of ominous guard towers and dog patrols before they entered a vast, dungeon-like, stale-smelling area. There they waited in a long line for what seemed an eternity. Murmuring voices echoed around them, but they did not speak to each other. Dee glanced at Dennis for reassurance. His tall, normally loose-limbed frame stood stiffly erect in his beige topcoat, his blue eyes stared straight ahead. He lifted a hand and brushed back his ash blond hair. He swallowed, and she saw his Adams Apple bobbing.

She felt her stomach clench when they reached the front of the line and surrendered their passports with the carefully drawn-up papers to the armed, grim-faced official. He studied the papers for a long time, and then looked up and studied their faces; and again, looked back down at the papers. Heavy dread gripped her, and then a memory flashed into her mind of a picture her Fifth Grade teacher had passed around the classroom. She saw herself at ten years old, frozen with horror as she stared at the picture, of emaciated children staring with haunted eyes from behind a barbed wire fence.

The Berlin Connection

The guard motioned them on through a turnstile to yet another depressing, dreary room, and then another, where they had to exchange their currency for Eastern Marks. Finally, their passports and papers were impersonally and miraculously thrust back into their hands. Trembling with relief, she hurried with Dennis across another huge room and out into the light of day. They moved through a desolate open space to the street beyond, where after some hesitation, they caught the appointed bus that carried them through dull, lifeless streets. People on the bus seemed dull and lifeless too; no one showed any curiosity, no one gave them a friendly smile. Dee turned her attention to her map and tried to match street signs.

They got off the bus a few moments later. All around them lay desolation. They started walking and she heard their breathing, their subdued, uncertain footfalls on broken pavement. They stopped a moment and Dee yet again consulted the well-worn map that had belonged to her grandfather. "It should be right here," she whispered. She looked up and pointed to a rusted iron gate across the road. "That must be it."

They crossed the street and went through the gate and into a vast, rubble-strewn cemetery that nevertheless provided welcoming shelter under the shadows of huge oak, maple and elm trees with low-lying leafy branches. Armed with information from her mother, they easily found the gravesites.

Unruly weeds crowded in everywhere. They stood in silence for a moment, gazing at the worn, crumbling headstones. "There's miraculous guidance in this," she told Dennis in a voice thick with emotion. Feeling a tingling, hushed reverence, she went on. "My grandfather came to the United States before the wars, Dennis. These are his people—my people. If he had stayed in Berlin, if I had been born here, I shudder to think what it would have been like to live through wartime bombs that fell on Berlin." Her arm swept the scene of substantial destruction. "Even the dead were affected."

"If your grandfather hadn't come to America he wouldn't have met your grandmother, and then you wouldn't have even been born," Dennis said flatly.

She looked up into his face and sniffed, suddenly aware of a dry, organic odor. "Where's the romance in you?" she asked with a hesitant grin.

He shrugged, didn't smile back. "It doesn't sound romantic to me to have bombs dropping on you."

She stared at him, at a loss. "That's not the point," she said, feeling the inadequacy of her remark. Frustrated, she turned away and wandered through the surrounding area in an attempt to regain her mood. Across a walkway the graves appeared newer and had obviously received care more recently. A dark-haired young man stood at one of them, head bowed, face crumpled, hands clasped together in front of him. Compassion rose in her as she watched him sink to his knees, bend his shoulders and pull bits of weed from the edges of the gravestone. She froze, not wanting to intrude in his space.

A moment later he stood up, turned and walked away, not looking in her direction. She watched him leave, waited a moment, then approached the gravestone. It looked new compared to many of the others. Knowing a little German, she read the inscription: *"Anita Mendenberg, Beloved Wife and Mother, 1920–1968."* She thought, *his grief is still fresh.* She stood pondering his caring gesture, absorbing his sorrow. After a time she turned and slowly retraced her steps to where Dennis was waiting.

"Let's go," Dennis urged. "I don't want to overstay the visa."

That afternoon, back in the Western Sector, they found a sidewalk café near the Brandenburg Gate and the Reichstag. But of course, blocking the massive structures and running the width of what she could see, stretched the Berlin Wall. She stared, brooding over the dark shadows it cast, the evil and destruction that had originated on the other side under the Nazis, and continued now under Communism. She felt a chill as her heartbeat slowed to its normal pace here in West Berlin. She had felt continuous anxiety during those few hours in East Berlin. Real fear had closed in like a vise. The other side of the Wall was only a brief walk away. But those who lived over there were a world away. What must it be like for them? She turned to Dennis.

"How did you feel about going into East Berlin?" she asked.

He jerked his head up from the map he was studying. His eyes were flinty. "That's a hell of a question to ask," he growled. "How do you think I felt? I still don't understand why you insisted on going." He went back to his map.

The Berlin Connection

Stung by his words, she stared at him a moment. Then she turned away, her gaze sweeping upward, taking in the lacy canopy of leaves above her. Their vibrant green, the soft breeze and the energetic bustle and chatter of people around her brightened her spirits. Whatever Dennis was feeling, he didn't want to talk about it now, nor did he want to hear any of what she had felt. She sighed and looked around, determined to concentrate on how sunny and fresh and clean her immediate surroundings were.

Her eyes fell on a dark-haired man finishing a meal at the next table. She looked harder. This was the man she had seen at the cemetery that morning in East Berlin. He frowned with tension as he pushed his plate away, then turned to some papers and began to read. She watched him, compelled and intrigued. What was behind his sorrow at the cemetery, his tension here? She wondered if it had anything to do with the Wall. Then she became aware of the curve of his jaw and the way the wind ruffled his hair. He moved in his chair, making notes on the pages he read.

"I'm going to call the office," Dennis said.

She pulled her attention back to her husband. "What? From here?"

"I told you there's an important project that needs monitoring, Dee. I have to check in once in awhile." He got up. "I'm going inside to ask for a pay phone."

She frowned as she watched him walk into the restaurant. *Great,* she thought. *I'm hoping to get pregnant, and his mind is on his work.*

She turned her eyes back to the young man at the next table and was startled, and embarrassed, to see his intent gaze focused on her. A quick jolt of adrenaline seized her, the most astonishing electric shock. Her heart pumped hard, spreading heat through her entire body. For a long moment their eyes held. The air shimmered, charged, between them. He looked at her as if he recognized her, knew her well, wanted to reach out to her. His mouth curved into a slight smile, his blue eyes held a softness that drew her in and compelled her to smile back. She couldn't take her eyes from his. He shook his head slowly as if he couldn't believe what he was seeing.

"You are American," he said, and took a pensive breath. His soft, faintly husky voice drew her in, too, like a warm robe on a cold night. Then he seemed to catch himself. "I am sorry," he said in heavily accented English. "I embarrass you. It's just that you remind me of… someone I knew."

She couldn't think how to answer him, so she nodded acknowledgment and summoned another smile. "How did you know I'm American?"

He shrugged and grinned. "I heard you speak before. With your – husband?"

She nodded. Her breathing felt shaky. His grin was sincere, boyish, wistful. She felt warmed by it; she welcomed it. He had looked so sad at the cemetery.

Almost as if he could read her thoughts, his face grew solemn, his manner formal. "I am sorry to bother you."

"Oh no, it's no bother. In fact, I thought I saw you earlier at a cemetery in East Berlin. I wanted to ask–"

"I must go." He rose abruptly, picked up his papers and rolled them up, then he walked over to Dee. He was tall, slim and solid, and she liked the way his clothes fit on his body as he moved. He held out a hand to her, she took it and felt the same electric shock, the same heat spreading through her. He looked down at their clasped hands and then lifted his eyes to hers. "Welcome to Berlin," he said. "I am happy to meet you." Then he turned and strolled off.

Startled, she watched him walk away. She wanted to call out. She wanted to bring him back. She wanted the wonder back. The sorrow she'd witnessed and wondered about at the cemetery held powerful appeal. And now this. He had said some things... intriguing things...She wanted to know much, much more.

Then a flood of loss and guilt swept over her. She was married; she and her husband were ready to start their family. She knew her reaction to this stranger, and his to her for that matter, was stronger than passing interest, and it bewildered her. She sat there, reflecting on what she had just experienced, and then her thoughts turned to her marriage. She truly felt blessed to have a good man like Dennis. Soon they would be a family. Although she had a good job, she believed that marriage and children were more important than career plans; she dreamed of quitting her job and settling down as a mother and homemaker.

Shaken, Erik strode away from his encounter with the American woman at the sidewalk café. He willed himself to relax, not look back. The East German

Secret Police, the Stasi, were everywhere, and it could be a crucial mistake to show interest in anyone in West Berlin. This was only his third trip from East to West, and they could interpret such a random conversation as something suspicious, a threat to security. For such a small slip, he could be detained, lose his visa, even be thrown in jail or killed. Many people had disappeared over just such a small slip.

But it had jarred him, seeing that American woman who looked so much like his mother did when he was a small child. He thought of his visit to her gravesite early that morning, the grief he'd felt there. He still missed her. He still felt her love, but all the secrets she had kept–and chosen to reveal right before she died–left him with so many questions. He felt betrayed, as though he had never really known her at all.

He walked with brisk purpose, looking neither left nor right, then hopped the bus on the corner. He had finished his business in West Berlin, and it had probably been a mistake to stop at the sidewalk cafe for a late lunch. His superior at the State sports equipment acquisition depot in East Berlin had told him to deal only with Henry Schrauder in West Berlin, but when he had arrived at the supply house, he had been told that Henry Schrauder was away for the day. He wondered if that had been a test. The negotiations with Herr Schrauder's replacement had been tense and difficult. But after several hours he had inspected the stock, made the arrangements for shipment, and by mid-afternoon, hungry and drained, he was ready to head back across the border. When he'd seen the cafe, he turned in on an impulse, sat down at a table

The Berlin Connection

and ordered a quick lunch. A harmless detour? He hoped so.

He hopped off the bus and strode toward the checkpoint, tension rising again. The guards at the gate had been inflexible and abrasive when he crossed to the West this morning and he hoped it would go better this time. Well, why shouldn't it? He was coming home. He wanted to sneer to express the sarcasm he felt, but he willed his face to remain impassive as the guard carefully scrutinized him and his papers. Then he was waved through.

He let out his breath and moved on. It still seemed a dream come true that he had been able to secure this position so soon after University that allowed him traveling privileges like this. After graduation came the meticulous training for two years, and last month, he had taken his first business trip across the Wall with his superior. Apparently he had passed their careful inspection, but he knew they would continue to watch him. He had his Communist card, of course, and he was determined to maintain the trust of the government. *My father's government.* The words drummed mercilessly in his head. His thoughts turned dismal. It would be so much easier for him if he did not hold the government in such secret contempt. But there it was.

He'd had to fight his father for almost everything he'd gotten. A harsh, autocratic man, his father. He remembered growing up, how his father had insisted on many things that he fought against. One was the strict military education he was forced into. He lost that battle. But he recalled another battle that had developed as a result of the private English tutor his mother had arranged for him. "But why?" Erik had asked her. At the time he found it hard to understand her determination on this one issue. Normally, she was passive regarding his education and submitted to his father on such matters.

She had shrugged and simply answered, "I feel somehow that it might serve you well in the future. But we mustn't mention this to your father," she had added. "He wouldn't understand. He would consider it a waste of time, I think."

He had agreed, and found that he had an aptitude for the language. It was a satisfying diversion from the strict State military education his father had insisted upon.

But later that year when his father looked over some of his papers, he had exploded when he saw the assignment written in English. "What is this?" he had blustered. "This is an outrage! A wasteful outrage! I forbid you to continue!"

He had argued with his father, and it had perplexed him when his mother stood silently by, saying nothing in his defense. So he stopped the tutoring sessions, but he had learned enough to continue on his own wherever and however he could, and he did.

He passed struggling dry sprigs of weed along the sidewalk, and stark, gray buildings as he walked. Sharp longing for the sandy beaches of his childhood near the Baltic Sea suddenly gripped him. He turned toward home, and his wife, Liesl. He had intended to go back to the office, but he decided it was too late now. He would go in first thing in the morning to report to his superior. Liesl would be home by now.

He rounded the corner with a smile of anticipation and approached the brick building that housed their apartment and several others, all distributed by the local government. They lived on the ground floor. It was small and dreary, and she had tried to brighten it with colorful cushions for the floor and curtains for the windows, but it was home because she lived there with him.

He turned his key in the lock and swung the door open.

CHAPTER TWO

"Liesl, are you home?"

"In the kitchen, Erik." She came to the door and greeted him with a happy smile. Her blue eyes sparkled with warmth. He smiled back as he came forward and swept her into his arms. Her body molded, as always, perfectly to his. It always felt so right to hold her. She was tall and willowy, but with an agile strength. She wore her light brown hair long and parted in the middle, and it flowed softly down her back. He lifted it with both hands and kissed her neck. She pulled back and her eyes searched his face. "You look tired and tense, Darling. Was it bad?"

Releasing her, he went into the kitchen. "I hope you didn't start dinner. The morning was very long, and yes, tense. I had a late lunch." He opened the refrigerator door, pulled out a pitcher of cold lemonade, poured it, then headed back into the front room.

She followed and sat down next to him on the sofa. "Tell me about it."

He put his glass on the table and pulled her into his arms again, nuzzling her neck. "It just took a lot of time and effort. The man I was supposed to see wasn't there today, and I had a hard time with his replacement."

"But the shipment has been arranged?"

"Yes, the shipment has been arranged."

"I'm glad. It could be much worse, you know. Every time you cross the border I worry–"

He put a finger over her lips. "I know." They didn't dare talk inside, since both knew there could be listening devices planted. They were common in many households. Everyone knew about the huge rooms full of files at Stasi headquarters. Anything suspicious could be used against them at any time. Even the young American woman he had met in West Berlin might be considered a suspicious subject to the wrong ears. He wanted to tell Liesl how much the woman looked like his mother, but he knew he couldn't. Instead, he lifted his finger from her lips and his mouth found hers. Soon their passion flared, as it always did.

"Are you hungry?" he asked against her lips.

"I can wait." She laughed, breathless. They rose and with their arms around each other, moved toward the bedroom.

Later, when they lay side by side, peaceful and satisfied, she gazed at him and traced a finger down his cheek. "I have news," she whispered.

He turned his head and looked at her. "What kind of news?"

"Good, I hope. I know our parents will be happy, and I wish your mother were here for this."

"I wish my mother were still here every day this past year. Just this morning I visited her in the cemetery again."

"I'm glad. She deserves your attentiveness, even now. I loved her too. My mother isn't nearly so warm, so easy to talk with as yours was."

He raised himself on his elbow. "And what would you talk about with my mother if she were still here?"

"Oh," she smiled wistfully, "I'd ask her what you were like as a baby."

He made a face. "A baby?"

"I'd want to know what it might be like for me in about seven months."

"A baby?" he repeated. His eyes widened. "You – "

She nodded. In her smiling eyes was a question.

"You're sure?"

"I was at the doctor during my lunch hour."

"But why didn't you tell me? You must have suspected."

"Yes, but I didn't want to tell you unless I knew for sure that it was true. And now I know for sure. And now I'm telling you. He'll be born in October, I think. Are you happy?"

For a long time he was unable to speak as he gazed at her, his own face washed with the depth of his feeling. Finally he uttered, "Oh, yes, Liesl. I'm happy. You'll make a wonderful mother." He kissed her, then he pulled back with a grin. "And how do you know we'll have a son?"

"Would you be as happy with a daughter?"

"Of course I would."

"Well, then. It will be a boy or a girl."

They laughed together. Again he turned serious, studying her face. It seemed to him to be suffused with radiance; she seemed to be glowing in a way he had never seen before. The wonder he felt became a living thing. He sat up and grasped her hands.

"I want to go for a walk before it gets dark." He jumped up and pulled her with him. She agreed with a laugh and within half an hour they were strolling down a pathway in their favorite part of the forest, hand in hand. The cool, still air smelled fresh and dense as shadows deepened. They walked along in silence for a few minutes, alert to cheerful birdsong around them.

"Do you remember the first time we came here together?" she asked him.

"Of course I do." He lifted her hand and kissed it. "You were trying to get me to chase you around that tree." He pointed to a large elm they were just approaching. "I told you that since I had just graduated from University, I was much too dignified and manly for such childish activities." He chuckled. "To be honest, though, I wanted to run and laugh, just like we did when we were children. I felt so happy to be with you. But it was a new feeling for me this time – different from when we were growing up."

She swung around to face him, walking backward on the hard-packed dirt pathway, hands on her hips. "You thought of me then as a little pest. Admit it."

He laughed and put his hands on her shoulders, pulling her close. "I admit it. Our fathers worked together and our parents socialized, and I had to endure your company. After all, you were two years younger than me—such a little girl."

She reared back and gave him an exasperated grin. He pulled her against him again, cradling her face in his hand. "No Liesl, the feeling that first day with you here in the forest was completely different from what I'd felt before. I remember I kissed you for the first time that day. I liked that feeling."

They walked on, and she said with off-hand innocence, "I'd been feeling that way for years, and I'd been trying to figure out how to get you to kiss me for years."

"Oh really?" he asked in feigned astonishment. They'd had this conversation a few times before, when the discovery of their love had been new and exciting. Now it seemed new and exciting all over again.

"Yes, really. I'd been in love with you since the first time I saw you, you know."

"Yes. I know," he said with a happy sigh. They strolled on in silence for awhile. He grappled with his thoughts and feelings, how to express them at this turning point in their young lives. "Liesl ..." he began. "Do you believe in God?"

She stopped walking and gazed up at him, her smile warm. "Why do you ask?"

He shrugged, struggling for words. "We don't remember much about religion, do we? After the war, when everything was in such dark turmoil, before my family and I came here to Berlin, my mother and I sometimes attended church in the Homeland. And she sometimes told me to have faith in a good power beyond our own. She said things were bound to get better. I feel that now—that we've been given a wonderful gift–a sign that things are bound to get better. It's a huge feeling. It fills me up. This child..." he placed his hand on her flat stomach and smiled again. "...this child is a gift from God. Is that a strange thing for a man like me to say? A man who has been raised in an atheist society?"

She gave a firm shake of her head and lifted her hand to his face. "No, Darling. It makes me happy to know you feel the same way I do. I remember my mother, too, used to take me to Lutheran Church services for a short time, until my father told us it wasn't good for his career. I always sensed that my mother was disappointed, but she didn't say anything, and neither did I. But I missed it. And I always sensed that God was still somehow with me. God brought us together." She looked down and gazed at her body. "Such a simple, normal thing between a loving couple, but to me it's more than that. Something between us is growing beyond our grasp, beyond our ability to understand."

He nodded, content that she understood completely, and looked up at the whispering leaves above him. Liesl was a miracle. A beautiful miracle. She was everything he had hoped to find in a woman: warm, exciting, thoughtful, compassionate. Smiling, he remembered the path that had led him to her.

By university he had gained an important victory over his father's iron will when he had refused to take a program that would develop a military career like the older man had. Since he had done well in sports, his father had finally agreed to a general sports scholarship through the German Gymnastics Sports Union.

His life would have been very different if things had developed the way he had hoped. But one day during training he had fallen off the trampoline and injured his knee. He flinched, reliving the nasty accident again in his mind, then the months of grueling physical therapy. He remembered how devastated he'd been during that time. After he recovered, his knee was never quite as responsive to the rigorous training, and he had to drop out of the program. Eventually he shifted his interest to general economics study at the University in Halle. This naturally assured a developing career position in sports equipment that included the travel he coveted.

"What are you thinking about?" Liesl asked.

"I was just remembering my accident. In a way, it brought us together, don't you think?"

"Of course."

They'd had this conversation before, too, but he needed to express his thoughts about it again. "Looking back" he said slowly, "I appreciated my background in sports training, but I'm glad I didn't excel as an athlete. That would probably have won me a position in one of the State sponsored sports schools. That life is one of driven sacrifice. It takes over everything else. To win for the glory of the State." He frowned. "I want to stay out from under the State's control as much as possible. And besides, we never would have had time to fall in love."

"Of course," she repeated with a grin. "It was during that time that you took a second look at me."

He glanced at her. As they continued walking hand in hand through the forest, he marveled that he could feel such love for her while hating everything their fathers stood for. Many times throughout his youth he had puzzled over where the contempt for Communism had come from. After his mother's revelations last year, he now knew. But he also knew that it did him little good to think about it.

He turned his head and gazed at Liesl again. She seemed lost in her own thoughts, yet he knew they felt the same about almost everything. They didn't even need to talk about it anymore. But these were such important issues. To agree so completely seemed such a miracle.

As if reading his thoughts, she nudged closer to him. "Remember how we felt when we heard of the student demonstrations in West Berlin? To be able to call for religious, political and economic reform seemed so wonderful."

He nodded. "Even though those students were violent, I felt such envy. They're struggling with their new democracy, but they're free to do it. Liesl, I wish we had the same basic freedom, but we know that in East Berlin it's impossible. In spite of privileges that came from our fathers' important Communist military positions, we have to keep silent, just like everyone else."

Again he marveled at their ability to think alike, and even pick up on each others' thoughts. While they were falling in love in the early sixties, one of the most surprising and wonderful discoveries he had made about her after careful, cautious probing, was that she felt the same way he did about the terrible new wall that divided Berlin. They had taken long walks in the forest then too, and discussed their feelings about their city, their country and the hopelessness of living in a Communist state. He had asked her how she had come to feel that way, since her father was as solidly committed to the Party as his.

She had just shrugged and said, "I see the way most East Germans live. It's very different with the elite in my father's circles. It seems to me they demand sacrifices in the name of Communism so we few can live the way we do. So I'll finish my education and then I intend to do something with it so that others can have a better life. But I would never tell my father that."

She had asked the same question of him, and he remembered telling her how he had picked up on little signs from his mother. He had always looked up to his mother and valued her judgment, and he had felt vague relief when he occasionally saw in her face a faint glimmer of distaste whenever his father expressed his autocratic Communist views.

Pain stabbed at him as he remembering his mother's death, and he slowed now and bowed his head. Liesl gave him an inquisitive glance, so he started walking again and put his arm around her shoulder. "I met a young American woman at the café in West Berlin where I had lunch this afternoon," he said as he kicked a small stone out of the pathway. "She reminded me of my mother, and now that you've told me about the baby, somehow I think she was a sign."

"What kind of sign?"

He squeezed her shoulder as they walked along. "Meeting that woman from America, the land of freedom, and learning of this little one inside you on the same day—this gives me new hope that anything is possible. Perhaps someday this child will know freedom. Who knows?"

"I'll just be happy if we can make a good life for our child," Liesl replied. "And I feel hopeful too, that some day, the world we know right here will change. In fact, I feel more than hope, Darling. Truly, I do."

CHAPTER THREE

After their trip to Europe, Dee and Dennis returned to Seattle where Dennis took a new job in computer sciences and they bought a new house, then began the business of settling down. She learned quickly that she had not conceived in Rome as she had hoped. And every single month after that, she suffered through a cycle of rising hope, anxiety and longing followed by plunging, aching despair that she was not yet pregnant.

Late that summer three of her old college girlfriends got together at her house. They all had babies, and the conversation revolved around feedings, diaper changes, and all the other daily details that made up being a mother. As she sat listening, Dee's little dog jumped up in her lap.

"I think I should learn to diaper this one," she attempted to add to the conversation, grinning. "He's still leaving puddles on the floor."

"Just wait till you have a baby," her friend Sally replied. "Then you'll be stuck like the rest of us."

Dee's gaze swept the laughing faces and her smile tightened on her lips. "I'd love to be stuck like the rest of you, but it's not happening."

Sally leaned forward and handed Dee her baby son. "Here. This one I'll share." The laughter sounded a little more strained to Dee, but maybe it was her imagination. She reached for Sally's baby and he came to her, unresisting. "See? You're a natural born mother," Sally observed. "It wasn't hard for Jim and me to conceive, but we did have a problem, as you know. I miscarried two babies before he was born. I'd be glad to recommend the fertility specialist we used."

Dee readily agreed. It was the first hopeful turn of events she'd had in a long time. She got the doctor's name and phone number and called the very next day to make an appointment. Then they started their round of tests. First her, then Dennis. It felt so hard, so scary. The weeks went by. Finally, the doctor told them he'd have the results for them the following Monday.

That weekend, she and Dennis both made an attempt to ignore the ominous presence. Neither one of them wanted to face the prospect of bad news. But it hung there anyway. She felt it, and she saw it in Dennis. He became increasingly quiet and moody.

Monday morning, the alarm rang, jarring them both awake. Dee listened with her eyes closed, then opened them to watch her husband reach over to turn it off. They were both still a moment, lying on their backs, breathing slowly and evenly. Then she turned her head as Dennis rolled his lanky frame to the edge of the bed and sat up, rubbing his face and head. His naked back was rigid, even in his sleepy state. She watched him pull himself to his feet and head for the bathroom.

A sense of dread overcame her as her drowsy mind cleared. Today the doctor will call with the results, she formed the words inside her head, and then they echoed again and again with loud reverberation.

She got up and went out to the kitchen to start breakfast. She and Dennis went mechanically through the motions of their morning routine. The coffee tasted bitter on her tongue and she put her cup down. Dennis rose from his chair.

"Dennis?"

"What?" His voice sounded strained, distant.

She waved her thoughts away. "Have a good day."

"You too." He went off to work and Dee was alone.

I wish I had a job to go to, she thought to herself. *I should start working again. It will keep my mind off this situation. What if we won't be able to have children?* Her breathing quickened as the full weight of that possibility hit her. She shook her head. *But I want children. So we'll adopt. Lots of couples do. I can't start working if we're going to adopt. I want to be home with the children while they're growing up. Why haven't we talked about this? Because we don't know for sure. There's nothing to talk about yet.* The thoughts jumbled around in her brain like wet clothing in a sluggish dryer.

The foreboding thickened, filling her. She forced her mind away from what she feared she already knew. *Oh, stop,* she chastised herself. *You don't know anything. And even if it is true, your big sister Donna would just tell you to get started on the adoption process. It's not such a big deal.*

The phone rang. She rose and moved toward it, reluctant, sure who was on the other end.

"Mrs. Sanders, this is Doctor Craig. I have the results of your tests."

She noted, without surprise, that his voice was subdued. "Yes?"

"I'd like to have both of you in my office as soon as possible to talk this over in detail."

Panic filled her. Her heart pounded painfully, thrusting adrenaline through her arteries. "Talk what over? What are the results?"

"Well, I'm afraid we found a real problem. There is probably no chance that you and your husband could ever conceive a child."

There was a long pause. She knew he was waiting for her to absorb this information. Clinical information. "No chance?" she finally asked, her voice hollow.

"No, it's pretty conclusive. Of course you could go for a second opinion. But why don't we meet and talk it over?"

She made the appointment with the doctor's receptionist, then called her sister. She felt like weeping, but she shared the information calmly. And just as she knew Donna would, her sister said in her usual brisk manner, "Well, get started on the adoption papers." She agreed, said goodbye, and hung up the phone.

The meeting with the doctor was just a formality. Their enzymes were incompatible, it seemed. She had antibodies that stopped and killed his sperm inside her. There was no known cure.

They left his office in silence. He went back to work and she went home, where the heavy black curtain came down over her. As she gave herself over to the pain, she closed her eyes and the tears spilled over and ran down her cheeks. A dark inevitability settled in. Four years into the marriage, she was now forced to accept that there was no hope for conception and pregnancy, one of life's major human experiences, one she had always taken for granted as a normal, natural right. While other young couples worried about birth control, she thought with irony, that was no longer an option for her and Dennis.

During the following months of mourning, she read everything she could get her hands on about infertility, and although there did indeed seem to be no hope, she felt comforted somehow by what she learned, that the vast majority of infertile couples had difficulty adjusting to their situation. Often, the marriage failed under the strain if the couple could not share their feelings.

Infertility felt like failure to her, it felt like defeat, but it was not necessarily a reason for her *marriage* to fail, she told herself stoically. She longed for closeness and shared grief with Dennis, she longed for a deep togetherness to rise from these ashes. But it didn't happen. Dennis remained caring and reasonable, but they did not delve beneath the surface of their disappointment. After all, she decided, they were both good people, and they would try to continue to be good to each other.

They discussed adoption and decided it would be the best option. They signed with an adoption agency. The end of one dream, the beginning of another. Dee got busy altering the spare room into a nursery with bassinet, crib, changing table with powders and lotions and stacks of diapers waiting. They talked about what to name the baby. The months went by. Sometimes they waited an eternity, and sometimes the time passed too quickly. She felt anticipation, she felt apprehension. She did not feel like a prospective mother.

But when the call came she felt immense relief. The waiting was over. Their daughter would be waiting for them at the adoption agency the next morning, they told her.

And she was. When they met her for the first time they both marveled: one week old and so terribly tiny, with soft, downy hair, impossibly sweet, clutching fingers, the hint of a milky warm smile. Dee felt the magnetic pull of recognition and connection. She turned to Dennis. "She looks like a Jill, don't you think?"

Jill gave a sudden hiccup, then cried out.

Alarm jolted through Dee. *I'm a new mother*, she suddenly realized. *What do I do now?*

They took their baby girl home and bit by bit, through awkward diaper changes, baths and feedings, Dee fell into the routine of mothering.

She spent hours late at night gazing down at the beautiful sleeping creature, overwhelmed by the love she felt for this precious gift. She wondered if Jill's birth mother would have been able to give her any kind of home. "Your mother is a stranger, and a stranger is your mother," she crooned softly. She thought often of Jill's birth mother, out there somewhere, feeling immense grief over what must have been the hardest decision of her young life. Admittedly, Dee thought of her at first as a threat. Irrational anxiety consumed her, that the birth mother would somehow change her mind, find out where they lived and come and take the child away from them.

Gradually, those feelings subsided, and she realized at some point that this child was hers to raise. And yet, somehow she knew that one day, at the other end of that long tunnel into the future, she hoped to meet this woman who had given birth to her little girl. She wanted the chance to thank her for her unselfish decision.

The tiny, wizened jerking creature bit by bit emerged into a plump, healthy, happily grinning baby, with an angelic face and wispy, corn-silk hair. When Jill was six months old they went to court to legally finalize the adoption. Dee dressed her up in a cute little blue flowered dress, and Jill looked chubby and rosy cheeked, the picture of health. Dee was determined the judge would see that Jill lived in a good home. She didn't want to run the risk that they'd repossess her baby.

She sat next to their attorney, strongly aware of the legal papers in his lap. She couldn't resist. She glanced over his shoulder at the legal typing on the papers.

She saw a name.

A moment later, noticing what she was up to, he got up and moved to another part of the room, leaving her feeling embarrassed and guilty. The memory stayed with her.

The weeks and months passed and Dee fell into the satisfying pattern of young motherhood with her other young mother friends. It was a happy time, perhaps the happiest she had experienced in her life. She and Dennis, good friends, were raising a sweet little girl.

But little by little, Dennis withdrew into his work, and she couldn't seem to pull him into the family she was trying to forge. She tried to tell herself he was building a career as all young men do, but this somehow seemed different. She didn't know how to talk about it but she knew somehow that she had to.

One cold winter evening she sat on the floor at Dennis's feet, Jill in her lap. Jill was a toddler and she was teaching her to play patty-cake. She glanced up at Dennis, assuming a moment of shared tenderness between the three of them. But Dennis was gazing stone-faced across the room toward the window, almost as if he wished he were outside looking in instead of sitting inside with them. She shivered, even though she felt warm in her long winter housecoat. She had seen that look many times before. It saddened her. It disturbed her. Resolute, she stopped the game and rose with Jill in her arms.

"Time for bed now. Kiss Daddy goodnight." She leaned Jill down to hug Dennis, then pulled her up again, holding her close. Jill laid her head against her shoulder, contented, cooing as Dee carried her off to bed.

When Dee came back to the living room, she sat on the floor in front of Dennis again, her cheek resting against his knee. "You seem so unhappy, Denny. What is it?" she asked earnestly. "Can't we talk about it? Can't I help?"

He shook his head, his eyes vacant, removed. "No. It's just work. You wouldn't understand."

"Try me." She prodded for hours, trying every way she could to draw him out. But somehow it seemed that she was pushing him further into himself. Her words, meant to be encouraging, were absorbed by Dennis as something to dismiss.

Whenever she saw an opportunity in the months that followed, she kept trying. He never insisted she stop pushing, never put his foot down or changed the subject. He either sat and listened in stony silence, or he got up and left the room. And so she felt like a failure with him.

Thick, gray fog crept in, leaving her lonely, isolated, desolate in the marriage.

One day she took Jill shopping at a large mall. Her little girl was having a wonderful time darting under the clothes. Dee smiled and told her to stay near. Then suddenly she realized that Jill wasn't there anymore. She stopped what she was doing and started looking for her. Concern turned to panic as she realized that Jill had vanished completely.

"Jill!" Frantic, she called out over and over as she searched, enlisting the aid of some of the employees in the store. Finally they came upon the child, hiding under a rack of clothing with a mischievous grin. The relief was overwhelming.

When she told Dennis about it that night after Jill had gone to sleep, she tried to convey her sense of fear and anxiety.

"I felt I had failed somehow," she told him.

"Failed? What do you mean?" he asked.

"I don't know." She put her arms around his neck and leaned into him, seeking comfort. "I guess I felt I had to answer to her birth parents for losing her so carelessly. It was an awful feeling," she concluded. But her explanation felt inadequate somehow.

"She's okay," Dennis replied, unconcerned. "She's safe in bed where she belongs."

"I know," Dee said with uncertainty. "But I love her so much. And I wish she had been born from our love."

"But she is!" Dennis said with a burst of conviction, impatience. "She's our child in every way that matters. Never doubt that, Dee."

She felt reassured for a few months.

Then one night when Jill was four years old Dee awoke in the middle of the night with sharp, searing abdominal pain. She started moaning in anguish.

Dennis raised himself on one elbow and peered down into her face. "Dee? What is it?"

"Terrible pain. In my abdomen. It's like gas pains, only much worse."

He climbed out of bed and came back with a bottle of liquid antacid. She raised herself with difficulty, and drank straight from the bottle. "I think that'll help," she said.

It seemed only a few minutes later when she woke again. "Dennis, it's worse. I can't stand it. I think something is really wrong. Can you drive me to Emergency?"

They called her sister Donna, who came over to stay with Jill, and Dennis drove Dee to the hospital where she was admitted for surgery.

They removed her near-ruptured appendix and she recovered fairly quickly. The days she spent in the hospital were a blur to her. She remembered Dennis coming once and reporting that Jill was at Donna's and that they wouldn't allow children in the hospital. When she came home after a week or two her mother was there to help her with Jill until she got her strength back.

Dennis rapidly spent as much time as ever at work, and the little time he was home he seemed remote, preoccupied. It hurt her that in spite of her medical crisis, he hadn't changed toward her at all.

Berlin, 1975

"Papa, when will Mama come home?" Jon asked, his huge blue eyes filled with anxiety. "May I go with you to see her in the hospital?"

Erik gazed at his five-year-old son, whose wheat-colored hair looked so like his mother's. He hoped his voice and manner seemed encouraging. He felt anything but that himself. "The hospital has rules we must follow, Jon. They are very strict, because they want her to get well and strong, and we want that too, so she can come home to us soon."

"But I miss her. Why is she there?"

Steeling himself, he answered slowly. "You remember we hoped to have a baby brother or sister for you. But something went wrong, and ..." he drew in a deep breath. "I know Mama misses you very much, but children cannot come to the hospital, and so I'll take you to see Hilda on my way to the hospital, and then later I'll come back for you and we can go home together. Let's put on your coat. We have to go now. Hilda is waiting for us."

After he left Jon in the care of his kindly neighbor, he drove his Trabi to the hospital. He hurried past Liesl's parents in the waiting room, barely acknowledging them on his way to Liesl's room. Three nurses and a doctor were bustling around the bed and he knew immediately that the anxiety level had increased since he had been here earlier.

"What is it?" he asked. He suddenly felt cold, so cold. "Is there a change?" He moved quickly to the bed, in spite of the nurses' efforts to block him.

The doctor took the thermometer from her mouth, read it, then lifted his troubled eyes. "She's very sick. She's lost a great deal of blood, and now her temperature has risen. We've been unable to control the infection or the bleeding."

"But you said she would improve after a few hours of rest."

"We thought the medication would have taken hold by now."

Liesl moaned and opened her eyes. Her face was pale, her eyes hollow and glazed, her breathing shallow, rapid. "Darling. My darling, come closer."

He bent over her and kissed her. He felt the fire on her skin. Panic welled up in him. He pushed it down, forcing a brittle smile. "Rest, now, Liesl. I'm here.

You must rest and get better. Jon sends his love and wants you home with us."

"Jon?" Her eyes widened in alarm. "Where's my baby? My baby!"

"Shh – you mustn't upset yourself," he pleaded, trying to keep the fear from his voice. "Rest now so I can bring you home to Jon. He needs us both." He gently stroked her forehead, aware that his hand was shaking.

"Please wait outside, now," the doctor urged. "She needs to be calm. I'll call you in a little while."

He turned and stumbled out to the sterile waiting room, his mind reeling with pain and confusion as he tried to explain the situation to her worried parents. Their anxious faces blurred in front of him and he swung his eyes away. "The baby – we lost the baby, and now –" He collapsed in a chair. He sat there for what seemed hours in his dazed state, unable to focus on anything but the fear. "Surely she'll be better soon. She has to be better soon."

She died only one hour later.

That night a huge, dark, empty hole opened, and it consumed him. It would be many years before he would emerge from it.

CHAPTER FOUR

Over the years, in Seattle, Dennis spent more time at work, so that he missed more dinners, movies, soccer games, birthdays, even family vacations– all became normal to their family pattern. Dee harbored a growing resentment like a piece of embroidery she was working on, watching for more furry fragments of yarn she could add to the whole picture. Money became plentiful, but pain and disappointment developed into familiar companions to Dee. Then he began to travel often to California's Silicon Valley on business. And she felt like a cruel shrew for continuing to communicate her frustration and anger.

"You're missing out on your daughter's life!" she repeated over the years. "Why can't you spend more time with us? Your work is killing your family!"

One Friday evening in 1989 Jill was out, and Dee remembered the times in recent years that her daughter had angrily stormed out of the house to be with her friends, a direct result of the tension between her parents. She scolded herself for being irritated with Dennis once again when he hadn't arrived home by eight that evening. *Just another big project with a big deadline*, she thought with resentment. Then she realized she dreaded his coming home. *This is not good*, she told herself. Jill had graduated from high school a year before and would soon be off on her own. *Is this what defeat feels like?* She wondered. There was no family anymore. Not really. And she didn't know if they could build anything meaningful between them once Jill was gone. Suddenly exhausted, she got up from the table to put the overcooked dinner away.

She was just sitting down to continue the novel she was reading when Dennis walked in the door. He hung up his coat, then turned to face her.

"Dinner is in the refrigerator," she said through tight lips. She didn't look up from her novel. He kept standing inside the door, so she finally looked up. His face held an expression of something indefinable—defeat, or determination. She couldn't tell.

"Why didn't you call to tell me you'd be late?" she asked.

"Doesn't matter. We need to talk, Dee." He walked over and sat heavily in the chair across from her.

"What is it?" she asked.

"I need to get out of this marriage."

"What?" She stared at him. Her heart began hammering.

He bent his head and looked at his limp hands hanging from his knees. "It's just not working between us. I don't know if it ever did."

"What?" she continued to stare at him, unable to comprehend his words.

"We shouldn't have to make such an effort, Dee. It shouldn't have to be so hard. From the beginning I never knew what you needed, or wanted. I just know you were never satisfied. So I just quit trying."

She knew her face registered the hurt and shock she felt. *This all feels so unreal. So abrupt,* she thought. *But wasn't I thinking the same kinds of things just before he came home?* She couldn't say anything. The silence lengthened between them. *It's not like him to rock this boat,* she realized. She felt a blurry buzzing in her head. Finally she asked, "Is there someone else?"

He hesitated, then nodded. "I think so. I don't know. But I want to be honest with you. She's someone I work with in California. When I'm with her I feel energized. She seems to appreciate what I say and do, and of course we have a lot in common because of the work. We understand each other."

"So you want to be free to pursue her?"

"I haven't thought that far ahead. I'm not having an affair with her or anything like that. I want you to know that. But I want to move out as soon as I tell Jill. This weekend, if possible."

So the marriage ended. Not with anger, but with resignation. Dennis' financial settlement was generous, and briefly she harbored bitterness about the guilt he must feel. But in the end, she reasoned to herself that they both felt the same way—they were too different—could not breach the gap between them. They had tried, and they had failed. Or the marriage had failed. She tried to tell herself all these things. If she were honest with herself, Dee admitted, in many ways she felt relieved. But she also felt abandoned, rejected. In the years that followed, she would experience bouts of emotional desolation and endless tears.

And somehow, occasionally over the years, the young man in Berlin flashed into her memory.

Seattle, 1993

"I wonder," Dee mused, regarding her pretty twenty-three year old daughter intently as she sat across the table from her, "when you find your birth mother, if you'll discover she's quite a bit like me."

They were seated at a window table in Charlie's Restaurant on Shilshole Bay, one of their favorites. Jill's reaction was immediate. Throwing her hands up and grimacing in mock horror, she declared, "Oh, heaven help me, if I find I have two overly emotional mothers on my hands." She shook her head with vehemence and squirmed in her chair.

"All mothers are overly emotional at times," Dee said, feeling defensive and glancing away. Then she softened, and her eyes moved back to rest on her daughter's face. Regarding Jill's face always pleased her; her clear blue almond-shaped eyes, gracefully molded jaw line, the wide mouth, the long smooth plaits of ash blond hair that swept back into a thick braid down the middle of her back. When she was a white-haired baby Dee knew she wouldn't look much like her or Dennis. She had grown to the same height as Dee, and in other ways too, she liked to think she saw a resemblance, if only faint. "The important thing to me is that she'd be as proud of you as I am. I know she would."

Jill folded her arms across her front. "Gee, what can I say to that vote of confidence? Thanks. It's strange, you know? The whole time I was growing up, my birth mother seemed like some kind of hazy fantasy. I had the usual curiosity about whether I looked like her and all that. But then when I got the information from the agency, every little piece of it seemed so real somehow. Like the fact that she had just graduated from high school before she had me. It took me quite awhile to digest it all."

Dee smiled at Jill with what she hoped was encouragement and understanding. Her daughter had written to the adoption agency with her inquiries more than a year ago and they had written back with what information they could provide by law, assuring her that if her birth mother contacted them, they'd put the two of them in touch. So far Dee was pleased Jill had shared her feelings about this, and knew she had heard nothing.

"I feel it too," Dee said. "That's what I meant about what she and I may have in common. The agency letter said she was a quiet girl with a soft voice. You know I tend to be that way, too. You're one of the few people who've seen my overly emotional side, and that's only because we lived under the same roof for over twenty years." She paused and grinned at Jill, who gave a little smile back to her, and encouraged, Dee added, "But basically, I'm quiet, even shy. You know that."

"But I didn't inherit shyness from you ... or from her, either."

Dee nodded, felt the familiar rush of pride and affection that accompanied thoughts of her daughter's self-assurance. "You are not shy because your dad and I were determined to encourage confidence in you, because we were so lacking in it ourselves. It isn't necessarily a biological trait." She pondered this, then added, "Quiet people often encourage confidence in others. We knew it would help get you over life's rough patches."

"Anyway," Jill went on, stabbing a potato wedge with her fork, "I'm not obsessive about finding her." She shrugged with some defensiveness, popped the wedge into her mouth and turned her attention to her next bite.

"Most adopted young adults are curious to meet their birth parents. To find out about their biological roots for medical reasons, if nothing else," Dee offered. She knew this wouldn't be an easy conversation, but every sentence suddenly felt to her as if she were walking through a mine field. She plunged ahead. "I think the files should be opened once an adopted child reaches 21. I mean that. You have a right to know."

"I think so, too," Jill agreed. "Of course, I realize she may not want to meet me, but that's a chance I'd be willing to take."

Dee nodded. "She may have a husband and children who never knew about you. No doubt giving you up was very painful for her. That whole time in her life must have been painful. She may not want to be reminded."

"I know."

"But I know you could handle whatever happened. And I also know it would all be worthwhile to her to know how well you turned out." She paused, watching Jill concentrate on the food on her plate. "The letter the agency wrote was revealing, I thought."

Jill looked up and met her gaze. "In what way?"

Her throat swelled and constricted, and she prayed she wouldn't get teary. She had to get it all said, and she didn't want her daughter closing off in the face of her ragged feelings. It always made Jill uncomfortable, she knew. Part of the annoying emotions she talked about. "They said she wrote quite a few times soon afterward, asking how you were doing, what kind of family you were placed in. She seemed to show a need to know what happened to you. She knew she had to get on with her own life, but she cared. That indicates to me that she never stopped caring."

Jill shrugged, but remained silent. Dee let the silence lengthen while they finished their lunch, gave her time to think about this. Finally, she said, "You know I'll help you all I can. If you want. And there's something –"

A young waiter came to take their plates away.

"Can I get you anything else?" he asked, smiling at Jill.

"No thanks," Dee answered quickly.

Jill turned her eyes up to the young man and smiled back at him. "It was good."

"Glad you liked it." He lowered his eyes shyly as he left the check, picked up their plates with another smiling glance in Jill's direction, then moved away.

Dee grinned at her daughter and leaned back. "A good chef appreciates a good waiter," she observed.

"You're right about that. They work hard."

Dee paused, then decided against teasing her about the handsome waiter. "I'm so proud of you, Jill. Ever since you were a child, you've shown amazing interest and talent in the world of cooking." Instead of conventional university education after high school, Jill had chosen to attend culinary school and pursue her career goals in this way. "Right out of culinary school you landed a great job in a great restaurant. That's quite an accomplishment. Do you still like it?"

"I do," Jill grinned. "I'm still learning so much."

"Well, I knew you'd like this restaurant. It's a lot like yours, don't you think?"

Jill nodded. "The food is. Different ambiance, though. Different view."

They had a window table, and at her daughter's remark they both looked out at the sailboats moored below, the water beyond. "It's soothing in a way," she said.

"That's what Dad says about the water in the Bay Area in California too," Jill replied. "It's different down there, a different kind of beauty."

Dee nodded her acknowledgment. Jill's remarks brought recurring questions to Dee's mind about Dennis. It had crossed her mind a few times that he had never remarried, and she wondered what had happened with the woman he worked with in California. He had never said, and she didn't want to ask Jill.

They lapsed into silence again, but it seemed a comfortable silence to Dee as they looked out over the sailboats and the water of Puget Sound beyond. It was calm today. Seagulls soared and wheeled in the cloudless autumn sky.

She turned back to Jill. "I was going to tell you something a minute ago. It was the reason I invited you out to lunch."

Her daughter's eyebrows raised in curiosity. "I'm all ears."

Dee swallowed. "Well, when you first told me you wanted to try to find your birth mother, I was glad for you. I encouraged you, and I was pleased when you wanted to share the letter you got back from the agency."

Jill opened her mouth to answer, but Dee held up her hand. "Hear me out," she said. "This isn't easy for me, and I don't know if it's anything at all, but I know I have to tell it. Because it's yours, not mine, if it *is* anything. But I have to tell it my way."

Jill nodded, her eyes intent on her mother's face.

"Since I read that letter, I've had a glimmer of something hazy—foggy–a memory of sitting in the courtroom when you were six months old, the day you were legally adopted. You know you were a week old when we got you, and then there was a six-month waiting period."

Jill's head lowered slowly in acknowledgment.

The beginnings of a smile cross her lips as snatches of memory rose in her mind. "After the six months were up, that day in court, we did everything we could to make a good impression of a happy home. Somehow I was scared to death they'd repossess you." She laughed. "So this was the last hurdle. Anyway," she pushed on, "I was sitting next to our attorney, and I couldn't seem to help myself – I glanced at the papers in his lap so often that he moved to another part of the courtroom. I was so embarrassed, I felt so guilty. That's the part I focused on, that's the part that stands out in my mind. Because I knew we weren't supposed to know the name of the birth mother." She paused. "But I saw it."

"You saw it?"

"I saw it. But that's the part that's hazy to me. I didn't dwell on the name, because I knew *I* didn't want to do anything with it, and I knew it would be twenty years or more before *you* might. So over the years I forgot about it." She paused and took a deep breath, watching her daughter's face for a reaction. "It's important to me that you know I haven't been keeping it from you. Only in the past few months have I thought about it, and wondered if it's even an accurate memory. I'm not sure I remember the name correctly. But as I said, whether it's accurate or not, I decided it's past time to tell you. It's your information, not mine. It's yours to do with what you want."

Jill's eyes had not left her face. "What is it?"

CHAPTER FIVE

"I'm not sure of the spelling," Dee told her daughter. "It's Insen." She took a stab at the spelling, continuing to watch Jill's face closely. She didn't seem angry, she didn't seem excited or happy. She seemed to accept what Dee had told her with casual interest.

"It's a start, anyway," Jill said. "If I want to pursue a search."

"I was hoping she contacted the agency by now." Dee lifted her shoulders in a little shrug. "But it's been over a year since you wrote."

Jill gave a brisk nod, then scooted her chair back from the table and stood up. "You ready?" She picked up the check.

"Sure." Dee rose and took the check from her hand. "This is my treat. I invited you, remember?"

Jill grinned. "I won't argue with you."

They walked over to the cashier and she paid the check, and then they left the restaurant and walked around the building to the waterfront. They passed a huge, stalwart maple, its stark branches still clutching a few leaves, flame-colored and translucent in the unseasonably warm sunshine. As they strolled along the walkway that skirted the shore, brittle, brown leaves swirled around their feet. She fixed her eyes upon Jill's shoes as they moved along. Her feet were long and narrow, just the right size, she thought, for the rest of her tall, willowy figure. She breathed in the bracing salt air and listened to the gulls crying, then she turned to look into her daughter's face.

"It seems like only yesterday when I taught you how to tie your shoes," she said softly. "You're still my kid."

"That'll never change, Mom."

"I know. And I want to support you if you do pursue a search. It costs quite a bit if you don't have any clues, doesn't it? Maybe the name, if it's correct anyway, will help you avoid all that."

"I don't know. Maybe. I don't think I want to do anything about it right now, though." Jill stopped and leaned over the railing of the walkway. "I guess I want to take some time to get used to the idea of the name and what I can do with it. I sent for a book I heard about that tells you how to proceed in detail. It cleared up a lot of questions I had. Even if they opened the records here in this state, the search would probably still take awhile. Things vary legally from state to state."

"Amazing. I didn't know that, Jill. You've learned a lot already, haven't you?"

"Guess so. One step at a time."

"Sounds sensible. I hope your birth mother is still right here in the area, though."

They fell silent, leaning over the railing together, watching the waves lapping the beach. *This wasn't such a difficult conversation after all,* Dee decided as they walked back to the car.

"Where to now?" Jill asked as Dee started the motor.

"Work," she answered. "I have an interesting new client named Mikhail Sommers. He's a retired gymnastics instructor and coach who was born in Eastern Europe. He lives at Sunrise Retirement Home, and we're working on his life story. It's fascinating – we've met for the overview already, and he's told me that he was a performer as a young man and he went through all kinds of adventures during World War II, running from the Nazis in Germany and then the Communists after the war. He saw a lot first hand. I think a story like his could be a best seller. Especially since the Berlin Wall fell and the Soviet Union broke apart."

"How did he get to America?"

"I don't know, but I imagine that will be an interesting story in itself."

"Sounds like you've got a good career started, Mom. I'm proud of you. Last year you did a family history about pioneer medical missionaries, this year you're doing a fascinating autobiography. What's next year?"

"Maybe a story about a reunion ..." she looked at her with a questioning smile.

Jill grinned back at her and shrugged her shoulders. Then she breathed deeply and gazed out the car window. "What a great day! I'm glad I've got it off. I've been working hard all week and I feel like being lazy. Think it's warm enough for me to sit out by the pool?"

After she dropped Jill at her apartment, Dee headed toward the retirement home where her latest client lived, thinking along the way about the young woman who had given birth to Jill. She thought of the trust the birth mother had put into the adoption process, that her baby could have a better life than she could have provided. Dee remembered the commitment she had felt to earning her trust, to raise this child to become a healthy, happy, productive adult. She thought of the countless times she felt she had failed that trust.

The beginnings of tears prickled her throat and nose as she pulled into the retirement home parking lot. Mikhail was standing outside the front door waiting for her with an expectant grin on his face, and she quickly wiped her eyes and climbed out of the car.

He walked toward her with his slow, smooth, erect gait and his bright smile. He carried his lean, compact body with strength and dignity. She knew he had to be in his early 70's, and she was impressed by how fit he looked. In the brilliant sunlight, his neatly trimmed brown hair had hardly a gray strand in it, and the lines and creases in his face etched their way down to a surprisingly firm chin line. He squared his shoulders, held out his hand and gave her a firm handshake. She returned his smile, wondering not for the first time how he happened to be living in a retirement home. He seemed too youthful.

"Well, Mikhail, this is a nice surprise, finding you right here to greet me as I drive up," she said.

He inclined his head in the dignified manner she had come to recognize as his trademark. He regarded her thoughtfully, blue eyes twinkling. "I look forward to our first real session," he said, his rich, accented voice reverberating heartily. "I see no point in waiting in my room when I could be out here watching for you. You are right on time, and naturally that pleases me to know I can count on your punctuality."

"Thank you, Mikhail." They walked back across the parking lot and through the front door. It felt much cooler inside. "Your story fascinates me. I look forward to hearing the first detailed installment. And I can already tell you'll be easy to work with. You have good instincts about organizing the segments of your life."

The retirement home provided a little office off the main front room, which could be used by residents and their guests. It contained a modest supply of the latest office machines, including a computer and printer.

She sat down at the desk and pulled her small tape machine out of her bag, then plugged it in. "You mentioned last time that you'd be agreeable to taping each session, then I'll take the cassette home and transcribe the material for the next session. That way you can look over what you talked about and add or subtract whatever you'd like."

"Agreed," he nodded. "I will try for chronological events, but I may jump around from time to time."

"In that case, I'll insert the material chronologically later."

"Fine, fine," he rubbed his hands together, clearly enthusiastic. "Shall we begin, then?"

She smiled at him and turned on the recorder. "Well, let's see how much we can accomplish today," she said briskly. "You were born in Riga, Latvia, correct? I'd like you to go into some detail about what your home city was like."

His eyes drifted to the window and he walked over and looked out at the trees with their almost bare, stark branches. "Riga ... ornamental city of majestic spires and domes, cobblestone streets, birch trees and bright flowers—red, blue, yellow, orange. Mention the name of my native home and at once, my thoughts flow back to it, like the powerful river Daugava that flows through its center to the Baltic Sea."

He spoke with slow and distinct precision. She could see what he was describing, so vivid were his verbal images. "My country, Latvia, together with Lithuania and Estonia, form the three Baltic States. All three countries are like the Russia of Dr. Zhivago – I remember bitter cold winters with huge piles of endless snow, warm summers with beautiful seaside resorts, colorful autumns and springs."

"Can you tell me about the history of your country?"

"The Baltics were a part of Russia until the end of World War I, and then they gained their independence. They were three sovereign countries until Communist

Russia overpowered them at the end of World War II. So they have been behind the Iron Curtain since then. Yet, I will always remember my native Latvia as a strong, independent country of proud, free people, people with laughing faces, people who love music, dancing, festive activities– because while I was growing up, during my most impressionable years, precisely the twenty years between my birth in 1920 and my adulthood, my country was free. And I was proud to reflect that freedom in my chosen life's work."

"Flying on the trapeze, right?"

He gave her a smile and nodded. It seemed to Dee that he lifted his countenance visibly, reflecting the pride he expressed. "From the time I was twelve years old and saw my first flying trapeze act at the circus," he continued, "I had pursued my fervent dream to become a flyer. I trained vigorously in gymnastics to develop strength, agility and discipline. Later I developed acrobatic skills. And then when I was sixteen, I felt confident that I was ready. I auditioned before a flying trapeze troupe, and they accepted me as an apprentice. My dream had come true – nothing could stop me now!"

He began to pace back and forth across the room, hands clasped behind his back, as she sat there, her mind alive with the energy of his words.

"How did your family feel about your work on the trapeze?"

His face fell, his bright smile faded; his words lost their smooth, lyrical cadence. "My parents were hard-working, conservative people who didn't approve of my chosen field, but when they saw how important this position was to me, they decided to support my efforts. My older brother also disapproved, so he went his way and I went mine."

"That must have been a disappointment to you," she offered.

He nodded silently.

"Tell me a bit about the details of your training."

"During my first year as an apprentice, my trainer, the head-flyer Jahn, pushed and drove me relentlessly, urging from me feats even he didn't realize I could accomplish. The catcher of the team, Oscar, encouraged me when I felt depressed and ready to quit. He helped me to believe in myself and my potential. In return, I developed unshakable trust in Oscar as we worked together. Even when I made a wrong move in flight, he covered for me and caught me every time. By the time we were ready to perform together as a team, I knew both Jahn and Oscar had accepted me as an equal." The musical rhythm of his words returned. "Every night I floated home from work. I loved the life of a flyer; I loved the physical and mental stimulation and grueling discipline, the exhilarating camaraderie with my fellow-performers. I absorbed the atmosphere like a sponge. I was still in high school, yet so impatient to leave it behind that I barely noticed that part of my life. In fact, during my last year in school, I traveled a great deal with the trapeze act, performing in circuses, fairs and variety houses throughout Eastern Europe." He chuckled. "My grades were so bad I barely graduated, but I didn't care. I was receiving all the education I wanted through my work. I remember our travels vividly during those times."

"Wasn't that the time of Hitler's rise to power, too? The late 1930's? Did you see any evidence of that?"

"Yes… I remember glimpsing signs of Hitler's rise to power. I remember how easy it was to ignore them." He shook his head. "Now, more than fifty years later, I feel the bitter irony as I remember my youthful, carefree innocence, and how quickly it was all to change." He stood in front of the window again, gazing out. "Memories of those deceptively simple, naïve pre-war days have sharpened their focus over time – even the exhilaration I felt when I performed. Why is that? After each swing on the trapeze, each twisting salto—summersault—with Oscar catching me, or each passage with Jahn crossing over me in midair, I returned to the bridge platform with the roar of applause echoing in my head. It never failed to trigger in me a surge of courage and pride, just hearing such genuine crowd appreciation." He turned to face her. She looked at him expectantly, saw his body give a slight shiver before he went on.

"After I graduated from high school, the act started to book regularly with the Salamonski Circus in Riga. The circus was housed in a large brick permanent structure, with one ring in the center of the vast round arena. Around the inside walls, the audience sat in three separate levels, with the best box-seats at ground level nearest the ring.

"My parents came sometimes to see my performances. I always got them box seats, and I always made a special effort throughout my act to flash a reassuring grin in their direction. I remember how my mother worried about the danger involved, as all mothers would, I suppose, but in my youthful enthusiasm I felt nothing but confidence and control. I was delighted by the success of my new career, and soon I moved out of my parents' apartment and found my own furnished place, right around the corner from the circus building."

Again he paused. Their eyes met and held for a long moment. His eyes were sparkling. Then he turned away and started to speak slowly, his voice hushed and full of emotion.

"And at this point in my life, I met Anita. She had an act at Salamonski as a rope dancer. I noticed her the very first night Jahn, Oscar and I began performing there. Our flying act was scheduled toward the end, and that always gave us time to watch the opening acts. Anita was second on the program.

"On that first night, I was standing in the gallery at the beginning of her act when she made her entrance in a sparkling blue costume. From that moment, I was captivated. She had dark, lustrous hair that fell soft around her shoulders, and her face had a kind of radiance and warmth under the spotlights, her shining brown eyes full of expression. As she walked with grace toward the rope, I followed the sway of her hips with my eyes. Then she ascended the ladder, moving in rhythm with the music. As she danced along the rope, the colorful umbrella she carried summoned a certain style – a quaint, charming quality that enhanced her physical presence. I remember glancing around at faces in the audience. All eyes were rapt and fixed upon her, and I knew I wasn't the only one charmed by her beauty."

He turned and blinked slowly, took a deep breath as if coming out of a trance. "Perhaps that is enough for one day," he told Dee, his voice returning to its earlier heartiness.

She nodded, turned off the tape recorder and stood up, then gathered up her material. She wanted to urge him to continue, but it was as if he had pre-determined how much to cover in one day. "I'll look forward to the next meeting," she said, meaning it sincerely. "I'd like to explore your relationship with Anita in some detail, if you're willing. It sounds as if she was significant in your life."

"Significant...yes." He breathed in. "I will think about it then. Until next time."

He walked with her out to her car.

Significant, she mused, as she drove home. *What did that mean, after fifty years of separation? Dennis had been significant. Would I feel the reverence I heard in Mikhail's voice after fifty years of separation from Dennis?*

But she was sure the memory of Dennis would never have the same meaning for her that the memory of Anita had for Mikhail. There had been too many years of too little communication, too much daily disappointment in her relationship with Dennis.

CHAPTER SIX

Dee pulled into her driveway, still thinking of Mikhail. She knew he had spent a great deal of time in Berlin during the war, and she knew his memories of that time must be powerful. Her own brief visit there twenty-five years before held powerful memories, as well. The divided city, the Wall, the visit to her ancestors' graves in East Berlin, the feeling of past and present evil, the freshness of Spring…the young German man at the sidewalk café. She shook her head, having realized at some point over the years that this man represented the nameless, faceless longing she'd felt most of her life. *Longing of an adolescent girl*, she admonished herself. But it had still rooted itself in that particular person's features–long forgotten, and in his strong reaction to her–long remembered.

She felt her face flush now at the memory. *Not relevant*, she thought. She'd need more than her own memories to fill in the descriptions and nuances and historical aspects of Berlin, she resolved, as she picked up her mail and went into her house.

She lived alone, and had since Jill had left home. Jill had found her own place two years before. She had a roommate and a career, a good start at life. Dee was certain Jill knew she had a mother who loved her, who'd always be there for her.

She sighed, knowing she couldn't go back and do it over. Didn't even want to, really. Her job as a mother was basically finished. The house was too big now, of course. But it had been home for many years, and Dee just wasn't ready to part with it yet. Somehow it was comforting to live in familiar surroundings. Her belongings were like old friends to her.

She moved through the living room, smiling at the colorful mementos of Jill growing up. Pictures, vases, muted hand-made pillows, all in shades of blue and green, and on the wall a large blue and green latch-hook mountain scene that Jill had created in a high school class. Dee had always been pleased at how it blended just right with the rest of the accents in the room. All of them were a little worn but still attractively placed, and there was always so much to be said for sentimental value. She picked up a recent portrait of Jill in a bright blue dress and a happy smile. She smiled back and replaced the picture on the piano. Then she moved into the large, cheerful kitchen.

As she fixed a salad for her dinner, her thoughts fastened again on that trip to Europe, before Jill had ever been a part of her life with Dennis. She saw a young Dennis again, getting up from the table at the sidewalk café and going inside to find a pay phone, so he could call the office in Seattle and 'check in.' She should have known how the marriage would end from that one incident…*Don't go there*, she admonished herself. She forced her mind back to her work with Mikhail and resolved to research the war years, as well as the postwar history of Berlin, especially the rise and fall of the Berlin Wall.

Mikhail lay on his narrow bed contemplating how effortlessly the words had come with Dee earlier that afternoon when he had introduced Anita in his reflections. He had noticed the resemblance between Dee and Anita immediately, of course. Every time he saw her he felt intrigued, and the memories came back in sharp clarity. But could he tell the story in detail? Dee had already seen that Anita was a special part of his past. And yet he wasn't even sure if he could open up to himself, let alone tell the story to this woman. Cautiously, he began to let his mind explore, and he sighed, remembering her face, her smile. As his thoughts receded drowsily into sleep, he wondered how he could have ever let her go, with so much of their history together unfinished. And now it was too late.

"I want you to see something," Dee declared with enthusiasm a few days later as she came through the door and into the large community room where

Mikhail was waiting by the window. Mikhail beamed at her, glad as always to see her. He had been thinking a great deal over the past few days about how much to tell her, and once he made up his mind, he was impatient for their next meeting.

She took off her coat and hung it on the rack inside the door, then turned to him with a grin. "It's cold out there," she exclaimed, rubbing her hands together briskly. "Let's sit by the fire a minute."

He glanced out the window again at the slate gray sky, then turned back to her and led the way to some large overstuffed brown chairs grouped in front of the cheerfully blazing fireplace. They took their seats and she rummaged in her large handbag.

"Here it is," she said, smiling and handing him a videocassette.

"What is it?"

"It's a travelogue of Berlin," she answered with enthusiasm. "I got it at the library and watched it last night. It's wonderful—there's a segment about the war, and it even covers the fall of the Berlin Wall four years ago and some of what East Berlin was like while it was closed off. I thought it might jog some memories of what it was like for you there during the war."

"But we have not reached that part of my story yet," he said.

"True, and I know how methodical you want to be about this. But I couldn't help myself. You see, after our last meeting I got to thinking about my own visit to Berlin in the late sixties, and I was eager to compare memories with you." She looked at him expectantly. "Would you like to watch it together now? It's only about half an hour long."

"Since you put it that way, I would be delighted. We can forego the chronology for today."

"Good. I was hoping you'd feel that way." She rose and walked over to the television and slipped the cassette into the VCR player.

Images soon played across the screen and he leaned forward to watch. They sat together in silence as a brief history of Berlin unfolded. He sat up straighter at the scenes of a bombed-out city. "That's how it was," he breathed. "I was there."

The video chronicled the post-war years of tension between Communist east and Democratic west, the vast migration of people from east to west, the building of the Wall to stem the tide, and the severe contrast between the two sides in the lives of German people that the Wall created.

Finally the sequence Dee had been waiting for played out before them, the crowds of cheering, exuberant people taking part in the ravage of the Wall and passing through newly opened gates to freedom. She had watched that part several times the night before, the part where the camera had panned a close-up of several people, their faces exultant as they passed.

Each time she watched, one face had always leaped out at her.

As she gazed at his movements, his features, his general likeness over and over with fascination, she had become increasingly convinced. The man was middle-aged, but he held an uncanny resemblance to Mikhail. It was as though she had been looking at a younger version of Mikhail. She wondered if she should point out the resemblance to Mikhail when it reached that point on the tape.

But she didn't have to.

As the camera panned the sea of faces and moved in for close-ups, she clearly heard his sharp intake of breath. "Rewind the tape a moment," he said in a hushed voice. She could see his fingers were gripping the arms of his chair. She rewound the tape and played the sequence once more. Then without a word, he rose from his chair and walked with a heavy tread down the hall toward his room.

For several moments she sat bewildered, waiting for him to return, wondering what to do. While she rewound the tape her mind whirled with unanswered questions. What had she triggered? Would he explain? Finally, unable to stand the suspense of waiting any longer, she decided to go knock on the door of his room.

As she walked down the long narrow hall, she was aware that no one was around, which didn't surprise her. This time of the afternoon most of the residents preferred to stay in their rooms. Hesitating a moment at his door, she lifted her hand and knocked. There was no answer.

"Mikhail? It's Dee," she called out. "Are you all right?" He didn't answer.

She wondered what to do now, and had almost decided to go ask for help when he opened the door and ushered her in. The room was small and Spartan in appearance, with only the barest of necessities: a narrow bed, a nightstand with lamp, chest of drawers, a bookcase, two straight-backed chairs, and a table on which stood a television and phone. She took it in quickly as he closed the door and then turned to face her.

"That young man on the tape. He looked so much like me." His eyes were troubled as they searched her face, as if she had the answer to a question he seemed unable to put into words. She remained silent, knowing she didn't need to say anything. He looked down at a sheet of paper in his hand. After a pause, he spoke again. "I have known since this came in the mail," he told her, holding out the paper toward her.

Her eyes questioned his as she closed her fingers upon the page. "Known?"

He nodded and she read the paper.

It was an official document of some sort, she realized, with the letterhead of the International Red Cross in Berlin. It was dated two years before. She scanned it, then looked up and her eyes met his again.

"This young man – Erik Mendenberg – he's asked that the Red Cross locate his father, last known address in New York City, then traced to Seattle. You?"

He nodded. "Evidently I have a son I never knew about. All the facts check out. I wrote back to the Red Cross telling them to relay information to this Erik that I indeed had a relationship with his mother, but that I had to flee Latvia in 1941 – leave my home and family behind, barely escaping a number of times as I crossed the borders under Nazi control. I intended to return when the war was over. We planned to marry."

She looked away, putting it together in her mind. "But you never could. From what you told me last time, the Soviets closed the border and absorbed your country as a part of Communist Russia." She closed her eyes. "I can't imagine what it would be like without a country to come home to."

"That's right. I could not go back. I couldn't live under Communism. I never heard from anyone I left behind again–other than one letter from my brother many years ago – until this letter came from the Red Cross."

She nodded again. "A result of the Iron Curtain's collapse." Her eyes turned back to him. "So you've been corresponding with Erik?"

He moved his head slowly from side to side.

Puzzled, she pressed him. "But his mother – I assume she is the beautiful lady you described the other day. Anita."

"I had planned to tell you about Anita today. And now it seems a foregone conclusion." He gestured to a chair and sat in the one opposite. "In order to answer both your questions I have to go back to the time I first knew Anita," he said.

She hesitated. Perhaps this was part of his story that he did not want to include in his autobiography. "May I record this conversation?" she asked him carefully. "Then I'll type it up later if you'd like, like I did last time."

"Yes," he answered. "I think that is a good idea."

She sat down opposite him, took out her cassette recorder and plugged it in. Then she looked at him and he nodded. She pressed the 'on' button and he began.

Riga, Latvia – 1938

Anita's effect upon him had been instant and profound. Up until then, he had been more interested in his career than in serious romance, or anything else for that matter. Training had taken all his attention, until he felt absolutely sure of himself on the trapeze. But from that first night, he wanted to meet her. In the days and weeks that followed, he flew through the routine with enormous assurance, especially when he knew she was watching their performance. Her presence in his life, however minor, seemed to heighten all his senses to peak performing capacity.

Gradually, during the course of daily training activity, whenever she passed him she offered a smile. For a few weeks he contented himself with this much. Then he noticed that she often stood nearby, watching as he practiced the routines with Jahn and Oscar. At those times he smiled to himself, anticipating a conversation with her after the training session ended. But she always disappeared before they finished.

Then one night after the evening performance he went over to the restaurant around the corner for a bite to eat. He opened the door and saw that it was crowded as always after the circus. The smell of warm food, the clamor of excited voices and the clatter of dishes assailed him as he scanned the room looking for a free table or someone he knew. All the tables seemed full.

When he saw her, she was looking at him, and their eyes met and locked for a moment. Then she glanced away, so he stood there, uncertain about whether to approach her. At last he moved forward, across the room toward her table. She looked up as he reached her, watching him with a shyness he found endearing.

"I'm Mikhail."

"The flyer," she acknowledged with a small smile. "I've been watching your act. You're very good." She picked up her coffee cup and raised it to her lips. "Anita," she returned, taking a sip, then setting the cup back on the table.

"The rope dancer," he nodded. "I've been watching your act, too."

She laughed with delight and gestured toward the chair next to her. "Sit down."

"You wouldn't mind? There doesn't seem to be room anywhere else."

"Not at all." She gazed up at him, and he stood there a moment staring at her, suddenly aware of her exceptional beauty at close range, too. She gestured once again toward the chair, this time with a question in her eyes.

He sat in the chair across the table, feeling dazed. "I guess I'm surprised to see you here alone," he offered, bothered by the sensation and determined to shake it off. "Your act was good tonight," he added with enthusiasm.

"Thanks. But I think it could use some improvement. If you have any ideas for me I'd welcome them." She leaned forward, her eyes bright with expectancy.

He moved closer, more relaxed now, and rested his forearms on the table. Here was a subject he felt sure of. "I'll be thinking about it," he said. He knew already that her act was limited, that she had taken it about as far as she could. But she herself had something special.

She nodded and her eyes drifted away. They scanned the room as if she were looking for someone. He thought he saw a hint of apprehension on her face.

"Are you sure you're not expecting anyone?" he asked, leaning away again.

"Not really." She shrugged and turned her attention back to him. "I just have a great deal on my mind right now."

He wondered if that meant she wanted him to leave her alone, but he decided to give the conversation another try before he made up his mind about that.

"How long have you been performing?" he asked.

Her face took on a kind of wistful expression as she considered his question. "I came here from Jelgava two years ago, when I was sixteen," she said. "I had great dreams of success in the big city." She propped her elbows on the table and rested her chin in her hands. "Like most little girls, I took ballet lessons. And then, the circus came through town regularly every summer, and I started thinking about using my dancing in a circus act. I got the names of some contacts here from the traveling circus people, then I trained the rope-dancing act under their supervision, and finally improved enough to get scheduled on the program here at Salamonski." Her eyes dropped to the table and she traced a scratch across the surface with her fingertip. He watched her face in the harsh, smoky light. The shadows of her velvety lashes cast a lacy pattern across her cheek. When she looked up again, her face had clouded. "It wasn't as easy as I thought," she declared.

He nodded. "A lot of discipline and hard work."

Her eyes met his and for a moment she seemed to want to say something. But just then the waiter came with her dinner. After he took Mikhail's order and left, she sat quietly for a moment.

"Go ahead and eat," he urged her, "or it will be cold by the time mine gets here."

She gave him a grateful glance and picked up her fork. "How did you become interested in flying?" she asked.

He grinned at her. "The usual boyhood dreams. I went to my first circus when I was twelve years old, and when I saw the trapeze act, I knew I wanted to be a flyer from that moment on." He saw she was listening with interest, her face animated, her lively brown eyes dancing. He began warming to his subject, wanting to make his story as entertaining as he could. "I never changed my mind. Over the years I trained in gymnastics and – "

He stopped talking. Her gaze had suddenly shifted beyond him and her face registered a startled, tense expression. He started to look around.

"I'm sorry," she said abruptly. "Forgive me, I have to ask you to leave."

He stared at her.

"Please. Leave now," she said, her eyes pleading.

"But my dinner."

"Please. Just go."

He rose slowly to his feet, and suddenly resentment took over. He wheeled and strode across the room, past all the crowded tables. Just before he got to the front desk he bumped into a man in a Latvian Army Officer's uniform. He caught a glimpse of blond hair and narrow, intense eyes as the man brushed past Mikhail.

At the desk Mikhail cancelled his dinner order and left.

Back at his apartment, he fixed himself something to eat. He couldn't get Anita out of his mind. Her behavior had disturbed and puzzled him. She had told him that she wasn't expecting anyone, and yet as soon as she saw someone she recognized, she dismissed Mikhail with actions that bordered on rudeness. Mikhail had had limited experience with how women think and act, especially growing up with one brother; she was the first woman who had truly intrigued him. He wondered if she'd explain the next day. If she did, he decided he'd probably accept her apology.

The next day when he went to meet Jahn and Oscar at the Circus for their daily training session, he found himself watching for her. She came in later with some other artists while Mikhail was going through his warm-up exercises. He knew she had to walk right past him to get to the dressing rooms, and when she did, she caught his eye, smiled and said hello, just as if nothing had happened.

"This went on for two or three more days," Mikhail told Dee, "and I became so confused I decided the only thing to do was to ignore her as much as possible. But every time I saw her she seemed to be looking at me with a thoughtful expression on her face.

"Then one night, everything changed."

CHAPTER SEVEN

The evening performance had gone well as usual, and Mikhail decided to go straight to his apartment around the corner from the circus afterward. He bounded up the stairs, eager for the quiet solitude that waited for him there. He didn't feel like being around anyone tonight.

After building a fire in the fireplace and fixing himself something to eat, he stretched out on the sofa and closed his eyes, remembering the mass of faces below him in the audience, smiling and wide-eyed. It pleased him to know he could give that kind of enjoyment to them with his midair soaring, twisting and rolling. He stretched, feeling the pleasant sensation of fatigue after a day of satisfying physical discipline and exertion.

He must have dozed off for a moment, because the knock on his apartment door jarred him awake, even though it seemed to come from far away. He sat up, wondering if it had been his imagination. Then it came again, more insistent this time.

He got to his feet and went over to open the door. She stood there with her hands thrust into her coat pockets. The corners of her lips turned up in a hesitant smile, and her eyes looked at Mikhail uncertainly. They stood staring at each other. The silence lengthened.

Finally, she said, "I hope you don't mind my coming so late. May I come in?"

He found his voice. "Of course. How did you know where I live?" He opened the door wider and she moved past him into the room.

"I asked Jahn." She drew in a breath and turned to face him. "I've been thinking about the other night at the restaurant," she said in a quiet voice. "I'm afraid I was rude to you, and I thought I owed you an explanation."

He nodded. "All right," he said mildly. He waited for her to go on, wondering why she seemed so uncomfortable. He extended his hand. "Let me take your coat."

She gave him a grateful smile as she unbuttoned her coat, slipped it off and handed it to him. He laid it over a chair and motioned her to sit down on the sofa. Then he went over and stoked the fire. It sprang to life again. He turned back to her. "Would you like some coffee?"

"No, nothing, thanks. I just wanted to clear the air between us." She looked up at him in the dimly flickering light, her eyes enormous and appealing. "The truth is, I'd wanted to meet you for quite awhile. I didn't want you to think after the other night that I wasn't even interested in being friends." She gave a little shrug. "After all, we see each other at Salamonski Circus every day." She smiled, and her whole face seemed luminous in the firelight. He smiled back, in spite of himself. "We should be friends, don't you think?"

"I wouldn't mind," Mikhail answered. He sat down in the chair across from her. "So what happened the other night?"

She turned her eyes toward the fire and gazed at it for a moment. For some reason he couldn't fathom, she seemed to be struggling in her mind over what, or how much, to tell him.

"Look," he told her easily, "whatever it is, you can tell me. I can be pretty understanding."

"I appreciate that," she answered with a sad smile. "I really do want to explain. It's just that I don't want to burden you with a lot of unnecessary information. I mean, we did only meet the other night."

He laughed. "Yes, but we're friends, remember? You said so yourself." He leaned forward, hoping his expression looked appealing and coaxing. He suddenly wanted very badly to know what she wanted to tell him.

"Yes, we're friends." Her smile deepened, and her eyes penetrated his with a softness that made him want to wrap his arms around her and comfort her. "You see, it's hard for me to have friendships."

"Why? Everyone seems to like you."

"It isn't that," she said quickly, lifting her hand in a gesture of dismissal. "It's – the man I'm seeing." She glanced down for a moment. "He's…possessive." She looked up at him again. "Do you remember the man you bumped into at the restaurant that night? The Army Lieutenant?"

Mikhail nodded slowly. "Vaguely," he answered.

"His name is Aleks Mendenberg. He comes from my home town. He's much older, but ever since I was fourteen, he's been the only man in my life. Our parents even expected us to marry. Then I moved here to Riga and since then he's been – difficult." She was speaking in a flat, toneless voice. "I suppose it's normal. He still wants to marry, and he's afraid I'll change my mind."

Mikhail leaned forward again. "You've opened yourself up to a much larger world," he said, trying to be understanding. "Naturally he'd feel threatened by that."

"But it's been so hard for me." While she talked she slipped her feet out of her shoes and folded her legs under her, smoothing her skirt. "Lately he's been more possessive than ever. He shows up and surprises me in places where he knows I might be. If I'm with friends he makes an awkward scene. The last time it happened, he almost came to blows with a man in my party, the husband of a girlfriend of mine, who was also there." Her voice rose with intensity. "He jumps to conclusions before he asks any questions." She fell silent and absently stroked the arm of the sofa as she leaned against it, and turned her head to gaze at the fire. He watched the fire's flickering light play along the curve of her neck. She looked so unhappy, he longed to find some way to reassure her.

"So you were afraid he'd make a scene if he saw me sitting at your table."

She turned her head and gazed at him as she nodded. Then she unfolded her legs and set her feet back on the floor. "I appreciate the chance to explain. And I apologize for the way I behaved." She rose to her feet and smiled. "Not many men would have accepted such a situation without question, as you did."

"I must admit you had me feeling pretty confused and resentful at first."

"I hope you don't feel that way anymore."

He stood up and moved toward her. "No, I don't feel that way anymore," he said. They faced each other, only inches apart, her gaze as steady as his.

Then suddenly she turned and said in a brisk tone, "Thank you for understanding. I should go now; I don't want to take up any more of your time."

Disappointment washed over Mikhail. He shook himself mentally and as he helped her with her coat, overwhelmed by her closeness. "I want to ask you something before you go," he said in a quiet voice. "How do you feel about Aleks now?"

She lowered her eyes a moment, then lifted them again to meet his, and the solemn expression on her face told him all he needed to know. Very slowly she reached up and touched his cheek with her hand. He pulled her into his arms and she didn't resist. He kissed her cheek and then she turned her head slightly and her lips brushed his. Her arms found their way around his neck.

"Stay," he whispered, feeling the urgency of his physical response. His fingers found a button on her coat.

She pulled back, shaken. "I can't. I want to, but I can't. It wouldn't be fair to you as long as I have this problem with Aleks." She gave him an anguished look, then swept past him to the door. The next second she was gone.

Not long after that, a man named Francis proposed an act to Mikhail. He and his female partner, Emma, had been performing elegant adagio, a combination of graceful, flamboyant lifts and turns. They wanted to expand the act with more versatility and for that they needed a more highly skilled acrobat. Since Mikhail had just finished a month of contracted performances on the trapeze and wouldn't be working for another month, he agreed to give it a try. They developed their act smoothly as a trio; Mikhail's acrobatic lifts and turns gave the routine just the diversity that Francis and Emma had been hoping for.

Then one day when Francis and Mikhail arrived to start training, Anita was there, and they watched her dancing on the rope with her umbrella for a few minutes while they waited for Emma to arrive. She was getting better, Mikhail observed. Graceful, sensual. She had the timing down to perfection, but he knew she could do no more with this particular act. Suddenly, an idea flitted into his head and he turned to Francis, whose eyes reflected the same kind of excitement Mikhail felt.

"How about a quartet?" Francis suggested with enthusiasm. "More combinations look better to the audience."

"That's just what I was going to say!" Mikhail responded, delighted with the thought. "She does look a likely choice, don't you think?" he gestured toward Anita.

As soon as Emma arrived, they put the idea to her, and she agreed. Then they asked Anita to join them and turn the act into a quartet. She jumped at the chance.

The first training session went even better than they had expected. Anita was agile and quick to learn. From the start she trusted Francis and Mikhail instinctively. Even some of the trickier lifts and turns she took in her stride. She and Emma worked well together, too. Both women had a natural dance style that came from their background training in ballet.

Everything seemed to fall smoothly into place. Mikhail and Francis decided to wear bright, stylized vests and the young women colorful, short-skirted native dresses with wide sashes at their waists. The quartet would pattern their routine after the traditional Latvian folk dancing.

Once Anita and Mikhail started training together on a daily basis, their relationship intensified rapidly, in spite of Aleks, and probably because of him, as well. A small pocket of apprehension had started pulling at Mikhail, and right after they finished training one day, he took Anita aside.

"What's the situation with Aleks now, Anita?" he asked her without preamble. "If we're going to be working together, I don't want him charging in here and disrupting things with his jealousy."

She looked at him with a slight frown. "I can't blame you for that," she conceded. He watched her as she turned her concerned gaze toward Francis and Emma. Then she dropped her eyes and said, "I've told him I'm not interested in marrying him anymore," she said carefully. "He was angry. He said he won't accept that." She lifted her eyes to meet Mikhail's steady gaze.

"Do you think he'll cause problems then?"

"I hope not. I have an appointment to meet him at the train station tomorrow morning to talk things over."

"What time?"

"His train arrives at ten. He's coming in from Liepaja, his military base. I'm going to tell him that it's over," she declared. "I just want him out of my life."

Mikhail pushed a lock of his hair impatiently back away from his forehead. "It sounds like he might not listen. You said yourself that he didn't listen the last time," he said.

She gave a little shrug and searched his face. "What can I do?" she asked with a troubled frown.

A protective instinct surged inside him. "Tell you what," he suggested, "I'll go see him and try to talk some sense into him myself."

Her frown deepened. "I don't think he'd listen to you any more than he would to me," she remarked with skepticism.

"He'd have to if I surprised him and showed up in your place at the train station."

She hesitated. "I don't know," she said. "He could be dangerous. He's pretty unpredictable."

"All the more reason I don't think you should go," he retorted. "It's worth a try, isn't it?"

She finally agreed. At ten the next morning Mikhail stood on the crowded station platform watching the train pull in from Liepaja. The air was cold, and he pulled his coat collar closer around his neck. People started to get off, and then Mikhail saw him, a tall blond man in uniform. He emerged from the train and stepped down into the crowd, his eyes scanning the mass of people. Mikhail made his way over to him through the throngs of men and women.

"Are you looking for Anita?"

The man turned sharply and eyed Mikhail with suspicion. "What business is it of yours?" he growled.

"She won't be here. She sent me to tell you she doesn't want to see you anymore. She wants you to leave her alone."

His eyes narrowed. "This is between Anita and me. You have no business –"

"I'm making it my business," Mikhail broke in. "She and I are working together, and I don't want you bothering her, disrupting her training."

The color deepened on the man's face and a look of pure rage passed over it. "Oh, you don't?" His arm trembled as he lowered it to his side. Mikhail's eyes followed the movement. He watched the man's hand lift his jacket aside, his fingers curl around a holstered revolver. "I ought to shoot you," he said in a voice thick with barely bridled tension.

Mikhail looked up quickly, prepared for resentment, but the glint of hatred in the man's eyes, the thin, tight line of his lips stunned him. This level of anger and jealousy defied reason. The man was an

Army officer. Yet instinctively, Mikhail sensed he was capable of shooting him then and there, and enjoying it, without thought about the consequences to his career. Especially if Mikhail showed any fear.

Mikhail leveled his eyes on the man's and held them there. "Go ahead." He spoke in a voice he hoped sounded controlled and confident. There were still crowds of people all around them, and he knew Aleks would be a fool to pull the gun out and shoot Mikhail in front of everyone.

The man glanced around uneasily. Then he sucked in his breath. "Tell Anita I still want to talk to her." He spun on his heel and strode away, flinging the words over his shoulder. "You haven't seen the last of me."

Mikhail stood watching him leave. He wasn't at all sure if he'd made matters better or worse, but he decided that at least the man wasn't going to go straight to Anita. He thought about going to her apartment and letting her know about the encounter, but he decided not to when he realized the Lieutenant could follow him there. Instead Mikhail went home to his own apartment.

She was waiting for him outside. She wore a lightweight coat, unbuttoned to reveal a pretty, form-fitting flowered dress, her dark hair a soft cloud around her face and falling gently over her shoulders. Wordlessly they climbed the stairs. Mikhail unlocked the door and let her in ahead of him. He closed the door as she turned to face him.

"Did you talk to him?" she asked, her voice stiff with anxiety.

"I talked to him."

"And?"

He hesitated. "I see what you mean about his being unpredictable."

"Why? What did he do?" Her voice rose in alarm.

He shrugged out of his coat and hung it over a chair. "He just let me know he was angry," he hedged.

She nodded. "I was afraid for you," she breathed, taking a step toward him. "I always sensed he was capable of violence." Their eyes met. "Do you think he'll stay away now?"

He held her gaze. "To be honest, I don't know. But at least he knows you mean what you say, now that he's heard it from someone beside yourself." He shrugged. "He wouldn't try anything violent, Anita. He's a Lieutenant in the Army, after all. He knows he couldn't get away with it. He has too much to lose."

She dropped her eyes and turned away. "You're probably right." She walked over to the window and gazed down onto the street. "I've been so afraid lately. There's something about the way he's been acting ..."

He saw her shudder a little, and he walked over behind her and put his hands on her shoulders. "Let's not worry about it anymore now, Anita. If he comes around again we'll just deal with it then."

She turned to face him. "Thank you," she said simply. He saw the unmistakable look of soft wonder in her eyes.

Desire for her flared. He moved away from her, suddenly uncomfortable about taking unfair advantage of her vulnerability. "I hope it helped." He turned to her and smiled. "Tell you what," he said, "let's go out and I'll buy you some lunch. We could both use a pleasant distraction, wouldn't you say?" When she seemed to hesitate, he added quickly, "Unless you already have plans for lunch."

"No, I don't have any plans." An impish grin spread slowly across her face. "I'd love to go out for lunch with you."

CHAPTER EIGHT

Mikhail had no particular destination in mind as they left his apartment. Perhaps his thoughts had flickered an image of the market in his mind's eye, but his only conscious thought was that he needed people around them. Back in the apartment he had become confused and unsure of himself. He wasn't exactly inexperienced where females were concerned. He had shared beds with a few in his youthful exuberance. Most of them, pretty, young and eager, had come to him out of the crowds, drawn to him, Mikhail supposed, because of the danger he faced each night performing on the trapeze. Some had told him they felt as if they could experience the danger themselves by getting as close as they could to him.

Yet, Anita was different. She was a woman, not a girl like those he'd known before. Her beauty dazzled him. The autumn sun was warm now, and she took off her coat and folded it over her arm. As they walked in silence he found himself admiring the grace with which she carried her beautiful body. He knew what he wanted from her, but it had to be different, more somehow, than it had been with any of the others.

"What were you thinking back at my apartment?" he asked her. "You were upset about Aleks, and then you seemed to shake it off. You've seemed happy ever since."

She turned and regarded him a moment, then she spoke, her eyes turning back to the street ahead. "I guess I just realized that I no longer have to consider Aleks. I'm free of him, and I can live my life now." She looked back at him and smiled. "I guess it was your involvement in the situation that made me realize that. Suddenly a huge burden has been lifted."

"I'm glad." He returned her smile and they lapsed into comfortable silence again as they walked along.

They reached the market. Several baskets of fruit lay in the narrow aisle ahead of them. With a playful glance in his direction, she impulsively gathered her skirt above her knees and leaped over them. He watched her with admiration. Her agile movement revealed her dancer's legs, toned, smooth and shapely. Momentarily disturbed by where the sight led his thoughts, he shook off the distraction and jumped over the baskets too, landing awkwardly on the cobblestones and stumbling a little. She reached out to steady him, and for a few seconds they stood in each other's arms. Her eyes sparkled with laughter, her face was alive with her radiant smile. He ached to kiss her, but he hesitated. She pulled away and scampered off.

"Some flyer you are." She laughed over her shoulder.

He watched her as she flitted away, thinking that she was like a down feather floating easily at arm's length, apparently attainable until he reached out with his hand. The movement caused currents in the air and pushed the feather just out of reach.

He followed her to a merchant selling pottery from his wagon. As she knelt to examine some colorfully painted clay pots displayed on the ground, the front of her dress fell away a little, revealing the swell of her firm, taut breasts, the skin tanned brown by the sun. Mikhail wondered how far the tan went. His eyes moved slowly up to her face as she knelt there. She was watching him, her face upturned, the same impish grin on her lips that he had seen in his apartment. He felt the blood rush to his face, and he spun on his heels and pretended to find something interesting in the crockery.

She stood up and latched her arm through his, nudging him gently to move on with her. They strolled along aimlessly among the colorful displays of food and jewelry and clothing.

Anita slowed her pace and lowered her head thoughtfully. "I wanted to ask you…" she began.

"What?" he asked. "Ask anything."

"It's nothing, really. But do you remember our conversation in the restaurant the night I interrupted you when I saw Aleks come in?"

"I'm not sure…"

"You were talking about your boyhood dreams," she prompted. "I'd like you to tell me about them now."

"Oh. Those." He grinned at her. "My dreams of becoming a flyer."

"That dream came true, didn't it?"

"Yes. It did."

"Any other dreams you want to share with me?"

"Today feels like a dream come true," he said softly.

"For me too." Her smile blossomed, and his heartbeat quickened.

As lunchtime approached, the streets became more crowded, but the people were all fleeting, shadowy figures moving near Mikhail and Anita, strangers to the world the two were experiencing together. When they felt hungry they stopped for soup and pastry at a sidewalk cafe. They talked of vitally important things, which later when summoned from Mikhail's thoughts, could not be recalled. Then they walked some more, down one street and up another, across a foot bridge, and on through a narrow alley toward an unknown section of town, attentive to nothing but each other. After awhile the streets all blended together as they walked on, absorbed in their conversation.

Time moved on for the rest of the world. Shop owners closed up for the day and the movement on the sidewalks slowed until Mikhail and Anita found themselves alone on an unfamiliar street. The chill of darkness gathered in corners and doorways.

"We'd better start back," he said.

They walked with purpose now, past the lengthening shadows. "Did Francis want us to train together today?" she asked suddenly as she slipped back into her coat. "I completely forgot the schedule."

"Me too." He laughed sheepishly. "I lost all track of time." Their eyes met and held, and they slowed their step for a moment. "Nothing we can do about it now," he added with a shrug. "I'll talk to him tomorrow."

They moved on until they reached a familiar area of the city, but they were still several blocks from Mikhail's apartment. He recognized a narrow alley just ahead, which ended at a wooden staircase. It climbed to a street parallel to the one they were on. It was a shortcut, and he motioned for her to follow him.

The alley was dark, but the street beyond the stairway was well-lit, and they walked quickly between the buildings. Halfway up the alley, Mikhail began to sense movement behind them. He tucked his arm around Anita's waist and hurried her along. Danger was a part of his everyday life, and his training for the trapeze had developed his senses as well as his body. And he sensed three dark forms closing the space behind them in the blackness.

"Hello, friends!" A loud, gravelly voice rang out and Anita and Mikhail came to an abrupt stop and whirled to face the three who stood a few feet behind them. "Out for a short walk this evening?" The men edged around the couple until they stood abreast at the bottom of the stairway, blocking the way. The streetlights above glared down eerily. Mikhail felt Anita tense. A short gasp escaped her lips.

"Stand aside, please," Mikhail said. "Let us pass."

"Not very friendly, are you?" said the one in the middle. "No wonder you've made enemies."

Mikhail didn't need to hear any more. Guiding Anita behind him, he half turned from the man and began speaking to the one on his right. "Now boys, I'm sure you don't want trouble." As if to emphasize a point, he raised his right hand shoulder-high. Suddenly he made a fist and pivoted left, swinging wide and catching the leader full on the chin. Surprise was Mikhail's ally as the man on his right, slow to react, received a short side kick to the knee. With a grunt of pain the man went down.

Mikhail pushed Anita rapidly through the men and up the first couple of steps. Then he felt someone grasp the back of his collar and yank him backwards. The leader had recovered quickly enough, and Mikhail could see the brass knuckles on his fist, closing in. Before he could make contact, Mikhail's right foot came up and landed a solid blow to the man's groin.

He eluded the half-hearted grasp of the third man and sprinted up the stairway behind Anita. He looked over his shoulder at their attackers and wasn't surprised to find they had no appetite for further confrontation. He turned to call after Anita, but the sight of her running down the street, her agile, shapely legs shimmering in the frosty moonlight, brought a smile to his face.

He caught up to her, and together, laughing with relief and gasping for breath, they stumbled the last block to Mikhail's building. They hurried up the flight of stairs to his door. As soon as they entered, she threw off her coat, crossed the room to the window and looked down on the street below.

"Do you think Aleks put them up to that?" she asked.

He stood inside the door and watched her a moment. Her figure was silhouetted in the window frame, her shoulders rising and falling with her breathing. Silently, he stepped up behind her and placed his hands on her waist.

"It doesn't matter," he answered gently. He felt her body relax as she leaned back against his chest. The room was silent except for the ticking of the clock beside his sofa. Moonlight filtered through the window, washing over them and filling most of the small apartment.

"Make love to me," she whispered.

His hands moved up her body and worked loose the first two buttons on the back of her dress. Slowly he slid the garment off one shoulder and gently kissed her there, and again on her neck. Her head rolled back onto his shoulder as she took a deep, steadying breath. He unfastened the remaining buttons and the dress slid down her arms and gathered at her waist. She turned and looked up into his face with wide, trusting eyes, yet eyes that now revealed an unmistakable hunger.

He lowered his head and brushed her lips with his. A quick, challenging smile crossed her face as she reached up, her fingers burrowing into his hair, pressing him closer, crushing his mouth against hers.

By the time she left his apartment in the morning, they both knew it was just the beginning.

"In the weeks that followed, Anita and I spent every free moment together," Mikhail went on as he paced the room. Dee continued to sit and listen, captivated by the warmth of his memories. "We polished the act with Francis and Emma, and we all felt exhilarated with our progress. Within a month, we were booked to perform our new adagio quartet at Salamonski for the month of December.

"During this time, neither Anita nor I heard or saw anything of Aleks, and we both felt enormous relief. It seemed we were now free to be together as we both wanted, and life was beautiful. I felt a perpetual glow in her presence, and we shared as much as we could whenever we could, like any two young people in love. We were little more than children, really. Life was so good and my work was like play, after all."

"Your work was dangerous, though," Dee pointed out. "Weren't you ever afraid? Didn't you ever have any close calls?"

His eyes flickered and he looked away. "It was easy to ignore the danger involved in my trapeze act, Dee; I heard the occasional reports about a flyer in Paris or Brussels who was killed when he attempted a new trick on the trapeze. But I was always supremely confident about my abilities with the act, and Oscar continued to be rock solid in his catching skills. One night I did have a scare, though. I suppose I was distracted by my passion for Anita.

"That night one of the overhead lights started flickering just before I jumped off the bridge in my approach swing toward Oscar. He gestured to me with a sign. I knew I was supposed to follow his signals but

I did not acknowledge this one. He meant for me to go back to the bridge but I kept soaring forward and then I released the trapeze. At that moment the lights went out and we were plunged into darkness. I felt some hesitation as I reached for Oscar's hands, and that shifted the split-second timing. His hands barely caught one of mine. I slipped from his grasp and started plummeting, and I landed on the edge of the net and bounced off and onto the ground. I fell backward and landed hard, feeling intense jarring even though sawdust broke the fall somewhat. I lay there stunned a moment, listening to the alarmed outcry of the crowd, wondering if I had broken anything. Oscar dropped to the ground and assisted me off the floor and backstage while the ringmaster cried, 'He's all right, folks! Let's give him a big round of applause.'

"In the dressing room Oscar rounded on me. 'Poor judgment!' he shouted. "You were so eager to impress Anita you could have been killed! Do not let that happen again!'

"I suppose I could have been badly injured, or even killed. And in the morning every muscle in my body ached as I got out of bed. I moved my body slowly, testing for any permanent damage. After that, maintenance vowed to check the lighting every day before each performance and I followed Oscar's signs more closely.

Mikhail paused, a troubled frown spreading across his face. "And about that time we saw ominous signs of Hitler's rise.

"In November, since none of us had other work, Francis got a contract for our adagio quartet to perform in Munich and Berlin. Within a few days we were packed and on the train headed for Munich. As the miles sped by, Francis and Emma tried to explain the situation they had witnessed in Germany, a few months before, while they had been performing there as a duet."

"Hitler has complete control over everything," Francis said gravely, "and he's building up tremendous armed forces. Everywhere we go we see the straight-armed salute and hear the 'Heil Hitler'! And we're expected to follow suit," he grimaced, "any time we go into a German office. If we don't, we might be detained or arrested."

Hot indignation rose in him. "To hell with that," he snapped. "We're foreigners."

"But that's just it," Francis retorted. "He's not fond of foreigners. He wants a pure German race. That's one reason he's especially against the entire Jewish population."

"What's he planning to do?" Anita asked, her eyes wide and grave. She reached for Mikhail's hand, and hers felt small and warm in his.

"No one knows for sure," Francis answered. "But it looks to me like he's gearing up for all-out war. Look at what he's done so far. Just last year he marched on Austria, his own birthplace."

"And this year he occupied Czechoslovakia without a fight," Emma added, leaning forward, her voice low and urgent, her big blue eyes alive with apprehension. "And what about his campaign to get all Germans throughout Europe back to the fatherland?"

"What about it?" Mikhail said. "My family is of German descent – but my parents and my brother and I were born right in Riga. We've never known any other national loyalty. We decided to just ignore the order. What can they do? Round us up and force us to move to Germany?"

Francis stared at him a moment. Then he said slowly, in a low voice, "Mikhail, you may be making a grave mistake. If Germany occupies the Baltics next, you'd be counted among the German enemies." He shook his head with concern. "You'd be in a terrible spot."

Mikhail stared back at Francis, trying to absorb the enormous implications of his words. He glanced at Anita and saw the concern in her eyes. Then he said, "One thing I know for certain: I won't fight for Germany if there's a war. The idea is laughable!" Anita smiled and put her hand on his arm as if to reassure him.

Francis sat up and peered out the window. "Looks like we'll be in Munich in a few minutes. We'll probably learn a great deal more during this trip; the situation changes so fast these days. But remember," he cautioned, "in our profession it's crucial to remain neutral. Don't mix in politics – it's too dangerous. If we want to keep bread on our table we have to assume our contracts come from the world at large."

The train pulled into the station, wheezing and screeching. Anita and Mikhail, Francis and Emma watched out the window as it came to a stop. Francis gave Mikhail a knowing glance, and Mikhail nodded. German officers with swastika armbands seemed to be everywhere among the crowd.

They gathered up their belongings, disembarked and went about their business routinely as they could, finding their hotel and the nightclub where they were contracted to perform. The director and other artists they met there seemed pleased enough, but Mikhail felt disturbed and guarded to see so many uniforms everywhere they went, especially those with Hitler's swastika on the armbands.

One chilly, overcast day they were walking to work at the nightclub when they noticed a group of people moving along the street, right next to the sidewalk. They all had a yellow Star of David sewn onto their clothing. They were led by a German soldier.

"Jews aren't allowed to walk on the sidewalk," Francis explained in a low voice.

Mikhail felt a wave of disgust. "Whose idea is that?" he asked. Anita's hand tightened on his arm through the fabric of his coat.

"Hitler's." They walked a moment in silence as Mikhail thought about what that meant from his own experience. Memories crowded into his mind of a childhood friend he'd had named Joshua, and of his affectionate, boisterous family. He'd seen him for the last time just three months before, when Joshua had come to say goodbye. Joshua and three others were leaving for Palestine, he'd told Mikhail. They didn't like the growing menace of Hitler's regime. At the time Mikhail had thought Joshua's reaction a little extreme. Now he wondered.

"What will happen to them?" he asked Francis, nodding toward the somber group.

Francis thrust his hands deeper into his coat pockets and shrugged dispiritedly. "They send them to work that way. No one knows how far Hitler will go with this."

"The man is crazy!" Mikhail burst out hotly.

Francis put a restraining hand on Mikhail's arm. "Quiet down," he cautioned. "But I agree with you."

The dark, ominous presence permeated Munich, and they were glad to finish their two week contract and leave for Berlin. There they played the Europa House Theatre, and at first their moods lifted. In spite of the party uniforms everywhere there, too, Berlin was a clean and beautiful city, with a pleasant atmosphere and an underground subway system that Anita and Mikhail explored with enthusiasm.

Within a few days, though, the full weight of Hitler's influence pressed in here too. All the political propaganda pointed to relentless preparation for war. Some artists they worked with related to them what they'd heard and seen: Germany had the strongest war machine in the world. Freedom in Germany was part of the past; Hitler's dictatorship fell across the country like a heavy shroud. Even uniformed youth groups marched everywhere. Germany's Air Force Field Marshall Goehring's voice became a familiar radio fixture to Mikhail and his group as Goehring regularly reported on the growing strength of his forces. "I will give my arm to be amputated if one single aircraft penetrates German air space!" he often proclaimed over the radio with feverish pride in his voice.

They finished their contract and with relief, took the train back to Riga. When they arrived Mikhail gave first-hand reports to family and friends and everyone else who would listen. Francis' words about Mikhail's German heritage cast a further burden on himself, his parents and his brother when Mikhail reported what he'd observed and heard. Still, they decided to wait and see.

Mikhail and the others in the adagio quartet began a month of performances in the familiar comfort of the Salamonski Circus.

"It wasn't long before ugly reality entered my personal world," Mikhail stopped pacing and glanced at Dee. "In less than a year, September 1939, Hitler invaded Poland and all of Europe was at war." He sat down across from her and sighed deeply. "This is harder for me than I thought."

CHAPTER NINE

Dee knew he was approaching the hardest part of his story, the part that had changed the course of his life forever. She could feel the emotional strain in his voice, and she leaned forward with urgency. "Would you like to summarize for now, Mikhail? Perhaps later you can fill in the details."

He stared at her; his face became a stiff mask. "All right. Summarize. Let me see. In 1940 Communist Russia occupied Latvia. I knew about the evil of Communism from my parents' experience during the Russian Revolution. My father had been jailed unjustly and treated inhumanely; I made no secret of my feelings about that." He shrugged, his shoulders rigid. "So I developed a reputation among authorities as a man against Communism. I feared I'd be arrested and sent to Siberia. But I wasn't. I continued to entertain in Riga, mostly for Russian soldiers.

"Then after only a year, Germany overran the Baltics and forced the Russians out, and suddenly they became the occupying country. Now I feared that my family and I would be deported to Germany as prisoners of war."

Frustration began to rise in Dee. She wanted to penetrate the stark facts and find the living, day-to-day emotion behind them. But she had asked him to summarize to relieve the emotional drain she saw in him. "Your family stayed in Latvia when the war started, so the Nazis might accuse you of denouncing your German heritage? And for that you'd become prisoners of war?"

"Correct. I also feared Hitler's mobilization of all young Baltic men, and we'd be forced to fight for the Nazis on the Russian front. They desperately needed young soldiers by then. It was too late for my family to do anything about the possibility of deportation, but as an entertainer, I was labeled neutral. So I had choices. I managed to arrange a contract to go to Berlin to entertain with my trapeze act in May, 1941. I gambled that entertaining the German troops on their home terrain would be a loophole that gave me enough freedom of movement to stay one step ahead of the Nazis." He glanced at Dee and saw her look of puzzlement. "They allowed neutral entertainers certain privileges, you see, and as long as my papers were in order, my contract to perform theoretically took precedence over my citizenship papers," he explained. "Of course it was still a risk; anything was possible by then." When she nodded in understanding, he went on. "Because of this, for years I managed to evade the authorities on the question of my nationality. But I paid a huge price."

"Home. Family. Anita."

"Anita." The emotion began to creep back into his voice. "She wanted to come with me and we tried to talk Francis and Emma into joining us to perform our adagio routine. But by then of course, everything was in chaos in Riga. It was dangerous even for neutral performers to travel across the border into Germany. So in the end we decided I had to go alone. I told Anita she'd be safer in Riga. I promised her I'd be back as soon as the war was over and things got back to normal. It was a terrible time, and I hated leaving her behind. We had talked of marrying, and we would have if…" he lifted his eyes in a silent, heartbreaking appeal to Dee. "No one knew the war would last six endless years and change all our lives forever!"

"Six years." Dee fought to maintain her professional distance. "It's hard to imagine such chaos for six years. I'm trying to picture it. Tell me what that border crossing into Germany was like."

Swirling leaves outside the window caught his eye and he moved over to watch the wind gusting through the tree branches, almost bare now. For a long moment he stood silently gazing out the window, hands resting on the windowsill. Then he turned away, placed his hands on his hips, and lowered his head. He stared at the carpet. He said, "That first night on the train to Germany my thoughts returned over and over to everything and everyone I knew and loved. I saw them all diminishing and disappearing in the distance between us. On the other hand, I felt the train pulling me toward my own death as I approached the moment of confrontation with the border guards. Strong young men were all in uniform, so neutral performer or not, I was sure they'd see through my carefully planned ruse, arrest me, and ship me off to certain death as a Nazi soldier on the Russian front.

"I had arranged my contract and publicity photos in my suitcase on top of my citizenship papers. I stared straight ahead; tried not to watch the guard as he opened the suitcase and began to examine the contents. Then he thrust a glossy photo into my face and asked me questions about my act as a trapeze flyer. I gave as much lively detail as possible in an attempt to sidetrack his attention. But suddenly he seemed to realize he had serious business to attend to and impatiently put the papers back in the suitcase, slammed it shut and motioned me to continue on. The ruse had worked! I dared not show the smallest sign of the relief I felt." He lowered himself into a chair and leaned back. "That first incident gave me the confidence to keep going.

"For four years I felt like a rat in a maze. I was lucky, but unbearably lonely, running from one contract to another, one town in Germany to another. I evaded the Nazis simply because the chaos increased steadily during those years. The German soldiers always appreciated good entertainment, and they needed it more and more as the fortunes of war began turning against them.

The Berlin Connection

Toward the end of the war, the bombings over Berlin grew more intense and horrifying all the time. Again I was lucky. I contacted a friend in Prague and he managed to send me a contract to entertain at the circus there, where the bombings had stopped. But I had to get travel papers approved. I went to a Gestapo office and endured agonizing, tense moments there." His fingers gripped the arms of the chair. He squeezed his eyes shut. "I will tell you more details of all these things another time. For now I'll just say I made it to Prague where I stayed until the war ended.

"I yearned to return to Latvia and Anita. But it was not to be. After the war, Communists took over my country and all of Eastern Europe. I could not go home, no matter how much I wanted to. If I did, the Communists would uncover my history of outspoken rebellion during their first occupation in 1940, denounce me as a traitor and deport me to Siberia.

"So I escaped from Prague back across the border into Germany and found work as an entertainer in the Western section, for the American USO. I knew when I made that choice I had burned my bridges and could never go home again. I did try to write to Anita care of Salamonski Circus, several times." His eyes penetrated hers. "I'd heard many were fleeing Latvia for the same reason as I, and I hoped and prayed I could make contact with her so she could come to me. I never heard back from her. And then I ran into someone we both had worked with in Riga who told me he'd heard Anita had married." A suggestion of anguish etched his face.

"You must have felt awful to get that news."

"It tore me apart. She hadn't waited for me." He shrugged helplessly. "I also wrote to my family. My brother finally wrote back to me in America after I had been there a few years and told me to stop writing to them. His words implied it would cast suspicion on the family. He also said he'd heard Anita moved to Berlin with her family."

He rose and went to the window again. "In some ways I felt betrayed by them all. But wasn't I the one who'd left them?" He turned to face her. "I decided I had to keep moving toward a new life. So for four years I followed the routine with the USO, and during that time I applied to come to America, a long, grueling process. The CIA examined every detail they could find in my travel and border crossings—dates, places, activities, throughout the war. There were so many questions and delays over this that I was sure I'd never be approved. They told me later that they suspected I had been a spy. But after almost two years they satisfied themselves that I was who I claimed to be, and they cleared me to come to America.

"I knew how lucky I was, but of course I still felt torn. Because of the Iron Curtain, I never again saw my family and friends, or learned for sure what had happened to Anita. When this letter came from the Red Cross on Erik's behalf two years after the Berlin Wall fell…an old scar…ripped open again. But I felt elation at the same time."

Dee realized she had been so absorbed in his story, listening so intently, that she had forgotten to breathe through some of it. She felt lightheaded. She took a deep breath and asked, "How do you think Anita learned you were in America, Mikhail?"

"It must have been the letter I sent to my brother after I arrived in New York. I suppose he told someone who got word to Anita where I was.

"I received one more letter from the Red Cross two years ago in answer to my questions about Erik's mother. They told me her name, that she had given birth in February 1942, and had been married to Aleks Mendenberg." He paused. "She died in 1968."

"She died?" Dee felt a sudden surge of grief. "Oh, Mikhail. I'm so sorry. Do you know how it happened?"

"No." His eyes dropped away. "In answer to your other question, I have not corresponded with Erik. I told the Red Cross that the period surrounding his birth was a complicated time for me because of the war. I told them I might possibly be willing to communicate directly with him later, but not at that time."

"But it's been two years. Surely you want to now."

He looked up sharply. "Why? What good would it do?" His shoulders sagged in defeat. "Anita is gone. The son she gave birth to is over fifty by now. And he was raised under Communism, by a man I despise." His voice rose in agitation. "Aleks Mendenberg is the Army officer she claimed to be afraid of. The man I ran off at the railroad station." He shrugged. "Growing up, Erik was surely accustomed to spying, to informing on others. They all were. Repression, lies, evasion, lack of trust—all were a way of life, so it's hard to be anything but fearful, bitter and cynical under such a system. And just because it's over now does not mean that way of thinking has changed for these people. It will take a generation to recondition their thinking." He began to pace once again across the small space. "I have thought a great deal about this, Dee. I have nothing to offer him. I was unable to be a part of his life, to raise him with Anita, to be responsible for him. If I tried to tell him all this, imagine how he'd respond."

Dee sat in silence, feeling the tension, the anguish that he reflected. She thought about all he had said. Then she asked softly, "Do you know how he found out you were his father? Or how long he has known?"

"No." Mikhail shook his head and folded his arms across his chest. "But that is of little importance."

She looked away, lost in thought. Then she lifted her eyes to his. "It had to have been Anita who told him, some time before she died." She leaned forward. "Mikhail, think about what she must have gone through when she discovered she was pregnant. She must have been devastated by the helplessness of her position. You couldn't come back to her and try to help her even if you had known about her pregnancy. From what you told me about Aleks, he wanted to possess Anita, not love her. He must have gotten a great deal of satisfaction from the knowledge that she had to turn to him. Surely *he* didn't tell Erik that you're his father. On the other hand, he probably resented Erik because her pregnancy was the only reason Anita turned to him. So I think Erik grew up feeling his father's resentment, his lack of warmth."

She rose and took a step toward him, caught up in where her thoughts were leading her. "Now–imagine what Erik must have felt when she told him about his biological father in America–how relieved, or at least hopeful, he'd have been to know that his father was someone else, someone who probably would have loved him, cared for him as he did Erik's mother. Did you say she died in 1968? That was 25 years ago. He's had all this time to cultivate all kinds of hope about what you represent in America—and now he's free to reach out, to try for a connection. Can you imagine what that must mean to him?"

"No. I can't." The words were final, heavy. Mikhail turned away as if the emotional impact of Dee's words were too much for him.

"I can." Dee touched his arm, hoping to reach him. "Forgive me, Mikhail. I probably shouldn't be talking so openly about my feelings on the subject, but there's a reason." Her mind raced. Why did she feel so compelled to reveal her own family history? She pushed on. "As you know, I have a daughter. She's adopted. And over the years, we've talked often about her thoughts and feelings on the subject of her birth, the people she comes from. That's one of the things she's told me she yearns for– to fill in the gaps about her own identity, her own emotional and medical background. Erik would be no different. In fact, he'd probably feel it even more strongly, given what Anita must have told him about you."

Mikhail shook his head slowly. "Please, Dee. I know you mean well, but believe me, when historical events of such magnitude as World War II, Communist oppression, and the fall of the Berlin Wall are churning around you, you don't have the luxury of being concerned about your personal needs regarding relationships. The need for things like survival and freedom from tyranny take precedence, I assure you."

She stepped back, feeling stung. She shouldn't have offered an opinion, she realized. She had overstepped his boundaries. "Of course. I understand."

"And now I'm very tired. We've been through a great deal today, you and I." He forced a smile and opened the door for her. "But I'll think about all you've said, I promise."

She gathered up her belongings and moved through the door and out into the hallway. "I'll wait to hear from you then, Mikhail."

Berlin, 1993

The letter fluttered back and forth between Erik's fingers. He sat at his kitchen table, gazing at the clock on the wall in front of him, not really seeing anything at all. It had been two years, and not a word since the initial acknowledgment. He remembered how hopeful he had felt two years before. When Berlin became the capital of newly reunified Germany, he had bought this house in the former West Berlin, as a personal gesture of hope for the future. And he had reached out to the man in America.

He glanced down at the well-worn letter in his hand and wondered how many times he had read it in the past two years. His jaw muscles felt tense, but he got up and walked over to the stove, poured himself another cup of coffee, then looked out the kitchen window. It was windy today. He could see the laundry Frau Buchman had hung out in the back yard next door, dancing like marionettes on a line that had been strung from one end of the yard to the other. She was a good neighbor. When he had to go out of town on business, she always watched the house for him. And she knew his son by now. Even though he still lived in the former East Berlin, he came often to visit his father. When the house was new, the two men painted the walls, hung the pictures, moved his belongings in and arranged them in the proper places.

It was then, he remembered, that he told his son about the man in America. His son's grandfather. Jon had been stunned, of course. As stunned as Erik had been 25 years before when his mother first told him.

Had it really been that long ago? He closed his eyes and saw her lying in the hospital bed, looking pale and fragile. Every moment of that last encounter in her hospital room came back to him in sharp clarity, as if it had happened yesterday.

He had stood at the door, anxious and heartbroken. Finally he moved closer, seeing that her eyes were closed and her breathing shallow. But as he approached, her eyes flickered open and she gave him a wan smile. He saw that her brown eyes were faded and her gray-streaked dark hair had lost its luster.

"I was just thinking about you," she said, her voice reedy. It had long since lost the lilting musical quality that had lifted him with its familiarity during his growing up years. She raised her thin arm and he took her hand. It felt cold. "You know you are the best part of my life. You and Jon."

"I know," he said simply.

"But there was a time…a time that made it *all* worthwhile." She turned her head and in the silence that followed he watched a tear leak from her eye and slide down her temple toward her ear.

He found a damp cloth and brought it to her face and forehead, stroking her gently, saying nothing.

"Sometimes," she sighed, "youth and strength and love can last a lifetime…in one's memory." She turned her head and her eyes met his. "I want to tell you now, what I've longed to tell you all your life. And I hope it's not too late to make a difference for you."

He shook his head slowly, puzzled.

"Remember when I urged you to learn the English language in school?"

"Of course."

"It is because your father lives in America, and I hope one day for you to go there to meet him." She lapsed into silence, watching his face as he stood before her, his eyes wide and uncomprehending. For a long moment they stared at each other. Then he brought a chair close to the bed and sank into it.

"My father…is not Aleks…"

And he listened as she told him how her great love for Mikhail had persevered through all the years of separation.

And two years ago, he told his own son the same story. When Jon heard it he encouraged Erik to contact the Red Cross and see if they could find the man in the USA.

They did–plucked him out of the anonymity of American life as if he were one ant among many moving through blades of grass–and they contacted him. Something Erik thought impossible, they did so easily. And suddenly he was real. The Red Cross had reported that he had confirmed he was the man. But he had also told the Red Cross that he was not yet ready to communicate directly with his son in Berlin.

In the two years since, he had heard nothing. So little by little the hope drained away. In its place rose a growing bitterness. If Mikhail were not willing to respond directly, there was nothing to do but let the matter lie.

He remembered the effect his mother's revelation had upon him 25 years before. It explained so many things–why he had hated Communism growing up, why he had longed for freedom. He remembered hopeful discussions about that with Liesl on their walks in the forest. But still. For 25 years the man had seemed unreal, veiled behind a cold, dense fog. Now he had a name, a location. A man named Mikhail Sommers, he reflected, exists in America, in Seattle, Washington, who knows first hand about freedom – its high cost, and its value. Mikhail Sommers had run from Eastern Europe during the war and had never returned. Rather than live under Communism, he had chosen to leave behind everything and everyone he knew to make his way to freedom, to America. And whether we ever meet or not, his blood runs in my veins.

CHAPTER TEN

How Erik envied his father in America. How he longed to talk with him, try to understand better. He sighed, understanding only that it was pointless to dwell on such fantasies. It looked as though there would be no direct communication between them after all. He had felt the sting of rejection when he learned from his mother of the man who ran away. He felt it more sharply now. He should forget about it, Erik decided with bitterness, and continue on the course he had set for himself and his own son.

Erik thought about the long years following Liesl's death, before the end of Communism. With a few short-lived exceptions, those years had been as dull and gray as the cold, dense fog Mikhail existed behind.

Even the few brief relationships he'd had with women during those years had been dreary and meaningless. He knew he should have tried to find someone to help him raise Jon, but none of the women he'd met appealed to him. So raising Jon alone had been a mixed blessing. Their relationship had strengthened as he kept Liesl's memory alive for Jon, and that, thankfully, had muted the influence of Jon's surrogate parent, the East German State. Throughout school, Jon had been enrolled like the other children, in the Young Pioneers, and the activities had kept him busy, and relatively happy, in spite of the strong official policies that Erik tried to dilute.

Erik remembered one day when Jon, age six, had come home and said firmly, "The Wall protects us from American imperialists, our enemy, who would exploit us, Papa."

"Perhaps," Erik had answered. Over the next few months he had carefully and quietly put alternate thoughts in Jon's mind without arousing suspicion, and then in 1976, after much checking and questioning, Erik was approved to provide sports equipment at the Olympic Games in Montreal and Jon, who was almost seven, was approved to go along. They both had a wonderful, liberating time there, a brief glimpse of the freedom Erik continued to dream about. And it heartened him to see Jon's private attitude about the west subtly change, though Erik taught him how to act and talk in public.

And of course he made sure they spent as little time as possible with Aleks. Once his wife was gone, Aleks had seemed to lose interest in Erik and Jon, except to express his strong approval of Jon's activities in the Young Pioneers. That suited Erik. He purposely maintained his distance for Jon's sake, and for his own. As the years went by, what Erik observed of Aleks's activities, even from this distance, disgusted him. As a leader of the Party, Aleks was a corrupt hypocrite, grasping more power through deceit and treachery. Erik always declined invitations to join his father at his vacation hunting lodge. He knew such possessions were acquired through the sacrifices of the common people. He was determined that Jon grow up without such influence. And he did.

Jon also managed to get through University during the last four turbulent years surrounding the political upheavals, the fall of the Berlin Wall and Communism. Erik was delighted when Jon joined his own firm which had developed steadily out of the ruins of Communism. Both he and Jon were now successful capitalists, providing quality sports equipment for athletic games.

After the Wall had fallen, Aleks' corruption and that of men like him had all come out in an investigation. The East German people had been outraged to learn the extent to which they had been deceived by the Communist government. All the old Guard under Erich Honecker, including Aleks, was placed under house arrest. A year later, Germany was reunified.

Erik and Jon talked often during this period. In fact, they had exchanged personal experiences from this most amazing historical event, the fall of the Wall.

"I could not believe how different I felt walking through that gate that night," Erik declared in a hushed voice. "I had been through it countless times on business, tense and uncertain, and suddenly, the contagion of thousands of elated people pressed around me—euphoria, triumph, astonishment—and sadness that your mother could not have been here to see this."

"I, too—at Brandenburg Gate," Jon said, reflecting the emotion they both shared. "I climbed up on the top of that wall with so many others, all with our hammers and chisels. It was a moment I will never forget. The bright searchlights. All the people standing beside me on the wall, the sea of happy faces on the ground below. We shared something almost magical. The cheering and reveling and dancing—and chipping away through the night." His eyes were shining. "I wish you had been there with me. But I felt your presence, and Mama's."

Often, when Erik gazed at his son, Liesl came alive for him again, and he thought of her fervent certainty that change would happen. And then he remembered his mother's silent influence during the years he had grown up, before she died.

He put his coffee cup in the sink and moved out into the living room. It was here, some months ago, he remembered, where he'd had the conversation with his son regarding his mother's deathbed revelations about the man in America. He'd told Jon everything he knew himself. Jon was a good son, trying hard to be mature and understanding. Erik could feel Jon's compassion and concern as he'd told him the story. He remembered how gravely Jon had listened.

"Your grandmother was a wonderful woman, Jon. I wish you had known her."

"You have not talked much about her to me, though. Why is that?"

"I was confused, I suppose–long after the last time she spoke to me. For many years I tried to forget what she said right before she died. But now–"

"What she said?"

"Yes. And now I think you have a right to know, too." Erik sank into the upholstered chair he had just bought and leaned his head back. "Your grandmother had an aggressive form of cancer, Jon, that took her quickly. She knew she didn't have much time, and so she told me she wanted to put her life in order. She described the war in Europe, during the time I was born. She said it changed everyone's life forever. And she told me how it changed hers."

Erik glanced at his son in the chair across from him. He was leaning forward and listening carefully. Neither of them spoke for a moment. Erik took a deep breath and smiled. "Did I ever tell you my mother was a performer? No? She came to Riga as a young woman and trained diligently. She did elegant rope dancing with an umbrella, and later teamed with another woman and two men, a quartet, to perform what she called an elegant acrobatic adagio act. They toured throughout Europe before the war with that act. She fell in love with one of her partners. His name was Mikhail Sommers. He was my father."

Jon sat back, stunned. The silence lengthened as Erik waited for Jon to absorb this news. Finally, Jon spoke. "Your father? But that means – the man I thought was my grandfather –"

Erik nodded. "So you know how I felt when she told me."

"But what happened to him? Was he killed in the war?"

"No." Erik told his son then what his mother had told him, about Hitler's mobilization of young men in occupied countries, and Mikhail's flight across the border to perform in Germany. "He told her he'd come back as soon as the war was over, and they'd be married. And then he left. And she never saw him again."

"But by then –"

"By then I was coming."

"Did he know about you?"

"She told me he did not– she discovered her pregnancy a few weeks later."

"And Aleks?" Jon grimaced. Erik was not surprised, given the events right after the Wall fell and the public revelations about Communist corruption in the German Democratic Republic. It had been difficult for Jon to face the harsh reality about the man he thought was his grandfather.

"Aleks was also raised in Latvia. He had been from her home town, Jelgava, too."

"That I did not know. I thought he was German through and through," Jon lifted his eyebrows.

"He had been a serious suitor before she met Mikhail. Apparently he had taken her rejection badly when she chose Mikhail. But when Mikhail was out of the picture, he seemed to be sympathetic."

Jon scoffed. "Took advantage of her need, you mean."

Erik nodded. "He was mobilized to fight for the occupying country, Germany. He was on leave in Riga when he saw her on the street one day when she was far advanced in her pregnancy. She had been working as a seamstress for the circus, sewing costumes. He invited her to a coffee house, they sat down and talked, and he offered to marry her to give us a name."

"But how did he become such a high-ranking Communist after the war if he was fighting for the Nazis? Why was he not thrown in jail then? It would have saved everyone a great deal of trouble!" Jon exclaimed.

"Yes, given what we know now. But in those days everything was in such chaos. He convinced the Russians at the end of the war that his loyalties had always been with Communism, that he hated the Nazis, and that if he were given the chance he'd prove it. And as you know, he did. Many times over."

"But why did Grandmother agree to marry him?"

"It was hard for a woman alone in those days, and she was no different. Her parents wanted nothing to do with her since she left the small, conservative village for the dazzling big city. She had no one to turn to, so in the end she agreed to the marriage. Aleks told her he'd take good care of her as long as she never divulged the identity of the real father. That's why she waited until she was on her deathbed before she told me."

"She had nothing more to lose. And she'd gain your respect for her honesty?"

"Well, it wasn't that simple, Jon. I think she feared that Aleks would divulge the truth to me in a destructive way after she was gone. Use it as a weapon for his own purposes. She wanted me to hear it from her so I'd see Mikhail through her eyes, as a man who'd been caught up in events beyond his control. But when she told me this, everything I thought was true turned upside down."

"But how did you feel about Aleks as you were growing up?"

Erik closed his eyes and considered what to say. In the end, he knew he had to be honest with Jon about his feelings. He opened his eyes, letting his gaze fall on his son. "I thought about that a long time after your grandmother died, Jon. I remembered trying to love him, but I always despised his harsh and authoritative manner with me. I especially grew to loathe the militant Communism he stood for. And to be honest, I received strong undercurrents from my mother. Oh, she never said anything, but looking back, that is the only way I could explain it to myself then, and to you now."

"What do you mean?" Jon gave him a puzzled frown.

"Well, as long as I can remember, Aleks preached equality, sacrifice for the common good. And yet as I was growing up, I could hardly miss the way we lived, so much more luxuriously than the poor common people in East Berlin. Your mother and I both had fathers in privileged Party positions, and that entitled us to our own privileged positions. We both had a strong conviction that this was wrong, and we intended to use our positions as means to our own ends. Receive the privileges, especially the education, so that we could help the common people from the positions we later held. I chose to provide quality Olympics sports equipment and supplies to young athletes with dreams of a better life, not merely to glorify the GDR in competition. Your mother chose to supervise and train people to develop better quality foods in the processing plant where she worked. We pursued real goals, and even though the State controlled our work, we believed we were making the GDR a better place in our own small ways. They watched us, of course, but we never gave them reason to question our allegiance."

Jon nodded thoughtfully. "It explains a great deal about why I saw so little of Aleks while I was growing up. I never thought much about it at the time, but it makes sense now." He looked at his father, his blue eyes soft and warm. "So when are you going to try and find the man in America?" he asked, his smile a mixture of excitement and warmth. "I suggest you contact the Red Cross. The sooner the better."

And so he had. But it had been two years. In that time, Erik and Jon had become well established in their growing business. Erik had kept Jon informed about his contacts with the Red Cross, and about this last letter he had received. Jon had been supportive, but busy with his own pursuits. Now, his heart a jumble of bitterness and regret, Erik went over to his desk and put the letter in the bottom drawer. It was time to let it go.

CHAPTER ELEVEN

On the way home from her afternoon with Mikhail, Dee thought about the uncanny resemblance between Mikhail and the man they'd watched on the video as he walked through the gate of the Berlin Wall. There was no question: she knew he had to be the son Mikhail had learned about from the Red Cross, but she squirmed uncomfortably at her lack of professionalism. She had allowed herself to become emotionally involved, even to the point of intruding her own opinion about what he should do. How could she have been so presumptuous as to urge him to contact Erik just because of her own experience raising Jill? His emotional reaction to her heartfelt appeal, she knew, came from a vast, agonizing storehouse of memories.

What had he said? When historical events of such magnitude as World War II, Communist oppression, and the fall of the Berlin Wall are swirling around you, you don't have the luxury of being concerned about your personal needs regarding relationships.

Perhaps he was right. She thought about her own struggle over the years with her husband and daughter. She wondered how overwhelming outside adversity would have affected their relationships. Would it have destroyed the family sooner? Or could it have drawn them closer, strengthened their family ties? In the case of her relationship with Dennis, the seeds of destruction had started before Jill had even joined their family, so Jill had been affected as she grew up, and then added her own genetic tendencies to the mix.

Pulling into her driveway, she switched off the ignition and sat, immobilized. Her thoughts centered on Jill, and she felt the tears again. She had to concede that she and Dennis, in spite of their best intentions, could have somehow done better with their daughter's adjustments to the gradual failure of their marriage. But how? And how to stop the constant need for tears since long before the divorce?

A long time ago, Dee mused, when she was just a child, her cousin had been killed in a tragic drowning accident. For years afterward, every time she felt like laughing at an inappropriate moment or felt out of control emotionally, she'd conjure up a vision of her cousin's face and she was immediately composed and controlled again. It became a kind of ritual. She remembered how magically it had worked, even at her wedding. While she and Dennis were reciting their vows at the altar, an uncontrollable urge to giggle bubbled up out of nowhere, and she had squelched it instantly. The feeling just evaporated, and she had gone on to say the vows with caring and warmth.

Now she had the opposite problem. Over the four years she'd been adjusting to single life, she'd wished time and again that she could conjure up a lighthearted memory, a face or a name to squelch her grieving emotions, to control the swollen, red, contorted face, the wobbly voice, the weeping that erupted from nowhere and nothing, unbidden. It was becoming so tiresome. She wondered if she'd ever get through the feelings of grief and loss. She knew she and Dennis were better off apart, she knew she was moving forward with her life, she knew the worst of the turmoil was in the past. But she remained deeply and hopelessly stuck in these emotions.

Sometimes she thought she must be like her grandfather on her dad's side, by all accounts a morose man. She wished she could remember him. She was two when he died, and one thing she knew about his death: her dad didn't like to talk about it. Bit by bit over the years, her mother had filled her in on family lore. Grandpa's grief over his wife's sudden death from a stroke had catapulted him into a rapid decline.

"He died of a broken heart, just a few months later," Mom had told her. "After Grandma died, when we went to his house to visit, he'd always be lying on the sofa. We thought you little ones might cheer him up some. He had lots of grandkids.

"The other little kids, your older sister and your cousins, were afraid of him because he was so grumpy. But you weren't." Mom smiled at the memory. "One time you climbed right up on the sofa where he was lying, sat your little bottom down on his chest, and leaned over to peer into his face. He had been sleeping and he didn't show any signs that you had wakened him. So you put your fingers right up to one of his eyelids and lifted it. You were nose to nose with him, staring right into his eye. 'Are you there, Grandpa?' you asked, full of childlike concern. He stared right back. Didn't say a word. Everybody thought he was going to get angry and blow you right off him any minute. But he didn't. He just started chortling. He sat up, slid you down onto his lap, and said, 'What did you see in there, Dee Dee?' And you answered, 'I saw you, Grandpa.'

"He hugged you tight and rocked you in his arms for a long time after that, honey. I'll never forget the smile on his face."

Ever since her mother had told her that story, it had warmed her. To her it meant that her grandfather's response represented a valuable gift, something to be nudged out from just under the surface like buried treasure, something to help her feel special.

She wished her father had told her the story.

She remembered that her dad had been in the room with them, and she had glanced over at him. "Is that true, Dad? Do you remember that?"

He had nodded and smiled a tight, painful grin. Dee sighed. He had never been one to say much of anything to her, except: "Don't be easy with the boys," he'd told her. "Be a good girl." And he hadn't been interested in anything she had to say to him. So she'd felt shy, inadequate around him. And maybe because of her father's reticence, she'd always yearned for emotional intimacy with a man, without compromising the relationship sexually.

It was a hard balance to find. It always seemed just out of reach, as if she were a prisoner stretching her arm between the bars of her cell; obviously doing something wrong in her effort to attain the key to emotional intimacy, to grab it and pull it in close, to hold it to her. She yearned to peer into a man's eyes as she had with her grandfather, to search for what lay beneath the surface in order to really know the man.

She'd found the breakthrough in her relationship with her father one day just that past summer, when she'd visited her parents. Her father started talking about his own relationship with his father. She never knew what triggered his revelations, but in the telling of his painful memories, he'd set her free. He never knew this, for he died not long afterward.

"You know about how gruff your grandpa was with everybody in the family before he died, Dee," Dad began. "But I want to tell you the reason why. He drank. A lot. And he became so bitter and ugly after your grandma died that nobody wanted to be around him. When he landed in the hospital right before he died, nobody came to visit him but me. And so help me God, I wished for years afterward that I never had."

"Why?" she asked in a whisper. She rubbed her arms against the chill she felt, even though the day was warm.

He turned his head and looked at her. "I never thought I'd ever be telling this story." He looked away and stared into space. "I stood in the doorway of his hospital room watching him. His skin was as gray as his matted, greasy hair. I thought he might be dead already. Finally I walked over to his bedside and looked down at him. His eyes were closed, but they were kind of twitching. I reached out and touched his hand. 'Pop?'

"He opened his eyes slowly and looked up at me. His face twisted in a kind of ugly grimace. 'What are you doing here?' he growled at me.

"'I came to see if there's anything you want.'

"'Oh, now you want to help me. After all the times you looked at me with contempt when I came home from the tavern and asked you to get me another bottle. You're a lousy son. You always were. You were weak and spineless as a kid, and then you grew up and acted like you were better than me. Get out of here.' He raised his hand. 'You're worthless to me. You were never any help and I sure as hell don't need your help now.' His hand fell to the bed and he started coughing. He kept coughing, and then he started choking. And I just stood there watching him and I did nothing. I watched the breath go out of him, and I didn't even run for a nurse." He turned and looked at her again. "And those were my father's last words to me."

They sat in silence for a long moment. Dee tried to absorb the shock of her father's words, tried to reconcile the warm picture of her grandfather chuckling at her toddler antics with what she had just heard.

"Dad, he was not in his right mind. You were a good son to him. He was just too sick to know it."

Her mother interjected her thought. "The drinking. It was the drinking that messed up his brain."

Dee sat in the car, brushing away the tears. The memories still evoked powerful emotions. At least I'm not dying from this pain like Grandpa died from his, she thought. And my dad never passed on to me what Grandpa passed on to him. In the end he explained a lot about why he was so remote as a father. He was afraid.

And maybe I married a man who suffered from the same demons, even though his story is different. Whatever I feel isn't from missing Dennis, she reflected, remembering how lonely she had been lying next to him night after night. For years she had searched for what had been beneath the surface of Dennis, and she had never found it. She never come close to feeling emotional or sexual intimacy with Dennis. And she thought a glimpse from her grandfather had held the key. But instead, she realized after her father's story, that there was much more under the surface that she hadn't seen. The longing for what her mother had described that happened between her and her grandfather had been an incomplete, flawed picture.

Could she ever trust her longings? Could she ever recognize any man with only a glimpse of something under the surface?

If only she had learned to live with Dennis in harmony, in spite of his inability to reach out and reveal more of himself. She tried to imagine what it would have been like to lie beside him night after night, year after year, and feel contentment and satisfaction and love from him in their relationship with each other. She sighed, understanding that it was pointless to dwell on such fantasies. Anyway, she thought, it appears he's found a good life with someone else.

A small tap on the car window beside her head startled her. She turned and stared into the smiling face of her sister, Donna. Quickly, she rolled down the window.

"How long have you been sitting here?" Donna greeted her. "You were completely lost in thought. Did you forget I was coming over to pick up that video you promised to lend me?"

Dee looked around quickly, a little disoriented. The shadows were deepening in the yard, and she realized that she *had* been sitting in the car a long time. And forgetting everything else. And getting nowhere. "Sorry, Donna. I've got it inside for you. Can you stay for dinner?" She opened the door and climbed out of the car, and the two of them headed for the house.

"Not tonight. I promised Bill I'd be home to fix him something tonight. But let's go out sometime soon, when Bill has to work late."

She glanced at her sister, noting again how much alike the two of them looked—the same soft brown hair and eyes, similar tall, slim figures and ready smiles, but that was where the similarity ended. Donna had always been the practical, no-nonsense sister; Dee the hand-wringing, demonstrative sister, determined to explore emotional issues no matter how distressing. She unlocked the front door and once inside, turned on the lights.

"Go ahead, help yourself," she offered with a gesture toward the shelf where the videos were stored. While Donna went for the video she leafed through the mail and then she noticed the light flashing on the answering machine. She pushed the button. Jill's soft, tremulous voice stopped her cold.

"Mom, I think I've found my birth mother. Call me back, please."

CHAPTER TWELVE

She stood frozen by the telephone, not breathing. She lifted her head and stared helplessly at her sister who was searching her face from across the room. Her mind couldn't seem to absorb the simple words Jill had spoken.

"We were just talking about this at lunch the other day, and she said she was taking it slowly, one step at a time. How did it happen so quickly, that's what I'm wondering." She moved to a chair and sank into it. "Am I ready for this?"

Donna sat down in the opposite chair and leaned forward. "This isn't about you, Dee. This is about Jill, isn't it?"

Dee looked at her sister, her mind churning. "Of course. I guess my first reaction was purely emotional. In my head, I know that this is about Jill's own process of discovery – who she is, what she's about. And besides, Jill is a grown woman. She has every right to learn these things now, without anything feeling like a threat to me or my shared past history with her. Those things, good and bad, can never be taken away from my own memory, or Jill's. I want to be a support to her, the loving support I've always tried to be. It's as simple as that."

Donna smiled with encouragement. "It's a big step, though." She rose and went to the front door. "Thanks for the loan. I've got to run."

Dee nodded, then got up and went over to give her sister a hug. "See you soon."

"Good luck. Go call Jill; I'll let myself out."

After Donna left, Dee stood there a moment, gathering her thoughts. Then with slow, deliberate movements, she walked over, picked up the phone and dialed her daughter's number. Jill answered on the second ring. Her voice was soft, as if she couldn't quite catch her breath.

"Jill? I just got your message. How're you doing? What's happening?" She willed her voice to be cheerful and encouraging.

"Mom, thanks for calling back. I've been a wreck."

"How did this happen so soon, honey?"

"Well, for the last few days I've been thinking about the last name you gave me, and the more I thought about it, the more I realized that I wanted to see where it might take me. I guess I'm ready for anything, because I just did it. No hesitation. Remember how the letter from the agency said that she had been a recent high school graduate when she gave birth? Well, I decided to call all the Insens in all the nearby phone books and pretend I was updating the roster of 1970 graduates to prepare for the Puget Sound Area high schools' 25th anniversary reunion in a couple of years. There's been some publicity about it in the paper lately. I'd just tell the person on the other line that we lost track of her and needed her current name and address."

"I thought you wanted to go through an intermediary when you were ready, and then they'd make the initial contact."

"Well, I could still do that. I'm just doing what I call preliminary research for now, I guess. Eliminating the dead ends. And it seems to have paid off. I found someone in Everett whose daughter graduated from high school there in 1970, married a few years later and moved to Arlington. I called every Insen in every local book, and that was the only one that fit." Jill took a deep breath. "Her name is Karen Connors now. Her mother was very nice. Said Karen has two children. Gave me the address and phone number. Mom, I think she's the one. Don't you?"

"It does sound possible."

"What do I do now? I've been sitting here for hours, feeling scared all of a sudden. She never seemed real to me before. Now suddenly, I may have been talking to my birth grandmother. I may not only have a birth mother but two half-siblings. All the possibilities I'd thought about intellectually are so scary and real now."

"Flesh and blood."

"Yeah. Not fantasy anymore. I'm not sure I'm ready for reality."

"I want to repeat what I said to you the other day, honey. I understand the need you have, and the huge risk it feels like. But whatever you find out, you are a terrific young woman, one any woman would be proud to have as a daughter."

Jill gave a little laugh. "I know you feel that way, mom. You're prejudiced."

"I don't know about that. I just know that if things don't turn out the way you'd like them to, you are still you."

"But my feelings are so jumbled and – and like I'm in pieces right now. I want so badly to feel like a *whole* me."

"You will. Just give it the time it needs." She squeezed her eyes shut and breathed deeply in an attempt to calm her mind, to say the right thing, and for a moment she could smell the milky, powdery scent that had been Jill, a tiny baby, after her earliest baths. Suddenly she winced at the memory of her first attempt to clip Jill's impossibly tiny fingernails. She saw the infant's red, contorted face and heard her irate howl as Dee accidentally cut into her skin, drawing blood.

"I have to absorb every step of the process as I go along, right?" Jill was asking.

Dee's mind came back to the present, and she answered, "I'd say so. But I imagine how overwhelming this must feel to you. I feel it myself. And I'm with you every step of the way. As much as you want me to be."

"Thanks, Mom." There was a pause. Dee could tell Jill was gathering her thoughts. "Okay. I guess what I need to do now is contact the intermediary agency. I don't want to be the one to make the first contact. I'm feeling too shaky."

"That sounds really good. Keep me posted."

After she hung up, Dee sat there a long time. She felt numb, exhausted, and emotionally overloaded, all at the same time. And a little scared, herself, about the outcome. She really did mean what she'd told her sister Donna. She wanted to be a support to her daughter; she'd always felt about Jill the fiercely protective instincts of a mother bear. In this situation, especially, Jill needed her.

She realized in the weeks that followed that she needed the time to absorb all she had learned – first, from Jill about the possibility of finding her birth mother, and second, from Mikhail, about his son in Berlin, who had tried to make contact with him in America. Both situations tugged at her heart, and yet in her heart she knew she was secondary to the dramas that quite possibly would play themselves out around her in the weeks and months to come. She knew there was nothing she could or should do in either case, except to lend support.

Her working sessions with Mikhail were becoming progressively more absorbing and satisfying. Every time she came to work, she gained more insight about why the life he had led affected her deeply. Against the backdrop of the horrors of the war in Europe,

Mikhail had left his old life behind and struggled to find his way to something good again. Dee knew he had come to America alone. She pondered that a great deal. She had always taken her family and friends for granted, just as she had taken the freedom she enjoyed in America for granted.

"What did you do in America? Did you ever marry?" she asked him one afternoon.

He shook his head slowly. "I had opportunities over the years. But I was so busy learning the language and the ways of my new country. At first in New York I worked several warehouse jobs, loading and unloading freight from trucks. I didn't need to know much English for that."

"Did you contact fellow-Latvians who had come to America too?"

Again he shook his head. "I deliberately stayed away from Latvian community activities. I've known some Latvians who never bothered to learn English because they stayed only among their own kind. I didn't want to be like that. I wanted to embrace my adopted country and learn as much about it as I could. I was so grateful to be free in this country. And I had a plan." He paused. Dee knew by now it was for effect, mostly. It meant he was about to reveal something he considered important, and that she was to lean forward and listen intently. So she did.

"When I had saved enough money and learned enough English," he continued, "I opened my own acrobatics school."

"How long did it take to reach that point?"

"About ten years. Then another ten years to build up the excellent reputation and the large student numbers. I'm proud to say I trained many outstanding students over the years. We did well in competitions, exchanges. It was a busy, satisfying life."

Dee sat up straighter. "How did you happen to come to Seattle?"

He looked away a moment and frowned, as if troubled. Then he turned his eyes back to her. "Some of my students went with me to the Olympics in Montreal in 1976," he said. "It was a wonderful experience. And it opened my eyes to something else. Olga Corbut revolutionized American attitudes toward gymnastics. By that time I knew I was tired of teaching acrobatics, and was ready for a new challenge more compatible with my background and training in Latvia. But how to introduce the new sport, when I had established such a following in New York? I decided to start fresh somewhere else. I had done it so many times before in my life, I was not afraid of another new start. The west coast appealed to me, so without much hesitation I chose Seattle. The timing seemed right, so I left New York for good and relocated."

She sighed and propped her elbows on the table, chin in hand. "You have certainly had a full life, Mikhail. But has it been lonely for you? No wife? No family here?"

He frowned. "I don't allow myself to think of such things. I stay busy. I'm glad you came to help me with my life story. But I suppose you wonder who'd be interested. No children to leave such a legacy." His eyebrows lifted as he gazed at her.

She felt her face flush. It seemed Mikhail wanted to forget their discussion a few weeks before about Erik Mendenberg. "I'm sorry Mikhail. I shouldn't have asked such a personal question."

"On the contrary," he smiled. "That's probably why you're good at your work. You ask questions I suppose a reader would ask." His eyes dropped and he studied his hands. "I have had many students, here and in New York who all expressed interest in my life in Europe before and during the war. The idea grew since my retirement a few years ago. When I decided it would be a good project while I am still in good health, you were here, and you had the right skills and credentials to help me."

"And you never wanted to return to Latvia? To Europe?"

His eyes widened in amusement and his mouth twitched at the corners. "Why would you think that? I've returned many times to Western Europe. I went to the Olympics in Munich in 1972. I've spent a great deal of time in London and Paris. I have many friends throughout the world. I've certainly thought of going back to Riga after the breakdown of the Soviet Union, but I know I'd hardly recognize it now, and that makes me sad. So lately I've thought a great deal about going to Berlin since you submitted your challenge to me. About the man named Erik." He looked at her pointedly.

She blinked. Neither of them said anything for a moment. Finally she asked, "Have you come to any conclusions?"

"Not yet. I want to wait until after the New Year before I talk about it further."

The holidays passed uneventfully. Jill had been seeing the intermediary, a woman named Nicole Brewster, in a series of counseling sessions, and had agreed to wait until after the holidays to try to make contact with her birth mother. She'd told Dee that Dennis was in California, and so mother and daughter both made the rounds of family gatherings feeling somewhat preoccupied.

Then one day in January Dee got a call from Dennis. "My company wants me to move to California permanently, and I'm going to do it," he said without preamble.

The silence lengthened over the phone. She could hear his shallow breathing on the other end. She wondered if she should feel something. She knew she should say something.

"When did this happen?" she asked.

"Well, you know I've been going and coming for years now. When I'm here I live in my condo; when I'm there I live in a company-owned apartment. I think I really want to try to make it permanent in California. It'll probably be a good move for me, and there's nothing holding me here."

She bit back a retort that she might have made if they were still married. It had taken her four years to feel enough emotional distance to hold her tongue. But they could still push each other's buttons on occasion. She thought their daughter needed him now, but she tried a more diplomatic approach.

"Did Jill tell you she thinks she's found her birth mother?"

"She mentioned it. Said she has an intermediary working on the leads now. Any new developments?"

"No, she's taking it slowly ... but this is a vulnerable time for her. She could use as much emotional support from us as we can give. I think it was hard for her at Christmas, with you gone. But I truly don't mean to lay a guilt trip on you, Dennis," she quickly added. Then she hesitated. It had been a little easier lately to talk about their daughter's life in depth, since Jill was on her own now. "In fact, I'd like to talk Jill's situation over with you, Dennis. There's a lot about this that's kind of like an emotional mine field."

There was a silence on the other end of the line.

She pressed on. "Especially if you're leaving for California soon. When are you going?"

"I'm not sure yet. There are a few loose ends to tie up here first." He chuckled, and she briefly wondered why. "I guess some time this Spring."

Another silence. "I'd like to talk to you though, whenever you'd like. Do you want to come over for dinner, or meet at a restaurant?"

"Whatever you say."

"Let's let Jill cook the meal, where she works." They had met there periodically over the years, and Jill was feeling comfortable about their efforts at friendship in order to keep some contact. They were still Jill's parents, after all, and Dee knew that Jill should see the evidence of that whenever an opportunity presented itself. They decided on an evening and a time to meet for dinner, but as they said goodbye and hung up the phone, Dee wondered if she had made a mistake by wanting to talk things over with Dennis. Instead of avoiding an emotional minefield, they might be walking right into one.

CHAPTER THIRTEEN

A few evenings later she sat at a booth in the restaurant where Jill was now Head Chef. She gazed around the familiar dining room with a kind of motherly pride. It had a pleasant ambiance; the walls were decorated with warm, muted green wallpaper and polished oak, the coordinated tables and chairs positioned strategically with candles that cast a warm glow. Since it was still early, there were few people at the tables, engaged in relaxed conversation. She knew the place would fill up quickly in another hour or so. The food was truly wonderful; everyone she talked to who had eaten there agreed. Never mind that they knew her daughter created the meals in the kitchen. Dee had seen it many times. It was spotless; Jill had enthusiastically given her a tour of the features and equipment. She inhaled deeply, savoring the delicious aromas that wafted from that direction.

Dennis approached, his lanky stride still so familiar to her after almost thirty years. Beside him was a woman she recognized immediately as his sister, Amy. She lived across the country in New York and had visited rarely over the years. Dee smiled and stood up, noting Amy's dark tailored suit and crisp white blouse, her short sleek blonde hair; Dee thought Amy reflected the poise and confidence that came with a successful career.

"Well, Amy, this is a nice surprise. What brings you all the way across the country?" She reached out and gave her former sister-in-law a hug. As always, Amy's response felt stiff and formal. But as she moved back, she smiled at Dee in return.

"I flew in yesterday to visit. Dennis told me he had plans for dinner with you, so I invited myself along. I hope that's okay."

"Of course it's okay, it's always good to see you. How long has it been?"

"A few years, anyway," Amy replied as she sat down. Dee sat next to her while Dennis sat across from the two women.

Some things never change, Dee mused with a sensation something like relief passing through her. Dennis probably thought Amy would be a good buffer for the two of them. And she had to admit, she didn't disagree. She hoped Amy's presence would make the evening more comfortable.

The Berlin Connection

"How late are we?" Dennis asked with a tight smile. "When we were married you always let me know to the minute when I was late."

Dee smiled in amusement. "I don't mind these days," she said pleasantly. "This is one of my favorite places to be." Another button safely avoided, she thought with relief.

"Does Jill know you're here?" he asked.

"I think so. I called her earlier to tell her the time. She'll be so glad you're here too, Amy."

A waitress came up to the table with a bright smile and a bottle of white wine. "Hi, you're Jill's folks, aren't you?"

"Yes, and her Aunt Amy. But I don't think we know you," Dee answered with a returning smile. "Have you worked here long?"

"Just a few weeks." She raised the bottle. "Compliments of the chef."

"How nice," Dee responded as the young woman uncorked the bottle and poured the wine into Dennis's glass. "Jill told me to tell you she's planning the menu, and I'm to give you the royal treatment."

They all laughed as Dennis took a sip, then nodded his approval.

The waitress poured the wine all around and after she left, Dee glanced at Dennis. She was pleased to note that he had relaxed visibly.

"So," she said briskly, lifting her glass. "A toast. To a bright future." They touched glasses and sipped their wine, then she asked, "Any more news about your move to California, Dennis?"

He shook his head. "I fly down again on Sunday. I guess I'll start laying the groundwork for some time in April or May."

She nodded. "Lots to do between then and now, I guess."

He shrugged. "Nothing I can't handle. I've always done well with work pressure."

There was a brief silence and she was conscious of moving emotionally away from the painful memories from the past. She drew in a deep breath, pleased that it was so much easier by now to sit face to face with him and not feel the old resentments about how often he had put work pressures before family. Family pressures, she corrected in her mind. He never handled those as well. But he was here now, and she knew they were both supposed to be removed in many ways from what she wanted to talk to him about. First and foremost, Jill was an adult, even if she was their child. She turned to Amy. "Did Dennis catch you up on Jill's news?" she asked.

Amy nodded. "She thinks she found her birth mother, right?"

"Looks that way. She'll come out to talk when there's a lull."

Amy's face turned grave. "I hope you don't mind if I give you my point of view," she said slowly. "Dennis already told me you wanted to talk about what might happen if she meets her birth mother."

Dee looked at Dennis, her eyes questioning. He glanced away briefly.

"You've been in on things from the beginning, Amy. I won't mind."

The Berlin Connection

Amy nodded shortly. "Dennis is not sure Jill needs her parents' involvement in this."

Dee frowned in surprise, and looked at Dennis again, but directed her words to Amy. "I thought you wanted to give your point of view, not Dennis's. But let's talk about that, Dennis. Why do you feel that way?"

"Well, she's a grown woman," he said somewhat defensively. "I'm not sure she needs us for any of that."

Dee took a deep breath. "Not directly, no. But she really needs to know we'll be there for her. Especially if things don't go the way she hopes. This woman could really not want to be found. She could react badly to the whole thing. Jill could feel devastated if she rejects her—I've read it's like being rejected for a *second* time."

"You mean if she tells her she doesn't want anything to do with her?" Dennis lifted his wine glass to his lips slowly and looked around the room. She knew this gesture well. She knew it meant he didn't want to be talking about this. She churned inwardly, suppressing an impulse to demand that he look at her, listen to what she was saying. It had never worked in the past, and she knew she should just say what she had to say and try to enjoy the rest of the evening.

"That could happen, Dennis," she said carefully. "And if it does, I think we should let her know she can always count on us, talk things over with us, even though she is grown up and on her own. She still needs to know she matters to us, no matter what."

He looked at her for a moment in silence. "I'll be here. For a few months, anyway. And I think she knows she can count on me, even after I go down to California to live."

"It needs to be said in so many words, Dennis. She needs to hear the words to truly feel the reassurance."

Amy broke in. "Let me ask you something, Dee. I may be overstepping my bounds as an aunt but I was hoping you'd explain it to me from your point of view."

"Explain what?"

"Well, I know the language about the need for emotional support and all that. But I don't really understand it."

Dee hesitated. "I just thought maybe Dennis and I could both say something to her together tonight if we get the chance."

"Okay. I agree. But why does it matter so much to you, really?"

"She's my daughter, Amy." She glanced at Dennis. "She's our daughter."

"And now after all this time, there's another mother hovering in the background. What if she's overjoyed if Jill finds her? How would you feel about that?"

Dee sat back in her chair, off balance. She twisted her napkin in her lap. Amy had never probed like this before. For as long as she'd known them, Amy and Dennis had both been closed off. Now suddenly, Amy seemed almost aggressive about discussing emotional issues. Dee didn't know if she liked her own defensive feelings. After all, Amy wasn't the woman who had raised Jill. She'd never been a mother at all. "This isn't about me, Amy. This is about Jill."

"Yes, but I'm asking you. What if the other mother wanted to be part of her life? Would you feel threatened?"

"Of course not." She took another sip of wine as she gathered her thoughts. Resentment tugged at her. Suddenly she was on the losing side of an emotional debate. But Amy was, after all, Dennis's sister. Of course she'd side with him. She shook her head. This wasn't about taking sides. She reminded herself that she had chosen this public place in an attempt at reasonable dialogue. "As I said, this is about Jill and her feelings. And I don't expect to be friends with Jill's 'other mother' as you put it, either. But we do have a great deal in common. I've always known she cares for Jill, from somewhere out there." She waved her arm in the air. "But if she became a reality to all of us," she said slowly, "I guess when the time is right, I'd just appreciate an acknowledgement from her that I'm the mother who raised her. Just as I'd acknowledge the birth mother for…"

"For what?" Amy leaned forward, a look of earnest sympathy on her face.

She thought about that. "For giving her up. It was an unselfish, caring thing to do. I assume she knew she wouldn't have the resources to raise her. She was so young."

They sat in silence for a moment. She looked at Dennis, who was glancing from her to Amy and back, looking even more uncomfortable than before.

"Maybe you'd better just leave it alone, Dee," Amy said at last. "It might be another one of those situations that you think would end harmoniously with everyone smiling happily at one another, but reality is another matter, isn't it?"

"Reality? Which reality are you talking about?"

Amy turned to Dennis. Dee's eyes darted across to Dennis. She could tell he was struggling to find words. She knew from all the times over the years when she had pushed a conversation, that foremost in Dennis' mind was fear of confrontation. Now it seemed that Amy had left something for Dennis to say.

At last he spoke. "We didn't end up happily ever after, hard as we tried to do the right thing, the best thing, in the face of reality. It went on for years, and it kept getting worse." He stopped, breathing hard, visibly attempting to calm himself.

Amy broke in again. "Now, apply that to the birth mother's situation. She could be overjoyed. She could try to make up for the lost years. She could feel afraid to face the reality of your role. She could ignore you. We can't just tie things up into neat little packages. This situation in varying degrees could go on for years, too, with no easy resolution."

Dee's eyes widened, sliding her glance back to Dennis again. "But that's exactly what I'm talking about. That's why I think Jill must be so scared. If it doesn't work out…and even if it does…"

Dennis nodded, calmer now. "So we're in agreement. We try to let her know we'll be there for her without crowding her space or putting our own spin on it."

"Is that what you think I've been doing?"

The Berlin Connection

"I think you like to be involved in any kind of emotional situation. You thrive on it." His face softened. "Look, I don't want to start anything with you. I was just trying to point out that we really are not involved in this."

The waitress came and put their dinners down in front of them. "Jill said she'd be out to spend a little time with you in a few minutes. It's slowing down in the kitchen now."

Dee smiled up at the young woman with gratitude. She wondered if the waitress could tell she had interrupted a strained situation between the three of them. She looked down at her plate, at the beautifully presented meal, and again her pride in her daughter's culinary talent took over. The three of them murmured words of approval and enjoyment about their identical meals, and for the moment Dennis's last words faded.

But as they fell silent, the question rose up and filled Dee's mind. What was Dennis trying to say to her? It didn't sound at all like the Dennis who had frustrated her so with his reluctance to discuss an issue. His sister had seemed to give him encouragement to speak his mind, and she was glad of that, of course. He was participating. He was pointing out what he considered to be a concern. But she couldn't quite get it.

"Let me see if I understand you," she said after a few moments, laying her fork on her plate and gazing at Dennis, eyes narrowed. "We all agree that Jill needs emotional support about this, no matter what, but that I should hold back and try not to give her any message that my own feelings are some sort of burden on her."

He nodded slowly. "Sort of a balance between what I'd call your 'in your face' involvement and what you'd call my 'lack' of involvement."

She held herself still while she absorbed this. After all the years of his lack of involvement, he was expressing his emotional point of view. She should be relieved, but instead, the familiar resentment and frustration gnawed at her, only this time it was for opposite reasons. How strange, she mused. How confusing, too.

"Point taken," she said stiffly. She bent her head and concentrated again on the savory meal on her plate. She picked up her fork and started to eat. Once more the three of them fell silent. Dee tried to clear her mind of everything but the delicious blend of flavors in the meal her daughter had prepared for them. She was almost finished and looked up to see Jill walking toward them and she smiled, grateful for the welcome distraction. Amy stood up as Jill approached. Jill reached out to give her aunt a hug.

"I'm so glad to see you, Aunt Amy." She sat down next to her dad and smiled at them all. Dee felt like she was basking in the sunshine of her daughter's presence.

"Hi, honey. I'm glad you could come out and join us for awhile."

"Me too," Jill said as she turned to her dad, reached over to brush his cheek with her lips. "Hi, Dad. How'd you manage to get your sister to visit us after all this time?" She waved her fingers at their plates. "Finish your dinners, you three. How do you like the food tonight?"

Dennis grinned at her. "Very good, as always. What's it called again?"

"Chicken Dijon with rice, Dad. Very simple. You've had it quite a few times."

"Very good," he repeated. "Your aunt came to visit because I'm leaving in a few months and she wanted to see us all." He ducked his head and finished his last bite, then pushed his plate away and sat back. "Have you been busy back there?" he asked.

"Not too. About normal."

Seated across the table from Dennis and Jill, Dee observed the two of them. How often had they indulged in small talk while she'd sat by in frustration, knowing they had important things to discuss and neither one of them wanted to begin?

She breathed in. "Jill has 'issues' as they say, to work out," she said.

Jill looked at her sharply. Bad beginning, she thought.

Amy said brightly, "I heard you think you found your birth mother, Jill. Are you glad?"

Jill hesitated. "I don't really know, Aunt Amy," she said, her tone cautious. Dee smiled wryly. Her daughter was a little confused about Amy's openness, too, she observed. "I guess I'm more scared than anything."

"I can imagine," Amy said. "Sort of like a big adventure?"

"I guess."

Like an African Safari? Dee wondered with frustration. "Well, we all want you to know we're there for you, if you need to talk, or …" Dee trailed off, hoping Dennis or Amy would respond with more emotional support to Jill's admission that she was scared.

Dennis squared his shoulders, then said, "I won't be leaving for awhile yet, but after I move to California you know you can call or visit any time you want, honey."

Dee sighed, her feelings jumbled, knowing that was all he'd say, and that she should be satisfied. She hoped Jill was too. As she knew he would, Dennis smiled and changed the subject, and the rest of the time Jill was with them, the talk was light and pleasant. And later, as she drove home, she reminded herself again that whatever she and Dennis had been trying to find in each other had never been there.

CHAPTER FOURTEEN

"Mom, my intermediary just called." Jill's voice trembled softly through the phone line. "She's made contact with Karen, and Karen says she *is* my birth mother."

It was only a week after their dinner with Dennis and Amy. Dee could barely grasp how quickly this had happened. She felt the jolt of adrenaline; her heart began to pound harder. "Oh, honey. This is the breakthrough you've been hoping for, isn't it?"

In the silence that followed she could hear her daughter swallow. "I guess so," Jill's reply was breathless. "She told Karen about me–the bare facts, anyway. She told her I wanted to meet her." Jill fell silent again. Dee wanted to reach through the phone lines and hold her daughter, stroke her smooth, silky hair.

"What now?" Dee finally ventured.

"I don't know. Karen told Nicole she needed to think about it, talk it over with her husband. I don't know if he's aware of me already or not, I mean that she gave birth to me. Nicole says to just be patient, give her time to absorb it all. It could take some time, probably more time than I'd like. She reminded me that *I've* had time to absorb developments about *her*, and now it's her turn."

"It sounds like good advice."

"I know. I'm really not sure if I'm ready anyway. Nicole says each step needs to be processed, and this is quite a step, isn't it?"

"Yes, it is. For me too, so I can imagine how much more it is for you."

After they hung up, Dee thought about the situation throughout the evening. She couldn't sleep for a long time that night, and then she woke up thinking about it. She tried to decide if she felt any of the things Amy and Dennis had tried to warn her about, but all she felt was confusion. She only knew for sure that she didn't want her daughter to be hurt. This is something she needs to do, Dee reminded herself. It's enough for me to just be there for her. It will work itself out, and my feelings, whatever they are, should stay in the background.

A few days later, Dee met again with Mikhail. She found him restless and unsettled. "I want to tell you my decision about contacting Erik in Berlin," he said brusquely. "But first you'll need more detail about why it's been such a difficult decision. What it was like for me during the war, when I was constantly on the run."

Dee started the tape recorder and then waited in silence. He rose from his chair to pace the length of the floor, hands clasped together, head lowered. He stopped abruptly and turned to her. "You can't imagine the way I felt from one day to the next, trying to stay ahead of constant danger, not only of being found out, but of being killed. I will try to explain with a few incidents." He ran his hand over his eyes and gazed up a moment, his face a mask of pain as though conjuring up some unspeakable scene.

"In Berlin the allied bombings came more often and with more intensity toward the end of the war. All of us who lived in Berlin had to get used to it – the unpredictability, the horror. In that sense the first experience I had was the worst, by far." He shook his head and continued. "I thought often about what I'd do when the bombings started while I was there, and I knew most people planned to go to the basements, but it seemed to me that if a bomb dropped on the building above me, it would collapse and bury everyone underneath. So I made up my mind to find cover at a big wide park just across from my hotel. I reasoned that if I lay flat on the ground under the trees, I'd survive.

"That night, right after I finished my performance I felt tense and anxious. I went back to my room and changed into street clothes. Almost immediately, what I had feared came to be. I heard the sirens wailing around me. I ran out into the hall and down the stairs. I got to the park across the street. I heard the planes coming. I saw a wide, shallow hole just ahead of me. People were running for cover all around me. I reached the grassy basin and dove to the ground. I covered my head with my hands. The whistle of the bombs sounded ear-splittingly close. I braced myself for the impact. The blast was deafening. Tremendous pressure ripped through the air, pinning me against the ground like a giant, brutal hand. More blasts followed, then there was silence. I couldn't move. I don't know how long I lay there—a long time.

"Finally, the all-clear siren sounded, and I got up and looked around. What I saw will haunt me till the day I die. I stood in shocked silence at the sight. I remember swallowing against the nausea that rose in my throat. Scattered all around me on the ground lay mangled, bloody pieces of bodies – arms, legs, torsos – unbelievable carnage!

"A man came toward me and shouted in German. 'This is what the Americans started doing – air bombs!' He was gesturing wildly at the scene. 'They create tremendous pressure when they explode above the ground—they pull anything apart that isn't lying flat. Those people must have been standing!'

"I squeezed my eyes shut tightly, but I knew I could never forget such a sight. Or the sounds of hysterical moaning and wailing that filled the air. Or the ugly smells."

Dee closed her eyes and swallowed. "Horrible," she breathed.

He turned to face her. "Yes," he acknowledged as he stood clenching and unclenching his hands. "As I said, the first is always the worst. Many other experiences like that followed. I lived for the day I could get out of Berlin." He breathed deeply, collecting his thoughts. "I heard that even though the Germans occupied Czechoslovakia the Allies weren't bombing in Prague. In the fall of 1944 I finally managed through a friend to get a contract from the circus there, but I knew that getting out of Berlin safely would be a huge hurdle. German soldiers controlled the Czech border, and I had to get permission from the high-ranking German official in charge of travel authorization. One wrong word could mean my execution, or at the very least, mobilization into the German Army, which I had up until then managed to avoid. I have no words to convey the anxiety I experienced as I hovered uncertainly in that Nazi office, waiting to hear the decision that truly meant my life or death.

"This particular officer had every evil Nazi trait anyone could imagine. Looking at him as he sat behind his desk so smugly, I knew that even if I said and did everything 'right', he still might deny permission on a cruel whim. All Nazi officers I had ever seen were everything you are likely to have heard – arrogant, brutal, with their own ways of reasoning. I stood before him and lifted my right arm in the detested salute. 'Heil Hitler!' I said.

"He raised his arm and repeated the salute, then curled his hand into an impatient, beckoning gesture. I walked over and put my papers on the desk in front of him. He sat staring at me with annoyed indifference.

"'This is a contract for me to perform my trapeze act at the circus in Prague,' I explained, willing my voice into control. 'I understand I need your signature to cross the border.'

"He picked up the form and read it over. I stood very still, breathing deeply, watching him. He picked up his pen and glanced up, his eyes cold. 'We have circuses here. Why do you want to go to Prague?' he asked me.

"'Only for one month,' I tried to evade the question. 'Then I'll return.'

"'But why Prague?' he persisted.

"'I have a contract. Work here is scarce.' I prayed my shaking hands would not betray me. He looked down at the form and frowned, as though he were about to sign his own death warrant. I felt my heart pounding heavily and suddenly I hated this Hitler Party man who literally held my life in his hands. He moved his hand toward the signature space, then hesitated once more and looked up at me, his eyes narrowing.

"'Surely you could find work here,' he said in a reasonable voice.

"'This contract in Prague was arranged some time ago," I answered. 'They have me scheduled on their program and they're expecting me to honor the contract.'

"The silence filled the room as he stared at me, considering my words. At last he abruptly lowered his eyes to scratch his signature on the paper. Without another word he thrust the paper toward me.

"'Thank you, sir.' I lifted my arm in the salute, turned on my heel and walked to the door. As I left the building, I felt the weight of the world lift from my shoulders."

Dee looked up. "I felt the tension and the relief you described," she murmured, "almost as though it had happened to me."

He nodded. "It happened decades ago, a lifetime ago. And yet for me it happened only yesterday."

He turned away and again, his head lowered briefly. She knew he needed to compose his thoughts, that there was more. A moment later he turned back and confirmed her thoughts. "One more incident should suffice. After I got to Prague I honored the contract at the circus there and then I found ways to prolong my stay: another contract, forging an extended visa— I was desperate to avoid going back to the chaos in Germany, where I'd be trapped when the war came to an end. And the war *was* coming to an end, everyone knew it. For me it was just a matter of waiting and watching in Prague.

"Then came the heartbreaking news that the Russians had penetrated my beloved Riga for a second time, and in the chaos there, Baltic citizens were fleeing to the western European countries. As I said before, I didn't want to live under the Russians again, any more than I wanted to live under Hitler's Germany. Western Europeans were happy the Allies had taken over. I hoped that my dilemma as an Eastern European would somehow be resolved when the war was over. But I knew nothing of the decisions that were already being made. In February, 1945, Roosevelt, Churchill and Stalin met at Yalta and signed the pact that prepared for the war's end. Those decisions set a course in motion that changed the structure of Europe for nearly half a century.

"As I said before, I worried about Anita. But if it looked as though I might never be able to return to Riga, all I could do was wait until I was in a place where I might be able to send for her.

"Over the winter, we artists who lived at the hotel in Prague all kept looking for any work we could find, waiting for something to happen to end the war. No one knew what to expect and life seemed to float and drag forever—how can I describe it? We were in a kind of pressurized limbo. Rumors flew: we heard repeated news reports that Americans were only thirty miles from Prague, and hope soared. Then we heard with dismay that Russians were closing in on Prague as well as Berlin. But either way, it would all be over in only a few more days or weeks.

Suddenly in March 1945, the Czechs in Prague took matters into their own hands. They revolted against what little German control was left. Almost overnight, the atmosphere in Prague turned ugly and violent. We heard the sounds of constant gunfire throughout the day and night. Czechs hunted down Germans all over the city. Vigilantes roamed the streets, gunning people down without even asking questions. They assumed that whoever didn't speak Czech must be German, or German sympathizers. We were ordered to stay in our hotels and off the streets if we didn't want to get shot.

"Inside the hotel, many of us sat together in the lobby hour after hour, day after day, listening to the gunfire and other sounds of violence and death out on the streets. It quickly became clear to us that the revolution was a hundred times worse than the war itself. Order had completely disappeared. No one was safe. Anything could happen.

"One morning armed, uniformed Czechs entered the hotel lobby and assembled everyone. They announced that they were ordered to protect us. That gave us some measure of relief, but the days dragged on endlessly. The fighting in the streets continued. Finally one day the armed guards confirmed what we had been too afraid to even think. The *Russians* were entering Prague and taking over the city. I can't tell you the despair I felt. No one could understand what had happened to the Americans. Why, when they were so close, had they stopped short of Prague and let the Russians enter instead? Sick with dread and disappointment, I drifted aimlessly through the next day or two. Random gunfire still echoed through the streets outside.

"One day I wandered down some steps that led to a basement area where I had never been. At the end of a long hall a handful of men sat together smoking. They wore civilian clothing. I walked toward them and one man spoke to me in German. 'What are you doing here?' he asked grimly.

"'Curiosity,' I answered. 'How about you?'

"'We were arrested,' he mumbled.

"I heard the sound of footsteps behind me and turned to see armed Czech soldiers marching toward me. I didn't recognize any of them.

"'On your feet, *now*!' one of them ordered the men, motioning with his rifle for me to join them. 'We need to move out to the courtyard. There are Russians in the building.'

"'But I don't belong to this group,' I protested in halting Czech.

"'You do now,' he barked, pointing his gun at me and the others. 'Even if you're not German, it's obvious you're a German sympathizer. Move.'

"As we walked through the door, one soldier threw a callous remark at us. 'We're going to take care of the lot of you while we still have time.'

"I tried to protest in Czech but they pushed me forward with brutal force and I almost stumbled. As my eyes accustomed themselves to the glare of daylight, I saw that we faced a concrete wall. Before I had time to digest this, they had us all turn and line up against the wall. We were facing a firing squad. All the soldiers were aiming their rifles at us. I stood frozen against the wall and my blood turned cold. I knew I was only seconds from certain death.

CHAPTER FIFTEEN

"Suddenly the courtyard door burst open and a Russian officer marched through it, followed by two soldiers with automatic rifles and three Czech civilians. I recognized one of them just as he recognized me. He spoke rapidly to the Russian officer, who called me over and I managed to clear myself on the recommendation of the Czech who knew me. I felt weak with relief. I walked swiftly through the door and started climbing the stairs when the sudden, sharp report of machine gun fire penetrated my ears. I winced and squeezed my eyes shut at the sound. All I could see were the tense, frightened faces of those Germans." His hands trembled slightly. "That was another nightmare moment I have never been able to forget."

Dee sat straighter in her chair, gazing at him as he stood so erect, a stance she was becoming increasingly familiar with, his hands clasping and unclasping, his chin jutting slightly forward. She said, "You have been able to put it all behind you and maintain a tremendous amount of dignity and confidence. Can you explain something of your feelings since then, as the years went by, about the three incidents you just described? Did they ever fade?"

He sat down and pondered her question. At last he spoke. "After each of my close calls, things happened so fast I couldn't think much about any of them. I did not want to slow my life down, because then I'd have to feel that reaction of horror, and it might keep on washing over me like a hundred huge waves, finally drowning me." His eyes penetrated hers beseechingly. "The last thing I wanted to feel was the overwhelming senselessness of life. My battle, my personal battle throughout the war, was to make it through alive. It was that simple. I fought so hard to push down how close I had come to death countless times—the ragged, filthy roar of guns, bombs, airplanes—the sheer helplessness of not knowing what to do, when the slightest action or decision might have been fatal.

"But I couldn't bury it completely. At night especially, right before I fell asleep it came back, over and over, like a disaster scene one replays on a video movie in the peace and safety of one's own home. But how different it is to watch it in a movie when you know it's not real, and to live through it, when you don't know what will happen next."

She continued to gaze at him. "The will to live is a powerful instinct," she breathed.

"As I said, if I had thought more deeply about it, I'd begin to doubt that life had any meaning. I knew so many people in that atmosphere who asked 'Where is God?' But I chose to believe. I suppose you'd say that the meaning, the guidance, comes to this moment. I still live and breathe, and because of me, Erik lives and breathes, and you want us to meet and ..." he shrugged helplessly.

She shook her head. "But I don't understand, then, if you really feel that way, why has it been a difficult decision for you?"

He shrugged again. "Too many years have passed. I had set my course, turned my back on the past, sure in my heart that was my only choice. Then once the Wall came down, I looked down that long, broken road back and felt there was no way to the past anymore. He had contacted me, that is true, but I felt it was easier to ignore him, pretend he didn't exist. But then your comments about your own daughter... I realized I wanted to do what I could to help Erik feel whole—for Anita's sake. I did not want him to feel my rejection any more, no matter what the past was like."

She nodded, smiled warmly. "I think you're making the right decision, Mikhail. And if you take it one step at a time, perhaps it won't seem quite so daunting." She watched his face, and thought she detected uncertainty. Indeed, she realized that he had revealed more uncertain feelings than she ever thought she'd hear from him, and that he wasn't accustomed to talking about his feelings at all. "Have you thought about when you might like to contact him?"

His eyes met hers. "As you said, one step at a time. I think we should finish the book first. I think we can do it in a month or two. Then I'd like you to go to Berlin with me."

Her breath caught with the surprise she felt. "Me? Oh, Mikhail, I don't know. This is such a personal journey for you. I don't think I'd even feel right being involved in my own daughter's search for her birth mother. Except to lend my support, of course."

"This is different. This is a case where I'd need an objective eye, an interpreter of the emotional landscape, if you will." He shrugged and turned away. "Give it some thought. We will have time to talk more about it as we proceed with the book."

She smiled. "Fair enough. Now let me gather today's material and transcribe it for you. The next time we meet we can go over it more carefully."

The next day Mikhail called her at home. "I've been going over my notes and realize I have much more to say about the years after the war," he began. "Some of it is quite technical, and will probably go slowly. So I hope that you'll be able to work an extra day every week. Is that possible?"

Dee didn't hesitate. "Of course. I'd been thinking of accepting another client, and now I'm glad I didn't. I really want to concentrate on this with you so we can finish it properly, and so let's step up the hours."

"Good. Tomorrow, then?"

"Yes, tomorrow's fine," Dee replied.

And so she immersed herself more deeply into Mikhail's story. In a way she was glad, because she didn't want to think about her own family situation—her ex-husband leaving for California soon, and her daughter anxious about a possible meeting with her birth mother.

The weeks flew by. Dee barely noticed when buds appeared as winter gave way to a glorious spring. By May Dennis had packed up his things and left Seattle for California, and a week or so after that, Jill called her one evening with a breakthrough.

"Mom, Nicole and I met today. It's been so long since she heard anything from Karen, but today she gave me a message she just received."

"What is it?"

Over the phone, Dee could hear Jill's soft sigh. "Karen evidently felt she needed to write me a letter before she decided anything. She's been working on it, and she plans to mail it in the next day or so. I don't have a clue what she might say, do you?"

Dee thought a moment. "Not really, honey. Except maybe some background information, reasons for her decision to give you up, and maybe even the decision to see you or not?"

"I don't know. I just don't know, Mom. Why is it taking her so long to make up her mind? It feels kind of like the jury being out. What is it they say? The longer it takes the more likely the verdict is not guilty?"

"That's right, and that can only be good. Karen really just needs time. But please, Jill, don't think of it as guilty or not guilty. That's so final. There are so many ways this could go. And through it all, you'll still be you."

"I know. You've told me that before, but I don't know what that means anymore. It's been four months! I feel like a piece of me has been missing for a long time anyway, and the waiting erodes away all the edges even more."

"I know it's hard to wait, but –"

"Listen, Mom. I have to go. I'll call you when I get the letter, okay?"

"Okay. I love you, Jill."

"Love you too."

She hung up the phone, wishing with all her being that there was something she could do to ease Jill's feelings. She knew this limbo, this prolonged period of obsessive thoughts and emotions her daughter was going through must be necessary until there was some kind of peaceful place on the other side. She knew that only a meeting with Karen would bring that peace, and until then… she mentally shrugged and resolved to put it aside. This was Jill's journey. All she could do was be there for her and support her through this. But it was proving to be so hard.

The next morning she went to another regular appointment with Mikhail. They had been working hard, and she knew his story was almost finished. She found herself wondering with increasing interest when he might be ready to contact Erik.

He was waiting for her outside, as usual. He had taken to walking her around the gardens of the retirement home each time she came, showing her the new blooms of azaleas, rhododendrons and other colorful flowers. It delighted her that he expressed such an interest and she told him so.

He smiled with irony. "You know," he said, "in some ways the past few years have been hard, gearing down to the slower pace of retirement. But in other ways, I'm grateful for the time I've been given to appreciate such things as these flowers, and to reflect on my life." He gave her a long, pensive gaze, then he looked down and pointed at the tight buds emerging from a shrub next to them. "I find it interesting to watch day by day as new life develops from these plants. The colors and textures and scents are a wonder, are they not?"

She nodded silently.

After a moment he went on thoughtfully, "I suppose my life feels a bit like that to me at this stage. It's been a process of self-discovery to write about my past, and I've learned some wonderful, enlightening things about life itself that I wouldn't have learned, if I had continued the constant drive for accomplishment and activity. I never had the chance to develop relationships with people other than those I worked with or had common interest with. Now I find it stimulating to explore the personalities and interests of all different kinds of people here at the retirement home. Many of them are older than I am, and I must say, wiser. Their children and grandchildren come to visit, and I've enjoyed getting to know them, too."

He walked on a bit, then looked up into the sky. "I've wondered lately if I have grandchildren, perhaps even great-grandchildren. It's possible, I suppose. I didn't ask when I sent the reply to the Red Cross two years ago. Now I think it's time I do." He nodded briskly and rubbed his palms together. "Last night I composed some ideas for a letter I thought we might write today."

"Today?"

He turned to her and grinned. "Yes, today. I think we've covered all I wanted to from my past, and to be honest, today I feel more like looking toward the future."

She followed him inside and sat at the word processor. "Will we send it through the Red Cross again?"

"Yes, I think that's most direct. We know he'll get it, and then I'll get as quick a response as possible too. Now that I've made up my mind, I feel impatient to get on with it. Shall we begin?"

My Dear Erik,

It has been over two years since I received the letter from the Red Cross. I must apologize for the long delay. Receiving that letter was a shock, and I felt I needed time to think through all the implications, the news that I have a son I never knew about, and never had the chance to raise and care for.

During this time I have been writing my life story. The woman who has helped me put the words together encouraged me to contact you again and after much reflection, I have decided to do so. I only hope this will open the lines of communication.

As I told the Red Cross to relay to you, I did indeed have a special relationship with your mother. We had planned to marry when the war was over. I realized when you contacted me that she somehow learned I had made it to America after the war. I am guessing she told you I had to leave Latvia and stay on the run throughout the war in order to avoid being mobilized for the German Army and sent to fight on the Russian front. I had many close calls, but I did make it through.

Then for a few years after the war I kept watching the signs that I could return to Latvia, but gradually it became clear that my country would remain under the oppression of the Soviet Union, so finally I made the decision to not come back at all. Erik, I hated Communism, and by then, you see, the Communists knew my political views. By then I had heard your mother had married and I felt I had no right to intrude in her life. But I must say, had I known you existed I would have come back even though it would have meant risking the real probability of being sent to Siberia. Even without knowledge of you, it was one of the hardest decisions I have ever made in my life.

But how do we know for sure about these things when we look back after so many long years? It was a turbulent time to live through, to say the least. The main thing I want to convey to you is that I cared deeply for your mother, and would have for you, as well. As it was, I felt I had no choice but to turn my back on my life in Latvia and start a new life somewhere else.

I am still amazed that you found me and trust that the Red Cross conveyed my message back to you that I needed time to think about your existence and what it would mean before there was any more communication between us. At first I did not think I could develop a relationship with a man who has lived his entire 50-plus years under Communism. I see by the facts I was given that the man who raised you is someone I *met when I first knew your mother. To be honest, I am uneasy about this. We had an unpleasant association. Beyond that, I wonder many things, and since you sought me out, I can only guess: When did you learn that I am your biological father? Did your mother tell you? How did she learn I settled in America? What is your relationship to the father who raised you? Are you married? Do you have children? I have much to learn about your life and views in general.*

Given these questions, I will leave it to you as to how we should proceed. I will only say further that I have thought long and hard about what I could lose in not attempting to meet you, and because Latvia and all of Germany are easily accessible now, I would be open to a chance to take the first step at some time in the near future and come to Berlin whenever it is convenient for you. After that I suppose we could take it one step at a time. Please advise me if this is possible from your point of view.

Yours sincerely,
Mikhail Sommers

"It's a good letter," Dee declared when they had finished. "And it should get the results you want, don't you think?"

He frowned. "He knows I hate Communism. I might not hear anything depending on how he feels about that. We can only wait and see."

Dee nodded and rose. "Do you want me to come tomorrow?"

"No, I think we will just take some time off now. I need to go over what we've written and make sure I've said all I have to say." He smiled. "I will call you in a few days."

CHAPTER SIXTEEN

A week later, Erik sat at the sidewalk café he frequented near the Brandenburg Gate. He had been here many times over the years since it was close to his shop and most of the other businesses he dealt with in the former Eastern sector that was now part of the reunified Berlin. Taxes were high on both sides of the city, but the situation was far better here than before the Wall fell. He remembered the countless times he had crossed from East to West at Checkpoint Charlie when the Wall was still in place and heavily guarded. Now most of it was torn down, and this part of the city showed signs of development where it once had been bleak and dismal, although the "no-man's land" on both sides of where the Wall once stood remained largely untouched.

It had been a good day; he had finalized another big contract. He breathed in the heady scents of spring; the memory of stale air, congested with stinking fumes that had been part of the old Eastern sector receded. Leaves were filling out on the trees, and the flowers were in bloom in large, ornate containers along the sidewalks. He sensed more fresh possibilities and new beginnings.

He caught sight of his son striding down the street toward him and his conscious well-being increased. Jon was a good-looking young man, he thought with pride, and a very nice young man. He was lean and sturdy as Erik had been as a young man, but his hair was more wheat-colored and straight, as Liesl's had been. He had a habit of swinging his head and impatiently brushing back a lock of it that kept flopping down over his forehead, and he was doing so now as he approached Erik's table.

"Have you been waiting long?" Jon asked with a smile as he took a seat across from Erik.

"Not long at all," Erik grinned at Jon. "It's been pleasant here, watching the people and the signs of spring."

"You look pleased with yourself. Did you do well with the Velten team people?"

Erik nodded. "Just as we'd hoped. A five year contract. Uniforms and equipment all around. This new beach soccer team is doing well—better than we'd hoped." He rubbed his palms together. "They confirmed today that their support is building steadily since last year, so they can afford to buy the best now."

"So of course they came to us." Jon extended his hand and shook Erik's, the two men grinning at each other. "It feels good, doesn't it?"

"It feels good," Erik nodded again. "And how was your day?"

"Not bad. I followed up on the leads we'd developed, and there are a few that show real promise." He gave his father a speculative glance. "But that can't be why you asked me to meet you here tonight. We always go over the business developments at the end of the week, and it's only Tuesday."

"Do you have plans for tonight? I don't want to keep you."

"Nothing that won't wait. I'm meeting Inga for a drink later, but I said I'd call her."

"You've been seeing quite a bit of that young lady, Jon. Anything serious?"

Jon shook his head. "She's fun, but no, nothing serious." He paused and waited, giving his father a long, measuring look. Jon had always been comfortably patient when he sensed some news, and Erik laughed at this thought.

"I won't keep you waiting any longer," he said. "I have some amazing news to talk over." He reached into his pocket and pulled out an envelope. "This was in the mail today when I got home. I felt so good about it I couldn't stand still; that's why I called you and asked you to meet me here. I needed a brisk walk to think and work off some energy." He handed the envelope over to Jon.

Jon's eyes widened at the printing on the envelope, and he looked up to meet his father's gaze. "It's from the Red Cross."

Erik nodded. "A letter and a picture from Mikhail. At long last."

"What does he say?" he asked as he took the papers from the envelope. He looked at the picture and Erik was pleased to see his reaction was one of astonishment. "He looks so much like you, it's uncanny!"

"That was my reaction. There's no doubt that we're related, is there?" Erik gestured eagerly. "Read the letter and see what you think."

Jon scanned the page. Then he looked up, his eyes soft. "Almost exactly what you had surmised, or hoped, from what Grandmother told you. He didn't know about you, he would have come back if he had, and in spite of some apprehension, is proposing to come here to meet you! How do you feel about that?"

Erik looked away a moment, his animated eyes turning troubled as they followed people moving along the sidewalk in front of them. He weighed his words carefully. "Of course, I'm glad he finally answered. But it's been two years. Why could it have taken so long?"

"He said he needed time to–"

"Two years? He's not a young man. He could have died during that time for all we knew." Erik gave a quick shake of his head. "If this had happened earlier, I would have been overjoyed. And as it is, I *am* pleased to hear from him. But now I feel I need time, too. He raised some concerns that I'm not sure I've thought through myself."

"What? About Aleks?"

"Yes. Aleks is languishing in prison, as he should be. This has nothing to do with him. I've been expecting this to be a simple, pleasant reunion between two

The Berlin Connection

people who'll start fresh from the first meeting. But Mikhail is obviously troubled about that complication from their past. I think perhaps in reality, my presence will bring up some disturbing memories that he'd have to face before we could move forward. I guess that's why it's taken him two years to answer me."

Jon nodded, deep in thought. "But he *is* finally agreeable to the meeting. *That's* where you start to build your own relationship, not in his past memories."

"There's something else, Jon. You know I've been in negotiations with some people in Florida, in the USA."

Jon nodded. "A huge contract, and complicated. But I thought they'd stalled."

"They called just today. They want me to go over there to observe their teams, assess their needs. It could take a few weeks."

"Are you serious? What about the daily operations from this end?"

"I could leave you in charge. You know what needs to be done."

Jon leveled his gaze on his father. "It would be possible, I guess. And I know you don't want this contract to get away. But the timing couldn't be worse."

"Maybe not. Maybe if I wait awhile it'll give me a chance to think more about Mikhail's letter. I could contact him from there just as easily if I have some time, after I've thought things over. "

Dee slowly approached the door to Jill's apartment, her apprehension mounting. Jill had called her a few minutes before at home and told her the letter from Karen had arrived. She asked her to come to read it and talk it over. Dee had been relieved to have the time, and she drove the ten minutes, trying to ignore her anxiety and concern. Jill's voice had seemed bewildered, but resigned. That didn't sound too hopeful.

She knocked on the door and took a deep breath. Jill opened it almost immediately and then led the way through the entryway into the small kitchen.

"I was just pouring myself some tea. You want some?"

"Sure, tea sounds good."

"The letter and a picture are in the living room on the coffee table," Jill waved an arm. "Go on in and read it. See what you think."

Dee went through the door into the next room, scarcely registering the few small attractive pieces of furniture and wall hangings that always before had given her pride in Jill's decorating talent. She sank onto the sofa and picked up the picture of Karen. Her heart leaped. Here she was, then. The face that smiled up at her was pretty, with bright eyes and a natural, easy appeal. Her blonde hair was short and smoothly styled. She vaguely resembled Jill. She laid the picture down and picked up the letter written in small, neat handwriting that filled two pages.

"Dear Jill,

Ever since I heard from Nicole that you wanted a reunion, I've thought of little else. I am of course happy to know you're well and have a good life. I've wondered over the years, remembered each birthday, and thought of how you might look and sound growing up. I'm so thankful to your parents for providing a life that helped you grow and thrive, and from what Nicole tells me, they've encouraged you in your search process.

My story is typical, I guess, of young girls from that era. Your birthfather and I knew each other in high school, and when he found out about you, he was not supportive. My parents encouraged adoption. Since I was only eighteen and barely out of high school, I didn't know how I could make a good life for the two of us, so I did what I thought was best for you, and then I tried to move on. But I want you to know that in my whole life I have never done anything harder than signing the adoption papers. I felt I had no choice.

I went to college and met Bill, my husband, there. We married when I was a sophomore. I never went back to finish my degree, as we had a baby a year after our wedding. That baby died. I went to work for a few years, and then when I felt stronger, we had two more babies. They are Gwen, 15, and Joe, 13. Both are healthy and active. They keep me busy.

My husband knows about you, but my children don't. That's why I have to postpone a meeting, Jill. I feel they'll take this hard if I tell them without getting some counseling about the best way to approach the subject with them. I do want to meet you at some point and I will try to make it happen as soon as possible, but right now I can't say when that will be. The time in my life when I gave birth to you was extremely traumatic for me. In some ways I'd like nothing better than to forget, but the day I heard from Nicole about you, I felt such joy and relief that I know your existence now has nothing to do with what I went through back then. I truly feel a bond with you, and long for a day when we can meet. Please be patient. I will stay in touch with Nicole–she says she'll help me sort things out until the time comes when we can all go forward after the best possible preparation.

Till then, Karen"

While Dee was reading, Jill had come in and placed the tray of tea things on the coffee table, then sat in silence, waiting for Dee to finish. When she did, Dee looked up, her eyes wide, her thoughts scattered.

"What do you think?" Jill prompted.

"She looks ... and sounds from the letter ... like a very nice person," Dee offered carefully.

Jill rose and paced the small room. "But more waiting, Mom! I don't know about this."

"Surely you see her point of view. Her children are teenagers. They have their own issues. I'm sure you remember those days, the feeling that the world revolved around you."

"Selfish, you mean? Self-centered?"

"I was the same way as a teenager, too," Dee said softly.

"I suppose." Jill sighed, then sat down again and picked up a magazine, distractedly leafing through it. Dee smiled inwardly. A coping mechanism she remembered Jill developing some time during her teenage years. Jill threw the magazine back down and lifted her hands in a helpless gesture. "But it's the waiting that's killing *me*! Is that so wrong?"

"Of course not." Dee picked up the letter and scanned it again. "She says she felt joy and relief.

That's what you need to focus on. She really wants the meeting to happen. It's just not the right time for her yet."

Jill gazed across the room thoughtfully, then picked up her teacup and took a sip. "She lost a baby after she gave me up. Imagine how she felt about that." She looked at her mother. "What's your guess? Even more guilt, like she was being punished or something?"

Dee gazed back at Jill. "I'm sure that loss added to the loss she felt about you. That's probably why she waited before the other two children came along. Her husband must have been a big support to her during that time, don't you think?"

"Mmm. Wonder what happened to my birth father." She shook her head firmly. "I don't really care about him. I'm guessing he was your typical love 'em and leave 'em, from what she said." She looked at Dee. "And what about the grandparents? Do you think they insisted she go through with the adoption?"

"Could be. Times were so different then. Young women were just not keeping their babies like they do now. I think her parents anguished over the best thing to do. I know I would have. But today? Times are different," she repeated.

Jill sighed with exasperation. "It's been so hard to think about anything else these past few months. I don't know how I'm going to keep living this way."

"One day at a time," Dee answered, feeling the triteness of her words. "And try to remember, whatever happens, you're—"

Jill leaped to her feet. "Don't say it!" she cried. "If I hear you say that 'I'm still me' one more time,

I'll scream!" Her breath came in great gulps and she glared at Dee. Stung, Dee stared back at Jill, her eyes wide, her heart pounding. "I just hate it!" Jill ranted on. "Don't you understand? I don't *know* who I am! I'm nobody! If abortion had been legal back then, she'd have flushed me down the toilet! As it is, she abandoned me when I was born and she's abandoning me again! I don't fit into her life in any way, her teenage kids are more important than I'll ever be." She picked up the letter and poked at it with her finger. "Did you see this? The part about 'the subject'? I'm just 'the subject' to her, and she won't ever want to see me as anything else!" She threw the page down with disgust.

Stricken, Dee continued to stare at her daughter. Jill was breathing hard, glaring at her as if she were an enemy. The charged silence lengthened between them. *It wouldn't do to remind her that* I'm *her mother, I guess,* she decided through the haze of pain.

Jill's eyes lowered in defeat. "Maybe you should go now. As you can see, I'm not handling this well," she said quietly.

Dee rose to her feet. "All right," she managed in a shaky whisper. "I understand. This will take time to digest. Call me," she finished lamely as she moved past her daughter and out the door into the bright sunshine. She closed the door and stood with her back against it for a moment, feeling drained. She sucked in air, then held her hand to her mouth and squeezed her eyes shut, willing herself not to cry.

CHAPTER SEVENTEEN

Dee spent the next few days feeling restless and apprehensive. Since the day she'd left Jill's apartment, she hadn't heard a word from her daughter, and her thoughts were consumed with the heartbreaking scene Jill had made. She played the exchange over and over in her mind, anguishing about what she might have said or done differently to reassure her daughter. She longed to call her, but she held back, knowing instinctively that Jill needed time alone to sort out her feelings, and then she'd hear from her.

She had plenty to do to try and keep her mind occupied, since Mikhail had turned the manuscript over to her to prepare for submission. After she finished it, she called Mikhail to tell him she was sending it off to a publisher. He was delighted, and that made her feel better. But now there was nothing left to do but wait. She had intended to call another potential client and tell him she was available to start on his project, but she didn't feel quite ready for that. She thought of calling one of her friends or her sister, but she just didn't feel like doing anything for awhile.

The phone rang and she eagerly picked it up, hoping to hear Jill's voice. But it was her sister, Donna.

"What's new?" Donna asked. "Have you finished the work for Mikhail yet?"

Dee filled her sister in. "So I'm at loose ends at the moment, trying to decide what to do next," she finished.

"You have another client lined up, though, right?"

"Not yet. I guess I haven't felt like pursuing anything." She sighed.

"What's wrong, Dee? You sound really down."

She hesitated. "It's Jill." When she finished describing the letter from Karen and her daughter's reaction to her own comments, her voice caught.

"Oh, Dee. I'm so sorry. Isn't that just like a kid to take it out on good old Mom? Good old Mom is safe to dump on."

Dee didn't have the energy to reply.

"What now?" Donna asked gently.

"I don't know. Wait to hear from her, I guess. Oh, Donna, I feel like I've lost her."

"No, no. You haven't lost her. This is just a bump in the road. But you need to stay busy. You can't sit around the house moping. Let's meet at the Mall.

I have to buy a new outfit for a business dinner we're going to this weekend."

"I don't think so, Donna. I'm not very good company. But I guess I'll call that new client, set up an appointment. Got to keep the money coming in."

When they hung up, she sat staring at the telephone, then jumped as it rang again. This time it was Mikhail.

"I'm going to Berlin," he announced without preamble. "I decided not to wait for a letter from Erik, and now that we've sent off the manuscript, I want to make the flight reservation. But I did not want to do anything until I extend the invitation again to you. I really cannot do this alone. I need you with me."

"Berlin? But Mikhail, wouldn't it be better to wait to hear from Erik?"

"Why wait? He could hardly be surprised, since he got my letter. The Red Cross confirmed that they delivered it successfully. I just got off the telephone with them. They gave me his number and address in Berlin, and I tried to call him but there was no answer. And now that I decided to meet him, I don't want to wait a moment longer." He paused. "So will you come with me? It would be a working trip for you, of course. I would pay all your expenses."

Berlin. The timing probably couldn't be better, she decided. She suddenly felt excited, energized. "All right, Mikhail. I'll come."

"Wonderful. I was hoping you'd say that. When would you be available?"

"The sooner the better," she laughed. "It's a good time for me to get away."

"Then I'll call you again as soon as I make the reservations."

"All right. And thank you, Mikhail."

"No, it is I who must thank you. Whatever happens in Berlin, this reassures me that I won't have to deal with it alone."

"I just hope he's there to meet us," she said. She hung up the phone, smiling. *It's good to know I'm reassuring somebody,* she thought. She got up to look for her passport, mentally calculating whether it was current or not. She'd had to renew it for the trip she and Dennis and Jill had taken to Mexico when Jill was sixteen, so it should be fine.

A week later she found herself in a Boeing 747, in the spacious First Class cabin on the upper deck. Mikhail's seat faced hers.

"I've never flown First Class before, Mikhail," she grinned as the powerful plane lifted from the ground. "This is a real treat for me."

He smiled. "I'm glad," he said with hearty warmth. "There is much more room to stretch your legs, and sleeping is more comfortable during the long flight overseas."

She sighed. "I still can't believe we're really on our way."

They talked a little about the rising anticipation Dee felt to see Berlin again after 25 years. Their gourmet dinners were served on real china with excellent wine in real crystal glasses, then Mikhail dozed and she watched a movie for awhile. The plane moved smoothly through the air, the vibration calming and pleasant, the First Class amenities a delight. She wanted to remember and enjoy every minute of this new experience.

But her thoughts kept wandering back to the conversation she'd had with Jill on the telephone right before she'd left. It hadn't been very satisfying.

"I'd hoped to hear from you by now," she had ventured cautiously.

"I know." Jill's voice had been so listless. "I'm sorry, Mom. I just didn't have anything much to say."

"I understand." Dee paused. "I'm calling you because I have news of my own." She waited a moment, hoping for some audible response, then when it didn't come she went on, attempting some brightness. "Mikhail invited me to travel to Berlin with him. He's paying my way—he says it's part of the research for his book. We're leaving tomorrow."

"Tomorrow? How long will you be gone?" No change from the indifferent tone.

"Just a week. Jill—if you—"

Jill broke in, as if she knew what Dee was trying to say. "Okay, have a good trip."

"Okay. I'll call you when I get back."

A trip to Berlin. Something she didn't do every day, she thought, disappointed that her daughter hadn't really seemed to care. Well, Jill was immersed in her own problems, her own life. She'd made it clear she didn't want Dee to hover. So here she was, flying to Berlin. There was nothing she could do for her daughter now, and it seemed they needed more time apart.

She tried to focus again on the excitement she wanted to feel, but then her thoughts drifted to Erik. She wondered if they'd even be successful in meeting with him. And if they did, would Erik be cold, harsh? Since he'd had to wait two years for a reply from Mikhail, he might feel the kind of resentment Jill had shown when Karen had put her off. Any number of things could happen to turn this into a frustrating experience.

Mikhail had dealt directly with the Red Cross. He had said he had an address and telephone number for Erik, but nothing more. She wondered if Mikhail did this sort of impulsive thing often. Given his years of discipline in business and physical training, she found it hard to imagine. But maybe he felt he had nothing to lose at this stage of his life. Even so, she found it strange that after putting off a reply all that time, when he finally did send a letter, Mikhail hadn't waited long enough to wonder if the timing was right for Erik to meet with him. She knew Mikhail hadn't learned anything about Erik's life in Berlin from the Red Cross, so they were truly flying blind. Talk about an adventure, she mused. In spite of her concerns, she felt rising anticipation about witnessing this kind of reunion between father and son.

When Mikhail awoke, he seemed restless and uncomfortable. Aware of his fidgeting, she tried to ignore it; didn't want to embarrass him by drawing attention to it. He finally unlatched his seatbelt and awkwardly rose from his seat, lurching forward, almost stumbling. Alarmed, Dee jumped up and moved to steady him. "Can I help you, Mikhail? Are you all right?"

The Berlin Connection

"I have to walk. I'm feeling a bit stiff. It is nothing, really–just these old bones protesting. I must go to the rest room." He shrugged off her steadying arm and started up the aisle with jerky motions. She followed him with her eyes, unsure if she should leave him to negotiate the walk on his own. Slowly, she sat down as she assured herself he was almost there.

As she watched him open the door and disappear inside the rest room, she was assaulted with doubts about taking this trip with him. She knew he had some health problems related to aging. Since her father had died suddenly and her mother was still in good health, she had no close, personal experience with elderly people who needed medical or caregiving attention. Apprehension gripped her. This journey that had seemed an exciting adventure now appeared fraught with daunting hurdles. What would she do if he had some kind of health crisis? The flight crew could help, but what about when they got to Berlin?

She remembered the day he had stayed in his room after viewing the video of Berlin. She had been sure at the time that there was something wrong with him, then found him in his room, deeply distressed. Now she realized Mikhail was still dealing with the same emotional response to these developing circumstances, Erik's existence. It seemed, Dee reflected, that an elderly person had difficulty navigating this kind of emotional territory, and anxiety translated itself into physical reactions that might be much more complicated than in a younger person. A chill swept over her, and then she chided herself. Her sister would accuse her of borrowing trouble in her usual melodramatic way, she thought. If anything did happen, that was all the more reason why he needed someone to accompany him. Until then, she'd just assume that they'd experience nothing but good.

She watched the rest room door. It remained closed for a very long time. She was about to summon a flight attendant to go check on him when the door opened wide and he reeled unsteadily out into the aisle. Alarmed, she rose and walked swiftly toward him, holding out her arm as she reached him, placing it behind his back. He peered at her, his face white and drawn.

"Mikhail, let's get you to your seat. Are you all right?"

He nodded and they moved slowly toward their places. He lowered himself awkwardly and she buckled his seatbelt, then turned and sank into her own seat. In silence, she watched his labored breathing. His eyes were closed.

Finally he spoke. "Before I awoke from my nap I had a bad dream. Now I feel uneasy. I want everything to go well. I want to find him without any trouble. I want the meeting between Erik and myself to be a pleasant one. But I have my doubts."

"Doubts?"

He shrugged and opened his eyes to look at her. "This man is supposed to be my flesh and blood. But he was raised under Communism. I cannot expect that he'll accept me, accept my reasons for abandoning him and his mother. Could that be why I have heard nothing from him yet?"

She reached out and took his hand in hers. It felt cold, clammy to the touch. "It's too soon, Mikhail. You didn't give it enough time before you decided to go to Berlin anyway." She squeezed his hand. "But it's good you're talking about this. It's a big step you're taking. A leap into the unknown. It's only natural that you'd have doubts."

"I hope you understand why I felt it was necessary for you to accompany me." His eyes searched hers, beseeching.

"Of course I do. Whatever happens–" She was about to say, "you'll still be you," and she stopped herself, appalled. This was not the same as Jill's fears, and even if it were, that was not the right thing to say in any case. "I'll be here, to listen, to support you. You know I'm glad to be here with you, and we'll see it through together."

His smile was hopeful, trusting, unguardedly childlike. She squeezed his hand again, with what she hoped was reassurance.

"I've never experienced fatherhood," he went on. "I don't know anything about raising a son. I'm sure he had some resentment that I wasn't there for him when he needed me."

"But that's good, isn't it? I mean, he'll finally come to terms with all that he couldn't explain when he was growing up. Maybe he sensed it, and couldn't explain it. Now the two of you can explore that together." She breathed deeply. "I know you're doing the right thing, Mikhail. You're in a position now to make something right that you had no control over at the time. Communism was the evil here, not you. If you'd been able to go back and be a family with Anita and Erik, you would have. Better late than never, don't you think?"

He shook his head. "I just don't know. We are strangers, after all. But it's too late to turn back now, is it not?" He gave her a weak smile.

"Don't worry. We'll see this through. It'll be fine. You'll meet him, and you'll see for yourself what kind of man he is. As you said, he's your flesh and blood. That counts for a lot, I'd say."

They lapsed into silence again. It occurred to her that this man who had told his story to her, detailing the strength, the determination, the instinct to survive in a hundred different ways, was expressing his fear and uncertainty to her in a way that he had never done before. And she knew instinctively that it was her job to try to buoy him with strength and determination of a different kind during this trip. If she didn't, he might not survive this ultimate challenge.

Neither of them slept after that. They eventually spoke a great deal of cheerful, satisfying things each had experienced in the past, both hoping to instill something positive into the next few days that somehow now loomed as almost ominous. The legacy of Communism, she mused uneasily.

A few hours later they descended toward Berlin through clear blue skies. She looked out the window and saw they were flying low over dark forests of trees that looked like oak; flat, lush terrain, then charming red tile rooftops.

"Can you see?" she asked Mikhail.

He nodded. His seat was farther from the window and he craned his neck and leaned forward. "I've never seen it from above," he said. "The last time I was in Berlin it was nothing but rubble. It'll be good to have new, better memories of this city."

Soon the plane landed with a slight bump. It was almost 5:00 in the afternoon Berlin time; in Seattle it would be early morning. She had been up all night, she mused. They had agreed earlier that jet lag was something they'd have to get through before they could do anything else, so a good night's sleep was the first order of business for them both. She turned to Mikhail and gave him what she hoped looked like a cheerful smile, but she feared it probably looked as groggy as she felt.

"We're here," she declared with anticipation.

"I'm glad the waiting is over," he breathed. "Now we will see."

CHAPTER EIGHTEEN

After going through Customs and claiming their baggage, they took a taxi into the city. Mikhail told Dee he had reserved a hotel on the Kurfurstendamm, the glamorous shopping avenue in West Berlin. The address he had been given for Erik was not far from there. Riding through the city, she felt a surge of excitement as she gazed at the tree-lined streets and quaint buildings. Colorful spring flowers bloomed everywhere in large pots along the sidewalks.

"This is just as I remember it," she remarked. "Everything looks new and clean, doesn't it?" she asked. "I guess it was all rebuilt after the war."

Mikhail nodded with some distraction. "I remember this section. I knew it well. After the bombing it was nothing but rubble," he said. "Soon we will approach the Kaiser Wilhelm Church. That was bombed too, of course, but I read that it was left half destroyed, as a memorial."

"I remember touring it in 1969. It definitely makes a person stop and think about the horrors of war. The photos I saw inside the church showed vast landscapes of bombed-out areas in the neighborhoods around the church."

He turned and gazed at her, his eyes intent. "I remember. I was in the midst of it." He looked out the window again as the taxi kept pace with the stream of orderly traffic on the bustling street. "It was in this area. But as you say, the vast landscape of rubble defies normal identity, and most of the bombing episodes blurred together into one. I remember countless performances of my trapeze routine in a large arena near here, then heading back to my hotel afterward, then the alarm piercing the air. I remember racing to the nearest bunker to wait out the bombing. I remember sitting for a long time among the crowd of others, feeling more closed in and uncomfortable than anxious. Towards the end the bombings happened more often. The whining of falling bombs and rumbling explosions outside, whether near or far, became exhausting. We were all in a numb state of despair. I told you much of this, I'm sure. But being here brings it back to me." He turned his eyes outside as the cab continued down the street.

"When it was over and the alarm sounded the all clear, I remember coming out to see the city consumed by smoke and flames and rubble. Many times we heard the alarm again, so we had to turn around and hurry back to the bunker for more waiting. The rest are snatches of memory.

"One morning I left the bunker yet again and picked my way through the chunks of cement, bricks and boards, trying to find the arena or the hotel, something that looked familiar. Smoke and dust drifted everywhere and it was hard to catch a good breath. I remember coughing and coughing. I passed one woman with a scarf tied over her mouth and nose, and a scarf tied over her hair. I remember she had a broom and was trying to sweep the rubble off the sidewalk in front of her door. German sensibility in the midst of German chaos." He shrugged, shook his head and looked down at his hands on his lap.

"I think that woman gives a powerful message of hope that this should never happen again. And so does the Kaiser Wilhelm Church," Dee said with conviction.

"One can hope," he said. He raised his eyes to hers. "What else do you remember about Berlin?"

"Checkpoint Charlie, of course. The Wall through the city was a horror in its own way. We walked along Unter den Linden near the Brandenburg Gate and stopped at a little sidewalk café there…" she trailed off, remembering the young man who sat at a nearby table there so long ago. She felt suddenly melancholy, wondering what had become of him, sorry she'd never know. "The flowers were blooming all along the sidewalks there, too."

He nodded. "We'll try to visit that place, I think. But first we must get our bearings and a good rest overnight. In the morning we'll call Erik."

The taxi pulled up in front of the hotel, and soon they were settling into their respective rooms on the same floor.

The next morning as she entered the lovely dining area, wonderful aromas of sausage and ham greeted her. She marveled at the elegant, well-appointed room. High ceilings and tables with bright yellow linen tablecloths gave the room a sunny glow. Lavish bouquets of pale yellow irises and roses were everywhere. The room was filled with people, and she was glad Mikhail had thought to make a reservation at the desk when they'd checked in. Her eyes swept the room again. She spotted him and headed to the table where he sat near the window.

"You look rested and refreshed," she said. She could see his eyes were sparkling with anticipation.

"The breakfast buffet looks wonderful," he replied with a smile. "I just got here myself, so we'll go over together, if you'd like."

He escorted her to the buffet, where eggs, breads, sausages, ham, fruits and cheeses were all lavishly displayed. They brought their plates back to their table and sat down to eat. They talked a little while they enjoyed their food, then Mikhail pushed his plate forward and leaned back with a sigh. "We can walk from here to Erik's address easily," he said. "I remember this area well. Just off this street is a little chapel I used to visit occasionally during the war. No doubt it was bombed at some point, and of course I have no idea if it was rebuilt after the war. But I would like to see if it's standing now."

"Of course," Dee agreed. "Did you call Erik this morning?"

Mikhail gazed around the room before he turned his eyes to meet hers. He nodded shortly. "I was awake early, and called before I thought he'd leave for his work," he replied in an off-hand, brisk way. He paused. "There was no answer."

Dee felt a jolt of alarm. If they couldn't contact him, the whole journey might be a wild goose chase. She wondered why he didn't seem as concerned as she felt.

He stood abruptly. "We will find our answers, Dee," he said, and strode across the room as if driven. She rose and followed him, feeling confused about Mikhail's sudden action, but reminding herself once again that she was just along to lend support. Certainly she had to follow Mikhail's lead, since he had made it abundantly clear that throughout his life, he had made strong, forceful decisions in much more chaotic circumstances than these. Even though at his age he sometimes showed a kind of faltering, he still had deeply ingrained habits of strength and confidence in his decision-making process. It was not her place, she felt, to suggest a different method to accomplish his goal.

She followed him through the hotel lobby, out the main doorway and down the stairs onto the sidewalk. After a brief pause to orient himself, he turned to acknowledge to himself that she was with him, then set off at a remarkably fast pace. This was no leisurely stroll, Dee mused; she knew he expected her to stay with him. While they stopped at the corner and waited for the light, Dee gazed at all the people passing by at an equally brisk pace. She knew this was supposed to be a street for glamorous shopping and strolling, but she saw little of that around her. The morning breeze felt almost fresh, but Dee expected, from the humidity, that in the afternoon the weather would turn warm. Perhaps that was why people were hurrying to finish what chores they needed to accomplish before it became sultry and uncomfortable.

When the light turned green, they crossed the street and headed down a side street away from the Kurfurstendamm. They walked in silence and the traffic sounds faded on this quiet residential street. Dee sensed that Mikhail was absorbing his surroundings, measuring the past against the present, memory against reality. She wished he'd talk to her, but they were walking too fast for her to even ask questions as they went along. They turned a corner and Mikhail stopped abruptly. "There it is," he said, breathing hard.

She saw it too, then turned her head to watch his face as he gazed with rapt attention at the small red brick chapel at the other end of the street. It seemed to her somehow that finding this chapel had been his only purpose. He started walking again, slowly and deliberately. They went around the building and entered a small courtyard in the back. It was completely enclosed, and inviting in its lush greenery. Red brick walkways meandered among the carefully groomed lawns. Mature, leafy oak and maple trees lent a cool shady repose to the pleasant surroundings.

The Berlin Connection

Park benches were placed at intervals, and Mikhail moved toward one and sank down onto it. Dee sat next to him. The silence was restful, serene.

"What a beautiful place," Dee said softly. "It's like a natural cathedral."

"It is just as I remember it," Mikhail replied in a hushed tone. "Of course it must have been completely rebuilt some thirty or forty years ago." He smiled, remembering. "I used to come here to pray. My prayers were answered when I found a way to get to Prague before it was too late." He bowed his head and clasped his hands in his lap. She felt awed by the peaceful surroundings and by the knowledge that he had been determined to find this place again to pray for a successful outcome once more in his present circumstances.

Her attention was drawn across the courtyard to a young woman pushing a small child in a stroller. She was walking away from them, toward the exit at the other side, but before she reached the opening, she stopped and knelt beside the stroller to give a hug to the child. Dee was aware of Mikhail's head lifting and she looked at him and smiled to see his eyes riveted upon the scene of loving warmth between mother and child. Then as they both watched, the woman straightened to a standing position again, and raised her arms and head in a position of supplication, or worship, or both; Dee couldn't be sure. She and Mikhail turned to one another and exchanged a smile at the emotional scene.

"They're a sign, I think, mother and child, are they not?" Mikhail offered. "Connection between the generations cannot be denied, even when it comes late in life, as it is with me."

She nodded as she watched the young woman push the stroller out of the courtyard and move beyond their sight.

They rose and walked out of the courtyard. Mikhail continued down the street with Dee at his side. He walked rapidly, noting the names of streets at each corner.

He finally stopped. "This is the street," he said. "The house should be just down the block." They walked on until they reached a small, attractive beige bungalow with a red tile roof, shrubs flanking the house, and flowers planted along the walkway to the sidewalk. Mikhail took a deep breath and they moved up the walkway and climbed the short steps to the porch, then he rang the doorbell. No sound came from within. He rang again and they looked at each other. "We'll have to get the address of his place of work from the Red Cross," Mikhail said. "We can find a taxi."

"Let's try the neighbors," Dee suggested. "They might know the address."

They went to the house next door and rang the doorbell. A stout, middle-aged woman came to the door and gave them an inquiring smile. "May I help you?" she said in German.

After a brief conversation with Mikhail, the woman invited them into the front room while she went to an address book and got the information for them. She spoke a moment to Mikhail, and his smile faded. Dee could tell he was disappointed by what the woman said, and she found herself wishing she understood the language better. After a moment they left her with their thanks.

"What did she tell you?" Dee asked as they walked along the street and back toward the Kurfurstendamm.

"She said Erik told her that he'd be away on a business trip for some weeks," he said gravely, then he smiled and suddenly his face was transformed. "He is in Sports Equipment. The name is 'New Beginnings.' He and his son are in business together. She thinks his son is at the office. His name is Jon."

She returned his smile with relief and delight. "Well, we can meet him then," she offered. "What a wonderful surprise – you have a grandson!"

They found a cab on Kurfurstendamm and Mikhail gave the address. They rode past Kaiser Wilhelm Church and its surrounding modern buildings, then on down the wide street that bustled with activity. Everywhere Dee looked she saw little boxy cars called Trabis, a holdover from East Berlin production which she read had ceased two years before. She and Mikhail spoke little as they took in the sights of what she assumed were the beginnings of new development everywhere.

After a few moments they turned onto Unter den Linden Boulevard and continued on past the Brandenburg Gate where the Wall had once blocked access. Dee remembered reading the English version newspaper just that morning about the seventh anniversary of President Reagan's visit to Berlin in 1987, and she commented about it to Mikhail.

The Berlin Connection

"At that very spot," she pointed, "Ronald Reagan gave his speech: 'Mr. Gorbachev, tear down this wall!' How much has happened since then."

Mikhail nodded. "And President Kennedy gave a speech there not long after the Wall went up, right? Some thirty years ago he said, 'I am a Berliner.'"

The cab turned onto a side street and proceeded on until it stopped in front of an attractive storefront with windows displaying sports equipment of all kinds. Mikhail paid the driver and they got out of the cab and entered the building. A bell gave a little jingle as they opened the door onto a large showroom with sports equipment neatly arranged on shelves and tables. A sandy-haired young man approached them with a wide smile of greeting. Then his smile faded to a look of stunned surprise. His step faltered and he moved toward them more slowly until he stopped in front of them. He said nothing, his wide blue eyes riveted on Mikhail's face. Mikhail was equally silent, staring at the young man Dee could see had to be his grandson.

CHAPTER NINETEEN

The young man smiled again, almost shyly, and lifted his hand to brush his hair back from his forehead. "You are Mikhail," he said in German, then he repeated the phrase in English with quiet conviction.

"And you are Jon," Mikhail answered heartily, nodding, holding out his hand.

"This is such a surprise," Jon exclaimed, taking Mikhail's hand in both of his and shaking it. "The resemblance between you and my father is nothing short of amazing. I saw your picture recently, of course. But in person – the smile, the gestures, the voice." He broke off and then started again. "I never dreamed you would come here so soon." He shook his head. "But this is unfortunate. My father is away—ironically, in the USA, I'm sorry to say. How is it you've come here like this, without telling us of your plans?" His grin softened any suggestion of admonishment.

Mikhail's smile faded to a troubled frown. "Yes, your father's neighbor told us." In the silence that followed, Dee stepped forward. "I'm Dee Sanders, Mikhail's assistant," she offered and she and Jon shook hands. "May we find a place to sit?" she asked, gesturing toward Mikhail. "All the travel …"

"Of course," Jon answered quickly, then he moved to the front door and turned over the *OPEN* sign so that it read *CLOSED* to the outside. "We can talk. Come with me to the office."

They followed him through the display tables to a door in the back, then entered a small room with a desk and chair, some filing cabinets, and two chairs facing the desk. Jon walked around and sat down, gesturing. "Bitte, take a seat, both of you. This is so amazing, to have you here."

Mikhail sank into his chair and said, "I apologize for surprising you like this, Jon. It was my idea to come to Berlin. I tried to call your father from Seattle, but there was no answer. Dee can tell you, from that moment on, my impulsive behavior astonished her. But I felt driven; there's no other word for it. Once I decided to come here I could not be persuaded to wait until I could contact Erik directly and make the plans with him. Since I knew from the Red Cross that he had received my letter, I simply had to come, and hope for the best. It was only when we arrived here yesterday and couldn't get him on the telephone again, that I started to feel uncertain. But I'm more than pleased to meet you. Imagine! I didn't even know you existed before this morning."

"You say you spoke to my father's neighbor?" Jon asked.

Mikhail gave a quick nod of his head. "We went to the home address I had been given by the Red Cross. Of course no one was there. Dee suggested we try the neighbor, a kindly frau next door. She told us your father was away on business. She also gave us the address of your business here and told us that you, Erik's son, would most probably be here. She told us your name."

While Mikhail spoke, Dee tried not to be obvious but she couldn't help staring at Jon. It warmed her heart to see that he was leaning forward earnestly, his expressive face illuminated by a wistful smile of wonder. "Yes, Frau Buchman," he nodded. "She has seen me coming and going often. My father bought his home soon after the Wall came down. We'd been living in East Berlin before that. I was born here. I have stayed here for now, to be closer to the changes. It is exciting, you see. I stood on top of the Wall the night we declared our freedom, almost four years ago."

He paused, his eyes never leaving Mikhail's. "You would understand, I'm sure, what we were feeling. When the Wall came down, everything changed for us. Not for everyone, of course. It takes time to put free enterprise in place after almost fifty years of Communism. But my father's business gave him a foothold, one could say, on free enterprise. He had been successful under Communism, outfitting State teams. The GDR had been good to us, you see. But still, we longed for freedom …"

He trailed off, then smiled. "I am talking on and on. And I haven't even told you the most important thing. About my father's business trip." He sobered, leaned back in his chair. "I talked to him by telephone just last night—morning for him. He's been in the USA, in Florida, negotiating with beach soccer teams there. We feel we're at the beginning of a new area of success with this sport. Details still have to be worked out, but he says it's a critical business maneuver, to bring our equipment, the right equipment, farther afield. He told me last night that he intends to travel throughout the Florida beach areas, as long as he is there, and use one or two successes to build momentum." He sighed. "So you see it would be quite difficult for him to come home. He's been there a few weeks now, and it appears he'll stay for some time to come."

"I see," Mikhail said slowly. He glanced at Dee, who remained silent. "Of course I'm disappointed, but I see now I shouldn't have come without arranging a time with him." He stood abruptly. "I must not take any more of your time, Jon. I'm sorry to barge in on you like this. Forgive a foolish old man."

Alarmed, Dee saw the clenched jaw, the tears pooling in Mikhail's eyes before he turned away. She wondered if she should follow Mikhail's lead, but before she could decide, Jon leaped to his feet. "But he did say he would call every morning before he leaves for the day–surely you can stay until I talk to him," his voice rose into a plea. "And if he doesn't call tonight I'll call him. If it's too late in the evening for you I'll contact you in the morning. We have so much to say to each other. I could tell you much of what you want to know, and I have many questions ... and I know many of my father's questions, as well. If you would permit me to ask them."

"You are a polite young man, Jon," Mikhail took his seat again, clearly relieved. "Of course I'll wait until you talk to your father. And I would permit you to ask any question you'd like. I came all this distance prepared to do just that with Erik, I assure you." He turned to Dee. "And my assistant has many questions for you as well. She brought a tape recorder for that purpose, if that would be agreeable to you. But I don't want to interrupt your business day. Perhaps we could make arrangements to meet for dinner?"

Jon eyed the tape recorder with suspicion. In that moment Dee could see Jon's old instinctive impulses from before the Wall. Then he grinned. "I trust you, of course," he said with conviction. "As it happens, I've finished the necessary paperwork already this morning, and I have no appointments for the afternoon. We don't have many people come in off the street. Most of our business is done by appointments, you see." He shrugged, then glanced at his watch. "I know a nice little sidewalk café near here. Perhaps we could walk over there for a quiet lunch."

"A fine idea," Mikhail replied. "But first, would you show us around your business? I'd enjoy learning about your chosen field from your point of view. And how is it you chose beach soccer?"

"My father has fond memories of the sandy beaches not far from Riga."

"Ah." Mikhail nodded. "The Baltic Sea. I performed my acrobatic act there once at a resort." He chuckled at the memory. "I'm not sure if you know this, but I had a gymnastics school in America for many years. So you see we have similar backgrounds, do we not?"

Jon laughed. "So I have been told." He waved his arm, gesturing toward the showroom. "Although this, I'm sure, is not as exciting. My father explained to me about you some time ago. He told me you had been a trapeze flyer with the circus in Latvia before the war."

Mikhail closed his eyes briefly. When he opened them, he spoke in a voice so soft Dee could hardly hear him. "Yes, I was a flyer. It was during that time that I met your grandmother." He breathed in deeply and rose to his feet. "We have much to talk about, do we not?"

"We do indeed." Jon led them into the showroom, and for several minutes, he pointed out and described various aspects of the business that obviously gave him great pride.

Dee looked and listened with interest, not so much to what Jon was saying about his work, but to the exchange between the young man and the old one. She imagined the man in between, the one who connected them, and she felt a sense of disappointment and longing. She shook it off, reminding herself that she was here to support Mikhail, not to satisfy her own curiosity about his son. Of course, she thought, if Erik's absence was disappointing to her, it must be far more to Mikhail. But what a joy to find the young man Jon, who seemed extraordinarily pleasant and likeable to her, and who could in many ways cushion the disappointment, as well as pave the way to a successful meeting with Erik in the future. She remembered the episode in the chapel courtyard earlier, the way that Mikhail had seemed driven to go there, to pause and to pray. These things do have a way of working out the way they're supposed to, she reminded herself.

Jon locked up the shop and they walked down the street to Unter den Linden, talking comfortably. They turned the corner and walked a few blocks to a sidewalk café. They found a table and a waiter came and took their order. After he left Jon resumed his narrative.

"The Brandenburg Gate is just over there, as you see. Even though our business was in East Berlin, we had been authorized to do business in West Berlin for many years, My father had been crossing the border at Checkpoint Charlie without problems since before I was born. Nevertheless, we always felt the tension, before and after, wondering if we'd be held up and interrogated each time. After the Wall fell, we could have moved to the Western sector but found we could build the business here in the East quickly with much less complication than before. The area used to be much shabbier, like everything else here. It starts to improve now, but still, it will take much time. Construction is everywhere, as you've probably already seen."

"I was in Berlin in 1969," Dee ventured cautiously. "I saw signs of tension then. It seemed so strange and alien to be dropped down in a divided city like this, but I remember feeling the need to see it for myself. The Wall had been established long enough to solidify the impact of the differences between East and West, and I definitely felt it."

Jon nodded with interest. "You will find it much different now. My father could tell you. I was born in 1969, so I grew up knowing only suspicion, secret police, being careful not to draw attention to myself. Even today, now that we know we're free, we still find it hard to shift our thinking. Your tape recorder is a good example of that. We're still cautious about what we say and do, for fear of reprisal. But I was more than ready for the fresh wind of freedom to blow through. Perhaps it was easier for me to make the change because I hated the Young Pioneers, the Communist organization I had to belong to."

Dee glanced at Mikhail, who remained strangely quiet. She remembered his comments about this very subject when he had argued that he didn't want to meet or get to know Erik. Anyone who grows up under Communism thinks differently from us, he'd said.

"How is it you hated the Young Pioneers?" Dee asked. "I thought the Communist society operated on some sort of brainwashing. Or is that too simplistic?"

Jon smiled. "A little. But my father, simply put, hated Communism because he hated the man who raised him."

"Aleks." Mikhail seemed to rouse himself and uttered the name with quiet contempt.

Jon nodded. "My grandfather was a Communist Party man in the most destructive sense of the word, and my father had to be obedient, but inwardly he rebelled, mostly because of his mother, he tells me."

Mikhail lifted his chin, his eyes revealing a mixture of warmth and regret. "Anita influenced his thinking, then?"

"Yes, in subtle ways, as I understand it. Do you know the story? My grandmother was far advanced in her pregnancy when Aleks persuaded her to marry him. She never loved him." Jon shrugged. "She died before I was born, and I knew nothing of this while I was growing up, but later, when my father told me the details, it all made sense."

"And your own mother?" Dee asked. "Does she feel the same way that your father does?"

Jon dropped his eyes to the table and fingered his napkin. When he looked up again his eyes were filled with sorrow. "My mother died when I was five years old," he said. "My father has kept her memory alive all these years, with pictures and stories. She was a wonderful woman, and yes, she hated Communism too. She dreamed of a better life for the common people. But she died giving birth. The baby died too. GDR hospitals were not so good, you know, in those days or even in recent times."

The waiter came with their food and drinks, and they turned their attention to the meal. Dee felt dazed by all the new information, disoriented, far from reality. Fork suspended in her hand, she lifted her head and gazed around at the people sitting at nearby tables, and the crowds passing along the sidewalk. She couldn't imagine how Mikhail must be feeling, since he was so emotionally involved with the story. She remembered him comparing it to a long, broken road with a bridge to the past in one of their conversations, and she imagined that right now he saw that bridge as Jon.

"Jon," Mikhail said quietly, "I had asked your father about Aleks in my letter. Do you know anything about him?"

Jon shook his head, took a drink from his water glass. "Not much. I saw very little of him growing up," he answered. "My father saw to that. He thought of Aleks as uncaring as a father, corrupt and deceptive as a political leader—he had risen in the ranks of the party and he wielded his power in an ugly way. My father told me recently that he and my mother both hated the hypocrisy of those powerful men. They all preached sacrifice to the common people, while they lived in luxury. He also told me that my grandmother suffered as the wife of such a man. She never said much, but Erik felt her influence strongly. How else can I explain my father's rejection of Aleks and all that he stood for? But at the same time, he had to be careful not to raise suspicion.

"At any rate, shortly after my father married and left home, his mother developed cancer and died. Then Aleks and my father saw little of each other for some time. I'm told Aleks tried to influence my activities while I was growing up, but my father avoided him as much as possible and so gradually Aleks lost interest and I suppose he devoted his life to the Party. After the Wall fell, he was arrested and imprisoned. He will not be released any time soon."

The Berlin Connection

Mikhail closed his eyes. Dee and Jon looked at him. No one spoke. The silence stretched out. Then Mikhail opened his eyes and gazed directly at Jon. "How did your father find out about me?" he asked.

Jon sat up straighter in his chair, leaned forward. "My grandmother told him, right before she died. She told him how you had met, of your German heritage, your decision to leave Latvia, and finally how she heard you had made your way to America after the war. My father told me he would have liked to ask more questions, to discuss the subject at length, but she died before that could happen. He also said he felt confused and bitter for some time afterward. So he tried to forget about it."

"Until the Wall fell."

"Yes."

The three talked easily into the afternoon, until the weather turned hot and humid. As they rose to walk back to the shop, Jon said, "I'll leave a message for my father in Florida. When he calls me back, tonight I hope, I'll tell him of your visit to Berlin. Then he'll decide what to do."

"Perhaps he could fly to Seattle from Florida?" Mikhail suggested. "I'd go to Florida myself to meet with him, but I fear my stamina is fading quickly."

"Of course," Jon answered with sympathy. "Perhaps he could come to you. In the meantime I'd like you to be my guests here for as long as you like, until we know something for certain."

"Well then, Dee will give you the hotel phone number and we'll wait there for word from you.

Traveling tires me more than I thought it would. I'll go back now and rest. Shall we meet again tomorrow?"

"And may I bring a tape recorder?" Dee asked.

"I'll try to overcome my earlier influences," Jon answered with a smile.

CHAPTER TWENTY

Three days later they flew back to Seattle.
On the flight, Mikhail slept a great deal, so Dee was mostly alone with her thoughts. She tried to read, but found she couldn't focus on the page. She kept thinking of their talks with Jon. How open and candid Jon had been with them, even letting her record their conversations. In spite of what he had said about people in the former Communist countries still being generally guarded in their conversation, he had shared his thoughts and impressions, much of them on tape, as if he had known her and Mikhail all his life.
Jon had driven them around parts of the huge city in his little Trabi, and it had been wonderful to see Berlin through his eyes and learn from one who knew

it well. They drove through the forested Schlosspark, Tiergarten, once a wildlife preserve– "Where my parents often walked together," Jon told them. They passed the Olympic Stadium– "Where Hitler held his 1936 Nazi propaganda games." He gestured expansively. "I must say, in spite of the complex layers of history," he concluded with pride, "Berlin is genuinely a city for young people now. There is energy here in the freedom that thrives after all the years of repression. One sees everything, from artistic creativity to a great night life."

They parked the car and walked to the Brandenburg Gate to study the plaques memorializing those who died trying to escape from east to west while the Wall divided the city. A short walk away stood the imposing stone-gray, bullet-pocked Reichstag Parliament building, where governing bodies, including Hitler's Nazi party, had ruled. "The building is 100 years old. They have plans now to make this a center for the people," Jon told them.

"As it should be," Mikhail responded. And then he had claimed exhaustion. Dee surmised it was as much emotional as physical. Now flying home, she reflected that she too felt as if they had been in Berlin for weeks instead of days.

In fact, it was hard to realize it had only been a few days since she had talked to Jill in Seattle. Even though the visit to Berlin had taken much less time than she had anticipated, she was anxious to get back, to see if Jill had heard anything at all from her birth mother. She doubted there was any news, and besides, she still felt there hadn't been enough time to smooth over her daughter's anxious outburst the last time they had been together. It no longer hurt to think about it–she knew Jill had been lashing out at the situation, not her. Dee had just been a handy outlet. But she didn't want to complicate things by being too involved.

Mikhail stirred and Dee looked over to see him gazing at her with wide and troubled eyes. "He said he was bitter." His voice was a growl.

"What?"

He slumped in his seat, seeming to shrink into himself. His eyes never left her face. "I've been awake for some time, thinking. Jon said Erik was bitter when his mother told him about me. I'm sure that's why he didn't arrange to speak to me by phone when he talked to Jon. I'm afraid he'll never accept me."

"Oh, Mikhail. Your presence in Berlin was a huge surprise to him. Jon said so himself. So he has a lot to think over. It's bound to take him some time to come to terms with all of it. And Jon did say Erik plans to call you in Seattle before he leaves Florida."

He pulled himself up straighter, waved a hand dismissively. "Suppose we leave this subject for now. I need to think more about it, and then in a few days, when I've rested ..." He caught her eye. "There is something else I want you to think about, Dee. I have never known you to be anything but sincere and honest in all your words and actions. You came highly recommended to me through the retirement home where I live. When I get home I plan to call my attorney and change my will. I have a son and grandson I wish to acknowledge. I want everything in order, as quickly as possible. And, if you will agree, I'd like you to be my Executrix."

"You mean you want me to carry out the terms of the will, when …"

"When the time comes. Yes."

"Are you sure? You have no one who'd be more suitable?"

He shook his head. "Who could be more suitable than you?"

"Let me think about it, Mikhail." She smiled with a bewildered shake of her head. "We both have a lot to think about, don't we? This has been quite an eventful trip."

The plane landed in Seattle on schedule a few hours later, and after the cab dropped Mikhail at his retirement home, she continued on to her house. As soon as she got in the door she called Jill. Briefly, she told her about the trip, then asked if she had any news of her own.

"Nothing new, Mom. I'm still in limbo."

"Can we have lunch together tomorrow?"

"I'm sorry, Mom. I have plans. I'll call you in a few days."

"Okay, honey. Take care." She hung up the phone, feeling unsettled and hurt. She knew she needed time to get back to normal. Jet lag was taking its toll, and after a quick meal, she went to bed. But at three in the morning she was wide awake again, thinking of Mikhail and Jon, and wondering how Mikhail must feel about not meeting Erik.

Lying in his own bed, Mikhail had troubled dreams. He kept thinking of Anita, and of Dee, and in his dreams, their faces and bodies kept sliding into each other. How could they be so much alike? He had known Anita over a long period of time. He had known Dee … it was too confusing. When he met Erik he'd find out immediately if he too saw the resemblance. Of course Dee and Erik would indeed meet. He would see to it.

The next morning he called his attorney and asked him to draw up a new will specifying the changes. The attorney said he would and made an appointment to come to the retirement home and have Mikhail sign it the next day. Then Mikhail called Dee.

"You slept well last night?" he asked her.

"Not really. I guess it'll take another day or two before the jet lag passes. How about you?"

"I too was awake. I had much to think over." He paused. "Dee, I made an appointment for my attorney to come see me tomorrow. He'll have a new will for me to sign. You need to sign it too. Can you come at 2:00 in the afternoon?"

His determination again surprised her. "Are you sure this is what you want, Mikhail?"

"I could not be more sure of anything," he answered with conviction.

"All right then, I'll come."

The next day, after the attorney left with the newly signed documents, Mikhail and Dee walked the grounds of the retirement home. It was a sunny June day, and zinnias, petunias, geraniums and roses were in full profusion all around them.

"It's not so hot here as it was in Berlin. I'm grateful for that. The heat seemed so oppressive there," Mikhail remarked. "Of course it could have been partly the memories of the place. To me I suppose it will always be an oppressive place. The bombs, the sense of disaster everywhere…"

"But now you have new memories of Berlin, Mikhail," Dee reminded him. "Jon seemed such a nice young man."

"Yes," he answered, a wistful smile enlivening his drawn face. Dee looked closely at him. He still seemed pale to her, but she supposed he was still not over the effects of the trip. "He's all I could have hoped for," he went on. "I wonder how long it will be before I hear from Erik."

"It could be awhile."

"Yes." He stopped and clasped his hands behind his back, then looked up at the sky. He spoke slowly, his words measured. "I'd like you to be with me when I meet him for the first time, Dee. I want to see if he notices something about you."

"Me? What would he notice about me?" Dee was again aware of the way Mikhail deliberately prolonged any drama in a conversation. As always, she decided to let him guide their way through this one. His eyes met hers, and his gaze felt intense on her face. "He would see a resemblance."

"What do you mean?" She took a step closer.

He moved over to a nearby park bench and sat down. Dee sat beside him. He resumed his concentrated gaze upon her face. "If you had ever met Anita you would know."

"Anita?" Now he had her complete attention.

"His mother. Anita. You look very much like Anita."

Dee's eyes widened. "I look like Anita?"

He nodded. "That's why I felt so easy with you from the first – comfortable telling you my story. It's strange. But after all, I've been through so much that's strange in my life. I suppose it could be fate. Some forces of nature drive us to complete our destiny. Do you believe that?"

She turned her head and pondered the fragrant roses beside the walkway. When she looked up she still felt the force of his gaze and she breathed in deeply. "Wow. I don't know, Mikhail. I will say that I'm a praying woman, and when I saw you praying in the courtyard of that church, it moved me deeply. I felt I was involved in something larger than just us. I guess I'm trying to say that I believe God guides us if we ask Him to."

He nodded, satisfied. "Dee, you asked me some time ago why I wanted to write my story. The idea started around the time I heard from the Red Cross that Erik was trying to contact me. That brought back so many memories of Anita, so I suppose I had it in the back of my mind that I owed it to Erik. Then when you came to help me, I immediately saw the resemblance. And later when you encouraged me to contact Erik I felt I could not deny the 'guidance.' And look what has happened since then. All we have to do is wait for Erik to call." He nodded again, emphatically. "We'll see if this particular destiny is completed when he calls."

They sat side by side in comfortable silence, each thinking separate thoughts about destiny.

Events seemed to move so quickly after that, they took Dee's breath away. That very evening, Mikhail called her, his voice filled with excitement. "Did I not tell you, Dee? Erik just called me. Just now, from Florida. He's coming in two days to see me."

Dee felt her heart beating harder and she caught her breath. "That's wonderful, Mikhail. How did he sound? What did he say?"

Mikhail chuckled over the line. "I think you're almost as pleased as I am about this. And Erik sounded pleased, too. He apologized for not being prepared to talk to me when Jon told him we were in Berlin. He needed time, he said. But now he seems impatient to see me too. He laughed and told me he was jealous of his son that he was the first to meet me. But no. He's happy. He's happy."

"Of course he is."

"It was so good to hear his voice. He told me what flight he'll be on. His plane arrives at noon. And I told him I'll be at the airport to meet him. I didn't tell him about you. I simply said I had a surprise for him. As I told you before, I want you to be there with me when I meet him."

"I'm honored, Mikhail. I'd love to be there to witness such an amazing reunion."

"Naturally, I have two surprises. I'll tell him of my will, too."

"Well, there's no hurry for that."

"I'll call you tomorrow morning with the details. I must go and collect my thoughts. Thank you, Dee. This wouldn't have happened without you. I appreciate your friendship – and your part in my destiny. I feel as if my life is just beginning again."

"I owe *you*, Mikhail. As I say, I feel honored to be a part of your story."

Dee awoke the next morning thinking about the conversation she'd had with Mikhail the day before. She was eager to hear from him, but the phone didn't ring. Early in the afternoon she called him. But there was no answer. He didn't have an answering machine, so she hung up after a dozen rings, wondering where he could be. When she called him again later, he still didn't answer. She began to feel uneasy. She ignored the nagging apprehension, but it grew throughout the afternoon.

Finally, late in the day, her phone rang. She picked up the receiver.

"Dee? This is Eunice Hanson, the manager at the retirement home."

"Oh yes, Eunice. I've been trying to reach Mikhail all day. Do you know where he is?"

"Actually, Dee, I'm calling about Mikhail." Her voice held a grave tone.

Dee felt her heart lurch. Cold, heavy dread fell on her like wet snow. "What is it, Eunice?" Her words felt forced. "Is he ill?"

CHAPTER TWENTY-ONE

Dee gripped the receiver tightly, not daring to breathe.

Finally, Eunice spoke. "I'm afraid I have bad news, Dee. Mikhail died in his sleep last night."

"What?" Her pulse started racing. "Mikhail died?" Her mind protested. *Something is wrong here, he can't be dead. He told me just yesterday that he felt like his life was beginning again.* She said the only thing that made any sense to her. "There must be some mistake, Eunice. I just talked to him yesterday."

Eunice's voice was calm, sympathetic, but firm. "I'm afraid there's no mistake. We found him early this afternoon. He hadn't come out for breakfast or lunch so I phoned, then knocked on his door. When he didn't answer I investigated."

"Oh, dear God. How did it happen?"

"We think it was a massive heart attack. But his face was so peaceful, I'm sure he didn't suffer."

She heard Eunice's voice, but couldn't make sense of the words. She felt her thoughts skidding around, trying to find leverage. She was aware of the silence on the other end of the line. Eunice was waiting for her to respond. "A heart attack? Did he have heart problems?" She rubbed a hand against her eyes in an attempt to focus.

"Not that we know of. He seemed to be in good health. But he was 74. Perhaps he needed medication and didn't know it. Dee, I'm calling because as you know, yesterday I was one of the witnesses who signed his new will. I telephoned the attorney and he told me Mikhail named you his Executrix?"

"His new will. Yes." She felt the tears springing to her eyes, and sharp pinpricks in her nose and throat. She jumped to her feet, winding the telephone cord around her body as she attempted to pace. Exasperated, she moaned, "I can't talk about this on the phone. I'll come right over." She unwound the phone cord.

"I was just going to ask you to come. We'll be in his room. See you here in a few minutes then. Thank you, Dee."

She put the phone down, her eyes swimming with tears, her breath coming in quick, shallow gasps. *Mikhail dead?* She grabbed her car keys and raced out the door. The retirement home was just a few minutes away, but she wondered if she should even be driving. Everything blurred in front of her, and she turned on the windshield wipers, then realized her mistake. She was reeling from shock and disbelief. Total disbelief. The familiar landmarks moved past her more slowly than usual, the light at the corner turned red and she stopped and the wait seemed intolerably long, so urgent seemed her need to get there. She pulled into the parking lot, jumped out of the car and ran into the building. How often had she done this before feeling calm and confident, she wondered, looking forward to meeting and working with him? Her thoughts raced as she hurried down the hall toward his room. She passed one or two residents along the way, barely acknowledging the look of sympathy on their faces. They feel the loss too, she realized. He was their neighbor. She wondered fleetingly what kind of conversations he'd had with his neighbors. She didn't know.

She stopped in front of his door and took several deep breaths, wiping tears from her face. The door was slightly ajar. She pushed it open.

"Eunice? It's Dee."

"In here, Dee."

Dee walked through the door and into Mikhail's room, and immediately felt the emptiness, the loss of his powerful presence. He wasn't here anymore. Eunice, a large, stately woman with dark hair, nearing retirement age herself, was sitting across the room with a man Dee recognized as the caretaker of the retirement home grounds. They both rose from their chairs and came forward to meet her. The two women who scarcely knew each other clasped hands. Dee's throat caught in a short sob. "I just can't believe this has happened," she said in a voice that felt weak and watery.

"Yes," Eunice replied, her tone somber. "When someone dies so suddenly like this, it's such a shock to us all…" She trailed off, then turned to the man next to her. "Do you know Dan Monroe, our grounds caretaker? He was a friend of Mikhail's," Eunice offered.

Dee attempted a smile toward Dan and held out her hand. His face was strained, filled with sorrow. His silver hair looked disheveled, as though he had run his hands through it many times. He reached out and clasped her hand. She could feel the rough calluses from daily yard and garden work, and she vaguely remembered Mikhail telling her he and Dan had found much in common and become good friends. She looked around the room. The bed had already been stripped.

"I called you as soon as I could," Eunice said, guiding Dee over to a chair. "We had some standard procedures to go through first with the State. As I told you on the phone, I knew to notify you because of the will we signed yesterday. But I'm at a loss as to who else he'd want to be notified. He wrote absolutely no reference information."

"You've been helping him with his life story, I know," Dan prompted, sitting across from them on the bed. "He told me how happy he was with your work."

Dee nodded woodenly. "We finished the manuscript a couple weeks ago and I sent it off to a publisher."

Eunice cleared her throat. "Was there anyone he talked about with you—family, close friends…children who live out of town?"

Dee's eyes widened. Her hands flew to her mouth. "He has a son he never knew," she whispered. "His name is Erik Mendenberg. He was born during World War II, in Europe. Mikhail only learned about him recently." The story poured out of her, an anchor she could attach her thoughts to. "That's why we went to Berlin, to make contact with him. He wasn't there, but we did meet his grandson, Jon. Then, just yesterday, his son called him from Florida. He's been in the United States on business. He's flying to Seattle tomorrow." She looked at Eunice, then Dan, who were both listening intently, their eyes filled with sympathy. "His son is coming here to meet him tomorrow," she repeated helplessly. "Oh, how awful for Erik. What will this do to him?"

"Can you contact him in Florida?" Eunice asked.

Dee searched her mind for anything Mikhail had said about a phone number in Florida. "I don't know. But I know Mikhail had his grandson's business number in Berlin. If we find that, he'll get word to Erik." She stood up and found an address book on the table by the telephone, then she checked her watch. "It's almost midnight in Berlin. He won't hear my message until he gets to work in the morning."

"You can try, anyway. If he's there he'll know how to contact his father. Then they can decide what they want to do."

"I know he'll want to come," Dee said, her mind racing ahead. "But what tragic circumstances for Erik.

He was so looking forward to meeting his father for the first time. He doesn't even know he and Jon have been named in Mikhail's new will."

"Then perhaps they'll both want to come."

"Oh my God, how awful this is!" Fresh tears flooded Dee's eyes. "Mikhail was so excited about meeting Erik for the first time. I just talked to him about it yesterday after he got off the phone with Erik." She rummaged in her purse for a tissue.

Eunice stood up and put an arm around Dee's trembling shoulders. "Do you want me to look in the address book for a number in Berlin?" she asked gently. "What did you say the name was?"

"Mendenberg. Look for a phone number in Florida too." Dee handed the little book to Eunice. "I'm a wreck. I'm sorry."

"It's understandable, Dee. You've had a shock." She flipped through the pages. "There's no number for a Mendenberg in Florida. But here's a business number for Jon Mendenberg in Berlin. Do you want me to call it?"

Dee nodded mutely. Eunice dialed the number and handed the phone to Dee. After a few rings Dee heard Jon's voice giving a message in German. She waited for it to end, then said, "Jon, this is Dee Sanders, Mikhail's assistant. I'm calling from Seattle with news I'd rather not leave in a message." She stifled a sob, then plunged on. "I'd like to talk to you directly as soon as possible," she said, adding that she'd continue to look for his home telephone number and asking him to call as soon as he got her message. She gave him the number and hung up the phone.

"What time does Erik's flight arrive tomorrow?" Eunice asked.

She shook her head. "I'm not sure, I think he said noon. Is there a note anywhere by the phone?"

They searched some papers. "Here it is. You'll want to keep this nearby, Dee," Eunice said, and handed her the slip of paper.

Dee glanced at it, then slid it into her purse. "I'll need Jon's number, too. I'll try to get his home number when I get back to my house."

"Is there anyone else he might want to notify?"

"I know so little about Mikhail's contacts and friends myself—but as far as I do know from his life story, he never married, and all his relatives are still in Latvia, his native country. It's been behind the Iron Curtain until recently, so he hasn't been in contact with any of them for decades." She shrugged. "Let me go home and think it over, and I'll look through his address book carefully. I have a copy of his manuscript at home too—I'll see if that jogs my memory."

"I'll try to think if he told me about anyone else who'd want to be contacted too," Dan offered.

"Maybe some of the other residents will have suggestions," Eunice added.

The next few hours went by in a blur. Dee called her daughter and her sister from home and told them the news of Mikhail's death, then tried to get Jon's home number from information in Berlin. There was nothing listed. She calculated when he'd be arriving back to the store, and decided she'd have to wait until then, which would be around 11 p.m. or midnight here in Seattle. She sighed. This is so unreal, she thought. Only yesterday ... she kept replaying in her mind conversations from the past few days with Mikhail. It was so hard to believe he was gone. A heart attack probably did cause his death, but even so ... she remembered his sickly paleness and shakiness in the plane on the way to Berlin. All the emotional turmoil he must have been feeling, she mused. That must have caused his death. He just wasn't able to handle it and his heart went into overload.

She looked through Mikhail's address book, but the names and places made no sense to her. Maybe she could decide which names to call tomorrow with Eunice, she thought. She dropped the book back into her purse and pulled out the slip of paper with the flight information on it. No information at all about the hotel where he was staying in Florida or where exactly the flight originated. She paced the room, wondering where Erik was at this moment. Perhaps Jon would have more information. At 11:00 pm she tried Jon's number again. The message machine again picked up so she dropped the phone back into its cradle and checked her watch again. It was now 2:00 a.m. in Florida. Perhaps it would be better to wait to tell Erik in person. She remembered Mikhail telling her that Erik would recognize her. She didn't know about that, but she knew she would recognize him. She shivered, dreading the moment she'd have to deliver the grim news to him, face to face. No, it would surely be better if he got the news before he left for Seattle. That would give him time to digest everything.

She jumped when the phone rang. "Hello?"

"Dee, this is Jon Mendenberg." His voice sounded strained, urgent. "I just got your message. You sounded distraught. Is it Mikhail?"

"Oh, Jon, I'm so sorry. Yes, it's Mikhail. He died in his sleep last night. They think it was a heart attack." She could hear Jon's sharp intake of breath.

"A heart attack? Mikhail died? But this is dreadful. Are they sure it was a heart attack?"

"It seems the likeliest cause."

"Had he been ill? He looked a little shaky when he was here, but I thought it was because of all the excitement. I never dreamed …"

"Thank goodness he got to meet you, Jon. It meant so much to him. But you're right, the excitement may have been more than his heart could take. I don't know." She lifted her head, her eyes sweeping around the room as she tried to gather her thoughts. "But Jon, your father is arriving tomorrow at noon, and I was hoping you'd be able to get the news to him before he gets here. It would be such a shock for him to hear it from me, when he gets off the plane. I mean, he thinks he's meeting Mikhail at last, and…"

"Yes, he was so happy, so filled with anticipation. I spoke to him yesterday. But he is not in Miami anymore. He left there last night and flew to Atlanta. He plans to take a plane this morning from Atlanta to Seattle. I don't know how to reach him."

"You don't know where he's staying in Atlanta?"

"No." He lapsed into silence.

"There's nothing we can do then?"

"Well, I suppose we could call the airport hotels, but…"

"There must be a hundred of them. Atlanta is a central destination in the United States for connecting flights." She hesitated. "Jon, there's something else I need to tell you. You'll want to come to Seattle, too. Mikhail named your father and you in a new will. He just signed it yesterday." She felt tears brimming her eyes again. "It's just so hard to believe. He signed the will yesterday and he's gone today."

There was a silence at the other end of the line. Dee could hear the faint static as she waited for his reply. When he did, his voice was a whisper. "I don't know what to say. I'm stunned, Dee. He named us in the will?"

"Yes. He was very positive about that decision. He had no other relatives, and he was so impressed, and proud–both of you and what you told him about your father. He named me as Executrix. It falls to me to carry out the terms of the will. And I am honored to do so."

"I'll come," he said simply. "Will there be a funeral?"

"I don't know yet. There's so much to think about, I've been in such turmoil since I heard the news. I went to his retirement home and spoke to the manager and the caretaker. But we haven't made any plans yet. I'll just have to take it one step at a time. The first step is meeting your father at the airport at noon tomorrow, and telling him the awful news. He and I will have so much to talk over. I just hope I'm up to the task."

"It's a hard thing, I know. I wish I could reach him before he arrives, but I'm afraid it will be your task, as you say, to give him the news. I'll wait for his call, and

I'll have tentative flight information about when I'm to be there."

"He'll be arriving at noon, that's about twelve hours from now, seven in the evening your time. He'll probably call you two or three hours after that."

"All right. I'll be waiting at home. And I'll be thinking of you both. Dee, I just … Mikhail was a remarkable man. I'm so thankful I was able to meet him before … before …"

"He felt the same, Jon."

After talking a bit longer with Jon, Dee hung up the telephone feeling charged with adrenaline and completely drained at the same time. She wondered if she could actually sleep tonight. There was so much to think about. She couldn't imagine how she would get through the meeting with Erik, the conversation. She had been so happy for Mikhail, so excited to meet Erik, and to see the reunion between the father and son. And now this. It just didn't seem real.

She got up and went into the kitchen, fixed herself a cup of tea. Sitting at the kitchen table, she pondered Mikhail's life. He had lived such a rich, fulfilling existence, had picked up the pieces after the war and accomplished so much by developing a successful gymnastics school in this country. If he had been able to go back to his native country all those years ago, he'd have picked up the pieces with Anita and raised a family. She wondered if Erik truly understood why he couldn't go back. Mikhail had been so sure he would have been deported to Siberia because he hated Communism. It was hard for her to imagine that, having been born and raised in a free country.

But surely Erik would understand. She could give him a copy of Mikhail's manuscript. He could read all the twists and turns of his father's life and decide for himself how it was. He could probably interpret some of the issues that Mikhail had tried to explain to her, but that she couldn't fathom. According to Jon, Erik had certainly walked a tightrope under Communism in East Berlin, and somehow had used his position as a springboard to a better life in spite of the obstacles. Perhaps he'd think Mikhail could have made it work, too.

She rinsed her cup at the sink and went in to get ready for bed. Before she turned out the light she glanced at her watch. After midnight. She wasn't sleepy at all. She kept seeing Mikhail's face, the delight and anticipation as he looked up after signing the new will. She had never observed such an expression on his face before that moment. He had really warmed to the idea of having a son and grandson, his heirs. It was as if he felt whole, felt he could help Erik feel whole, and contribute something positive to his future.

Lying in bed in the dark, she thought of Jill's search for her birth mother. She knew Jill longed for that kind of wholeness, too—to explore her heritage, to finally know the people she was linked to biologically. Jill wanted to hear her birth mother's story, know her personally, find out how much they had in common. That kind of bond couldn't be achieved with an adoptive mother. Dee wasn't part of the biological link. She examined her feelings about this. Did she feel left out, envious? Maybe a little. But she had raised Jill and shared a mother/daughter love, as well as countless special moments with her. She remembered Jill's first steps as a baby, her first day at kindergarten, her first best friend Maria, her childhood illnesses, her first boyfriend. No one could take those shared memories from her, or from Jill. But now Jill was an adult, and she had a right to uncover the other part of her story.

Suddenly Dee realized that she was the only one she knew of to tell the other part of Mikhail's story to Erik. She sat up in bed, her eyes wide, overwhelmed by the magnitude of the task ahead. She didn't feel equal to it. Fresh tears slid down her cheeks and she brought her hands to her face and sobbed. It felt to her as if Mikhail had abandoned Erik all over again, and he had abandoned her, too. She had been so attached to him and his story. The emotional involvement she'd felt had sustained her and strengthened her during the months they had worked together. She'd felt she was finally moving beyond the divorce, and building a life of her own. And now she felt as if everything was being wrenched away from her. She felt empty, inadequate, less than whole.

She lay back down and eventually drifted into a fitful sleep. Early in the morning she awoke with a heavy feeling of dread. Memories of the day before rushed in. Mikhail was truly gone, and she felt truly alone.

CHAPTER TWENTY-TWO

The plane slowly descended over the city of Seattle, and Erik leaned toward the window, marveling at the lush greenery and sparkling blue waters below, the passing downtown skyline. The sky was perfectly clear and blue. Snow-capped mountains shone in the distance. Erik's sense of wonder and anticipation increased. A slow smile spread across his face. How amazing, he thought, to be in this beautiful city, where my father lives–to realize that so many things are happening so quickly now.

Once events had finally started moving, it seemed he'd become swept up in something that felt like a whirlwind. He could never have predicted that Mikhail would fly to Berlin! Looking back, he realized that he had reacted in a childish way by not wanting to arrange to talk to Mikhail by phone from Florida while his father was in Berlin with Jon. At first he had felt resentment—'Let him wait a while—he made me wait two years while he got used to the idea of a son,' he'd thought. But after Jon's report of their time together and all the things they had discussed, Erik had changed his attitude.

When Erik called Mikhail in Seattle from Florida, his voice must have reflected his enthusiasm, and he heard relief and joy in Mikhail's response. He felt he would have recognized Mikhail's voice anywhere. The warmth, the pride in it was unmistakable. He sat back in his seat and his grin widened as he recalled the conversation.

"Why did you fly all the way to Berlin without even calling to let me know you were coming?" he'd asked Mikhail.

"Impulse," Mikhail had answered. Erik shook his head. How much of Mikhail would he recognize in himself? Impulsive behavior? Erik almost laughed out loud. There wasn't any of that in him. "It developed in me during my years of living in a free country," Mikhail went on. "And of course, I learned to make quick decisions when I was on the run in Nazi Germany."

"I have much to learn from you," Erik responded. "I have many questions for you when we meet."

"I will answer them gladly. And I have many questions for you."

Erik was glad he'd taken the flight from Miami to Atlanta last night so he could get a good night's sleep there. This morning he felt refreshed and energized,

The Berlin Connection

and his flight to Seattle left on schedule. He spent much of the past few hours in the air thinking of his mother's revelations right before she died. Even though she'd been very weak, the tenderness and affection in her words told him a great deal. He knew how proud she was of her son, how glad to finally tell him of his real heritage, and how proud she felt he should be of the man she had loved. She never blamed Mikhail for not being able to come back to her. She knew he would have if circumstances had not kept them apart. And Mikhail had made that clear as well, in his letter to Erik, in his voice when they had talked on the telephone. Because of Mikhail's decision to finally contact him, he felt all his old doubts and even bitter feelings ease away.

The plane touched down and Erik took a deep breath. He was only moments away from meeting the man he had waited so long to face.

Dee stood at the gate of the United Airlines flight from Atlanta, watching the plane taxi closer. It seemed to her she was standing in a dream, with a hazy mist drifting in front of her eyes. She had hardly slept the night before, her mind felt dazed and dull, her eyes, she knew, were puffy from weeping. And she stood here woodenly, waiting for the plane to bring a man face to face with her, a man she had never even met, so she could give him news that still felt so devastating to her.

Earlier this morning when Jill had called she'd tried to put her feelings into words.

"How are you doing, Mom?" Jill had asked, her voice warm and comforting over the phone. It felt so good to have Jill's concern, and she basked in it a moment as she gathered her thoughts.

"I guess I'm numb," she answered. "It just feels so unreal. That's the only way to describe it. And now I have to go to the airport and tell Mikhail's son that he lost his father before he even had a chance to meet him."

"I keep thinking about it, too, Mom. I mean, I keep wondering how I'd feel if that happened to me with Karen. Cheated? Robbed? I don't think those words even begin to describe it." Jill's voice softened to almost a whisper. "I think the hole in my life would feel even bigger."

Dee realized she wasn't all that numb after all; she felt irritation at Jill's self-absorbed analysis. She told herself to shrug it off. There was some basis for comparison, after all. "I know," she replied. "I feel I've lost an important part of my own life, too. Mikhail had become a dear friend." She sighed. "I don't know how to face Erik though. This is going to be so hard."

"Is there anyone else who could go? The manager at the retirement home?"

"No. I worked closely with Mikhail these past few months. He told me his life story in painstaking detail. He told me himself that there's no one else he talked to about it in such depth." She gave a little cry of exasperation. "If only Erik had been in Berlin when we went there to find him. If only he and Jon had been together then, and again when I got hold of Jon last night. They could have come to Seattle together.

I could have gotten myself together somehow if I'd had a day or two more to get used to this shock before they got here. As it is …"

"I guess both of us have to deal the hands we're played, Mom. Here I am, waiting and waiting, and for you, and for Erik, things are happening too fast."

"Yes. If they were happy developments, that would be one thing, but …" She swiped at another tear. "I better get dressed, Jill. I have to meet the plane soon. Say a prayer for me, okay? And for Erik?"

"I will."

And here she stood, in the terminal. Her attention returned sharply as the first group of passengers began to trickle through the doorway and walk toward her.

She kept her eyes fixed on that door.

The line of passengers slowly made its way up the aisle of the airplane. Erik was barely aware of the murmuring around him as he inched forward, carrying his bag. When he'd left Atlanta it had been stifling hot and humid. He wondered what the air would feel like here in Seattle. Somewhere he had read that temperatures were mild here year-round. He'd like that, he was sure. The fresh air, the mountains, the many bodies of water throughout the region that he had gazed down upon as the plane flew over the area, enchanted him. He could understand why Mikhail had chosen to settle here. He looked forward to asking him about that. He had so many things to ask, he wondered if it would be hard to begin. Jon had said he was easy to talk with face to face; had asked many questions himself. He hoped his own experience with Mikhail would be as effortless.

But he was nervous, now that the moment was at hand. He took another deep breath as he passed through the door and onto the ramp toward the terminal.

The other passengers moved quickly now, and he kept pace. He went through the door and paused to get his bearings. The brightly-lit terminal was crowded with people. His eyes passed over the crowds, vaguely aware of people greeting one another, or moving on down the concourse toward baggage claim. He stood there, searching for the one face he had memorized from all the times he had studied the picture Mikhail had sent him. Where could he be? He began to feel apprehension creep into his jumbled thoughts as he scanned each face.

He noticed, then, a woman approaching him, looking at him steadily, her manner purposeful, her face wreathed in anxiety. His heart slammed against his chest.

She approached him slowly, aware of his wide shoulders, his lean, sturdy frame, the way he stood with dignity, head held high. She realized with a shock that his resemblance to Mikhail was truly remarkable. Then she saw the bewildered recognition on his face, and suddenly a great calm descended over her. He did recognize her, just as Mikhail had said he would. She stopped in front of him and gave him a tentative smile.

"Erik?"

His eyes remained fixed on her face, intense blue eyes that were so like Mikhail's. They were less creased around the edges, and a few less lines were etched along his brow and on either side of his mouth. His dark hair curled at the neck just the way Mikhail's had. There was not a hint of gray in it, just like Mikhail's. She waited, watching him, while crowds of people moved and chattered around them. The silence between them stretched out as they gazed at each other. "I know you," he said slowly. "I recognize you. Where …?"

She collected herself then and her smile brightened. "My name is Dee Sanders," she began. "I came in Mikhail's place." She paused, uncertain how to go on. She drew in a deep breath, gave a short laugh. "I'm told I look a little like your mother?"

"Yes. Yes, you do. Mikhail saw it too, of course." He drew himself up, shook his head in confusion. "You say Mikhail sent you?" He began to scan the crowd again. "He could not come?"

"No." She followed his gaze, trying to buy time, aware of the pleasant cadence of his German accent, so unlike the harsh tones of some she'd heard in Berlin. "I'm his assistant …"

His smile widened as his eyes met hers again. "You are the woman who came with him to Berlin? The one my son Jon met?"

She nodded, lifted her hands in a helpless gesture. "But I'm afraid I–" she stopped, looked away.

His smile faded as he seemed to absorb what she had said. "You looked distraught when I first saw you walking toward me. Please." He took her by the arm and led her to a row of nearby lounge chairs, where he put his bag down and motioned her to sit, then lowered himself next to her. "Tell me. Is he ill? Is that why he sent you?"

She shook her head and looked away again. "I'm so sorry, Erik. I don't know how to tell you except to just come out and say it." She swallowed, lifted her eyes and looked straight at him, willing herself not to cry. "Mikhail died. Just two days ago."

She saw the confusion in his eyes. "But that cannot be. I talked to him two days ago. He seemed very well. His voice was strong, filled with … happiness."

She nodded, her sad eyes searching his face. "Yes, he was so happy to know you were coming to–" her voice broke. "—to meet him at last."

"Then how–"

"It happened that night while he slept. We think it was a heart attack." She turned her eyes away and gazed across the busy, crowded room. "They found him in the morning. They called me that afternoon, yesterday, from the retirement home where he lived. When I got there they had – he was already gone. I talked with the manager there for quite awhile, and we agreed you needed to be contacted right away. But I knew you were in Florida, and we found no phone number there for you."

She paused, glanced back at him, met his gaze, then hurried on. "So then I tried to call Jon in Berlin. By the time he called me back, he said it was already too late to contact you. That you had flown out of Miami to Atlanta, and he didn't know how to reach you there." She stopped as she saw his face dissolve into such pain and bewilderment that she wanted to turn away.

Instead, she leaned forward. "It's been a nightmare. And I'm so sorry you had to find out about it like this. I wish with all my heart that we'd been able to tell you before you came here."

He gave a confused shrug. "I would have come anyway," he said with quiet conviction.

"I'm glad. But you would have had time to – absorb the shock and disappointment. When I talked to Jon he said he'll come too, as soon as you contact him."

"Jon will come too?"

"Yes. The thing is, Mikhail had written out a new will and named you both his heirs. He was so impressed, and proud, when he talked with Jon about you in Berlin."

"Wait." He frowned and held up a hand. His voice rose sharply. "I cannot keep up with you. You are telling me that Mikhail is dead. I've thought of the moment when I'd be meeting him for years, and here I am in Seattle, expecting it to happen, and you are telling me that he is dead and that Jon is coming. This is …"

"I'm sorry." She lowered her eyes, swallowed hard. They sat side by side in silence, both of them staring straight ahead. A little boy was crying, his mother attempting to calm him. An elderly couple walked past, the last of the passengers to deplane and head toward baggage claim. At length Dee turned to him, and saw such a mixture of raw emotion passing over his face, she reached out a hand to touch his arm. "Erik, I know I'm doing this badly. I just don't know if there's a good way to say all this, that's all. Perhaps I can answer any questions you have."

The Berlin Connection

His shoulders sagged. "Of course. Let me – let me sit here a moment. I'll try to ask questions as they come to me." He attempted a brief smile, then looked away and took a deep breath. After a time he glanced back at her, his face a reflection of confusion and anguish. "You must be sad about your own feeling of loss," he said softly. "Tell me about your relationship to him."

She gazed at him, aware of his thoughtfulness, his ability to look beyond his own feelings of loss. "I'm— I was helping him to write his life story," she began. "We'd been working on it for about a year. We just finished it a few weeks ago and I sent the manuscript off to a publisher I know about who might be interested. I have a copy of it for you, if you'd like."

He gave her a sad smile. "I'd like very much to read it. After that I'll have many questions for you. I'm sure you know things he would have told me that he may not have put in the book." He regarded her with a certain wistfulness that almost broke her heart. It went unsaid that he was mourning the loss of all the answers he would have gotten from Mikhail personally. "In the meantime," he said slowly, "I'd like you to tell me about the last time you saw him. You say he was happy?"

"Yes, he was happy. We'd just signed the new will he'd had drawn up. He named you and Jon heirs, as I said, and I'm to be the Executrix." She shook her head. "The timing … I just can't get over it. He died that very night."

He nodded. "A cruel twist of fate."

"Tragic, but …" She sat up straighter, remembering.

CHAPTER TWENTY-THREE

"He talked about fate," Dee reflected. "About how he had come to the decision to contact you. He told me that after you tried to connect with him two years ago, he decided to write his life story. The memories of Anita were so strong, he said. And then when he met me ... he told me the day before he died that I looked like Anita, and that he'd felt comfortable sharing his story with me because of that. He said something about completing his destiny, that because you attempted to contact him, and I looked like Anita, it all came together for him. That he owed it to you to tell his story."

His eyes caught hers. "He owed it to me? He said that?"

Suddenly she realized that Mikhail had wanted to contact Erik all along—and yet he'd hesitated for two years, because he'd needed to clarify in his own mind that it was the right thing to do. He needed to relive his story and talk it out with someone. She gave Erik a sad smile and her throat swelled; the tears brimmed again. "When you called him that evening, he was so happy. Then he died in his sleep." She bowed her head. The tears slid down her face and she brushed them away.

Erik's voice brought her back. "He told me he had a surprise for me. I think he meant you'd be with him, and I'd see the resemblance."

"Yes. That's what he said to me. And I told him I'd be honored to come to the airport with him. He made me feel so much a part of the whole thing. In other circumstances I'd have felt like an intruder. But I felt I could help. I'm grateful for that."

"I don't think he'd have made the flight to Berlin, either, if you'd not been with him for support," he said with quiet confidence.

"I suppose you're right. But it was more than that. He was pretty shaky on that plane. I was afraid he might be really sick."

"What happened?"

"On the flight over, he had an episode of some kind. I thought he might be having a stroke, or a heart attack." She rubbed her forehead, remembering. "He'd just awakened from a nap. When he got up to go to the rest room, he seemed terribly unsteady, but he refused my help. He was in the rest room a long time, and then when he finally came back he seemed pale and weak, his breathing not quite right. It scared me a little, but he recovered pretty well by the next morning. That was the day we met Jon."

"So you think it may have been too much for him?"

She nodded. "I think he must have been emotionally overwrought by everything awaiting him in Berlin – his past, his future... and it affected him physically."

They sat in silence again, and then he stirred.

"So much to take in," he said faintly. He stood up, picked up his bag. His eyes met hers. "So much to think about. I think I need some time. I left the hotel reservations to him. Do you know if he made them?"

She gave a helpless shrug, rising. "There are some nice hotels near his retirement home. I imagine we could go to any of those, and I live nearby."

They started walking down the concourse. "Fine. After that we'll visit the retirement home, yes?"

On the drive into the city, he spoke little. He gazed out the window and Dee sensed his growing despair, so she tried not to interrupt his thoughts with talk. As they pulled into the parking lot of the hotel she'd decided on, she glanced at his impassive face. She wondered if the hotel seemed as cold and uninviting to him as it did to her. She almost said something, but then she remembered the kind of buildings he was used to in East Berlin and she remained silent. They went in and registered him.

"Please come with me, Dee. I'd like you to be here when I call Jon." He glanced at his watch. "It's late night there, but I'm quite sure he's still up, waiting for my call."

When they got to the room he went straight to the telephone, tossing his bag on the bed. Dee sat down on a nearby chair and watched him punch the numbers, then he waited a brief time and began speaking German rapidly with an anxious smile. Dee observed his features as he talked. His emotions ran from warmth, sadness, even excitement, all seen clearly on his expressive face. She sighed inwardly and felt her heart swell with the same feelings he conveyed, almost as if she was reunited with an old and special friend. Because of Mikhail, she thought. Because of Mikhail. It was a comforting thought.

He hung up the phone. "He's flying in day after tomorrow at ten in the morning. We'll meet him at the airport?"

"Of course," she said, and she clearly saw the relief in his eyes.

The retirement home where Mikhail had lived was a modest one-story structure that looked like an overgrown ranch-style home surrounded by vast lawns and colorful flower gardens. Erik's face brightened as Dee pulled her car into the parking lot. She turned off the ignition and said, "About fifty residents live here. Most are typical middle class people of modest means. The huge appeal is the grounds. I think anyone who likes flowers would be drawn to this place, don't you?"

"I do and I am," Erik responded. When they got out of the car, he stood a moment, gazing at the lush, vivid grounds. "The flowers here are quite remarkable," he observed. "The roses and blooming shrubs, the rich green foliage." He sniffed the fragrant air with pleasure and then glanced at Dee, grinning with some embarrassment. "I must confess, after living all those years in a place where there was little beauty, I savor something like this."

Dee smiled back, pleased that he'd comment, let alone notice. "Mikhail loved walking in the rose garden over there," she pointed past the arbor where they could see a profusion of red, pink, yellow and white rose bushes set among neatly trimmed walkways. "That's where we were when he told me his thoughts about you … about destiny …" she trailed off uncertainly and started moving toward the front door. His gaze lingered on the rose garden a moment, then he followed her.

The reception area was empty. The office door behind the front desk stood ajar. To the right was the large community and dining room; to the left, the hallways leading to residents' apartments. They went to the office door and knocked. Eunice sat at her desk, and she rose to greet them as they entered.

"You must be Erik Mendenberg," she said with a tentative smile, introducing herself and offering her hand. "It must be so difficult for you. I'm sorry you had to come here only to be met by such shocking news."

"It is a shock," Erik acknowledged, frowning. "I hardly know what to think, except that I'm glad to be here to help in any way I can. Although he was my father, I never knew him, as I believe you know. I imagine you feel the loss in a more distinct way than

I do. My loss is ... ill-defined, I suppose you could say. The loss of what might have been."

Dee watched him as he talked, impressed not only by his grasp of the words he spoke, but the meaning behind them.

The caretaker came through the office door just then. Eunice introduced him to Erik and the two men shook hands. "I've asked Dan to join us because he and Mikhail were good friends," she explained. "Perhaps he could help with the sorting process."

"Anything I can do, just ask," Dan said as they all took their seats.

"We could use some help, I'm sure," Dee agreed, smiling at Dan.

"Before we do anything else though, I'd like to set a date for the funeral. It could be right here in the chapel, if you agree."

"Thanks, Eunice. Erik just checked in at the hotel, and he called his son Jon from there. Jon will be flying in from Berlin the day after tomorrow in the morning."

Eunice consulted her calendar and said, "Then shall we say Monday at one? That should give us all enough time to prepare. I'll be happy to coordinate with a funeral director and put a notice in the newspaper if you'd like."

Dee looked at Erik and he answered quickly. "I appreciate that. And Monday is fine." He rose, an impatient appeal crossing his face. "I'd like to go to his room, now," he said.

"Of course." Eunice found the key in a desk drawer and rose to hand it to Dee. "If there's anything either Dan or I can do to help, please let me know."

Dee and Erik didn't speak as they walked slowly down the hallway toward Mikhail's room. As they approached their destination, she felt a sense of tension from him, flowing like lava toward her silently. She was sure his life's largest questions still clamored for release. And Mikhail was no longer there to answer them. Erik's heart must be breaking, she thought.

They reached Mikhail's doorway and she glanced at Erik before she placed the key in the lock and swung the door open wide, then stepped aside to let him pass. He hesitated, then finally moved forward. She followed him and closed the door. They stood quietly a moment, absorbing the room and its meager contents. She watched his face as his eyes passed over the stark mattress, the bedside table and lamp, the chest of drawers against the opposite wall, the bookcase, the small table where the telephone and TV sat, the two chairs beside it. He breathed deeply, then moved around the room, touching items as he went. He picked up a book from the nightstand, leafed through it briefly and set it down again. At the window he stood very still and stared out as if seeking a peaceful refuge from turbulent emotions. Then he turned to her. His face reflected confusion.

"There are so few personal things in this room. No pictures. No mementos." He waved a hand in the direction of the nightstand. "That book tells me nothing about him." He gazed around the room once more. "And yet I feel his presence, Dee. How can that be?" She glimpsed in his eyes the depth of his inward struggle to understand.

"He did have a powerful presence," she acknowledged. "When I first arrived here yesterday and saw the bed had already been stripped, it stunned me. The room seemed so empty. Of course I had never been in here without him. But now... I feel it, too. In many ways, he was larger than life."

He nodded. "How I wish I had known him." He looked around again. "And yet, for me ... I mean, the fact that I'm here at all ... here in this naked room, here on this planet ... is because of him. So in a strange way, I feel whole for the first time in my life." He shrugged. "It's hard to put my thoughts into English words."

Her heart turned over as she realized she had heard similar thoughts from Jill, and the smile she gave him was warm and heartfelt. "You're doing fine."

His face closed off abruptly. She stood and watched as his effort to understand his thoughts warred with all the years he'd spent guarding his thoughts. Then slowly, he continued, almost in spite of himself. "All my life, you see, I felt there was something missing. Something, perhaps, that my mother was not telling me. It was a shock, of course, for her to finally reveal to me that the man who raised me was not my father. But then I began to feel the truth of it. The man who gave me life was the one I had been missing all my life." He lifted his hand, swept the room with his arm. "I'm standing here in this room where he lived. That tells me he was real. This is all real." His eyes settled on hers. "Please understand, Dee. All those years under Communism, we had to suppress our thoughts and feelings. It feels strange to express them now, even here in America. But after all, this is a free country. I know that's why he came here." His eyes softened. "And I look forward to reading his story, about his particular fight for freedom. I want to hear what you have to say about him and what he was like in detail."

They gazed at each other for a long moment. "Openness seems to come to you pretty easily," she said, probing carefully. "I remember Mikhail telling me that since you were raised under Communism, he was afraid your thoughts and feelings would be conditioned differently from ours. That lies and evasion and lack of trust permeated your society."

"He was right," Erik said without hesitation. "I hated having to live like that."

"You would have understood each other," she said. "And your son Jon seemed open to Mikhail, almost as if they already knew each other. I was so glad to get to know him a little in Berlin." She pulled her eyes away from his and glanced around the room. "It's your right to go through Mikhail's things, you know. Learn what you can of him. Decide what you want to keep and what to dispose of."

"There's no one else?" He gestured toward her. "You're the Executrix of his estate, you said. You know of no one else with some prior claim to mine?"

"No. I know little about his recent life. Most of his conversation and his book centered on his early life, and then the war. Whatever things he acquired, whatever friends he made here in America are pretty much a mystery to me." She gazed around the room. "There's not much here, I know. But I imagine there are some things in storage someplace. Eunice could probably give us more information. But she was at a loss, too, about people from his past to contact. I do have his address book. I'd like to go through that with you today. And there may be other papers and letters that will shed some light on the last few years he spent, people he knew. Maybe Dan can help with that, too."

He rubbed his eyes, then sank onto a chair. "It feels overwhelming. There's so little to go on."

"I'll help as much as possible. We can begin by talking more with Dan and Eunice, whenever you say. And then we'll call the attorney who just drew up his will."

He gave her a pained smile. "I don't know if I'm ready for this yet. Perhaps we can begin after we eat something. Is there a restaurant nearby where we can talk all this over?" He stood up.

"Of course. In fact, the restaurant where my daughter works as a chef isn't far from here. She's probably there now, and I'd like to introduce her to you."

"That sounds fine. I know nothing about you, Dee. I'd like to hear more about your family, and your life. You have other children as well?"

She shook her head. "No, only Jill. She's 23, pretty and bright." She gave a little laugh. "Of course, I'm prejudiced."

"And your husband? I'd like to meet him too."

"My husband and I divorced a few years ago. He just moved to California recently, so no, you won't be meeting him. We *are* still friends, though."

He nodded. "That's a good thing, when you remain friends for the sake of the children, and for your own sake, I think."

"Yes." She led the way to the door. They stopped in the office briefly to arrange a more in-depth talk later with Eunice and Dan, then they decided to walk to the restaurant, since it was only a few blocks away. A stream of traffic passed them as they walked along. Erik thrust his hands in his pockets, deep in thought. Dee glanced at him. On his face was a bewildered frown. They continued to walk in silence a moment longer. When Erik spoke his voice was filled with confusion.

"All this seems surreal to me, Dee. I came to meet my father and he's not here. I have hundreds of questions for him that he no longer can answer. I've learned almost nothing yet of who he was. I keep wondering how I got here, how this all happened." His voice rose in frustration. "I'm trying to put the pieces together. I mean, I sent an enquiry to him through the Red Cross, and then I waited two years for him to respond directly to me. Why did he take so long? And how did he finally make the decision?" He stopped and reached out to take her arm. "Please, Dee. Can you explain? I need to understand."

Dee looked down at his hand on her arm and lifted her eyes helplessly to his. How could she describe something she didn't understand completely herself?

CHAPTER TWENTY-FOUR

"I guess it came piece by piece," she began. "First of all, there was a video tape I got at the library a few months ago. It featured Berlin, and the events surrounding the collapse of the Wall. I intended to bring it to Mikhail to watch, since he'd been talking about the time he spent in Berlin during the war. I watched it alone the night before. The crowd surged through the gates, every single person exultant and joyful. Somehow one man stood out, caught my attention. He looked so much like Mikhail I was stunned. I played the segment over and over again. He walked right by the camera, looked right into the lens.

"I couldn't wait for Mikhail to see it. I didn't know it was you."

Erik frowned. "Do you mean you saw me on the video?"

She held up a hand. "Wait. I don't want to get ahead of myself." Her eyes followed a passing car. "I didn't know your relationship at that point. He hadn't spoken of you at all." She gave him a pensive smile. "Then the next day when I watched the tape with Mikhail, I didn't have to say a word. He made me stop it and play it over. Later that day he showed me the letter from the Red Cross, and then we talked about it all."

They continued to stand in the middle of the sidewalk. He dropped her arm, turned away, hands on his hips, head lowered, staring at the sidewalk while he digested this. Dee blinked rapidly. How many times in the past had she watched Mikhail move his body in the same way? She stared at Erik.

He turned back to face her. "You saw *me*?"

She nodded. "It had to be. Were you there? Maybe I'm making an assumption, but try to remember what you were doing that night. Do you remember the camera you walked by?"

"No." His troubled eyes remained riveted on her face. "I didn't notice the camera. But yes, I was there, at Bornholmer Strasse. Of course I had my papers, but I didn't need them. We were all so happy, so excited, and yet apprehensive. If I had seen the camera I'd have thought the authorities were tricking us and wanted proof we East Berliners were breaking the law and would soon be arrested."

"I never thought of that," Dee breathed, stunned.

"Only later we dared to believe we were living through a huge historical event. But I never even saw the camera, Dee." He gave a little cry of exasperation, then shrugged in an effort to dismiss the disturbing thought. "So. Do I understand you to say that when you observed me on the video you saw my resemblance to Mikhail?"

She nodded, watching his eyes soften. "Immediately. But at that point I didn't know he had a son. It was Mikhail who made the connection."

He shook his head, pondering. Erik's eyes shifted toward the traffic, as if it held some fascination for him. Across the street a bus pulled up and a cluster of people got on. Dee could smell the acrid diesel as the bus roared away. As the sound faded she could hear a dog barking somewhere nearby. Finally Erik spoke. "A video. And I never even saw the camera," he repeated. "And because of this Mikhail decided to respond to me?"

"Well, it took him some time to decide, but yes, that was the turning point."

He lifted his eyes and gazed at the leafy green trees lining the street. "This will take *me* some time to think about." His eyes dropped and fixed themselves on her face. "But then, everything about this day has been, as I said, surreal. I suspect some things are beyond explanation."

After a moment he walked on. She followed him. Neither of them spoke until they reached the restaurant, went inside, and slid into a booth across from each other. Dee leaned back, pleased to see the attractive room again, this time washed in sunshine and emitting the delicious aromas of late lunchtime. A pretty young waitress arrived and filled their water glasses, then handed them menus.

"Is Jill here?" Dee asked, still feeling a bit shaken. "I'm her mom."

"Oh, hi. Yeah, I'll tell her," she said with a bright smile.

As she turned and walked away, Dee watched Erik. A look of bleak bafflement passed over his face. He picked up his water glass and drink deeply. He set the glass down, glancing around the restaurant. "This is a nice place," he commented. "But there are no tables on the sidewalk outside, as in Berlin."

"There are in some places, just not on this street," Dee answered, aware of the enormity he was attempting to set aside for now. She couldn't blame him. "I guess the sidewalks aren't wide enough. That's one thing I noticed about Berlin. The sidewalks are so wide."

She looked over his shoulder and saw Jill coming out of the kitchen door and approaching their booth. "Mom? Hi." Jill glanced at Erik, giving him a hesitant smile as he rose to his feet and faced her.

"Hi, Jill. I'd like you to meet Erik Mendenberg, Mikhail's son." Her tone turned solemn. "We've just been to the retirement home to see his father's room."

"I'm so sorry for your loss, Mr. Mendenberg. I didn't know Mikhail, but Mom tells me he was a really nice man."

"Thank you, Jill. I am glad to meet you, and I appreciate your kind words." He gestured toward the table. "Sit, please."

Jill slid in next to Dee, and Erik sat down again. "This must be so hard for you, Mr. Mendenberg," Jill offered.

"Call me Erik, please. Yes, it is strange and sad. When I came I was so happy to finally be meeting this man I had never known. Your mother told you the story?" When she nodded, he continued. "I had hoped for a chance to get to know him, to ask questions, to fill in gaps I had wondered about all my life…"

Jill suddenly gave a startled little cry and Dee perceived something like an electrical current coming from her daughter as she sat next to her. Jill was leaning forward, nodding energetically. "I know what you mean," Jill said. She glanced at Dee uncertainly, then rushed on. "Did Mom tell you I'm adopted, and I've found my birth mother?"

Erik glanced at Dee with surprise and interest. "No, we had not spoken of this."

"We haven't met yet. But I know the feeling … I mean, that you can't wait to ask questions, and all that."

Erik chuckled. "And all that. Yes." He tilted his head to one side. "You are a lucky young lady to have two mothers, you know."

Jill sat back. "Two mothers?"

"The mother who gave birth to you and the mother who raised you."

"Well, I don't consider the woman who gave birth to me a mother in any real sense of the word, since she doesn't want to get to know me, or even meet me."

Erik looked at Jill thoughtfully. Then he said, "My son Jon is about your age. His mother died when he was five, so he remembers little of her. We both still miss her very much. Not having any mother at all leaves a big hole in one's life."

"Yes, I can imagine," Dee murmured. She turned to Jill. "Erik called Jon in Berlin a little while ago. He'll be flying here in a couple of days. Then the funeral is Monday. Can you come? Another young person would probably be reassuring to Jon. Maybe the two of you will be able to spend some time together."

Jill said to Erik, "If you think I wouldn't be intruding. You have so much to do in a short time."

"I'm sure he'd like to meet you." He leaned forward. "Tell me. Why do you say your birth mother does not want to know you?"

Jill frowned and gestured toward Dee. "Mom and I have talked a lot about this. I contacted Karen through an intermediary about six months ago. But she says she's not ready to meet me yet." A touch of sarcasm crept into Jill's voice. "I guess she still needs more time to get used to the idea of me. She did write me a letter, though. A very nice letter," she added softly. She stood up. "But right now I feel pretty frustrated about the whole thing."

Erik held out a hand, gesturing for her to stay a moment longer. "You know, Jill, it took two years for Mikhail to write me a letter. I imagine it was a similar process for your biological mother – to come to terms with the memories. I know how hard it is to wait, though. Especially since I didn't know if Mikhail would ever respond. I hope for your sake that you'll meet this lady before too long." His brow furrowed, his voice grew intense with feeling. "And then you will have a blessing—and a challenge. I envy you."

The Berlin Connection

Jill's thoughtful smile warmed Dee's heart as she watched this exchange. Clearly, Jill felt Erik's empathy. Then Jill's smile faded. "She has a husband and two children to consider," Jill said. She lifted her shoulders. "Well, I know you have lots to talk about, so I'll leave you to it. But if you want, I'll take your order and get it started right now." She smiled brightly.

He grinned. "I like a real American meal. I had many hamburgers in Florida these past weeks."

"Two of the gourmet hamburger specials then. They're really good here."

They watched her as she walked away. "A pretty, bright young lady, just as you said," Erik remarked, still smiling. "I think you must feel blessed."

"Yes. As you said, blessed, and challenged, both. I was pleased that she opened up to you like that, Erik," she observed. "She doesn't often share her feelings about her search for her birth mother."

"There seems to be one coincidence after another in our life experiences, Dee Sanders. I'm not even surprised anymore." He turned his water glass in circles on the table, his expression one of puzzled delight. Then he shrugged. "Jill seems to see a kindred spirit in me," he said simply. "Although I'm a generation older and I grew up under Communism, it feels easy here for me to talk about my similar circumstances, and I could see that probably put her at ease. And now I understand more clearly about Mikhail's letter. I think when you talked with him about me you helped him understand how I might be feeling. Because of your own daughter."

Dee fingered her napkin. "We did talk about it, yes."

He nodded, his eyes intense. "After you saw me on the video. Months ago. So even then it took him some time to decide. As you indicated."

"Well, he wanted to finish the book, for one thing."

He closed his eyes briefly and sat very still. When he opened them again, he said, "I was also glad you introduced the idea of Jon to her. He really would appreciate her company while we are here, I'm quite sure. But before we think about Jon's arrival, we probably need to decide what to do tonight and tomorrow."

"Let's go back and talk further with Eunice and Dan, then we'll go to Mikhail's room and look for a safe deposit or storage key. There's also a copy of his manuscript that you can take back to the hotel."

"That would be wonderful. I'll try to finish it tonight. Then I'm sure I'll have a better idea how to proceed."

"Yes, I think you're right. I'll feel better once you know what he wanted you to know." She reached down into her purse and took out Mikhail's address book and a pen. "Maybe we'll find some names here to call. I'll check off the ones we want to ask Eunice and Dan about. It'll be a place to start, anyway."

After they finished lunch they walked back to the retirement home and stopped briefly in the office to talk to Eunice and Dan once more.

"I want to read the manuscript of Mikhail's life before I do anything else or make any more decisions," Erik explained to them.

"Probably a wise move, given that so much is happening in such a short time for you," Eunice agreed. "The reading will help to ground you, I'm sure."

"Feel free to call me if you have any questions or thoughts about it as you go along," Dee offered. "You'll finish it in a few hours, I think." She sighed and felt the prickling of tears. Her voice broke. "It still feels like a bad dream to me, Erik. You should be hearing what you need to hear from Mikhail, not me. You shouldn't have to make decisions in the wake of Mikhail's sudden death."

To distract herself from further tears she consulted the address book. "Eunice, Erik and I went through some names and addresses here and checked off possibilities. Maybe some of the names will be familiar to you." She handed the book over to Eunice who scanned the pages, shaking her head. Then she passed the book to Dan. He looked through the pages carefully without saying anything, and Dee was afraid he wouldn't recognize any names either. But then he pointed to an entry on a page.

"This one," he said. "Sam Gordon, in New York City. Sounds vaguely familiar, so it wouldn't hurt to try to reach him. Other than that, I'm drawing a blank. Maybe you'll find recent letters in some drawers."

"Well, it's still early enough for me to call some of these names with East Coast addresses while Erik is reading the manuscript. Then I'll try some of his gymnastics students. There must be rosters somewhere. He told me they always encouraged him to write his life story. I'll look around a little when we get the manuscript in Mikhail's room."

"Tomorrow morning I'll call the funeral director, and I'll need your help with the obituary some time soon," Eunice said.

They said their good-byes to Eunice and Dan, and then went to Mikhail's room and found the manuscript. They decided to search further the next day. After dropping Erik at the hotel with a promise to call him in the morning, Dee went home feeling exhausted. It was still early evening, but all she wanted to do was go to bed. She knew she needed to call the East Coast connections before it got too late, though, so she started in. She called the number for Sam Gordon first. An elderly woman answered the phone.

"I'm sorry to call you so late, but I'm trying to reach Sam Gordon. Is he available?"

The woman answered, "I'm Sam Gordon."

CHAPTER TWENTY-FIVE

"Sam Gordon?" Dee asked stupidly.

"Sam is short for Samantha, my dear. What is it you want?" she asked in a richly modulated voice.

"My name is Dee Sanders. I'm calling from Seattle and I'm trying to locate friends or relatives of Mikhail Sommers. Did you know him?"

There was a long pause. In the silence, Dee suddenly felt as if she'd been running up a steep hill.

"Yes, I knew Mikhail," the woman finally answered in slow, measured tones. "He moved there several years ago, but we stayed in touch." Again, an awkward pause. Dee opened her mouth to say something, but the words wouldn't come.

"Has something happened to him?" the woman asked at last.

"Yes, I'm afraid I have bad news." She swallowed. "Mikhail died two days ago of a heart attack. I'm sorry." When the woman once again did not respond, Dee continued. "His funeral will be here on Monday. Do you know of anyone else to notify?"

The answering voice was brisk and businesslike. "I'll think about it. I won't come myself; I'm confined to a wheelchair. But thank you for the information. Do you have a telephone number where you can be reached?"

Dee gave it to her and then the woman thanked her and hung up. She put the phone back in its cradle, pondering the strange, brief conversation. Well, she had done all she could. Maybe at some later date, Erik would want to talk further with the woman.

"Please, Dee, I need to understand."

A tremor of heat prickled her scalp, remembering Erik's words, and she smiled to herself. Then she dialed several more numbers, all of which had been disconnected in the years since Mikhail had moved from New York. It seemed he hadn't kept in touch with anyone except Sam Gordon. She sighed, wondering why not. She'd probably never know. His death was still so hard to comprehend. She felt a fresh stab of pain at the loss. But now there was a new element in the mix, Erik. That gave her some degree of reassurance. Once again she marveled that he was so open with his observations, his questions. She sensed that Mikhail would have been as relieved about that as she was, and she felt his approval like a blessing. She fell quickly into a deep, restful sleep.

In the morning she awoke refreshed, thinking of Erik. She wondered what he had thought of Mikhail's book. She hoped it had given him some comfort. The telephone next to her bed rang. The bedside clock said 7:30.

"Dee? Erik here. I hope I'm not calling too early."

"No, I'm awake. And glad to hear from you. Did you get much rest? Did you finish the book?"

"Yes to both questions. I finished the book around midnight, and I fell asleep almost immediately after that." Dee warmed to the enthusiasm in his voice. "I took many notes and wrote down many questions. And I wrote out a short biography for the newspaper notice that I'd like you to correct or add to, as you see fit." He sighed audibly. "I feel I know my father better now, and I'm eager to talk it all over with you. How soon can we meet?"

"I was just going to jump in the shower, so I'll meet you in the hotel coffee shop in an hour."

Jump is the operative word, she thought as she headed to the bathroom. She could feel the energy and the lift of her spirits as she stood under the warm spray and shampooed her hair. She dried and dressed quickly and then she scrutinized her face in the mirror. Much better, she decided. The puffy eyes were gone, the color was back in her cheeks, the drawn expression replaced with a cheerful one.

She found him already seated in the coffee shop. As she crossed to his booth, he rose to greet her and with a smile he reached out both hands to grasp hers.

He said nothing, just gazed into her eyes for a long moment. His eyes were clear, steady, intensely blue. It seemed to Dee as if he saw something no one else could see. Something even she couldn't see. She gave him a puzzled smile, and with a quick, embarrassed laugh he released her hands. They slid into the booth across from each other.

"I want to thank you, Dee." He spoke with a gentle shyness that touched her. "In so many ways I feel you are, and have been, the right person in the right place at the right time. As I said on the telephone, I think I know my father better now. But it's more than that. I feel I know you. Somehow the phrasing of his story reflects your personality, too, I think."

She sat back. "That surprises me, Erik. I mean, both you and Mikhail told me that I remind you of your mother, right? His story is a tribute to her in many ways. Could it be her personality that you see in the phrasing?"

The waitress came and took their order. When she left, Erik repeated her question thoughtfully. "Do I see my mother's personality in your phrasing?" Slowly, he shook his head. "His descriptions of her ring true, of course. Except that he saw her through the eyes of young romance, and I saw her through the eyes of a child, a son. But her personality was in many ways different from what I've observed in you. The surface resemblance is striking, but you grew up in America. You're used to openness, freedom. My mother – held back, as we all did. There was an underlying sadness, like melancholy music, in her everyday routine. Naturally, now, I understand it much better." He shook his head. "No. I do not see my mother's personality in Mikhail's story." He pulled a picture out of his shirt pocket and handed it to her. "I thought you'd like to see the physical resemblance for yourself," he said simply. "I think she was about the same age that you are now."

Emotion swelled in her as she looked at the picture. She felt the pull of understanding, of connection with this woman. It was more than the physical resemblance, although she did indeed look like Dee. Her hair and eyes were a soft brown, her smile and the oval shape of her face were similar to Dee's. But there was a subtle sadness in the smile that Dee recognized from her own history. What was the sadness from? Loss of hope? An ache of longing welled up in her, to know this woman who died too soon, before hope could begin again. "Yes, I do see it," she said, and handed the picture back with a cheerless smile.

Erik studied her reaction as he took the picture. Then he nodded and leaned forward. "What was Mikhail like when he described to you their early life together, Dee? Falling in love, youthful enthusiasm, dreams of the future – before the war changed things so drastically for them, I mean? That interests me a great deal."

She gazed at him a moment, aware that his words followed a similar path as her thoughts. "What was he like? Transformed, I'd say. He seemed to be reliving it as he spoke about it. His eyes shone with emotion, his face lit up. He was in love with life – Anita, his career, his youth and freedom. He never quite got over all those things he lost during the course of the war. And during the years after the war, when he was trying to figure out a way to get back to Latvia, the gradual realization that he had to make a choice about whether to live under Communism or find a new life – that was almost as bad for him as leaving Latvia initially."

"The war did terrible things to millions of people." Erik's face was grim with new awareness. "The way he described Berlin and all the bombings he experienced – it seems a miracle that he survived it at all. So many did not."

After the waitress brought their food, he lifted his fork with a thoughtful frown. "One thing I wondered about as I read of his early years: why so little mention of his family left behind in Latvia? What happened to his parents? His brother? Why did they not take in my mother when Mikhail had to leave? They had been together for years. Surely his family was a part of that, to some extent, anyway?"

She took a sip of coffee, then put the cup down. "I don't know. He said very little about it. I take it your mother didn't either? Do you know anything at all about her parents?"

"She told me she had come from a small town in Latvia, and pursued her own life in Riga. She lost touch with them some time during the war. But Mikhail's parents were right there in the city. It seems strange that he didn't interact with them more."

"I gathered from him that they didn't completely understand his choice of career. His parents tried to be supportive, went to his performances, but his brother had different goals and interests."

"It makes me want to look for pictures of his early life, mementos, that sort of thing. I doubt there's much, since he had to leave practically everything behind when he came to America, did he not?"

"Oh, that reminds me– there must be pictures and mementos from his life in New York, too. I had the strangest conversation with Sam Gordon, who, by the way, turned out to be a woman. Samantha."

He swallowed a bite of toast before he replied. "A woman? What did she have to say?"

"Not much. She said she knew Mikhail in New York. Didn't offer any details, but she did say they had kept in touch over the years since he moved to Seattle."

"Is she coming to the funeral?"

"No. She said she's in a wheelchair. But her response was so lacking in emotion, I wondered if they'd even been friends, except for the fact that they did stay in touch. She really didn't seem distressed about his death. She said she'd think about other people who might have known him, and she'd give them my phone number if she thought of anyone. But it made me want to look for pictures of her, of possible clues to his life in New York, aside from his acrobatics school, that is."

Erik laid down his fork and said, "Well, we have a great deal of work to do. When we finish here, shall we go right back to his room and begin the search?"

Later, when they entered Eunice's office at the retirement home they went over the newspaper notice together, and Eunice promised to phone it in while Dee and Erik went on to Mikhail's room.

Eunice had instructed them to set aside only the items they wanted. The rest would be cleared away at a later time. But as they stood in the center of the room, Dee glanced at Erik, suddenly disoriented and unsure of herself. Neither of them spoke for a long time.

"I don't know if this is right." He said the words slowly, in a voice so low she could barely hear him. He turned to her, his face a mask of confusion and pain. One hand reached out to her, and she extended her hand to his in response. Their fingers entwined. "I mean, I know this must be done, but I feel so …"

"I know. Me too," she said. Her throat began to sting. Blurred memories of Mikhail flooded her mind, and she couldn't focus on a single one of them. So she gestured toward the chest of drawers with her free hand. "Do you want to start there, and I'll take the bedside table?" she asked, her voice thick with unspoken emotion.

He nodded silently, and they moved apart to begin opening drawers. "What would you be doing today, if you weren't here? Tell me about your normal life," she said.

"Oh, I'd be calling on clients, potential teams for beach soccer, if I were still in Florida."

"Yes, Jon told us about that while we were in Berlin."

"Once we get back, he and I will be coordinating plans to get equipment and uniforms to them. There will be much detail work to finalize."

The Berlin Connection

"Is it on hold for now?"

"Yes. I finished most of the calls I had intended to make. I called the rest to tell them I'd be in touch at a later time." He turned to her. In his hand he held a ring of keys. "Did he drive? Did he own a car?"

"He never said. I assume not." She moved over to inspect the keys more closely. There were three. "No car keys there. One is to his room. Another to the outside door. And this one looks like a storage locker key. It could be here on the property, or it could be from a facility somewhere else."

He laid the keys on the dresser and continued to work through the drawers. She turned back to her own task feeling even more disheartened. She couldn't shake the feeling that they were trespassing, and she knew Erik felt the same way. On the other hand, she mused, someone had to claim the items and there really did seem to be no one else. The drawer she looked through contained his wallet with identification and a few membership cards: one to the library down the street, one to a fitness gym; health insurance and credit cards. Presumably Erik would find documents to go with some of these cards. They continued methodically checking drawers and shelves and books in the bookshelves, placing items of interest on the bed. Then they moved to the closet where they sorted through the clothing items, and finally, the bathroom. By lunchtime they had some possible items of interest to pursue, but they agreed there was in that stark room far less than a man of his age and experience would have accumulated.

The Berlin Connection

After lunch they approached Dan and asked if there were any storage facilities on the premises. "Oh, yes," he said. "Mikhail had a storage compartment, just like all the rest of the residents." When he led them to it, the key they had found opened it.

It was an area of approximately four feet wide and four feet deep, filled to capacity. They looked at each other, then started pulling out and briefly examining items: boxes full of letters and papers, two photo albums, one from what appeared to be the early period in Mikhail's life before and during the war in Europe, and the other from his first years in New York; and equipment from his days as a gymnastics coach and instructor. As they sorted they spoke in hushed, urgent tones, their wide eyes meeting often, the anticipation rising between them. Here indeed was the bulk of Mikhail's former life.

CHAPTER TWENTY-SIX

Three hours later they had sorted through everything to their satisfaction and put things in two piles: one to go through in more detail and one to have hauled away. They agreed to pile the items they wanted to sift through into Dee's car. When they finished, they headed to Eunice's office to let her know they were leaving. They drove with the items from Mikhail's room and storage area to Dee's home, and there they began to carefully examine each of them together.

They sat side by side on her sofa, going through a thin photo album that seemed newer than the few pictures in it. One of the pictures was a small family portrait Dee presumed to be Mikhail with his parents and brother. He had been around ten, his brother in his early teens. Another was a picture she recognized as him as a young man, standing with his brother who was dressed in a uniform they assumed was of the Latvian Army. Others were of Mikhail in his costumes as a circus performer.

"At every age I see myself," Erik said. The wistful expression on his face brought a smile to Dee's. "But why did he not show you some of these pictures when he was telling you his life story, Dee?" he asked her.

She shook her head in bewilderment. "I have no idea. They would have made a wonderful addition to the story, don't you think?"

"No doubt. Look at this one of him as a child. Someone in his family must have sent it to him after he arrived in America." He turned a page of the album. "And this one. Publicity photos for his trapeze act at the Salamonski Circus in Riga, it says." His breath caught. He pointed to the next picture, and Dee looked more closely. There stood Anita in a sparkling costume, holding a decorative umbrella, posing as if she were dancing along a suspended rope. In spite of the worn and creased paper, they could see that her face was luminous, her eyes shining with the vibrancy of youth.

"I have never seen this picture," he breathed with emotion. "How lovely she is. How young – and filled with hope for the future."

"Before the war changed so many things forever," Dee said softly.

He lifted the glossy picture from the page and continued to gaze at it as if he wanted to memorize every nuance. Then he turned to her, his eyes questioning.

"But I cannot understand why these pictures weren't used to enhance his story. It seems to me he'd be eager to share them with you as he did the story itself. That he would have spent a great deal of time poring over them, discussing with you which ones to use where."

Sadness passed through her like a dry wind. "Maybe he wasn't ready for that. Maybe that was coming next. First he uncovered the memories, and that was a painful process in itself."

"I wonder how long it was before he told his story to you that he looked at these pictures."

"I'm guessing a long time." The pictures would have been such a great loss, she couldn't imagine him deliberately excluding them. Her gaze drifted as she remembered how it was to work with him. "He didn't seem to need much help to get the memories flowing. It was fascinating the way he paced, his head held high, his hands on his hips or behind his back. He had such a dignified air about him." She turned to Erik. "Your manner is very similar, you know. It's what struck me when I saw that video of you at the opening of the gate of the Berlin Wall, and then again when we met at the airport. I want you to see it for yourself."

A warm smile nudged the corners of his lips. "Well. It pleases me that you tell me all these things." He looked down at the picture of Anita again. "A picture paints such depth," he said sadly, shaking his head. "She missed so much in life,"

"He did too. They should have been together."

"Yes. And here we are, trying to piece together what might have been. Or, as you say, what should have been."

They continued on over the next pages. As the pictures represented times in his life that he had talked about in great detail, she passed on parts of Mikhail's story that they had left out of the book. Erik listened and asked more questions as if her words were treasures uncovered in a huge vault he'd searched for all his life.

The later album was much thicker. They examined photos of children of various ages in acrobatic poses, publicity photos of his school in New York, and some black and white snapshots they presumed were of social gatherings. One in particular caught their attention because it had been enlarged. It showed Mikhail in his late forties or early fifties, his arm around the shoulders of an attractive woman of about the same age. There was another couple in the picture in the same pose. The four of them stood side by side, smiling happily.

Dee lifted the picture and held it next to Erik's face. "Looks just like you, all right," she remarked. "Too bad it's not labeled," she added. "He seemed to be great friends with these people. Do you suppose this is the female Sam?"

They compared the photo with others and found shots of the same people in many of them, seeming to cover a period of ten or fifteen years, through the 1960's and into the '70's. The woman they guessed to be Sam held herself gracefully in each picture, and they speculated that she might have been a ballerina.

"I wonder if there are more albums somewhere," Erik mused when they turned the last page. "When did he move here to Seattle? There is nothing here to represent that part of his life."

The Berlin Connection

"I remember he told me he decided to open a gymnastics school in Seattle after he brought some of his acrobatics students to the '76 Olympics in Montreal and saw Olga Corbut, I think."

Erik's head shot up sharply. "Jon and I were in Montreal for the '76 Olympics. I handled the GDR teams' sports equipment. "To think we might have seen and recognized one another!"

"It never occurred to me that you could have crossed paths at some point over the years," Dee said softly. "But it's true. You surely would have recognized one another if you had … in fact, he told me he'd been to the '72 Olympics in Munich too."

"Liesl and I wanted to go. But we could not–Jon was small. It was a period of tightening restrictions. But after Liesl died my status with the State improved somehow."

They set the albums aside and turned to the boxes of papers and letters. Much of them were unimportant, but there were many brochures and award certificates of his gymnastics school events in the ten or fifteen years before his retirement in Seattle; and letters, which they pored over in more detail, but which mostly yielded little insight.

One neatly bound stack had letters which were postmarked throughout the years. The entire stack was from Sam. Dee and Erik took turns reading the letters to each other. The tone was cordial but not especially warm, asking him about his progress with the gymnastics school in Seattle. Many of her letters referred to her physical improvement after an accident, then admonishment that Mikhail should not blame himself any longer; that she had forgiven him.

"Forgiven him for what?" Dee mused. "It sounds as though he was responsible for an acrobatic accident?"

Erik lifted his shoulders in a little shrug, then peered once more into the box. "What's this?" He pulled out a pale blue parchment-thin envelope from the bottom of the box; this one was from his brother, from Latvia, sent to Mikhail in New York, dated 1965.

"I know Latvian from my childhood," Erik said.

"Dear Mikhail," he read,

"Life has been in chaos since we were deported to Germany by the Nazis, somehow managed to survive, and then returned to Riga at war's end. I received one letter from you after that; I cannot find it now. But since I wrote down your address in my book, I am writing to you to inform you of our parents' accidental deaths in recent months. Also, you must not write again, for my children's sake. The weather is cold here."

Erik turned to Dee. "The next sentence is blacked out. Then it continues. *"The picture albums you asked for are not coming. I recall our early years, and am sure you do too. Perhaps these few memories will suffice.*

"Regarding your question about Anita: I heard she married and moved to Berlin some time back. Your brother, Nick."

"Well, there's the reference to your moving to Berlin," Dee commented.

"Yes." Erik leaned back on the sofa and put his hands on top of his head. They sat in silence a moment. "The letter also implies why he didn't have more pictures from his early years in Latvia. And why he did have those few. They came with this letter." He pointed at a sentence on the page. "Notice how guarded the language is. Typical Communist style."

"'The weather is cold.'?"

He nodded. "Also the reference to his parents' 'accidental' deaths. I am guessing they were deported to Siberia."

"How awful," Dee whispered. "Mikhail did tell me his father hated Communism."

"A family tendency," he commented cynically. He set the letter aside, then reached for another box.

The afternoon fled by swiftly. When they finished, she sighed. "It seems this answers some questions and asks a lot more, don't you think?" She stood and looked down at him. "I'm feeling stiff. I need to move around a little. How about some dinner? I'll cook here if you'd like."

"I'd like. And I want to help." He rose to his feet and followed her into the kitchen.

"Let's see what's in the refrigerator. I know I have wine," she offered, opening the door.

"A glass of wine sounds good," he said, picking up a framed picture of Jill on the kitchen windowsill. "She is a lucky young woman," he repeated his earlier sentiment. "And a lovely one. I'm eager to introduce Jon to her. They might be friends."

"She is a friendly person, and I'm proud of her for that," Dee said. "There was a time when she was a teenager that I swear she didn't know how to smile. She was sullen and uncommunicative, like most kids her age, I suppose." She shrugged and handed him the bottle of wine, a corkscrew, and glasses from the cupboard. "But thankfully she got past that stage. Did Jon go through anything like that?"

He thought about this a moment as he opened the bottle. "It was different for us, I think," he replied. "Because of our repressive society. He was obedient, if slow to communicate. His upbringing under Communism trained him well. Outwardly. He and I had little opportunity to talk openly together but we understood each other."

As they prepared the dinner together she listened carefully to his words and his implications. What he said and didn't say. She kept imagining Mikhail in this conversation, his reactions and contributions, his observations about Erik growing up in East Berlin with Anita, without Mikhail himself. She was struck by Erik's presence in her home, especially since she had never invited Mikhail. Theirs had been a business relationship that had developed into a friendship as he progressed through his story, and then the trip to Berlin that they had shared together, of course.

They ate on the patio which looked westward over a sheltered back yard. Early evening shadows lengthened. Dee had planted trees, shrubs and flowers when the house was brand new, and now they had grown into the place, lending a mature and cozy atmosphere. There were three birch trees, their top leaves still dappled by sunlight, and an evergreen that she'd planted as a seedling in the back corner by the fence. Over the years they had all grown substantially, and she liked to think that someday, long after she was gone, the evergreen would tower over everything else;

an enormous, sheltering and benign landmark in the neighborhood.

"You have birch trees," Erik observed. "I remember my mother telling me often about the birch trees that were prevalent in Latvia."

A pang of disappointment jolted her, and she puzzled over the reaction. Then she sensed her face, and in fact her whole body, warming as she inwardly acknowledged her attraction to Erik. From somewhere came the memory of long-ago similar stirrings at a sidewalk cafe in Berlin. All these years she had carried that memory of mutually startled recognition. And Erik inspired the same recognition: in her imagination, then and now, she recognized the romantic ideal, a man so likeable, so smart, so good-looking and easy to be with, whom she could truly know, inside and out.

And he had recognized his *mother*. She groaned inwardly with embarrassment, and yes, disappointment. Then she shook off the reaction. He was here because of Mikhail. She had offered her support, just as she had to Mikhail. *Stay focused, Dee,* she admonished herself.

"I am remembering a time in Berlin," Erik continued, his voice musing. "I have not thought of this for a long, long time. It was about a year after my mother died. I stopped for lunch at a sidewalk café." He turned to her, his smile as warm as his voice. "I met a beautiful young American woman there."

Her heart began to pound. It was as if he'd read her mind. But this was even more than that. "You met …"

"She looked like my mother. I was stunned at the resemblance. And now I've met another lovely lady, all these years later, who brings back so many good memories of my mother."

Her skin tingled and she shivered. "Erik. Was it near Brandenburg Gate? In 1969?"

His smile faded. "As I recall," he said slowly, his eyes steady on hers.

"I was there that year with Dennis, my husband. I remember meeting a young German man at a sidewalk café near the Brandenburg Gate."

He leaned forward. "You? You were there?" His voice was hushed, urgent.

"You ... were reading some papers. Dennis went into the restaurant to call his office in Seattle. I looked over and you were staring at me. You ... had the most ... stunned... look of ... recognition..."

Erik sat very still for a moment, watching her. In the lengthening silence their eyes held. Then he reached across the table and took her hand. "Could life be that strange," he asked, "and wonderful?"

The warmth of his smile turned her heart over. "All these years later, all that's happened in between, and here we are on the other side of the world, in the same place at the same time, again. And the mystery about why you seemed to recognize me ... is solved." Her throat tightened. "But I felt...I don't know...I felt I recognized you too. That's why..."

The warmth of his smile increased, the warmth inside her increased. "We both remember," he whispered.

She pressed his fingertips urgently as she recalled a crystal-clear image. "I did see you earlier that day," she said, "at the cemetery."

His eyebrows lifted.

"You were visiting your mother's grave, and you looked so lost and alone, I was caught up in the scene. After you left, I went over and saw the grave, the inscription. *Anita Mendenberg.* The dates of her birth and death."

"And Mikhail never knew?"

"I never put it together until just now."

CHAPTER TWENTY-SEVEN

The sky softened and shadows disappeared completely as the sun continued its descent. They finished their dinner and talked in hushed tones about the coincidences of life over another glass of wine, and then coffee, smiling often into each others' eyes.

"These days have held so many emotional revelations," Erik finally concluded with a deep, satisfied sigh as he rose from his chair. "I think we need to talk of other things for a time. How far are we from the water? I'd like to see the sunset over the ocean."

Dee stood up and nodded her agreement. "We could walk to a point not far from here to see Puget

Sound and the islands and mountains beyond. We can't see the ocean; it's farther west, beyond our view, but the sunset is often pretty from here. I'll show you a map of the whole Puget Sound area before we go."

They picked up the dishes and moved into the kitchen. Together they stacked them into the dishwasher. Then she led him to a map on the wall of her den and pointed out where they were in relation to downtown Seattle, Puget Sound and the Olympic Mountains on the peninsula to the west, and the Pacific Ocean beyond. After that they started off on their walk to the bluff nearby overlooking the water. They strolled down long blocks of substantial, attractive houses with neatly manicured yards of lush green lawns, colorful shrubs and flowers.

"The map you showed me helped a great deal, Dee. I see how astoundingly beautiful this part of the world is." He grinned at her in delight. "The mountains, the bodies of water so nearby. I had no idea how much there would be to see and do, all within easy reach."

She nodded happily. "People ski in the winter, and climb mountains, swim and sail in the summer. And that's just the tip of the iceberg," she said, and they laughed together at the tour guide rhythm of her voice.

"You have lived here long?"

"Born and raised." She tilted her head inquiringly. "Jon told Mikhail and me quite a bit about life in Berlin," she said. "I'd like to hear from you though, since you have a broader perspective. What have the changes been like over the years?"

He frowned and breathed deeply. "There was oppression, suspicion. One could not trust his neighbors." A pensive smile crossed his face. "But Liesl and I knew...we could trust one another, right from the first. She and I agreed on so many things, and we talked often about the changes we'd like to see," he recalled, his voice hushed.

"You loved her very much," she said, feeling stirrings of tenderness again, drawn as always by the sound of his voice. "That's so rare, so special, to have that kind of relationship, especially in the environment you describe."

"We knew it was a miracle." He glanced at her, his eyes alive with memory. "There is a forest within the city limits of East Berlin where we used to walk, so we wouldn't risk being overheard. In our position, I was always concerned about one or both of us being found out ... our viewpoint was in conflict with the State, you see. The threat was very real. We could have both landed in prison or worse. Then what would have happened to Jon?" He stopped to examine a rose bush, to breathe in the scent. Then they moved on.

"You had a good career with the State, you said, in sports equipment. What did Liesl do?"

"She also served the State. She supervised in a food processing plant. She believed it was important to serve others, especially since it took so long after the war to bring safe, nutritious food to the tables of the German people. Less potatoes and wurst, more fruits and vegetables. She worked toward that end. Because we were so happy together, we did have hope. She used to say she believed the future would bring changes neither of us would believe could happen.

And she was right." His voice dropped. "As long as Jon and I had Liesl, life was good."

"It must have been awful to lose her. She died in childbirth when Jon was five, you said?"

"Yes, I barely recall those gray years after she died. The only bright spot, of course, was raising Jon. And then suddenly, the changes were upon us."

"Did you ever imagine that Communism would collapse so abruptly? Mikhail told me that even he was stunned by the events of five years ago. It was what he had dreamed of, and then suddenly he didn't know what to think."

He ignored the question. "Mikhail should have responded to me," he declared, frowning. "I admit I was bitter about how long it took him. I couldn't understand what he was waiting for. To me, the Wall was still there between us, as it had always been."

Dee thought about this a moment. Then she said, "I think he believed it was too late for him. He had conditioned himself to turn his thoughts away from what he'd had to leave behind. It hurt too much to do otherwise." She slowed her pace, contemplating. "So he had to talk through his past, hoping that would help him change his mind. Ironic, isn't it, that even though he finally did change his mind, it turned out to be too late for him after all."

"If only he'd decided when the Red Cross first contacted him," he repeated.

"I know. As you told Eunice, you're experiencing the grief of what might have been."

"Yes. Right now I'm caught up in what needs to be done, and I keep busy with that. It's good to have you to work with, to talk things over. And tomorrow Jon will come. But I feel the grief and anger too, just under the surface. I feel Mikhail wasted two years getting used to the idea of what my existence meant for him, past and present. Two years," he declared, his voice rising as he stabbed the air in front of him with a finger, "in which we could have met, perhaps even become friends. So I will go back to Berlin with memories of him, but not in the way I expected."

"It must have been so hard for him, though," Dee countered. "He even had misgivings on the plane, Erik, before we got to Berlin. He told me he was afraid you'd have resentments that he wasn't there for you while you were growing up."

Erik shrugged. "I understand in my head that it was not his fault. But in my heart?" He frowned. "As I said, I felt the bitterness. Also that it took my mother so long to tell me about him. And that I didn't have a chance to ask her questions about it as they came to me. She was already gone."

They were approaching the bluff and a little park that overlooked the water. There were streaks of fiery gold and pink in the sky, accenting the wispy clouds the sun hid behind. They stood silently at a chain link fence gazing in silence out over the scene.

"Glorious," Erik breathed after a time.

"See the sailboats moored below? My ex-husband had a sailboat there for awhile. He lived on it. He loved the life."

He turned to her. "You say he lives in California now?"

"Yes. He was transferred by the company he works for."

"And you're still friends?"

She nodded. "Somehow we couldn't live together under one roof, but we get along fairly well apart." She turned to him and saw the concern in his eyes. "It's better that way," she hastened to add. "We never had what you and Liesl had, even at the beginning. It was a good friendship … but …"

"I see." He turned back to gaze out over the water and the dark mountains beyond, in silhouette against the rose-colored sky. His words came with some hesitance. "Sometimes oppression is a good thing," he said. "I mean, Liesl and I found it easier to appreciate each other in the face of our … challenges. But it occurs to me that in a free society there may be no such challenges to offset the value of the relationship." He turned to her. "Am I making any sense?"

"Yes," she said quietly. "In fact, Mikhail talked about the challenges of oppressive society that overshadow personal problems, and so I've thought a great deal about that in recent months. I've decided it works both ways. I mean, we did have a challenge, too—not of oppressive society, but of oppressive circumstances. In our case, it proved to be too much. The relationship couldn't withstand the challenge."

"I'm sorry. I should not have judged the situation."

"You didn't judge, Erik. It was a good general observation." Their eyes met in understanding and she saw the softening in his.

The Berlin Connection

"In any case," he said, "we each have our children. Now that they are both young adults, we see our lives stretching backward and forward, beyond ourselves. I feel this strongly because of what I'm learning about Mikhail's life. How a thread extends from Mikhail through me, to Jon, and then to his future children, as well. And you share that with Jill also."

"Well, it's not quite the same. Jill isn't genetically linked to me."

"That doesn't matter. As parents, we have a duty to project the best parts of ourselves toward our children's lives … toward their futures. Jill already has that from you. And she'll appreciate it more as she grows more mature. It's as important a legacy in my eyes as the genetic link."

"Thank you, Erik. I'd like to think you're right. Time will tell, I guess."

"Time will tell." He thought a moment. "What you said earlier about Mikhail having to talk through his past? That fits, too, Dee. Do you see? I have two fathers. I choose to take on the best parts of both. Sadly, the political and cultural mood shaped Aleks to a large extent. From what Mikhail wrote about Aleks in his book, there was conflict between the two men about that, and about rivalry over my mother. I want to explore such things in Mikhail's past. Perhaps in that way I'll learn more about myself."

He moved closer and faced her, his eyes intent once more. Her heart began to hammer. "We should see this through, Dee. Together, I mean. Knowing that we met all those years ago proves this to me." He took her hands in his. "Will you do it? After the funeral, as soon as possible, I want to go to New York, to learn how Sam fits into Mikhail's life. Then to Riga, to see if his brother is still alive." Gently, he lifted his hands to cup her face. His eyes, full of warmth, searched hers. "You and I have a duty ... as friends," he said softly, "to explore the best parts of this friendship, do we not?"

His hands reached back to cradle her head, then gently he pulled her towards him and kissed her, and at once she could feel the sweet, sharp jolt of electricity, the sensation of warmth spreading through her like molten lava. She instinctively lifted her arms to encircle his neck. As they held each other, she felt her whole body melting into his. For once, she did not question her instincts. She only knew a dizzying relief at the ease and simplicity, and the rightness of this connection.

CHAPTER TWENTY-EIGHT

Later that night, Dee lay in bed thinking about all she and Erik had talked about and shared throughout the day. Uppermost on her mind was that kiss – it certainly wasn't the kiss a man gives his *mother*, she thought with wonder and delight. She had felt passion, and he'd made it clear that's what he'd felt, too. They had only spent two days together, but the unusual circumstances of those two very full days, she was sure, were fueling the intense feelings in both of them.

"Erik." She said his name softly, savoring the sound of it.

She closed her eyes and visualized him, pointing out the sliver of moon hanging over them, as they stood on the bluff and watched the sky darken and the first stars begin to glimmer. That gesture represented to Dee how attuned they both were to what they were sharing. Clearly, she felt enchanted. But how could such things happen on the heels of such devastation? Mikhail had just died. They were sharing the grief, the loss, the emptiness–and helping one another through all that. And they were also sharing amazing coincidences and discoveries, and basking in the glow of each one.

She probed opposing thoughts tentatively, as she'd probe a sensitive tooth with her tongue–was Erik authentically good and kind? Or did he have ulterior motives? Mikhail had been so sure about the influence of the Soviet system—the duplicity and deceit. Out of respect for Mikhail, she had to keep that in mind. But Erik had a successful business in Berlin. When he flew to Seattle he hadn't known that Mikhail had died and left his estate to him and Jon. And anyway, it seemed unlikely to Dee that there was any estate to speak of.

And now Erik wanted to go to New York with her sometime next week, he'd told her, and try to find out how Sam had fit into Mikhail's life. Then he wanted to go to Riga, Latvia and find anyone from Mikhail's family still left there. What would it be like for them, to probe a part of Mikhail's life that he'd left behind forever? Maybe it was something they shouldn't try to uncover. And yet, this was Erik's family, too. He had a right to find them and learn about them, if at all possible.

Before they'd parted tonight, she'd called Jill and invited her to go with them to the airport to meet Jon's plane. It had been Erik's idea. He said he thought it would be a good experience for Jill to be involved in the discussion about Mikhail and their time with Jon in Berlin. Jill had been reluctant, but had relented when Dee had persuaded her that she could help Jon feel more comfortable while he was in Seattle.

Her thoughts flew back to Erik, and how good she'd felt in his arms. She realized how much she'd missed the sensation of warmth and comfort that comes from being held, and how lonely she'd been all these years. She experienced a sudden tightening in her body. *Oh my*, she thought, pressing her palm to her lower abdomen, *I haven't felt that for a long time. It's as if he's thrown a match onto a pile of dry kindling and started a bonfire. Easy, girl*, she told herself. *It's nice to have those feelings, and I'm glad I'm still capable of those feelings, but I don't want to get ahead of myself and read more into it than I should.* But she felt so alive, so alert, in touch with the harmony of the universe. She wondered how she'd ever be able to sleep.

It seemed a minute later when she awoke to a new morning.

All the memories washed over her again, and she smiled, just as the bedside phone rang. She glanced at the clock. Again, it was 7:30.

"Good morning!" Erik's cheerful voice greeted her.

"We're getting into a routine already," she said brightly, amazed that she who had always taken a good hour to wake up, felt infused with enthusiasm and energy this morning.

An hour later when she saw him sitting at the booth in the coffee shop her heart picked up its pace. He stood up just as he had the morning before and gave her a warm welcoming smile, and extended his hands to grasp hers.

"We had a fine day yesterday, Dee. Thank you for that."

"Yes, we got a lot accomplished," she said with an answering smile. A wave of emotion rose to her throat. "I think Mikhail would be pleased."

"Yes." His smile faded a bit as he released her hands and they slid into the booth across from each other. After the waitress brought their water and took their orders, Erik looked into Dee's eyes and his tentative smile blossomed into one of unreserved delight. She felt she was being washed with sunshine and she smiled in return. *Now I know what it's like,* her thoughts vibrated through her body and bounced onto him. His grin evaporated. He leaned forward, his eyes earnest. "This entire experience," he said slowly, "has been overwhelming, Dee. Overwhelming." His face tightened. "I don't know how I would have managed if you hadn't been there to meet me at the airport."

"No need to—"

He held up a hand, palm facing her. "Hear me out, please. I appreciate your presence throughout this time. And I want to repeat what I said to you last night. I want to finish the business of learning all I can of my father, and I want to do it with you, if you agree. I trust you. I mean, given my experiences of life in East Berlin, those words don't come easily for me. All those years, I concentrated on my work and on keeping Jon safe growing up."

He leaned back and his eyes slid away from her face. "And now, as I said, we must concentrate on the business at hand. And not allow ourselves to be ... distracted. Agreed?" His tone was brisk, terse.

She sat back. A powerful image raked across her brain and she tensed against the onslaught. When Jill had been a teenager she'd had a brief interest in horses. On one visit to the ranch where Jill rode, she'd seen one horse inside a corral, racing frantically from one end of the fence to the other, eyes wild, trying to get to the horse Jill was riding. Dee had asked the owner about the disturbing scene.

"Separation anxiety, it's called," he'd told her.

At the time she'd related it to what she'd felt toward Dennis. Now she gazed across the table at Erik and took a deep breath. The image dissolved.

She answered, "I'm glad you trust me. And I'm sure you know it's mutual. I'm happy to help. I know things would have been very different if Mikhail had died without reaching out to you through Jon." She looked away, puzzling. "He seemed to be in such a hurry – first, getting to Berlin, and then once we got there, finding you. It's as if he knew his time was running out."

He reached for his napkin and it crumpled in his fist. "All the time he wasted before that." She heard the bitter tone in his voice. "I couldn't ask my mother, and now I cannot ask my father ... all the questions I have," he said.

"In an hour you'll be seeing Jon again," she tried to soothe. "I'm glad he can finally give you a face to face opinion of his impressions of Mikhail. How long since you've seen him?"

"Some weeks before you and Mikhail were in Berlin. It feels like years. Yes, it will be good to see Jon again. I've missed my son."

Their breakfasts came and they ate quickly, both feeling a sense of anticipation to get to the airport and meet Jon. They stopped at Jill's apartment and Erik waited in the car while Dee went to the door. Jill opened it without a smile, still in her pajamas.

Dee's spirits fell. "Aren't you ready, Jill? Jon's plane'll be here in less than an hour."

Jill's words were careful, casual. "I just don't think I should come, Mom. I'm sorry. I'm not very good company these days, and this is something I've never really known much about, so I feel you and Erik and his son will do better talking everything over without me."

Dee stepped back, stung. "But Erik felt this issue is something you have in common—because of Karen, I mean."

Jill folded her arms across her middle. "I suppose. It's not that I don't want to be a part of this later. I just don't want to go to the airport with you." She forced a smile. "Tell you what. I don't work tonight. Why don't you call and come by later with Erik and Jon—or I'll meet you someplace."

Dee sighed, trying to rein in her irritation. "Okay, then. We'll do it that way. I'll call you later…if you're sure."

Jill waved as Dee and Erik continued on to the airport alone.

"Do you think she'll meet with us later?" Erik asked after Dee explained.

"I think so. She just felt you and Jon had a lot of business to catch up on and she didn't want to intrude. In fact, once we pick him up, I think it would be best if the two of you sort some of this out together, without me."

"We'll have time for everything. Since the funeral is in two days and Eunice arranged for us to meet with the attorney after that, I think this weekend we should try to break away from some of this. Perhaps you and Jill could show us something of the Seattle you know, yes?"

They arrived at the airport, parked the car and found the gate just as Jon's plane taxied in. A few moments later the crowd was deplaning through the gate.

"There he is," Erik cried. "Jon! Over here!"

Jon spotted them and the two men came together, slapping each other on the back and beaming. Immediately, Dee could tell that they shared a great deal of affection and warmth as she stood by smiling and watching them together, chattering away rapidly in German, alternating good cheer and sadness.

"It's good to see you again, Dee," Jon offered, holding out his hand. "And I'm glad to be here, even if the circumstances are not to our liking."

"It's not a very happy time, I know. But it helps to be able to get through it together, so I'm glad you're here too. It's been strange, sorting everything out."

They continued down the concourse while they talked, Erik filling Jon in on some of their experiences of the past two days while Dee marveled to herself how each of their lives had been turned upside down in the week since she and Mikhail had gone to Berlin. Mikhail was suddenly dead, and here they all were, thrown together because of him, and without him.

After they picked up Jon's luggage, they drove to the hotel where Dee left them to catch up on their own for awhile. She swung by the library to rent out the documentary tape of Berlin that she had viewed with Mikhail a few months before, thinking perhaps the four of them could watch it together later. At home, she called Jill to persuade her to join them after lunch.

"Why don't you come here for lunch, Mom?" Jill countered. "I want to talk some things over with you, okay?"

"That'll be great, honey. I'll be there in half an hour."

Driving over to her daughter's apartment she found herself wondering how Jill would react to her mother's attraction to a man who wasn't her father. Since the divorce, Dee hadn't dated at all. She thought again of how little she and Erik actually knew about each other, and she determined to concentrate, as Erik had said, on the business at hand. After all, she felt so caught up in Mikhail's death and Erik's appearance, how could she not try to share it with Jill? The attraction was a side issue, after all. In any case, did Dee's involvement in Erik's life feel like a betrayal to Jill? She gave up trying to sort out such thoughts as she parked near Jill's front door.

Jill opened it at Dee's first knock. She was dressed, but she still didn't offer a smile. "Mom, I just can't do this," she said flatly. "I understand how you feel right now about Mikhail dying, and Erik and his son needing your attention, but this is your life, not mine. These are your friends, not mine. I just can't bring myself to get involved. I don't even care if you understand me or not, I don't–"

"I was just thinking about that on the way over here, Jill," Dee said, moving past her daughter into the living room. "I think I do understand how much emotional energy it's taking to wait for Karen's decision. But whether you like it or not, you're close to this too. I saw you come alive when you met Erik and started talking so easily about what you have in common. That's why I think it could give you some insight, even help you deal with your frustrations when you talk more with someone who's been through it too. Besides, I really need your perspective on this. I'm flying blind with some of this stuff. Please come with me. I think you could be a big help."

"What if I just plain don't want to?"

Dee made no response, just looked at her steadily. The mother and daughter stood facing each other for a long moment. Finally Jill blinked and puffed out an exasperated breath. "I've got lunch on the table. Let's eat, and then we'll go pick up those guys."

Dee grinned at her daughter, gave her a hug, and they headed toward the table.

An hour later they were back at the hotel. As they walked down the carpeted hallway toward the room, they glanced at each other. Dee gave Jill an encouraging smile, but Jill didn't smile in return. Sighing, Dee knocked on the door.

CHAPTER TWENTY-NINE

The afternoon offered sunshine and soft breezes as the four headed downtown for some sightseeing. They got their bearings on the observation deck at the top of the graceful 600-foot high Space Needle. Dee and Jill pointed out all the important landmarks and bodies of water as they strolled the circumference. Mt. Rainier to the southeast dominated both mountain ranges, the Cascades to the east and the Olympics to the west, which stood out against the clear blue sky like molded mounds of vanilla ice cream.

When they descended the elevator and walked to the car the tang of salty air beckoned them, and they drove on to the downtown waterfront, parked, and took a ferry boat across Elliot Bay to Bainbridge Island.

They walked up the steps to the ferry's deck and gazed out over the water as the boat's horn blasted long and low to announce their departure.

The Seattle skyline of high-rise buildings gradually receded as the ferry made its way across the sparkling water, and they all leaned against the railing to gaze at the scene. Then they wandered the length of the deck to take in the scene from the other end of the boat, seagulls swooping and soaring around them and calling to one another. The lush greenery of the island drew near.

"A rural scene," Erik remarked. "So near the big city."

They didn't talk much except to comment about the scenery, but Dee felt comforting relief to see that Jill was relaxing in the presence of these two such likeable men. In fact, she became aware that Jon and Jill responded to one another with friendly interest from the moment they met. Dee and Erik exchanged glances throughout the afternoon to see them enjoying each other's company. By the time the ferry docked back in Seattle the sun was low over the water and all four of them were pleasantly weary. They found a waterfront restaurant and the waiter led them to a window seat.

"Looks like we're going to have another beautiful sunset," Dee observed as they settled in, Dee and Erik across from Jon and Jill.

"This is a city of remarkable natural beauty," Jon said. "It was wonderful to spend the afternoon like this, and you lovely ladies are excellent tour guides." He stifled a yawn. "You wore me out," he joked, and Jill poked him playfully.

"Jet lag, Jon?" Erik asked with a grin.

Jon chuckled. "I heard a description of jet lag on the airplane," he said. "It feels like walking under water. I think I understand the feeling."

"You probably want to get some sleep soon so you can be as normal as possible by tomorrow morning."

Jon nodded, and the waiter came and took their orders.

"You two might be interested to know that tomorrow is a special day here in the US," Dee remarked. "It's Father's Day—a day to celebrate and honor fathers."

"Oh, that's right," Jill said. "I'll have to remember to give Dad a call." She turned to Jon. "My father lives in California," she explained.

"Well," Erik said pensively, "if my own father were here, I'd surely celebrate and honor him, and the fact that we are together." He turned to Dee. "Is your father still alive?"

"No, he died just last year. I miss him," she said simply.

"Me too," Jill agreed. "My Grandpa Ron was a good man. As good as they get."

Jon regarded her thoughtfully, his fingers absently smoothing the tablecloth in front of him. Then he said with a frown, "My grandfather Aleks Mendenberg is not a good man. He represented oppressive rules, restrictions, organizations and authority in the Communist society of East Berlin. I cannot imagine what it must be like to grow up in a free society, to enjoy your family, and not to feel suffocated." He paused, glancing at Erik. "I'm still trying to throw off the East German influence. It's not easy. My father is doing the right thing by trying to learn about our genetic influence, our genetic inheritance. Even though we didn't know Mikhail we probably are more like him than we realize." He nodded at Dee. "What do you think?"

"No question," Dee answered without hesitation. "I see gestures, facial expressions, physical features in both you and your dad that remind me of Mikhail."

"I was lucky to be born in America, but even I ponder those questions," Jill said slowly. "Who am I, really? How important is genetics, really? Am I, after all, living the life I'm supposed to be living?" She gazed at Erik and shrugged. "Complicated issues, but I'm hoping when I meet my birth mother I'll get some answers." She turned her eyes to Jon and briefly explained the legalities of adoption in the United States and her personal involvement. As she talked she gave Dee a tense smile, and Dee smiled back, trying to communicate warm reassurance.

Jon looked from Jill to Dee and back, his eyes questioning. The waiter brought their drink orders, and then Dee explained, "When Karen gave Jill up for adoption she signed papers and that legally ensured her identity and Jill's would remain sealed from one another, unless both parties want a reunion. Jill's working with an intermediary through an agency provided by the State of Washington. When they verified Karen's identity through legal channels, they called her and told her Jill was hoping for a meeting, and now Jill is waiting for her answer. It's been a few months."

Jon pondered this. Then he said, "In a free society it seems to me that Jill has the right to a meeting once she comes of age. It is her life, is it not? So why is this Karen hesitating?"

"The same reason Mikhail hesitated two years to answer my letter, I suppose," Erik answered. "As Jill says, it's ... complicated."

"In Karen's case," Jill added, a nervous hand toying with a tendril of her hair, "she has a husband and two half-grown children. The kids don't even know about me. She's trying to decide what's best for everyone concerned."

"It can't be easy," Dee murmured, sipping her wine.

Jon shrugged. "Time is the answer, I suppose. But it must be hard for you, Jill. I know from what my father went through that the waiting is frustrating – and in this case, tragic. I feel almost guilty that I was able to meet Mikhail, and my father wasn't."

Erik leaned forward. "You didn't tell me many of your impressions of Mikhail yet, Jon."

Jon sat up straight. "When Mikhail and Dee walked into the store, when I first saw him – I was utterly stunned. The likeness was amazing, wasn't it, Dee?"

"Yes, it was. Even voice inflections and speech patterns were the same. Amazing, because you were more exposed to the German language, and he grew up with Latvian."

The waiter brought their dinners and while they exclaimed over platters piled high with fresh fish, potatoes and vegetables, he adjusted the window shade as the sun dropped lower in the sky.

After some time, Jon continued, "It was so easy to talk to Mikhail. He was eager, open, so – emotional.

It surprised me. I had no real experience in dealing with any man on those terms, except my father, of course. It was good to be able to ask and answer questions." He took a bite of salmon and closed his eyes with delight. "Delicious. Fresh fish is wonderful here."

He went on to describe his impressions of the meeting in Berlin to Erik in detail, glancing at Dee for confirmation, and Dee kept nodding. "He told me he'd known nothing of my existence. He first went to your home, then Frau Buchman told him where to find the store. We talked of the Berlin Wall, how I stood on the top the night we gained our freedom. I told him what it was like to live under Communism, how our business grew after Communism fell. We kept staring at each other. I couldn't get over that he came all the way to Berlin, and you were not there."

"I know," Dee acknowledged. "His eyes filled with tears when you told him your father wasn't in Berlin. But he was so glad to meet you, Jon. You smoothed things over so nicely and put him at ease because you said you wanted to ask and answer his questions in your father's place. He remarked about it many times afterward. He was so tired from the travel, and yet so overjoyed."

Jon nodded with satisfaction and his eyes moved back to Erik. "I told him about my mother," he turned to Jill to explain, "and how she died when I was small. And he talked of his relationship with Grandmother. How much he loved her. How they had planned to marry."

"That's so sad," Jill murmured. "It would have been wonderful if she'd been alive so they could meet again when he went to Berlin with Mom. When did she die?"

"Before I was born," Jon answered. "I never knew her. But he brought her back to life when he talked about her." He sighed softly. "He was especially concerned about Aleks, my grandfather." He looked at Erik. "I told him he's in prison now for his political transgressions." Jon sat back and breathed deeply. "He told me of his life before, during, and after the war as an entertainer, then how he finally came to the United States."

"Jon, he has finished a manuscript of his life story," Erik told him, his voice rising with enthusiasm, pushing his plate aside. "Dee helped him write it. It's so amazing to read about all the things he went through in his life, and to realize how his memories link us to him. I hope you'll be able to read it before you go back to Berlin."

"I want to read it too," Jill remarked with a smile.

Dee glanced at her daughter, pleasantly surprised. "We were hoping to get it published," she added for Jon's benefit. "We sent it to a publisher I know who might be interested, but it's too soon to hear back yet. In fact, after the funeral we'll notify them about the change in contact."

"So we have one more day before the funeral. Father's Day," Erik smiled. "Any suggestions on how to spend it?"

"I have the video of Berlin," Dee said. "We can all watch that together."

"And later in the evening I'll cook dinner for you at the restaurant where I work," Jill added.

"Jill is a very good chef, Jon. You must sample something she's famous for."

"What's she famous for?" Jon asked with a grin.

"Everything on the menu," Jill quipped.

The sun sank below the horizon and not long afterward the waiter came and pulled up the window shades, so they turned their attention to the sunset's golden afterglow.

Soon they left the restaurant and drove home in the fading twilight. After they dropped the men at the hotel Dee and Jill continued on to Jill's apartment.

"I liked him, Mom," Jill said in a tone that teased. Dee glanced at her and saw her lips pulled sideways in a knowing smirk.

"They are nice men, aren't they?" Dee noted with pleasure the relaxed companionship she was sharing now with her daughter. She wanted to comment to Jill how glad she was that they both felt better for the day's distraction, but she was pretty sure Jill had gotten the message without her having to say a word.

The next day Dee awoke early, again filled with energy and enthusiasm, her mind on the previous day. She jumped out of bed, realizing this was the first day since Mikhail died that she had the morning to herself. She decided to go to church.

It was located not far from the retirement home where Mikhail had lived, and Dee had met the pastor once or twice during his weekly appointment to give the retirement home residents Communion. She assumed he was the one Eunice had called to arrange the service at the retirement home.

She found a seat and let herself be soothed by the music and the uplifting message, and sure enough, after the service when she greeted the pastor at the door, he drew her aside and said, "I was sorry to hear about Mikhail, Dee. I know the two of you had been working together this past year on his life story."

Suddenly Dee felt her throat constrict and tears well in her eyes. The reality of Mikhail's death overwhelmed her all over again. It was too late for him and Erik, and she prayed it wouldn't be too late for Karen and Jill. She thought again of her own longing to meet Karen, a deep personal need, always just below the surface.

She stopped at the grocery store on the way home and bought food for a light lunch. When Jill and the men to arrived, they ate lunch in the kitchen as a light rain fell outside, and then they moved into the living room to watch the video.

Dee watched the video again with renewed fascination. Here sat two people, she thought, who had lived through these very events that had sent shock waves throughout the world less than five years before. She could see that Jill was equally mesmerized as both men narrated from their own personal knowledge what they watched on the screen. Jon pointed with genuine excitement at himself among a crowd of young people lining the top of the Wall, their bodies illuminated by the floodlights, and Erik sat stunned to see himself as he moved past the camera at the Bornholmer Gate, gloved hands clasped in front of him, head lifting slightly in a hesitant but triumphant smile.

"I did not register that the camera was even there," he whispered. "But see how I look straight at the camera."

"That's the climactic moment, right there," Dee acknowledged, stopping the tape. "I'd like to hear about the months leading up to it. What was that like for you?"

CHAPTER THIRTY

"For more than a generation, people in the East felt the weight, the burden of daily life," Erik began, hushed excitement humming in his voice. "It had been next to impossible for so long to get to freedom in the west. Now we were all alert to a whisper of change. The cage door slipped its latch, just a little." He lifted two fingers and rubbed them together. "Perestroika and Glasnost gave us hope. Some border restraints relaxed.

"That summer before the Wall fell, what started as a trickle across loosening borders became a flood of people, trying to get to the West. They made their way to the West German Embassy in Prague. Thousands of them. Then the border closed again and they were trapped."

"Why was the border closed again?" Jill asked, genuinely puzzled.

"The authorities were afraid of losing control, of outright bloody revolution," Jon explained carefully, and it struck Dee anew what different lives Jon and Jill had lived growing up. "That seemed ever more possible as the tension mounted, and not in anyone's best interests. So the government made a strange decision and promised these people safe passage on a train from Prague to West Germany through East Germany. They wanted tight control in this situation. Naturally, we feared that all those on the train would be slaughtered as so many Jews had who had disappeared on trains during the war. But this time the whole world was watching the developments.

"And sure enough, the people on the train got safely through East Germany to West Germany, to freedom!" His voice rang. "Imagine how we felt. If they could do it, then maybe there'd be hope for all of us! Each new development encouraged us to demonstrate throughout East Germany. The Soviet leader, Gorbachev, by this time seemed to distance himself from the East German government, and when he came in October for the 40th Anniversary of the GDR in East Berlin, all my friends and I joined the demonstrations on the streets and cried out in unison, 'Gorby, help us! Gorby, help us!' We didn't know what kind of repressive measures they'd take. Tanks? Guns? Would our blood be spilled on the streets? But our numbers were growing, and we were determined—not only in East Berlin, but other cities

The Berlin Connection

in East Germany: Leipzig, Halley, Dresden– huge crowds of demonstrators filled the streets."

Erik continued, "And then the next thing we knew, Honecker, the East German Chancellor, was voted out as Party Chairman, and Egon Krenz, second in command, replaced him. Under so much pressure from the people he arranged to relax the travel restrictions. Miracle of miracles, on November 9, we watched it live on the television: it was announced that a new travel law would provide orderly passage from East Berlin into West Berlin for our citizens, to take effect immediately!" Elation rose in his voice. "Imagine what a surprise that was! We didn't find out until later that the law wasn't supposed to go into effect until the next morning when all the authorities would be in place to stamp exit visas.

"So crowds of us went to all the check point gates, just to see what would happen. No officials were in place that night, and it was amazing—amazing! I stood among a crowd that grew to thousands that evening at Bornholmer Street Checkpoint, all of us pressing and demanding passage." He chuckled. "I have to feel sorry for the Stasi guards that night. They didn't know how to handle this." His face tightened. "As Jon said, we knew there was always the danger that they'd open fire and slaughter us." He shuddered. "And then, just as the pressure became unbearable, the guards released the barriers, and we all moved forward in a crush of joyful shouting. Well, you just saw it on the video. Men, women, children, and me. It took us all by surprise." He lifted hands to his heart. "What a night!"

"Yes. What a night," Jon's voice was hushed with reverence. "I stood on the top of the wall at Brandenburg Gate with so many others, dancing and reveling. Almost all of us had hammers and chisels. We chipped, hacked, and pounded away at the wall until morning." His face was glowing. "It took a whole year, but that led directly to Germany's reunification."

Dee started the video again, and the four of them sat in silence watching the documentary play to the end. As she began the rewind, she asked, "And since then?"

"Reunification is building its momentum," Erik said with conviction. "Already we see signs of reconstruction and urban renewal. Bulldozing, scaffolding, traffic detours are everywhere. And it will be that way for many years to come. It's a glorious time in Berlin." He remained silent for a moment, thoughtfully rubbing his thumb across his chin. No one spoke. "And do you know," he finally said in measured tones, "I understand completely why Mikhail chose to leave the life under Communism behind. He'd surely have been sent to Siberia. Jon and I had a relatively comfortable life under the circumstances. But the system was so corrupt, so burdened with daily misery on all levels. We're glad it's crumbled, and it's all behind us."

Jon and Erik looked at each other, and their gazes held in the silence.

Jill and Jon moved to the dining room table and spread Mikhail's manuscript before them, reading the pages together while Dee and Erik cleared away the lunch dishes in the kitchen, then went over the picture albums once again, pulling out several for a display at the funeral.

After a time, Jill rose from the table and sighed. "Mom, it's wonderful," she said. "What you've done. It brings him to life."

The warmth of her daughter's praise brought a surge of pleasure to Dee's heart. "I wish you'd known him," she answered.

"And I wish I could be at the service to honor him. And," Jill gestured at the pages on the table, "I wish I could keep on reading. But I have to go to work. And I want to cook dinner for you at the restaurant later," she affirmed.

After she left Jon continued to read and Dee and Erik methodically worked through photos and documents, organizing them as best they could.

"Where are those letters from Sam?" Erik asked. "We should make a note of Mikhail's address from that time, so we can visit the place and find out if any of the neighbors remember him."

"Good idea," Dee said, and she dug in the box and pulled out the stack. "It's on Galer," she observed. "Near downtown, I think."

Later, after Jill cooked them a wonderful dinner at the restaurant, they tracked down Mikhail's former residence. Dee drove slowly down a street of shabby buildings and pulled over in front of a run-down rooming house. They got out of the car and stared at the two-story structure. Weeds grew rampant in the yard. Grimy white paint was peeling off the siding. Two doors at porch level stared at them like dark, gloomy eyes. Dee squinted in dismay and glanced at Erik and Jon. Both their faces were closed off, grim. No one spoke.

They climbed the porch steps and Erik knocked on both doors. They waited in silence. Finally they heard the muffled pounding of footsteps coming slowly down the steps. The door opened and an elderly man in wrinkled clothes, and badly in need of a shave, faced them.

"We understand a man named Mikhail Sommers lived here about three years ago," Erik said. "He had a European accent something like mine. Did you know him?"

The man continued to stare at them. Finally he opened his mouth. "Folks here come and go all the time," he said with a growl. "I doubt you'll find anybody on the block who knew him." He waved his arm toward the street, then he turned and abruptly closed the door.

They walked back down the steps to the street. "So much mystery," Jon commented, looking genuinely puzzled. He kicked at a clump of dirt on the sidewalk. Dee and Erik nodded, gazing bleakly at the sorry structure.

The next day at the retirement home they went back to Mikhail's room so Jon could see where Mikhail had lived. Eunice had told them that most of the furniture would be used by the next occupant and they had little of his personal belongings left to clear out, so they gazed forlornly at the dreary surroundings, saying little to each other. Then they made their way down the hall to Eunice's office where she and Dan sat.

"How did the residents take the news of Mikhail's death?" Dee asked.

"Most of them are in their 80s and 90s," Eunice replied, "so they were shocked, because they're so much older than he was."

Dan cleared his throat and gave them a grim smile. "Mikhail hadn't mingled with them much since they'd had so little in common."

The attorney arrived then and they all went into the chapel and took their seats in the front row.

About fifty elderly residents were already seated, and again it struck Dee that they were all so different from Mikhail. She couldn't tell if anyone besides the residents were there, but by the time the funeral was over and they turned around, it was clear that no one else had attended, unless they had slipped in late and slipped out early.

Afterward as Dee, Erik and Jon mingled in the nearby reception hall, the most bewildering revelation of all: each person they talked to who looked at the collage of pictures remarked that they hadn't known about Mikhail's life as an entertainer or even a gymnastics instructor. Erik and Jon were easily accepted as Mikhail's son and grandson, and weren't even questioned about the lack of family pictures.

"How did he end up in such a place, among these people?" Jon observed in a subdued whisper. "And why did he live before this in that filthy rooming house that reminds me of East Berlin? He had such vitality, such energy and sophistication for a man his age."

"And why had Mikhail not told any of them anything about his past life?"

Dan, Eunice, and the attorney approached them from nearby. Dan seemed to have been waiting for the question. "He told me he didn't want to stand out in any way," he said softly. "He'd felt his past life would be too different for them to comprehend, and he wanted to blend in as much as possible. True, he was much younger than most of them and had a foreign accent, but those were the only ways he wanted to appear different. And he never volunteered anything else."

"How long was he here before he hired me?" Dee asked.

Eunice answered. "About two years. None of us knew much. Dan was the only person he talked with, and he never had visitors that I know of, except you, Dee."

Dee's attention moved back to Dan. "I remember you picked out Sam's name in his address book, and you didn't know Sam is a woman. Did he give many details about other people his life in New York or before, in Europe?"

Dan considered the question, then shrugged. "He just mentioned his good friend Sam in New York, but I don't remember anyone else. He mostly told about his life as an entertainer, running from the Nazis in Germany, starting his acrobatics school in New York."

"But why was he here in the first place? Why didn't he live among the general population, in a nicer home?"

"He'd had some kind of health crisis. He never told me what it was, but I'll never forget the day he moved in. He was shuffling like many of the other residents. He was thin and his skin was kind of gray. I didn't think he'd make it. But little by little, he did improve."

"I really expected some of his old gymnastics students to see the notice in the newspaper and come," Erik remarked. "He told Dee he wrote his life story partly in response to their questions."

"More mystery," Jon observed.

"I'm ready to discuss the will," the attorney said. "That should clear up some of your questions. Shall we continue this conversation in Eunice's office?"

As soon as they took their seats, the attorney began. "There is a sizable inheritance," he stated directly, "kept in trust for you by one Samantha Gordon of New York City."

Erik, Jon and Dee sat stunned as they listened to his words.

He went on to read the detailed terms, then after he left they talked over this new development.

"It seems I had the right instinct to visit Samantha Gordon," Erik said, shaking his head. "She must hold the key to much of this."

And so, once again they agreed to telephone Sam and make an appointment to see her, then make plane reservations for New York. They left the retirement home and drove to Dee's together.

When they got there a message from Jill was waiting for Dee.

"Mom, call me at work. I can't stand it, I'm so excited! Call me!"

"What do you suppose that's all about?" Erik asked.

"Only one thing," Dee answered, explaining briefly as she led them into the kitchen and started coffee. Then she called Jill at work and sure enough, Jill had news about Karen's decision.

"Mom, she wants to meet me," Jill whispered. "I heard from Nicole about an hour ago. I'd told her to call me at work about any developments like this, so she did, and I don't know if I'll be able to concentrate, but that's okay because I can do all this cooking with one hand tied behind my back – Mom, she wants to meet me! Isn't that great?"

"So great, honey! So, when? Will Nicole set it up?"

"There's one hitch–that's why I'm calling you. Nicole wants to meet with both of us, you and me, in her office so she can fill in the details about Karen."

"Me? Are you sure you're okay with that, Jill? I didn't think it would be right for me to be that involved."

"Apparently Nicole thinks it's best this way. And God knows she's counseled a lot of people in this kind of thing. So yes, I trust her judgment." Dee heard a happy sigh coming from Jill, and she closed her eyes tight, then opened them again, turned to Erik and Jon, and gave them a thumbs-up sign and a big grin. They nodded, returning her grin. Over the phone Jill continued, "She wants us to come to her office tomorrow morning at 10. Does that work for you?"

"Yes, of course. I'll make it work."

There was a pause, and Dee could tell Jill was shifting mental gears. "I've got to get back to work. Say hi to Jon and Erik for me. I'll want you to fill me in on the funeral when I see you tomorrow, okay?"

"Okay. See you in the morning."

She hung up and turned to Erik and Jon with Jill's news. "So many developments, all at the same time," she said, shaking her head. "It's good to know things are moving for Jill now, too."

"Perhaps you'll need to postpone travel to New York until you know more from Jill?" Erik wondered aloud.

"I don't know that I even need to go to New York with you and Jon. Do I, Erik?"

"But of course you do. You're Executor of Mikhail's will."

"I guess I am," she said slowly. "I guess I am." She couldn't quite manage a smile. She poured coffee and placed the cups on the table in front of the men. "You're right about things hinging on Jill's developments. I want to be here for her if she needs me." She pulled out a chair and sat down across from them. "Could we wait until after the meeting tomorrow to call Sam in New York?"

Jon shrugged. "My return flight to Berlin will need to be changed in any event," he said, "since I'll have to go to New York now too. Mikhail named us both in the will, did he not?" he asked Erik.

"Yes, we three will all have to be there, whenever Sam agrees to meet with us."

"We need answers," Dee said with a frown. "What would have happened if Sam had died before Mikhail? And did she know about you two when I talked with her the other night? And why wasn't she surprised to hear about Mikhail's death?"

CHAPTER THIRTY-ONE

At 10:00 the next morning Jill and Dee entered Nicole's office. Jill introduced her mother to Nicole and they all took their seats. Nicole was a pretty woman of about 35. She wore a soft pink sheath and her long, curly red hair was pulled back behind her ears with shiny silver clips. She gave Jill a warm smile across the desk. Dee could see clearly that the two young women had built a bond of trust in the months that they had been meeting. Nicole had a relaxed manner and intelligent green eyes that she now turned to Dee.

"Jill tells me she's been keeping you up to speed on developments with Karen."

"That's right. I've been trying to be supportive any way I can."

"Good. That's so important." She folded her hands under her chin and Dee could see that the soft pink nail polish she wore matched her dress. "I called you in today because I wanted to describe the situation so you'll be able to see the kind of support and encouragement Jill needs at this stage. To be honest, it's getting a little tricky now, but I don't think it's anything we can't handle."

Jill leaned forward in her chair. Dee could feel her tension. "Tricky?" Jill gave a short laugh. "That's an interesting choice of words."

"I'll explain. But I need to go back to clarify things for your mother first." Again she turned her eyes to Dee. "I understand that Jill got the last name of her birth mother from you?"

Dee nodded slowly. "I was never sure about it, but once Jill decided on a search, if it *was* accurate, I felt it was her information to do with as she wanted." She could feel the tone of her explanation rising into a question.

"Yes, well, it's a little unusual to start with that premise. Typically what we at the agency do is get the information for the searcher, contact the person in question, and if they want to be 'found' they sign consent papers. Before we undertook the search, we had Jill sign papers, as well. So then both parties are free to make the reunion happen. No surprises. We don't need to be involved. But in this case, we contacted Karen on the basis of information Jill already had, and then worked with her to help her make her decision about whether she wanted a reunion with Jill or not.

The Berlin Connection

Jill could have contacted Karen on her own, but she chose to work through us, and for obvious reasons, I believe that was the best course of action, legally, morally and emotionally."

Dee could sense Jill stirring restlessly in her chair. She didn't blame her for the impatience she showed. But Dee recognized her own relief that Nicole was covering the issues with such professional confidence. She felt herself relax a little.

"Karen has made it clear that she wants a reunion with Jill," Nicole went on. "After the initial shock, she was ecstatic to be 'found' and to know Jill is happy and healthy, and she looks forward to meeting and talking with her. She's signed the consent form – but there are circumstances that you both need to be aware of; complications– that Karen has been getting ongoing counseling about. She's given her consent for me to share this information with both of you before we proceed."

"She does want a reunion though?" Jill asked, her voice trembling audibly.

"Yes, she does. Very much." Nicole paused, smiling, and let the full impact of the words sink in. Dee and Jill turned to each other with hopeful, tentative smiles. Then they turned their attention back to Nicole.

"But? What circumstances? What complications?"

"She wants to meet with you in neutral territory—a restaurant, just the two of you. She has full support from her husband on this, as you do from your parents, but she feels she can't tell her children about it any time in the foreseeable future."

"She can't?"

"No. She feels they'd probably be okay with the idea of a new, much older sister in their lives. But they'd have to understand the traumatic circumstances of Karen's pregnancy. And she feels so anxious about it, to this day, that she believes she'd botch telling them. And that would cause major trauma for them at their ages."

"Trauma?" Dee asked. "But what if she tells them years from now, after her anxiety is smoothed over, and they find out she's been keeping it from them all this time?"

"She understands the risk, and she's determined that she needs more counseling about all that. In the meantime, she feels there are things she'd like to talk over with Jill, in any case. Things that could help you, Jill, as a young adult."

Jill held up a hand. "Wait. Nicole, back up. What trauma? Exactly?"

Nicole's eyes softened. They never left Jill's face. She took a deep breath. "In those days they didn't have a term for it, but nowadays they call it 'date rape.'"

"Oh. Date rape," Jill repeated the words. They fell heavily, like stones. Dee could hear Jill swallow. The silence lengthened. Dee turned to Jill, finally, laying a hand on her arm, opening her mouth to say something comforting. But Jill shook off her hand and lowered her head. "Well, Mom," she said in a low, steely voice, "What do you think of the 'me' that came out of this development?" She looked up at Nicole. "Mom is fond of saying, 'You'll still be you.'" She gave a short, unhappy laugh.

Nicole said quickly, "It's true, Jill. That's exactly why I asked your mom to be here today. I want you both to understand once again that you're the same person you were before you got this piece of information. It doesn't change a thing." Nicole's voice was soothing, reassuring. "Karen and I talked for hours about this, and as you can imagine, it was very emotional for her. In a nutshell, she told me she went on a date with a guy in high school who was popular and good-looking, a guy every girl wanted to date, a guy who was charming and got good grades and the whole nine yards. Apparently he was also used to getting his way, and didn't understand the word 'no.' A lot of girls in the early '70's got caught in that kind of dilemma. The guy every girl wanted to date asked *Karen* out, then forced her to have sex with him, then couldn't see anything wrong with it. Karen was left feeling cheap and guilty. She felt that somehow she must have led him on. And then, on top of everything else, she found she was pregnant. She was devastated. Now, if *you're* having trouble understanding all the emotional fallout from that, imagine what her teenage kids would be feeling at this stage. That's why she wanted to take it one step at a time, and she wanted you to know her dilemma – why it's taken her so long to sort it all out emotionally."

She fell silent, let the silence stretch out. After a time she got up, came around the desk and leaned over to give Jill a hug. Then she straightened and said, "Jill, you're a wonderful, pretty, bright, engaging young woman. Any woman who gave birth to you, and any woman who raised you, would be proud of the way you turned out. That's what Karen wants you to know, too."

Dee's heart tightened as she thought about what Jill must be feeling. What Karen must be feeling. She longed to reach out to both of them. But her daughter was here now. "That's true, honey," she said. "You know it's true."

"Okay." Jill breathed deeply, then rose and paced the small office, Dee's and Nicole's eyes following her. Then she stopped in front of Dee. With a grin that didn't reach her eyes she leaned over and gave her mother a hug. "Forget the sperm donor, then, right? Glad you're here, Mom. This will take some getting used to, won't it?"

"As Nicole said, 'Nothing we can't handle.'" Dee blinked and sniffed back tears, patted Jill on the shoulder. Jill straightened and took her seat again.

"Now what?" Jill asked.

Nicole handed her a slip of paper. "This has the name and address of the restaurant where she wants to meet with you, and the date and time. If that doesn't work, she gave me some alternates."

Jill glanced at the page and looked up at Nicole, her eyes stricken. "But this isn't until September, Nicole. How am I supposed to wait three more months?"

"She wanted to wait till her kids are back in school, and until she has a few more counseling sessions. I agreed. From your point of view, it's important to digest this new information and think through the kinds of questions it raises, questions you'll want to ask Karen. She wanted me to tell you that by then she will be fully prepared to answer any questions you have, including more detailed genetic and medical background of herself and the birth father."

Jill raised her hands to her head and pressed the heels against her temples. "Oh, I wish I could just fall through a hole and slip into a coma until the reunion. I am so very tired of waiting, Nicole. I can't think of anything else. I don't want to think of anything else. I have no life until I meet Karen."

"I know." Nicole gave her a sympathetic smile. "How long has it been since you started the search?"

"Almost two years."

"Have you had a vacation since then?"

"No. As I said, I couldn't think of anything else. Takes too much emotional energy."

"Why don't you do that, Jill? Take a vacation. Seriously, you could use a little distraction."

"I doubt it would help."

Dee leaned forward. "As a matter of fact," she said, "I was going to ask about my own plans. Jill is my first priority and I want to be there for her. As it happens, though, a client of mine has died, and his son and grandson are in town for the funeral." She turned to Jill while she continued speaking to Nicole. "Jill has been a tremendous help and support to me over this, and believe me I've needed her. Well, long story short, I was named my client's Executor, and I have to go to New York with the son and grandson to execute the will."

Jill's eyes widened. "Mom, when did this come up?"

"The lawyer read the will yesterday right after the funeral. A woman named Samantha Gordon in New York City was a good friend of Mikhail's. She's holding the inheritance in trust, apparently, as well as the answers to a lot of questions Erik and Jon want to ask her about Mikhail. Jill, I could really use your help and support in this, and I know Erik and Jon would welcome it too. They were talking about going to Riga Latvia, after New York, to uncover whatever family is left there."

"Riga, Latvia? Mikhail's home town?"

"That's right. You still have your passport, don't you?"

"What? You want me to go with you? Oh, Mom, I don't know if I'm up for anything quite like that."

Nicole had been listening with interest, and jumped in at that point. "I think it'd be just the thing to take your mind off your own situation for the time being, Jill. Why don't you do yourself and your mother a favor and go along?"

"At least think about it, Jill," Dee urged. "I don't want to leave you at a time like this, and this really does seem like the perfect solution for all of us."

"When would I have to make up my mind?"

Dee dropped her eyes to her hands folded in her lap. "They were going to call Samantha as soon as possible and make plans to meet with her, possibly within the next day or so."

"Wow." Jill shook her head. "Well, let me sleep on it. But I want you to go without me if I decide not to go, Mom. Promise?"

Now it was Dee's turn to shake her head. "Why don't we both sleep on it? We have a lot to think about. And besides, if you're with me on this trip, we'll talk about Karen as much as you need to. She's important to me, too."

"Sounds like a good idea to me," Nicole said with conviction. "I'm really impressed with the way you're both handling this situation. It's not easy under any circumstances. Dee, your daughter will be a nervous wreck as the date of her reunion with Karen gets closer. It's important for you to keep listening, keep supporting Jill, especially at that point. Cautious optimism will be the watch-word. For now, though, this could be the perfect distraction for both of you. Take your minds off it for awhile. Don't you think?"

Later that afternoon, Jill went to work after promising Dee she'd approach her boss about taking some time off as soon as possible. Dee went on to Eunice's office at the retirement home where she had dropped Erik and Jon. They were waiting outside on the grounds, and when they got into the car they confirmed that they had arranged for Eunice to take Mikhail's calls till further notice. Dee explained Jill's new developments, and they all agreed it was time for Dee to call Samantha and sound her out about a meeting.

It was 2:30 by the time Dee called, 5:30 Eastern Time.

"Yes, my dear Ms Sanders. I've been waiting for your call."

Dee's eyes widened and she turned to the men and gave them a perplexed shrug. "Um. I have Mikhail's son Erik and grandson Jon from Berlin here with me. Did Mikhail tell you about them?"

"Not about the grandson, no. But two years ago he received a letter from the Red Cross and called me about it. So I knew about the son. We decided together at that time that the trust I was holding for him in my name should probably go to the son upon his death."

"Yes. He changed his will after he and I went to Berlin and met his grandson. The will stipulated that."

"I'm glad. I wasn't sure how he had arranged it by now. We weren't in close touch over the years since he moved there to Seattle."

"Erik and Jon have so many questions for you. We'd like to make an appointment to meet with you in New York to talk all this over, at your convenience, of course."

"I expected as much. As soon as possible, then?" Her voice was brisk. "Let's say Friday afternoon at the Russian Tea Room in midtown Manhattan, 1:00."

"Let me check with the Mendenbergs." She put her hand over the receiver and relayed Sam's suggestion. They both agreed, and she turned back to the phone. "We'll be there, and we appreciate your time and cooperation so much. This has been a hard time for all of us."

"I'm sure. I'll make the reservation for lunch then." Her voice softened. "Tell me, my dear. Did Mikhail ever write his memoirs? He told me he was thinking about it the last time we talked."

"Yes, he did. That's why he hired me– I helped him write it. It's being considered by a publisher right now. It's one of the last things he did before he died."

"Interesting. Please bring a copy to me. I would truly appreciate that."

"I'll see to it."

The next morning Jill called Dee and told her she was able to get the time off and had decided she was glad to get away. Dee hurriedly made the travel arrangements, and on Thursday morning the four of them headed for Sea-Tac airport to catch a flight for New York City.

CHAPTER THIRTY-TWO

"The streets really *are* canyons," Jill exclaimed, her face bathed in wonder. "Every building is gigantic. They're so crowded together, and they go on forever! It's awesome." She stopped and twirled around slowly, her arms outstretched, her face turned up, her gaze barely reaching the tops of the buildings. Dee smiled with pleasure and pride watching her lovely daughter, glad all over again that she was with these three particular people, that the four of them were making this journey together.

They walked the few blocks from the hotel to the Russian Tea Room, passing one famous landmark after another. They had already ventured out earlier in the day, strolling down Broadway to 42nd Street, then back in the other direction and into Central Park a ways.

The days were at their longest this time of year, with a full moon as well. The evening before after dinner they had taken the elevator to the top of the Empire State Building, where they could see the island of Manhattan spread out in all directions. None of them had ever been to New York City, so each familiar scene and structure was a delight for them all. The Statue of Liberty, the twin towers of the World Trade Center, the lush greenery of Central Park.

"Carnegie Hall," Jill now breathed in awe.

They rounded a corner. "There's our destination, The Russian Tea Room." Jon pointed to a door set off at the top by a dark red awning. They went into the building and immediately heard the musical strains of violins. They moved toward the sound and approached the desk, where they gave Samantha Gordon's name to the host. He was dressed in Russian garb, and he smiled and nodded in recognition of the name, then led them to a cavernous, elegant room with high ceilings, decorated in dark red brocade. Waiters in flowing dark trousers tucked into shiny black boots, and white balloon-sleeved shirts accented with red brocade vests, moved between the tables, as did the wandering gypsy violin orchestra in similar costume.

Dee walked slowly with the others, following the host and gazing at all the enchantment around them: vivid color and old world splendor at its most lavish. She had read somewhere that the Russian Tea Room was a place where the ballet greats had congregated along with celebrities of all kinds. She speculated then that Sam must have been a ballet great. How tragic, Dee thought, if she was, that she was confined to a wheelchair now.

They moved toward a table near the center of the room where a trim elderly lady sat gazing at them with interest as they came near. Dee could see clearly that it was the older face of the woman in Mikhail's pictures. Her posture was erect and dignified, chin lifted slightly. Her iron gray hair was pulled back in a chignon at the nape of her neck, accenting her long, regal neck. Her icy blue-gray eyes penetrated, missing nothing, but the smile remained soft.

Dee gave her a returning smile. "Hello. I'm Dee Sanders. You must be Samantha."

"I am indeed. Delighted to meet you."

Dee introduced the others, and Sam acknowledged each person, but her eyes slid back to Erik's face and held there, a look of wistful intensity upon her face. "You do look so like your father," she whispered.

"So I have been told."

She nodded briskly, gestured with one arm. "Please. Sit. I cannot rise. They seated me here and took my wheelchair away until I'm ready to leave."

She sat at an oval table; Dee took her seat at Sam's right and Jill sat beside her; Erik sat across from them and Jon at the other end. The waiter arrived to fill their water glasses and leave menus, then strolled away. Dee became aware of the delicate teacups and plates at each place setting. Speechless with awe, she simply gazed at the fragile china pieces, then her eyes swept the room once more, taking in everything in sight. Erik, Jon and Jill followed suit, and Sam seemed content to let the silence lengthen, listening instead to the murmur of nearby diners, the clink of china and crystal, the lovely violin strains.

At last Sam spoke. "A lovely room, isn't it? I don't come here so often anymore, but Mikhail and I used to frequent it in its heyday, throughout the '60's. It was opened by Russian immigrants in the 1920's for the ballet elite, of which I was one. A long time ago. A proud history." She paused, and her voice turned melancholy. "I understand the present owner is hoping to sell now."

Dee opened her large shoulder bag and pulled out the manila envelope with Mikhail's manuscript. "As requested," she smiled.

"Oh, thank you Dee. I shall read this with great interest."

"I have to say though, he didn't mention you—in fact he said very little about life in the United States, or his childhood in Riga, Latvia. He concentrated mainly on the years as an entertainer in Riga, then the war years, especially in Berlin and Prague."

Sam glanced pointedly at Erik. "Nothing about his son either, I assume."

Erik shook his head. "We're still sorting out the details of all that. It seemed he lived a full life in each of the stages. Riga, Berlin, New York, Seattle. And he left a great deal out. We were hoping you could fill in some of the gaps for us."

Samantha inclined her head. "I am happy to. But first I am curious about you, Erik. Please tell me of your background, and especially your meeting with your father."

"I never met him," Erik answered flatly. "I arrived in Seattle to meet him on Thursday, one week ago yesterday. And I learned that he had died two nights before."

The Berlin Connection

Sam frowned, shaking her head sadly. "How tragic. I didn't realize that."

"Dee met me at the airport with the news. It was a shock. So much has happened in such a short time."

The waiter came and took their orders, then Erik continued his narrative, with Dee and Jon filling in some details. Erik explained his early childhood in Riga, his background in Berlin, how Mikhail and Dee had traveled to Berlin and met Jon, and what had happened since then.

"Staggering," Sam remarked, blinking rapidly, lowering her head for a moment. When she lifted her eyes, she gave Erik her full attention, her expression soft, yearning. "It is the strangest sensation when I look at you, Erik. You bring him back to life for me. We were close at one time, you know." She closed her eyes briefly. "What can I do to help bring Mikhail into sharper focus for you—at least a bit?"

No one spoke for a moment. All four faces were turned toward Erik, who had lowered his gaze. Seconds ticked by. At last his eyes settled back on her face. "Did he talk about his youth in Riga, his life with my mother? That part is written in his book, but we can't understand why so little was said about his family. For instance, my mother did not turn to her parents when she was alone and expecting me.

"Dee and I found a letter from Mikhail's brother Nick, describing how the family had been deported to Germany in 1942, so that explains why she couldn't turn to them when she found herself pregnant. But it's all so sad. She met Aleks Mendenberg on the street one day by chance and he took her in. And that set the course of my life."

"And mine, too, for that matter," Jon added.

"Can you shed any light on those matters?" Erik asked.

"Your mother and father were two young people in love, Erik," she began. "But it was more than that. They clung to each other. He told me they felt alone against the world. They felt safe together. There were deep wounds in both their families of origin. I'm not surprised he didn't touch on that in his book."

"You mean it was more than their not having support?" Dee asked.

"Mikhail's family disapproved strongly of his whole circus lifestyle. They never understood it. His parents went to one or two performances, but his older brother had always belittled every interest Mikhail had. And then he became resentful whenever their parents showed the least bit of support toward Mikhail. So Anita did not get to know the family in the normal sense of the word." Her face tightened and she took a sip of water. "But the hardest part for Mikhail was the fear that his family would be deported to Germany–and they were, after he left. He learned later that Nick fought on the Russian front for Hitler while his parents were in a prison camp. After the war they arrived back in Riga, only to find themselves under Communism. Many people fled to the west, but Nick and his parents came back to the only home they had ever considered home—and life became hell for them there. So Mikhail felt guilty about that. He had escaped to the west."

"So his family could not have taken my mother in."

Sam shook her head sadly. "I doubt they even knew of her pregnancy. She may have met them once or twice, but when he called me about the Red Cross letter he received on your behalf, Erik, he and I speculated that they probably never knew of your existence.

"And as to your mother's family, there was abuse there, in the early years. That's why she came to Riga at such a young age. She never looked back."

"There was so much sadness in her life," Erik reflected, his expression a mixture of anger and compassion. Dee could see he was fighting tears, and she wanted to reach out to him. His hands clenched and unclenched on the table. "I sensed it always. She never spoke of her childhood, and seldom of the early years in Riga. And I can guess why she never told me Mikhail was my father until she was on her deathbed. She was afraid Aleks would sense the bond we shared that left him out, and use it against me."

Sam placed her hand on his. "They did have a great love, Erik. Even though she felt she couldn't talk to you about it sooner than she did. Never doubt that. I'm sure it brought her enormous comfort. They would have married if the war had not intervened and taken him away forever."

Erik's voice broke as he asked, "And you? Would you have married Mikhail?"

"Ah. That's another story, my dear."

Their lunches came at that moment, and they enjoyed the savory aromas and relished the flavors of Beef Stroganoff and Russian piroshkies, while the talk centered on New York City, places and events of interest, the history of the Russian Tea Room and Sam's early career as a ballerina. When they had finished, Sam pushed her plate off to the side, retrieved a cigarette from an elaborately embossed gold case, placed it in an enamel holder, and lit it with a flourish. Then she began her story about her life with Mikhail.

"I met Mikhail in 1963. He was an acrobatics coach and instructor and I was a teacher of ballet here in Manhattan. We did have a wonderful, rich relationship, full of fun and common interests. But to answer your question from before, Erik, neither of us was interested in marriage. We each had our schools to run, our students to teach. It was a full life. We were close, however. And socially we enjoyed the company of another couple, who were married. Roger and Daphne Thorne."

"They must be the people we saw in several of Mikhail's snapshots with you," Dee offered.

"Yes. They had a combination dance and acrobatic school. Our schools were all near one another's, and we were friendly competitors. There were plenty of students to go around– we all enjoyed a stellar reputation. As I said, we spent a great deal of time together socially when we weren't busy with our respective careers.

"Over the years we went on trips together–Paris, London, Madrid. In 1972 we went to Munich. You know what happened there."

"The Israeli hostage crisis, yes," Erik supplied. "A tragedy."

Sam nodded, crushing out her cigarette absently. "It was sobering, to say the least. We realized that anything could happen at any time, to any of us. That sort of thing. After that, we all began to question the wisdom of traveling without some kind of insurance. We had many discussions about it over the next three years. Neither Mikhail nor I had children," she looked at Erik, "but Roger and Daphne had one daughter. Sylvia. She was seventeen that year. She was covered as beneficiary in a life insurance policy of theirs already. But we all agreed that year that we each needed to buy an extra life insurance policy. Because of the schools, you see. Roger named Mikhail his beneficiary and vice versa, and Daphne and I did the same. We all trusted each other completely."

She paused and looked around the room. The others shifted uncomfortably in their seats. Dee glanced at Erik and saw the look of apprehension on his face. She knew whatever was coming was going to be bad.

"The following year, shortly after the 1976 Montreal Olympics, we were coming back from a weekend on Long Island," Sam continued in a monotone, her eyes staring sightlessly past Erik's shoulder. "Mikhail was driving. We'd stopped for dinner and drinks. It was almost dark by the time we got back on the road. He tried to pass a car. We hit an oncoming car head on. The two people in the other car lived through it. But Roger and Daphne were in the back seat. Neither of them was wearing a seat belt, and they were both thrown from the car and killed. My legs were crushed.

I don't know why, but Mikhail hardly had a scratch on him."

She stopped talking a moment.

"How tragic," Jill murmured.

Sam turned her eyes to Jill and nodded briskly. "Yes. There was a criminal investigation. Sylvia was eighteen by then and saw to it. She was devastated, and her feelings came out in rage. Mikhail went to trial. He was exonerated of all charges because it was dusk and the oncoming car hadn't turned on his lights yet, and it could not be proven that Mikhail had been drinking in excess. But of course he was devastated as well. Two dear friends dead, my own life ruined, and he naturally blamed himself. He was driving, after all.

"Sylvia threatened a civil suit when the criminal charges didn't stick. She knew about the insurance policy and was outraged that Mikhail stood to gain a million dollars upon the death of her father. That's when he signed the money over to me as a trust and made me promise to use it if I needed it for medical care or further surgeries, or home health care. I inherited Daphne's million dollars, so naturally I was fine financially. But Mikhail and I were never the same as far as our relationship was concerned. And his career suffered because of the publicity of the trial. Even though he was found innocent he decided he had to start over. So he moved to Seattle."

"Samantha, I don't know what to say," Erik stared at his hands, braced palms down on the table. "Such tragedy. Such waste. And Sylvia? Are you in touch with her yet? That was almost 20 years ago now. She'd be—what? 35 or so?"

The Berlin Connection

She stirred and sighed wearily. "She's moved on. She was terribly spoiled, Mikhail and I thought. But she didn't deserve to lose her parents like that, of course. She inherited a sizeable amount, married young, divorced, traveled a great deal, part of a jet set crowd, you know. Never had to hold a job or wanted to develop a career to my knowledge. I lost touch with her some years ago."

"So Mikhail had tragedy in Europe when he had to leave everyone and everything behind after the war, and then again when he had to leave New York after the accident," Dee murmured. "It certainly explains a lot. Why he didn't want to have pictures for his book. He didn't want Sylvia to think he was capitalizing on his life story in any way."

"Of course," Jon said with some astonishment. "It also explains why he lived the life of a recluse– in that squalid rooming house in Seattle. And why he didn't want to move out of the retirement home once he was healthy again."

"Healthy again?" Sam asked.

"Something happened to his health about three years ago, and that's when he moved to the retirement home. No one there knows exactly what, but he was in terrible shape, I guess," Dee said. "Near death."

Sam made a clicking sound with her tongue. "He probably was trying to drink himself to death after he retired," she said with resignation. "He always drank too much, and I was afraid that would happen once he sold his gymnastics school in Seattle. That school was his means of survival when he moved there. I'm only guessing, of course, but it fits with everything I knew about him. He had such an ego, our Mikhail. He couldn't stand to face those situations that made him feel any loss of control, and there were many, especially as he aged, I imagine–so he drank. Don't get me wrong. I loved him dearly. But he was deeply scarred. Deeply flawed, by life."

A thought flashed through Dee's mind and she sat there stunned. *"It was the drinking that killed him,"* her mother had said, about her own grandfather. Whatever failures and humiliations he had faced as he aged didn't give him the right to humiliate his son at the end, she thought with indignation. At least Erik hadn't had to deal with the deathbed verbal attack that her father'd had to face. Maybe it was better for Erik to be left with other people's impressions of Mikhail instead of his own, like her father had.

But then she thought about the Mikhail she had known. He had revealed so much of the good and strong sides of himself to her, seemed to trust her so openly. And she had never seen him take a drink in all the times she had been with him. He must have conquered some of the darker sides of himself that he'd wrestled with.

Well, she mused, doesn't everyone have dark sides they don't really understand or want others to see? I don't even understand myself that well sometimes.

Sam was gazing at Erik, the glistening of her eyes revealing her depth of feeling. "And you, my dear young man," she said softly, "I want to thank you. And express gratitude on Mikhail's behalf as well. You gave him his purpose once he regained his health. He found out about you, and he decided to write his memoirs for you," she turned her eyes to Jon, "and for you, and your children."

A chill of understanding and recognition welled in Erik. He knew something about that drive, that single-minded purpose to survive. In spite of the oppression of Communism, he and Jon had found a way to emerge as survivors. In spite of the attempts at oppression by Mikhail's family of origin, he had found a way to express his yearning for physical excellence, and that took him to new beginnings after the war. Erik shook his head slowly, his eyes drifting upward to the high, ornate ceiling, his breathing deep and full.

Before they left her at the Russian Tea Room, Sam told them she had made an appointment at her bank Monday morning at 11:00 to sign over the document that Mikhail had left in trust for her and they agreed to meet there. "It's been drawing interest all this time," she said with a smile. She also encouraged them to complete the journey and go to Riga after that, all four together if at all possible. "Perhaps you'll tie up many of the rest of the loose ends if you talk to Mikhail's older brother, if he's still alive."

"He sent the one letter to Mikhail in the 1960's. We can try and find the family through that address. That's all we have to go on," Dee said.

"Regardless, you'll also get a feel for the climate of that time and place before the war broke out, see for yourselves the environment in which he could thrive. And you, Erik—your early childhood was spent there. I imagine you'd want to see some of the old places you remember."

"Perhaps. I was only seven or eight when I left Riga. I doubt I'd remember anything much."

"You might be surprised," Sam replied.

In spite of her imperial bearing, Dee could see that she was a warm and caring person. Before they parted, Sam easily drew out both Jon and Jill, expressing a natural curiosity about their lives and interests.

After three hours together, Sam pleaded exhaustion. She told them she had an assistant coming with her wheelchair to bring her home, so with warm thanks, they rose and left her. Outside the building, they talked over their plans for the next few days.

"When do we each have to be home?" Dee wondered. "Are we all in agreement to go on to Riga as Sam suggested?"

"I really should be back in Berlin by the end of next week," Jon said. "I think that leaves time for Riga. Two or three days should be enough."

Erik nodded slowly, deep in thought. "I need to take stock of the business in Berlin, as well," Erik said. "Would you ladies be able to accompany us there from Riga, and then fly on to Seattle from Berlin?"

Dee and Jill exchanged a look, then Jill said, "I have two weeks." She lifted her shoulders. "Works for me," she said with a grin.

CHAPTER THIRTY-THREE

Jill and Jon were eager to explore the city, perhaps take a tour. Erik and Dee opted to head toward Central Park for a more relaxed wandering through the wooded pathways. They all agreed to meet back at the hotel by 8:00 p.m. for dinner.

Dee and Erik went through the south entrance to the park and headed down an inviting path. They strolled awhile in companionable silence under huge broad-leafed trees. After a time Erik remarked, "This forest reminds me a bit of the one in Berlin where Liesl and I used to go. It was there that we talked over all the problems of the world, agreed on how they could be solved, and fell in love in the process. It was the best time of my life."

"So you married your best friend," Dee observed.

With a smile, Erik nodded. "She proved herself to me, over and over again. Without Liesl, I never would have experienced faith and trust."

They moved on down the path through the trees, enjoying the sights and sounds of their environment—birdsong, dappled sunlight filtering through the leaves, even trickling water from somewhere not too far away.

"I was glad to know that Mikhail and Sam had a loving relationship," Dee commented wistfully. "I just wish it hadn't ended in such tragedy. What a horrible story she had to tell."

"But it explained so much, Dee." Erik's voice held quiet confidence. "From what I now understand about Mikhail, he'd have wanted to contribute something positive to society. He was doing that, enjoying his life in America—then it all turned on him. The very freedom he had found that represented opportunity for a better life—driving a car, vacation trips with friends, even drinking too much—was the means to his destruction—or so he must have decided after the crash. The only thing that still served him well was his work; acrobatics and gymnastics training that he could draw on from his youth. And so he moved to Seattle, and didn't dare attempt any kind of life beyond his work."

"And then he found out about you, and that motivated him to get his life—the best parts of it—on record for you. That became his purpose."

They fell silent again as Dee pondered what Erik had said. It struck her that Mikhail's purpose at the end of his life stood in stark contrast with her own grandfather's end. She glanced at Erik, hesitating. It was one thing to give opinions about what was happening to the people she cared about, but expressing her own vulnerable feelings about her own background felt like moving from the shelter of the forest into open terrain during a war. But trust had built rapidly between them, so she ventured softly, "My grandfather left a different legacy in my family. In a funny way, learning about it set me free."

Erik turned his eyes to her, slowing his pace. "How so?"

"He died when I was two," she began. "He had lived a hard life; tried to start several businesses that failed during the depression in the 1930's, had several children to raise, and started drinking to ease his troubles. As his children grew, my dad, the oldest of seven, had to take on more responsibility to keep food on the table, keep the family going. And yet it was never enough for his father. He criticized every effort his son made." She gave Erik a wistful smile. "My parents told me most of this not too long ago, shortly before my dad died." She wandered over to a park bench and sank down upon it. "By the time my grandfather died he was a bitter, destructive man."

"But how did that set you free?" Erik asked as he sat down beside her.

She bit her lip and looked away. The movement of a squirrel in the underbrush caught her eye. She watched it scamper away before she continued. "Growing up myself, I yearned for a dad who'd talk with me, show an interest in me, value me. I thought I must be doing something wrong because he always seemed just out of reach. I married a man who also was distant, distracted, who had similar responses, or lack of responses. I guess it was a choice I made. It seemed comfortable and familiar to me. I was a prisoner of my own subconscious." She shook her head and closed her eyes briefly. "Anyway, I was set free from that particular life sentence when my dad told me about a visit he made to the hospital the night his father died. When he came into the hospital room, Grandpa started shouting abuse at him, told him what a worthless son he'd been all his life. And then he started coughing uncontrollably, and then he died, right then and there. And he left my dad with that terrible legacy."

"Those early impressions stay with us sometimes, longer than we realize," Erik said in a reasonable, sincere voice. "No wonder your father was distant. He was afraid of saying or doing the wrong thing, afraid of the damage he might cause."

She turned her eyes to Erik's face. He was looking at her with tenderness and compassion, and relief caressed her like a soft breeze. "That's what I decided, too," she said. "My dad gave me such a gift—to open up to me like that at the end. I don't know why my husband Dennis was so closed off, but I know I unconsciously chose him because he was like my dad."

"And now you're free of that unconscious reaction?" he asked quietly.

"I think so. At least I understand why I have it, and what the family background is. Anyway, I think I could accept Dennis now as a true friend, just as he is. And I suppose I could accept a man as a friend who'd reveal more of himself as time went on, as well."

Erik put his arm around her shoulder. "You brought out many of Mikhail's thoughts and feelings in the process of writing the book. You're good at that, Dee. And because of Liesl, I trust you. That is my triumph over the oppressive society I came from. So we're both contributing something positive and productive–to each other, and to the world, are we not?"

A flood of emotions passed over her. He could not have said anything more meaningful to her. "We are indeed. Thank you, Erik." She closed her eyes again, settling into the curve of his arm. They sat together in comfortable silence for a time, and then they rose and continued down the path together.

At dinner that evening, the four laughed a lot and made energetic plans for the weekend in New York. And later in their hotel room as Dee and Jill got ready for bed, they talked of the issue of legacy, just as Dee had with Erik. Their conversation revolved for a time around Karen and the upcoming meeting in September.

"I've been talking so much for so long about wanting to feel whole, wanting a sense of my own identity to come out of this search for Karen." Jill was sitting on the bed, pillow propped against the headboard, watching Dee at the mirror as she applied lotion to her face. "But now this new information about my birth father—how do I face Karen if I remind her of him, Mom? What if I look like him? What if I have a son someday who looks like him? How is Karen supposed to deal with that?" She shuddered.

Dee walked over to the bed and propped the other pillow up so she could sit beside her daughter. She put an arm around her shoulder. "I think you're wonderful for thinking of Karen, Jill. That shows your true compassion. You'll never be anything like that guy who raped her on what she thought would be an innocent date."

"But I have half his genes!" Jill cried.

"Concentrate on Karen in this, honey. What strength she had, to go through with the pregnancy! I'm so grateful to her for that! She knew it wasn't your fault for being conceived, and she wanted you to have a good, positive life. And you do! And you know the same thing about her." Dee sighed. "Life is complicated, isn't it? At lunch with Sam, I could see Erik and Jon both struggling to understand what she told them about Mikhail's background and weaknesses. I mean, they already had ideas and impressions about Mikhail, and now they have to fit these new ideas and impressions into the mix. And how does that alter how they see themselves?"

"You mean Mikhail's drinking to escape his problems?"

"I guess. I mean, like Karen, he really had a lot to deal with, didn't he?"

"He did."

They sat side by side, eyes straight ahead, both sensing that this conversation might be too hard for them to face one another. "But even *I* got mixed up about my identity growing up, Jill—and I was raised in my genetic family."

"What do you mean?"

"I didn't get enough of the background story to feel I had a complete identity," Dee answered. "We are all evolving." And so once again she described the visit her dad made to her grandfather's hospital room, and how it reverberated down through the generations. "I had always wondered why I couldn't seem to get close to your dad or your grandpa," she finished. "And it made me feel so inadequate, like there was something wrong with me."

Beside her, Jill sat in silence for a time, mulling that over. "I guess I see what you mean," she finally said. "But your divorce was so traumatic on me. I felt like you and Dad were so self-centered not to see how badly it affected me. I remember the tension, the arguments; I remember you sobbing and Dad sitting in stoic silence. And I went a little crazy reacting to the stress of all that. I remember you telling me that an unhappy marriage was more damaging to me than divorce, but I never agreed with that. After the divorce I felt abandoned, cast adrift."

"But we tried so hard, both of us, to be there for you," Dee cried, distressed.

"I know you did. I just felt that way anyway. I guess that's one reason why I wanted to search for my birth mother." Jill turned confused, sorrowful eyes to Dee. "Why couldn't you have stayed together, Mom? Why was Dad's being too distant so hard to take?"

Dee dropped her eyes to her hands folded tightly in her lap. "I guess that's what I'm trying to tell you. Maybe if I had known the full story of my own background, I wouldn't have reacted to his distance so badly, and then we might have gotten along better over the years." She sighed wearily. "At least we're friends now, even if we couldn't live together, and I think the counseling we got helped us all to adjust to the divorce, didn't it?"

"I'm just saying it was a rough patch any way you look at it. I was eighteen, and had a good job, and a good start at life, but still, it was so hard for me ..."

"I know." Dee gathered her daughter into her arms and they both gave in to the tears. "We're still healing and learning, aren't we? That's a lifelong process, I guess."

Jill nodded, sniffling. "You were right, Mom," her tone of voice through her tears sounded heartbreakingly cynical. "This is a terrific way to distract me from the frustration of waiting for the reunion with Karen." She rose and moved quickly over to the sink, grabbed a tissue and blew her nose.

"We're both on emotional overload, aren't we?"

Jill nodded, came and sank down beside Dee on the bed again with a sigh that was heavy with sadness. "I see how I need other things to fill the time while I wait, but I think I want to balance this kind of talk with some fun tomorrow, okay?"

The weekend with Erik and Jon was filled with enjoyable excursions deeper into familiar landmarks in New York City: a carriage ride in Central Park, an elevator to the restaurant at the top of one of the twin towers of the World Trade Center, a ferry to the Statue of Liberty, then tours through several museums. By the time the weekend was over they realized they had barely scratched the surface and agreed to meet back at the top of the Empire State Building a year later, so they could continue their tour together.

"Just like 'Sleepless in Seattle,'" Jill said. "I loved that movie. It's all engineered by the kid, and you don't know until the last minute whether they'll get together or not."

"Great scenery of Seattle too, by the way," Dee said.

On Monday morning after making reservations for a flight to Riga, Latvia, they arrived at the appointed bank and the appointed time, finding that Sam was already there. The transaction took little time in fact, transferring funds from Sam's account to Erik's in Berlin after the will was verified and signatures were notarized. They thanked Sam again and she wished them well, and the next morning they caught the flight to Riga.

They landed in Copenhagen for a connecting flight to Riga. "Remember in Mikhail's book," Dee commented, "how he took an entertainer's tour with a circus one summer as a youth before the war? He got stranded in Copenhagen."

"He made a great many foolish mistakes on that trip, as I recall," Erik said with a grin. "Like getting lost on the way back from Tivoli Gardens and not being able to find his way to his hotel. And he missed the connection with his departing ship because he was supposed to meet someone downtown who never showed up. Those were happy, inconsequential, carefree mistakes. The kind of mistakes a young man makes gladly, just for the adventure of it."

"He had a good life during that time," Dee agreed. "And maybe we'll see something of the best parts of his life as a boy in Riga."

"What do you remember of your own childhood in Riga?" Jon asked his father.

"Not much." Erik's tone was suddenly wary. "My father was harsh, my mother sad. The muddled period during and after the war reflected itself in our family, I think."

They flew through clouds on most of the flight from Copenhagen to Riga, and as they descended toward the city the clouds became towering columns and canyons interspersed with tufts of cotton balls. Dee was disappointed she couldn't see much of Riga as they approached. She got an impression through the clouds of flat land that stretched in every direction. Then they touched down smoothly and eventually found their way into the rundown terminal, where they went through customs and found a taxi to take them into the city.

CHAPTER THIRTY-FOUR

Erik knew enough Latvian and Russian to get by for them all, and Dee felt herself relax as she sat beside Jill in the taxi's back seat and enjoyed the scenery. The driver pointed out landmarks and enthusiastically gave details in Latvian; Erik, sitting next to him in the passenger seat, translated for them.

"Many people still speak mostly Russian," he said as they rode across the bridge that spanned the River Daugava. "But Latvians are proud to be able to speak their native language again." From the bridge they could see the baroque skyline of the Old City where Mikhail had lived his first twenty years. Dee was able to make out the tapered, towering ornamental spire of St. Peter's Church that he had described in his life story. His voice came back to her. *"I saw with my own eyes, all three tiers of the church spire, burning like a torch during the first Russian occupation of 1940,"* he had said. *"I read it wasn't rebuilt until the 1970's."*

"I remember this river, this skyline," Erik's subdued voice brought her back. His face was closed, grim. They drove through the narrow cobblestone streets, observing buildings in bad repair everywhere, crumbling and dark with soot. Little restoration was visible, but Dee caught glimpses of former glory and a sense of magnificence, reminding her of the Paris she and Dennis had visited all those years before.

The taxi driver was speaking non-stop and Erik translated as fast as he could, telling of the emerging national pride of the native Latvians, even reporting an eager anticipation of the 800th anniversary of the founding of the city of Riga, some seven years into the future. "They're already planning huge song and dance festivals, just like the ones Mikhail participated in as a young entertainer before the war that he described in his manuscript," he said.

They passed a huge central park, lushly green and inviting. Dee recognized within on a wide plaza the tall, tapered stone pillar of the Freedom Monument that Mikhail had described. Dee remembered his words vividly as they passed the structure. *"During the first Russian occupation in 1940 I met a young woman who had just been released from six months in jail,"* he had said. *"When I asked her why she had been arrested, she told me Russian soldiers had caught her placing a wreath of red roses at the base of the Freedom Monument. She screamed and cried as they dragged her off."*

A few blocks later the taxi pulled up to the front of an impressive, elegant building about four stories tall. It had been freshly painted in a pastel green. Dee noticed all the connecting buildings had also been painted recently, in lively pastel pink, yellow and blue. "Here's the hotel he recommends," Erik told them, so they got out and collected their luggage, then climbed the steps and passed through the large, elaborately carved door into a dark, narrow lobby.

Dee gazed around, her spirits dampened by the peeling paint, and the water stains and grime on the walls and furniture that faced them. She knew it had only been three years since Latvia had been declared a free and independent nation, but she could also see it would take many years before anyone could distinguish progress after the damage that had been done under Soviet dominance. On the other hand, even the taxi driver had not curbed his enthusiasm about the better future Latvians anticipate as a free country. Give them time, she thought. They'll make it.

While Erik checked them in she glanced around the dim, shabby foyer. Would this place ever be ready for tourists? she wondered. The ornate, high ceilings were draped with electric cords that trailed from light fixtures and looped to wall sconces, then into adjoining rooms. Dee wondered how long before resources were in place to provide the things she took for granted in America. Would Latvians even know what kinds of useful, efficient items to buy, even if they did become more available? Obviously there'd be no television in their rooms, no advertising to inform Latvians any time soon.

Erik turned from the desk. "There's no restaurant here," he said. "But I'm told there are some two or three blocks down."

"I'm so tired," Jill moaned. "It's been a long flight from New York City, especially with the stopover in Copenhagen."

"Give us 30 minutes to refresh ourselves a little," Dee agreed. "Then we'll meet in the lobby to explore the city before it gets dark."

Dee and Jill's stark hotel room smelled slightly musty as they entered. It had two cot-style single beds, a two-drawer desk, a narrow closet with three wire hangers, tall windows with water-stained curtains, and again, cords draped from light fixtures on the high ceilings. Walls and corners had peeling paint, but the beds and bathroom were clean if rudimentary. Jill flopped on one bed, watching while her mother put a few things into the closet.

"I understand Erik's urgency, Mom, truly. I feel the same way about Karen," she said, her voice wistful. "I'm curious about her family just the same way Erik is curious about uncovering people here in Riga. But right now I'm just so tired."

Dee turned to gaze at her daughter. She bit back an admonishing retort and said instead, "I'm glad you're here, Jill. We all need your support."

After a time they went back to the lobby where Erik and Jon were already waiting.

"Can you ask where Salamonski Circus is? And maybe we can get our bearings and find how far away Mikhail's family address is for tomorrow," Dee suggested.

"I got the information already," Erik answered with a grin. "The circus building is no longer called

Salamonski, but perhaps we'll recognize it when we get there."

They walked along a narrow cobblestone street with tall, grandiose buildings on either side that flanked narrow sidewalks, allowing little sunlight to penetrate. The effect was gloomy but elegant, even magnificent. Dee sensed again that even though there was an enormous amount of work to be done on the gray, worn out buildings, the enthusiasm of the people would motivate them and get the job done. It might take years, but the potential was already here, waiting to be cleaned and polished. Then the tourists would discover this lovely city, bringing in much needed revenue. Again she heard Mikhail's voice, saw his erect stance, hands on hips: *"It will take Eastern Europeans some time to figure out what exactly their newfound freedom means, and how to use it to best advantage."*

Erik guided them by means of the map, and as they moved along Dee continued to feel Mikhail's presence strongly. It was all just as he had described it, even though when he had told his story his descriptions of the city had seemed larger than life to her. The Riga of his youth had been immersed in his own warm, bright memories of the best time of his life. He'd probably be dismayed to see what the Soviets had done to his memories, she thought sadly.

In contrast, Dee reflected, from the little Erik had said, his own memories of his early childhood in this city were bleak and dismal.

"Do you remember where your family home was?" Dee asked Erik.

"Somewhere farther out of the city, I think," he replied, smiling thinly. He said nothing further.

After two or three long blocks, they came to a corner café and went inside. Following a great deal of trial and error with the waiter, they managed to order a meal, which turned out to be savory stroganoff, much like what they'd had at the Russian Tea Room. When it came time to pay, they learned with dismay that none of their bank cards were acceptable. Erik pulled out some American bills and suddenly the man's eyes lit up. He gladly accepted what amounted to ten dollars for the four of them—the amount stretched to the equivalent of a hundred dollars here, the man assured them with effusive gratitude. He kept shaking Erik's hand and nodding with a wide grin, and they left the café laughing together, exhilarated. They had successfully crossed that hurdle.

The shadows had lengthened further but there was still plenty of daylight left, and they continued on in search of the circus building. Erik calculated from the map. "It's only a few blocks from where we are now," he told them. Few vehicles and people were on the street, and they saw no signs of workers leaving offices to head home. What few people they encountered had cheerful, pleasant appearances if well-worn, unpressed clothing.

"There's no corner groceries," Jill observed.

"I'm sure there's a central market where everyone shops, as there are in many large European cities," Jon replied.

They turned a corner and found the circus building halfway down the block. They approached it slowly and stood in stunned silence.

"I never dreamed it connects on both sides with the adjoining buildings," Dee said. "Somehow I'd pictured it standing alone, with a vast space all around it for—what? Parking? I'm just shocked at how small and inconspicuous it is."

As on the other streets they'd seen, all the buildings along the block were attached. Dee and Erik had seen the circus building in a picture or two in Mikhail's collection, but those pictures had not been taken from far enough away to see how small it seemed in conjunction to the others next to it. And all those years ago the building in the pictures had been almost white concrete, scrubbed clean. Now it was dark with soot, as all the buildings were, and the roof was dingy red tile, worn away over the years by the elements. The only distinctions the circus building had were the round pointed dome and two gray, dismal-looking performing horses prancing on their hind legs at the top of the flat part of the roof, next to the word "Cirks".

"So this is Salamonski Circus," Erik said in hushed tones.

"You're as surprised as I am? Your mother never brought you here as a child?" Dee asked.

"Never. I suspect my father wouldn't have allowed it." He moved forward to try the door but it was locked, and there were no signs announcing when it was open to the public. He asked a passing pedestrian if he knew when the circus opened and the man just shrugged and hurried on. So they took a few pictures and headed back toward the hotel to settle in for the night. They were all exhausted by this time.

Dee and Jill's hotel room had turned warm and muggy when they walked inside, so they opened windows to the cool night air. There were no screens on the windows but Dee decided it didn't matter. Their room was facing the rear of the building and as they gazed down into the courtyard, they were dismayed to see piles of concrete rubble throughout the area below.

"The pretty paint in front is just a façade," Jill commented. "Depressing. It sure makes me appreciate my own country."

During the night Dee was groggily aware of buzzing and shrieking near her ears, and when she awoke she could see the effects. Both she and Jill had angry red welts all over their arms, legs and faces.

"Yikes—they've been munching on us all night!" Jill cried.

"We've got to get something in a market," Dee said. "Riga mosquitoes must carry different toxins our bodies have no immunity against."

When they reached the lobby, again, the men were already waiting for them. They both gasped when they saw the angry red welts both women suffered. They gave them a good amount of sympathy and just the right amount of gentle teasing and then they all went in search of a restaurant. Over breakfast, while they talked about what they might or might not encounter at the address where they hoped to find the Sommers family, Dee absently scratched her arm, feeling unsettled as she realized how Erik's own cheerless memories contrasted in a disturbing way with his search for clues to Mikhail's carefree youth. But she knew from the way he interacted with them that he appreciated their presence. They were all great companions and they were all lending encouragement and support in the spirit of adventure. The encounter with Sam in New York had yielded real enlightenment. Dee fervently hoped this part of the search would be successful in equal measure, and what they learned at least give Erik some comfort and insight.

After breakfast they found a pharmacy and bought some salve, which the women applied with relief. Then they went in search of telephone directories for Riga, but found none. Erik attempted to get a number for the Sommers family on the phone, but soon hung up in frustration and pulled out the worn, aging letter from Mikhail's brother. "All we can do now is find the return address on this envelope and knock on the door."

Since the address was not far from the restaurant and Erik was beginning to get a feel for the Old City, it did not take them long to find the building. It was one connected with others along the entire block of the street, large and imposing with four floors and many apartment units. Unfortunately, there was no unit number on the envelope Erik carried and as they peered inside, they saw a small, narrow hallway with a run down, cluttered and dark staircase.

"You wait here on the sidewalk," Erik decided. "I'll go from apartment to apartment until I find someone who answers my knock."

Erik walked unsteadily down the dark, narrow, cluttered hallway, knocking at every door. No one answered. He climbed the stairs to the second floor, picking his way over piles of debris as he went.

Knocking on the doors again yielded no response. He climbed to the third floor, relieved that the others were not with him. The smell of damp mold was stronger the higher he went. This was discouraging business, he thought grimly, shaking his head. He stopped a moment and closed his eyes; at once his thoughts settled on Dee, a fleeting image of her smile. He felt a sensory stirring and rubbed his arms, glad she was nearby, grateful she had made this journey with him. A feeling of longing rose in him, so powerful it almost took his breath away. He yearned to hold her, to cherish her, to protect and comfort her, to build her confidence. He almost turned and went back down the stairs to the street where his future waited, and he looked around blindly, wondering why he was here, rummaging in the past in this dark, grimy hallway on the third floor of a building in Riga, Latvia. But it would be foolish not to see this through. There were only three units on each of the four floors, after all.

    He knocked on the nearest door and waited. After a time he heard some shuffling noises inside, and then the door opened wide. An extremely old, frail, emaciated man stared at him with squinting, blinking eyes. Before Erik could say anything, the old man's eyes widened, his face contorted with rage. "So you came back to see your family, Mikhail! Well, look carefully—this is all that is left of the family you betrayed."

CHAPTER THIRTY-FIVE

Shaken, Erik asked, "You are Nickolai Sommers?"

"Of course I am Nick, your brother. Little wonder you do not recognize me. I am almost eighty. A few years have passed, eh?" He pointed a gnarled finger at Erik, his eyes wild. "You are not welcome here!" he railed with a hostility that reminded Erik of a cornered rat. "You disgraced the family. You became an entertainer—an entertainer!– while I supported the family business with devotion and loyalty. You entertained Nazis while I was forced to fight on the Russian front. Do you have no idea how badly your family needed you? You turned your back on us and escaped to the west, to your own selfish pursuits. How did you find life in America, Mikhail? Have you grown rich?" He spat on the floor with contempt.

The Berlin Connection

From his shirt pocket Erik pulled the letter Nick had sent Mikhail thirty years before, and with a trembling hand he thrust it toward Nick. "I am not Mikhail," he said, willing his voice to be calm. "I am a son from Berlin whom Mikhail never knew. I found this letter from you among his belongings at his home in Seattle, in America."

Nick eyed the letter with suspicion, reached out slowly as if it was contaminated, then he snatched it away and peered at the writing on the envelope. His eyes slid back to Erik's face. "I wrote this letter, yes. Our parents were sent to a German prison camp in 1942 and I had to fight on the Russian front for Hitler, while you were entertaining Nazis! We lost everything!" His mouth distorted as he bellowed, and Erik could see stained and missing teeth. "Then when we came home after the war we had to live under Communism. Life was never the same in Riga, and you went to America! I was loyal to the State and got nothing in return." The words continued to pour from him. "Our parents were sent to Siberia when Father protested Soviet control. My wife died, my children deserted me."

Erik tried again, speaking slowly. "My name is Erik. I never knew Mikhail, but he was my father. He died before I could meet him. I was hoping you could tell me something about his early years."

Nick's rheumy eyes turned sly and he peered more closely at Erik. "He died? Mikhail died in America? There is an inheritance, yes? I am entitled to something. Surely Mikhail has gotten rich from life in America, while I have lived in this apartment for 40 years. Now the building's new owner is pestering me for rent which I cannot pay. Soon I will be evicted. Well?"

Dee, Jill and Jon waited a long time, standing on the narrow sidewalk outside the building, watching the stark contrast of sunlight and shadow on the street, while they talked quietly together. Finally after almost an hour Erik reappeared, his face grim. "I found him on the third floor. He was hostile and ... disoriented. He thought I was Mikhail, so I decided not to come for you to meet him." He looked around. "Is there a place we can go to sit and talk?"

They walked across the street to a basement café and ordered coffee and pastry. Then Erik told his story. When he had finished they all sat in silence a moment.

"Mikhail never said what the family business was," Dee finally inquired.

"Road construction," Erik answered. "During those twenty years of freedom after the first Russian occupation, much was done to improve Latvian roads. The family had a successful enterprise with more national contracts for business than they could handle. But the war and the two occupations destroyed all that. Somehow it's all confused in Nick's mind with what he considers Mikhail's betrayal." Erik puffed out a frustrated breath and stared at the coffee cup in front of him. "This man had been taken care of by the Soviet State as he aged, and after the fall of the Iron Curtain all that dwindled. This to me is one of the hard parts of re-establishing a free country. Until recently he did odd jobs for food, but he says he's too old to work now and has no resources. I gave him what American money I had in my wallet. I think it's probably enough to pay the rent for some time and to get the food and help he needs."

No one spoke. The four of them sat digesting what Erik had said.

Finally Jon stirred. "End of story?"

Erik gave him a long, thoughtful look. "I suppose. I could look for his children, but they never knew Mikhail. The family here was torn apart by Soviet control, and Nick's memories of Mikhail are full of resentment and anger because he escaped it all."

"No wonder Mikhail felt guilty for leaving," Dee sighed.

"Well, we knew it might be a depressing experience here," Jon offered.

"Yes." Erik nodded, setting his cup away and absently smoothing the tablecloth in front of him. "Here is evidence of another life destroyed by evil over which he had no control."

Dee leaned forward. "I remember telling Mikhail that, too, Erik," she said, "when he was caught up in remorse for not being able to know you, to raise you. Nazi Germany and Soviet Communism were the evils. He had no control over that."

She felt Jill flinch beside her, and realized she had touched on the one basic difference between Erik's story and Jill's. A huge, evil societal system was very different from one young woman's independent decision within a supportive society. But even so, that failed to change the result. Circumstances were circumstances, injustice was injustice, people and systems were flawed.

They left the café and wandered along, with no particular destination in mind. Riga was a pleasant city, well laid out with abundant flowers, green lawns and broadleaf trees among shabby, gray streets and buildings. At the central park they turned in and headed toward the Freedom Monument. They stood there a long time, speculating together what it had meant to Mikhail, what traits he'd had that had motivated him to move in a different direction from his family and the safe, successful business they offered, especially during the time when Latvia was free.

"And doesn't each of us spend a lifetime pursuing our own particular freedom and purpose?" Erik asked rhetorically. It was a question each of them took seriously.

In the morning they took the first flight from Riga to Berlin. As the plane touched down, Dee marveled that only a few weeks before, she had been in this city with Mikhail, searching for Erik. And now she was flying back to Berlin with Erik himself, and Mikhail was gone forever.

Erik registered Jill and Dee in a hotel roughly halfway between his house and Jon's apartment. He explained that he and Jon needed to catch up on business at the shop. "We'll take you to a nice Berlin restaurant later," he promised.

Dee and Jill spent the afternoon in their hotel room, relaxing and chatting together. Dee relished the luxury of a peaceful time of rest. But shortly before Erik and Jon were to pick them up for dinner, Erik called.

"Dee, I have news," he said in a quiet, grim voice. "Jon and I are at the prison hospital. It's about one hour from your hotel. My father, Aleks Mendenberg, sent for us here, and we both saw him and spoke with him briefly. He just died."

"Oh, Erik, I'm so sorry. How did it happen?"

"He was eighty. His time had come. Dee, we have arrangements to make, so I'm afraid we can't take you to dinner. It'll be late before we can get away. But I'll call you in the morning. We'll talk then." He paused, then his next words came in a rush. "I'm thankful you told me about your father's hospital experience with *his* dying father. It helped. I'm looking forward to talking it over with you."

"All right, we'll be here. Erik, I don't know what to say. I know you had strong feelings about his negative influence, but…"

"I must go now; they're calling us. Give Jill our apologies. We'll talk later." The line went dead.

Dee turned to Jill, feeling unsettled. "Erik's … father…Aleks Mendenberg, died just now. He had been in prison since the Wall fell…"

"What? Prison?"

"It's a long story." Dee turned away. "They can't come. They have to see to the arrangements."

"Wow. I guess they're glad they got back when they did."

"In a way, I suppose. They both had hard feelings about the man, though. It's been a stunning few weeks for them both. First Mikhail, the biological father and grandfather, and now Aleks, the man who raised Erik. They must be reeling."

"Maybe we should just go home now, Mom. Don't you think we'll be in the way?"

Dee thought about it. "I don't know. It's a shock. We'll see how they feel in the morning, what needs to be done yet." She looked at Jill. "How has this trip been for you so far?" she asked.

Jill shrugged and grinned. "It's been great. Jon and his dad are both good traveling companions, aren't they? I mean, there's no spark there with Jon, but I really enjoy his company anyway. He's easy to talk to, easy to do things with. We laugh a lot together. I wouldn't want anything more complicated right now anyway, that's for sure."

Dee nodded and fell silent, unwilling to get into her feelings about Jon's dad with Jill. The truth was, she felt more drawn to him every day, and she was surprised Jill hadn't noticed. Erik seemed to be responding instinctively to her, in all the ways she wanted and needed him to. It gave her great reassurance that they really did seem to understand one another. Every now and then he looked at her as if to say, "I know just how you're feeling, Dee." She felt comfortable returning the same kind of look, and she could see it reassured him as well. They didn't have to say a word. She was deeply grateful for his presence. But what if she and Jill had to leave now?

"What are you thinking about, Mom?"

"Just … all the things we've been through since Mikhail died. And now Erik and Jon have another huge development to deal with. Maybe we *should* leave tomorrow." She stood up. "Let's go to dinner. I'll tell you what I know about how Aleks landed in prison."

CHAPTER THIRTY-SIX

The next morning Erik called early and told Dee that he and Jon would be tied up all day at the shop, since they hadn't had a chance to catch up on work the day before. "Jon wants to ask Jill if she'd like to go out on the town with him tonight. Since this is the weekend, he thought she'd enjoy club hopping with him."

"Do you want me to put her on?"

"In just a minute." He paused. "We need to talk, Dee. I thought you and I could have dinner at one of my favorite places, just the two of us. I'll pick you up around seven?"

"Sounds perfect," Dee answered, concerned but pleased. She heard warmth under the strain in his voice, and all thoughts of flying back to Seattle vanished.

"Good. I'm sorry we can't show you our city today, but perhaps you and Jill would like to explore on your own. Most of what might interest you is on Kurfurstendamm, Berlin's famous boulevard for shopping. And I'd highly recommend KaDeWe, continental Europe's largest department store. It's a fascinating place to experience—for one thing, it's enormous, and it has one unusual surprise after another–and many choices."

"We've been looking over the brochures that the hotel gave us, so I'm sure we'll be able to find our way around just fine. I know this part of the city, Erik, since Mikhail and I stayed in a hotel not far from here on Kurfurstendamm." She caught Jill's look and decided to mention leaving after all. "But Erik, it sounds like you have your hands full here. We were thinking maybe we should leave pretty soon. You probably don't need tourists from America to take care of on top of everything else."

"Oh, no, Dee! We have so many special plans to share with you. I insist you stay, at least through the weekend. And so will Jon, I know. Here he is now, if Jill is ready to talk to him."

She handed the phone over to Jill and wandered to the window of their hotel room to look down over the street below. The trees along the sidewalk were the same full leafy green as they had been when she and Mikhail had been here less than a month ago. A shiver ran through her as she realized how much had happened since then. She remembered walking with him along the street, looking for Erik's house. She remembered the humid warmth of the morning, the church courtyard, the crowds of scurrying people. She remembered the sense of urgency and decisiveness Mikhail communicated on that day, without saying a word. His son had a slower, more relaxed manner in general, she reflected, but a similar style. The bright, penetrating gaze, the delight in his grin, the way he put his hands behind his back and lifted his chin, all similar tendencies.

Jill's voice pulled her from her thoughts. She turned to face her daughter, and saw that she was smiling with anticipation. "Did you hear me? I'm excited—I get to see Berlin's night life! I've been curious about it ever since I saw 'Cabaret'. I bet I'll see a certain flamboyance tonight, too—a lot of those places must be touting their newfound freedom."

"Sounds like fun," Dee commented with a thin smile, still a little distracted by her lingering memories.

She and Jill set off to see the sights and shop. They worked their way up to the top floor of the KaDeWe Department Store, and wandered through a multitude of foods and food services displayed there. After exploring the entire area and absorbing the sights and sounds and smells, they settled on butter fish, and sat down on stools at the counter. They had to point to the food they wanted because they didn't speak German and the waitress who served them didn't speak English. The food was delicious; tender and moist with aromatic spices. It didn't need sauce of any kind and with salad and fresh blueberries, the meal turned out to be a memorable experience for them.

In the afternoon they went downstairs to Women's Fashions. They had decided they both needed to buy something to wear that evening, and they had fun trying on various possibilities.

"Look at this sexy hot pink number, Mom," Jill exclaimed, holding it up in front of her. It was above-the-knees with spaghetti straps. "What do you think?"

"Try it on, Jill. If you get heels to match, you'll be a knockout."

They both decided it looked sensational, then Dee tried on a bright blue sleeveless sheath with simple lines in a soft fabric that clung becomingly to her figure.

Jill gave her a thumbs-up. "That's the easiest decision we've made in a long time," she said with a big grin. "We sure don't need a wrap since the weather's so hot and muggy." They left the store and headed back to the hotel, exhausted but excited, with their purchases.

Dee showered first and then turned the bathroom over to Jill, so when Erik arrived, she was ready. She opened the door and stepped aside with a smile to let him pass, noting the casual dark slacks and short-sleeved button-down blue shirt he wore with a dark tie. It seemed to her that he filled up the small space with his powerful presence as he turned and looked at her.

"You look beautiful, Dee," he said simply.

Up until this evening, she had worn mostly slacks and casual tops, so it pleased her that his blue eyes shone brightly as he gazed at her. She couldn't help flushing, and then she noticed how his eyes matched his shirt, and even her dress. Everything seemed to be in perfect symmetry this evening. "Thank you. You look pretty good yourself." An inexpressible joy lifted her as they stood gazing at each other.

Erik finally took a deep breath and looked around the room. "Where's Jill? Did Jon pick her up already?"

"I'm in here," Jill called from behind the closed bathroom door. "Jon's not coming for another hour, and I have a lot to do before that to make myself as stunning as possible."

"Well, do we get to see?"

Jill opened the door and twirled in front of them, her face aglow. Erik whistled. "What was the word you used? Stunning? Yes, I agree," he grinned.

"Thanks. This should be fun—the Berlin party scene. Just think: two weeks ago I met you and your son for the first time, and look how far we've come! I feel something enchanting is happening tonight. Do you feel it too?"

"Enchanting. Yes," Erik answered. Dee nodded. Standing beside Erik she felt a current between them, and had since the moment she'd met him. But she couldn't speak; her smile stiffened; she had to force herself not to turn to him at Jill's question.

Jill's glance skipped quickly between the two of them, then she turned away. "Okay you two, have fun. Don't wait up for me."

The Berlin Connection

They walked out and closed the door softly behind them, then started down the hall toward the elevator. "My son thinks your daughter is wonderful," Erik remarked. "I'm glad she's been an available companion through this whole experience, and that they've become good friends."

"Me, too. This whole trip has been a good distraction for her, just as I'd hoped." She had told Erik about the meeting in Nicole's office, the revelations about Karen, and the tentative plans for a reunion between Karen and Jill in September. Talking those things over gave her more reasons than ever to feel his warmth and understanding.

But now, suddenly, things felt different. The hair on the back of her neck prickled; her hopes were high for a romantic evening. But what if something went wrong between them? She tried to shrug off her old insecurities, but it seemed her instinct had taken over.

They reached the elevator and stood in front of it. Erik pressed the button. They both stared at the door. An awkward silence fell between them. Her throat felt dry as she tried to swallow. She could hear the elevator making its interminable, creaking ascent, stopping at each floor on its way to the top floor, the sixth, where her room was. Why couldn't she look at him, think of something to say? She had never been at a loss in his presence before. Why now? And why was *he* suddenly so silent?

The elevator doors opened and they faced several people, who stepped inside the elevator and turned to the front. Her anticipation and apprehension rose as the elevator started its slow descent and finally stopped at the main floor lobby. Erik took her arm at the elbow and led her across the crowded lobby and out onto the sidewalk. They walked the short block to a dark Volkswagen sedan. He unlocked her door and she slid into the passenger seat. She breathed deeply, trying to relax as she watched him walk around the front of the car to the driver's side. He opened his door and got in behind the wheel, then turned his face to her in the dark. She could barely make out his eyes, but saw they had narrowed with concern.

"I feel ... we have so much to say to each other," he said hesitantly. "So much that I don't know where to begin."

At once her tension evaporated. He had put his finger so easily on her feelings as well as his own. She nodded and said, "I want to ask you about Aleks, but I imagine what a painful, complicated subject it is for you. I want to talk about my fun day shopping with Jill, but that seems too trivial. I want to ask if you got caught up on your work today, and what all that involved." She lifted her shoulders and gave him a rueful smile.

He reached out, placed his hand gently against her cheek. As she leaned into his palm and closed her eyes, he said, "I want to ... how do you Americans say? Break the ice first." He moved toward her and brushed her lips with his. She sighed, breathless, eager, and yet relaxed and fluid as she moved into his arms. His lips were just as she remembered them, and suddenly her heart was pounding in her ears like waves against rocks. She wrapped her arms around his neck.

Finally he pulled back and said, "I was beginning to think this time would never come. I was beginning to think I had made a big mistake by telling you we should…ignore the attraction…and wait." His smile was endearing as he traced her cheek with his finger. "I was beginning to think Jill and Jon were going to be with us forever… even though I enjoy their company too, of course, it's not the same as what I feel with you. When I'm with you I'm drawn to you, always. I want so badly to touch you." He kissed her eyelids, her cheeks, her neck. "All day I knew we'd be alone together. And the day seemed endless."

"It was the same for me," she whispered, feeling her joy rise like a helium balloon as the words rushed out. "But we're bound to have strong feelings about what we're going through together. That's why I knew you were right that we should set this aside. I just didn't realize how hard it would be."

"Dee…my favorite place for dinner is in my home. I bought food for a small dinner party for two…"

"You don't have to…"

He put a finger on her lips. His gaze was intense. "Will you come?"

She let out a long, unsteady breath. She couldn't stop smiling. "Of course I'll come."

CHAPTER THIRTY-SEVEN

As they drove the short distance from the hotel to his house in silence, she closed her eyes and saw a younger Erik as he walked away from the sidewalk café all those years ago. She remembered her immeasurable yearning, to draw him back to her. And here he was. He pulled the car up at the curb and turned off the ignition.

"Did I tell you I was here with Mikhail?" she asked, her heart pounding. "He had your address, and we walked here from our hotel. The frau next door told us where to find Jon at your shop."

He nodded. "He told me himself, on the phone before I came to Seattle. It comforts me to imagine my father here. When I arrived home late last night after what Jon and I experienced at the hospital, I stood on the front porch a moment and imagined him filling the space beside me." He closed his eyes and his head moved slowly from side to side. She could sense his powerful emotion. She didn't know where his ended and hers began. He opened the door and got out of the car, then came around to let her out. As she rose, his arms circled her waist and they stood close together a moment, his forehead resting on hers.

"Let's go inside," he said softly.

They moved up the walkway and climbed the short steps to the porch. As he unlocked the door and pushed it open, he said, "Welcome to my home." The aroma of roasting chicken reached them. She turned to him, her eyes alight. "You already started dinner?"

"I hoped you'd come," he shrugged and grinned with engaging shyness.

He led her across the living room toward the kitchen, Dee glancing quickly at the comfortable furnishings: a large plaid overstuffed sofa and chair set, a floor lamp and coffee table, all pleasant and welcoming. In the kitchen she saw that the table was already set for two.

"Would you like a glass of wine? The dinner will be ready soon I think." He opened the refrigerator door. "Liebfraumilch," he said, holding up the green bottle. "Germany's best."

"That sounds wonderful."

He poured it into two glasses at the table, then handed her one and touched his to hers. "To more new beginnings," he said with a warm smile.

She grinned, knowing he meant more than his sports equipment business. "To more new beginnings." She took a sip. "It's good," she said.

He opened the oven door to check the meal, then they went back out into the living room and sat side by side on the sofa.

He tasted, nodded, then set his glass on the coffee table and took her hand. His eyes clouded and he looked across the room. "I need to get this out. I need to tell you what happened at the hospital." His face looked haunted. "It was depressing, Dee—so shockingly similar to what I had just gone through with Mikhail's brother in Riga. But I hadn't known Nick…and this man I did know—the once powerful, authoritative, cruel man I had known so well growing up, was now reduced to an ashen shell of himself." Erik turned his head and his eyes found hers. "I suppose you can guess what he said to me."

Dee set her glass on the table next to his. "You said something about my own father's experience with my grandfather in the hospital room …"

"Yes. I was reminded of that immediately when Jon and I walked into the room. Except Aleks was sitting up a little, as if waiting for us. His breathing sounded harsh, his voice raspy and filled with sarcasm." Dee absorbed Erik's words, drawn in again by his own gently accented voice. Her heart ached at the sad irony in his words as he told his story. "'My dear, devoted family', he called us in derisive greeting. 'It seems I'm near the end.' He tried to lift himself a little higher on the bed, so I went over to arrange his pillow for him. But he shook off my gesture. 'I want to tell you the reason I feel such hatred toward you,' he said."

Erik let go of Dee's hand and rose from the sofa, pacing the room as he continued.

"I stepped back from the bed and exchanged glances with Jon. We both knew what was coming." Erik sank into the chair adjacent from Dee, just close enough for them both to reach out and to touch hands. Their fingers entwined instinctively. He went on, "His eyes were fixed on me and what I represented. After the reaction I got from Mikhail's brother I expected him to confuse me with Mikhail also, to think he was back in time when he, Anita and Mikhail were all young. But his mind seemed as alert and clear as always, if twisted with hate.

"He did not waste time. It astonished me to see how much hate he projected, even in his weakened condition. He spat out the words with amazing strength for a man who was dying. 'Your mother was a whore, did you know that, Erik, my dear son? But no, you are not my son, and it gives me great pleasure to tell you this. You never behaved as a true son of mine. That is because, of course, the one who fathered you abandoned your mother and the State, ran away from his duty, was traitor and betrayer, the worst kind of cowardly vermin. That is the kind of blood that flows through your veins.'

"Dee, I answered him with a calmness I did not feel. 'I already know,' I said. 'I already know.' He stared at me as I went on. 'I learned the truth from Mother, many years ago.' I told him my impressions of Mikhail were quite different from his."

"He seemed to shrink into himself as he considered this. Finally he sputtered something about saving my mother from a life of shame by marrying her, giving us his good name. Then he turned to Jon but his words were for me. 'Well,' he said, 'that explains why you turned your son against me and the Party.'

"I was so proud of Jon, Dee. 'The truth speaks for itself,' He declared calmly, 'I have a better life now than any of us did under the GDR.'

"Jon and I stood there in silence a moment, watching him. He was deathly still. He said no more. After a moment he lifted his arm and gestured weakly as if to dismiss us. So we left him then and went out to speak with the doctor. He told us death was near, so we waited outside. I thought of calling you then, but I decided not to. I knew I had to sort through some legal details, and I didn't know how long that would take. About an hour later, the doctor came and confirmed that Aleks had died and told us what was necessary for us to do. I called you then."

"You said legal details," Dee ventured. "I hope the German government doesn't hold you accountable for his crimes, as his heir."

"No. His holdings had all reverted to the German government already. I had separated myself from him sufficiently for years, and that satisfied them. All I had to do was sign a document to that effect. And now it's behind me." He looked away, his voice distant. "But...I feel...overcome, Dee. By the bad memories. By the 'if only's'. If only I had been raised by Mikhail in a loving family. If only I had never known the ugly reality, the deception that Aleks projected all those years I was growing up. He is dead, and Mikhail is dead, and I only mourn the daydream of what should have been."

"You've been through so much in such a short time, Erik—it takes my breath away."

He looked down at their joined hands, then lifted his eyes, his gaze tender. "And you've been through it all with me. I can't tell you how much that means to me. And now—ah, Dee, I've imagined this. Just as I imagined my father standing on my front porch, I imagined you sitting here like this, in my home."

"When did you imagine such a thing?" she asked, moved.

"When we were together in your home. I almost said something to you then, but I knew it was too soon. But then," he paused, his smile filled with urgency, "I felt from the moment I saw you at the airport that I'd known you always, that there was never a time I didn't feel we were connected, close, in touch with one another, in spite of the ocean that separated us. Being together feels so right to me, Dee. So satisfying."

She nodded, the enchantment flowing inside her like a soothing, peaceful river. "It's like we see the best parts of each other, and it all makes sense. The pieces all fit."

He stood and gazed down at her, then he pulled her to her feet and into his arms. They stood together for a long moment as he kissed her, his mouth moving against hers with a rising passion they both felt. When at last they drew apart they were breathless. "This is the beginning, Dee. We're making new memories," he said with quiet conviction. He lifted his hand and smoothed her hair back with infinite tenderness. "I want to experience the next memory now. And I have a feeling it will be perfect."

The next evening Dee and Jill took a flight back home to Seattle. Each were lost in her own thoughts, and talked little. Dee's head and heart were filled with Erik and the passion they'd shared the evening before that had left little time or inclination for dinner. When he'd taken her back to the hotel later, he had gathered her in his arms and whispered against her hair, "I don't want to lose this love we've found, Dee."

Dee had nodded, dazed and happy. "You don't have any concerns about what we feel for each other getting all mixed up with what we've been through together since Mikhail died?"

Erik had considered her question seriously for a moment. "We climbed mountains together," he'd said slowly. "Now, if we have to be apart for a time, I want to savor what we found, and then when I come back to Seattle it will be an exciting time of discovery and exploration for us, will it not?"

Dee continued to lose herself in the memories while Jill dozed beside her during much of the flight. She thought of the drive to the airport, and of the four of them waiting at the gate for the flight to be called. Thankfully, the special glances Dee and Erik gave one another seemed to be lost on Jill and Jon as they chatted happily.

"I'll be coming to Seattle soon, Dee," Erik had said. "As soon as probate is finished we need to conclude what's left of the estate."

"And we need to follow up with the publisher about his manuscript, hopefully about that same time," Dee added.

"How soon, do you think?"

"A few months."

"A few months, then. And I'll call you often in between," he smiled.

"You won't mind a big phone bill?"

"It will be a pleasure. We owe it to ourselves," he glanced at Jon and Jill, "as good friends, to stay in touch."

Dee looked out the plane window, noting the vast ocean below. *An ocean between us,* she thought. *Will we be able to hold on to what we've found,* she wondered as she closed her eyes, *or will it fade with time and distance? Time will tell. But he's coming back to me.*

Jill stirred in the seat next to her and Dee opened her eyes and turned to her daughter. "Been sleeping?"

"No, just dozing. I've been wondering if I can get back to reality now. This has been a great little diversion. But the routine of work, and the anxiety about meeting with Karen in a couple months, it's all there again. In a way I can't wait to get back to it. In a way I dread it."

"Hopefully you're refreshed and ready to tackle everything again," Dee smiled.

"Hopefully. Time will tell."

"Time will tell," Dee repeated.

Three months later, on a morning in September, Jill called Dee at home.

"Wish me luck, Mom, she said in a shaky but cheerful voice. "I'm on my way."

Dee laughed with delight. "You sound pretty good, honey. No butterflies?"

"Oh, yeah. Lots of butterflies. But I've been waiting for so long, I'm ready for anything. And Nicole says Karen is ready too. She's had lots of counseling about how to handle everything, especially with her kids. She hasn't told them yet, but they're back in school and busy with their activities, so that takes some pressure off her for now."

"Any word on when or how she'll tell them?"

"Well, I guess she's been talking it all over with her husband, too, and he says she should meet with me first, get a feel for this relationship, and then tackle the next step."

"What does Nicole say about that?"

"She agrees. It's good to take it one step at a time. But Nicole tells me Karen is definitely ready to meet me and talk everything over. That's always been the biggest step."

"It sounds like her husband is a good guy. He'll be with her when she tells her kids, I assume."

"I think so. I'll ask her." Dee could hear Jill's sigh over the phone. "I have so many questions to ask her, I've written a list. Is that silly?"

"No, it sounds wise. You have lots of ground to cover, after all."

"Thanks again for all the snapshots you gave me the other day to pass on to her. I'm sure she'll appreciate them, and they'll give me lots of stories to tell her too, about what my life was like growing up. It was a nice thing for you to do, Mom. And I'll call you as soon as I can with a full report."

All afternoon Dee's mind was on her daughter, wondering how the reunion was going. Strong feelings warred in her: anxiety and excitement, worry and joy, all at the same time.

Then, at about 8:00 that evening, the doorbell rang.

Dee opened it to find her daughter standing in front of her, and glowing. Dee stood there a moment, smiling, her heart warming at the sight. Her daughter had never looked more alive.

Then she yelped. "What are you doing, ringing the doorbell, Jill?" she scolded with a grin, grabbing Jill's hand and pulling her into the house. Jill laughed and threw herself into Dee's arms. "Don't tell me," Dee hugged Jill hard. "It went well?" She pulled back and looked into her daughter's shining eyes. "It went well."

Jill nodded vigorously. "As good as it gets, Mom. I had to come and tell you. And I rang the doorbell because I felt like if I came screaming into the house I'd scare you half to death."

"Oh, right," Dee scoffed, pulling Jill with her into the kitchen. "Tell me everything. Start the beginning. No, just tell me whatever you want."

Jill flopped herself at the kitchen table. "Well, let's see. We were both on time and we gave each other a big hug and a smile. We couldn't stop staring at each other, examining each other for similar expressions and traits and features, you know, and I asked her tons of questions about what her likes and dislikes are, and how she feels about Bill Clinton, and what her favorite color is, and all kinds of things like that. She asked me the same kinds of things, and she loved the snapshots. She cried when she leafed through them, Mom. She was really touched. She said she wants to meet you some day."

Dee went over to the teakettle heating at the stove. After she poured the tea, She closed her eyes and smiled with contentment. "That means a lot to me, honey. Whenever you think the time is right."

"She said she wants to thank you for doing such a wonderful job raising me. I told her sometimes it wasn't easy. And she told me where she thinks I got my talent as a chef—she found out for me that my birth father is almost all French. How about that?"

"So she contacted him about you?" Dee set the cups of tea in place and sat down across from Jill.

"Yep. Just to find out some things about medical history and all. I guess he was okay with it. She didn't go into detail, except to say he's still in the area and doesn't really want any contact with me. That's fine with me." Jill's eyes narrowed with concern as she sipped her tea. "But there was one thing she told me that made me glad I contacted her for purely practical reasons, Mom. She just found out she has heart trouble. They keep it under control with medicine, but still, she's only in her 40's! Anyway, it's something I'm glad she told me to be aware of."

"For sure. It's a really vital piece of information."

"Anyway, we sat and talked for three hours. She had to go pick up her kids and drive them to soccer practice. But before she left she told me she'll call me again soon. She says she hopes to arrange a meeting with her husband and kids before too long."

"That's great news. Oh, Jill. I'm so happy for you. It turned out about as well as you'd hoped, didn't it?"

"Yeah. It did. I went home and wrote down my thoughts and everything we talked about so I wouldn't forget. And then I came over," she finished cheerfully, producing a small notebook from her handbag. "Want to hear some of what I wrote?"

A few weeks later, Dee received a call from an editor about Mikhail's manuscript. The publisher had accepted it with enthusiasm, even adding that it was all the more powerful because it would be published posthumously.

Dee explained to him that Mikhail's son was coming to Seattle from Berlin in the near future to tie up the legal details regarding Mikhail's estate, and needed to be the one to sign the contract.

"We'll mail it to you in the next few days, and you can go over it together, then. Congratulations, Mrs. Sanders. We'll look forward to working with you and Mr. Mendenberg in the near future."

Dee called Erik right away. It was late evening Berlin time. "Erik, we sold the manuscript!" she announced. "They're sending the contract here in the mail. Can you come soon? I need you."

Erik's voice was warm and happy on the other end of the phone, on the other side of the ocean. "It's what we've been waiting for," he said.

EPILOGUE

Dee drove carefully, observing the speed limit, watching the traffic, making a conscious effort to focus on every detail. This day had been coming almost her whole adult life, and she didn't want to spoil it with a ticket or an accident along the way. Finally she pulled into the parking lot, stopped the car and turned off the ignition. She took a deep breath and glanced at her watch. She was twenty minutes early. No surprise, really. Ever since she'd gotten up this morning she'd been a nervous wreck, trying on several different outfits before she decided on one, forgetting to eat breakfast until 10:30, then rushing at the last minute to finish getting ready, then leaving in plenty of time to account for possible traffic jams, then finding herself here early. She'd just sit here, composing herself. Erik always told her, you must be composed. So she would be.

Ever since he had come back to tie up the rest of the legal details regarding Mikhail's estate, and to set up regular meetings with Dee to guide the editorial and legal process as Mikhail's book moved toward publication, their time together had been magical. They had worked together as a team, and they had fallen even more deeply in love.

Dee and Erik talked often about Mikhail being the connecting link between them and their loved ones, because of his pursuit of freedom. And now their relationship created an environment in which their mutual pursuit of freedom could thrive.

Dee glanced at her watch again. Time to go in. She stepped out of the car, brushed herself off, and before she could move toward the building, Jill drove up and parked beside her car. In the passenger seat Dee could make out another woman, one who had become familiar to Dee from the many pictures Jill had shown her. Tears welled in Dee's eyes and she swallowed them down, resolving again to be composed, to make Erik, not to mention her daughter, proud.

Jill and Karen got out of the car and approached her. All three of the women had wide, radiant smiles on their faces. Dee stepped forward.

"Mom, this is Karen," Jill said. "Karen, I want you to meet my mom."

Dee and Karen moved into each other's arms and into a healing, heartfelt hug.

"Thank you," they both whispered in unison.

Made in the USA